DARK BLADE FORGED

THE DARK BLADE TRILOGY, VOL. 1
TYREAN MARTINSON

WINGS OF LIGHT PUBLISHING

For all the warriors who fight battles the world doesn't see

Contents

Chapter I: To the Watch Tower

As dusk lost the last edges of light, and the heavens darkened to cloudy night, Dan heard his mare's hooves clack on cobblestone. After many hours traveling on the dirt roads, they must have reached the outer edge of a Watch Guard Tower, but he could only distinguish silhouettes reaching into the obsidian sky. The heat of the afternoon had given up its battle to the evening chill. Weary from the ride, Dan struggled to sit upright. The nearness of the keep's walls gave him relief. He leaned forward, forced his sore legs to tighten, and his mare picked up her pace to match the strides of the horse ridden by Watch Guard Quinn, the stocky, sandy-haired man who had taken Dan and his two fellow recruits from their homeland. As apprentices to the Watch Guard, they would become set apart from nation or city-state, at least for a time.

Quinn's leather armor rustled as he turned to glance over as Dan drew near. He waved toward the shape of the building up ahead. "We're almost to the outer defenses."

Dan's tiredness gave over to nerves and excitement. The next moments could transform his whole life. He had to create a favorable impression and was not sure if he had with Watch Guard Quinn. The warrior had an inscrutable countenance. Quinn carried a blade of power and he had taken them on a day's journey with no signs of fatigue. Dan had been struggling not to slump in his seat for several hours, and his doubts fell heavy in his thoughts. He knew his blade, while of fine make befitting the son of a merchant baron, was nothing compared to one of the legendary weapons of power. Even so, he hoped. The King had sent them here. If his apprenticeship established his abilities, he could leave his past and join the legendary inter-kingdom agency of the Watch Guard, through which men and women worked to safeguard ancient secrets and protect all the kingdoms of Aramatir from the misuses of power and sorcery.

He cast about for a technique to intrigue Quinn, to impress him. "I did not observe anyone on duty as we approached. Are there magical wards?"

Quinn chuckled quietly. "Your sight is not trained enough to notice our protections." He clucked at his mount and moved to the lead position again.

Embarrassed, Dan fought to see more in the gloom. How did Quinn maneuver so easily? Was it related to his blade of power? Some swordsmen gifted with such blades had remarkable abilities that resembled magic, although they swore they did no sorcery. Dan could barely discern sufficient details to measure how close the keep was in relation to him. Thankfully, his mare had no trouble trailing Quinn's horse. Behind him, the other two horses click-clacked onto the stone path, carrying their riders.

The three of them had not spoken since that morning, not since the skinny redhead dressed in tradesman robes had made an attempt at conversation and found both Dan and Alex to be curt. Dan felt bad about that. Farrald, with his freckled face and soft-spoken demeanor, might be an agreeable fellow. But he had no desire to start a conversation with Alex, who had every reason to be angry with Dan, and who traveled at the rear.

Torchlight brightened a barbican ahead, a defensive, walled structure that loomed above the portcullis. They were here, wherever here was. Without having a compass or a map to consult, Dan wasn't sure. Watch Guard Towers were situated in various countries, both within and at the borders, and sometimes doubling as lighthouses along the coastlines.

Nobody here cared about his background. He would have a chance. Could he prove his worth? He clenched his dark fingers on the reins he held and then willed them to relax. He had to. He would not return to his parents. While his father had ambitions and clever plans to gain more influence within the prestigious court of nobility, Dan would rather live away from such politics and the gatherings full of flattery and manners. He wished for purpose, for time filled with the necessary training to protect others. If he could become a Watch Guard, he would be called to a higher purpose than any single nation offered, and he would be free from his father's machinations.

Ahead of him, Quinn paused outside the building and tilted his head up to speak to a hooded figure above them. "Three trainees and Quinn reporting." His craggy face, lit by the blaze of nearby torches, seemed awake and lively, as if they had been out on a pleasant afternoon excursion and not riding from daybreak into the depths of night.

"Marked." A woman's husky voice answered him.

Dan strained his eyes and made out an armored silhouette standing on the rampart. She wore a hood that shrouded most of her upper body, and the torch smoke appeared to twist around her.

Before them, the iron grating rose, drawn up by pulleys. The sharp ends of the portcullis reminded Dan safeguards came in many forms, like strong ramparts, heavy doors, guards, and strategic planning.

Quinn beckoned to Dan and the others. "We've arrived, gentlemen." He smirked at his closing choice of word for them, clucked at his horse, and proceeded through the opening.

Dan's stomach churned with anticipation, hope, dread, and longing, all at once leaking out of him, leaving him hollow. With his fists clenched against his fear, he leaned forward, and his mare stepped through the archway. Dan noted the tiny holes above him, prepared for defensive strategies, and then refocused on the courtyard ahead.

He could hear the other horses following, then the grinding of the portcullis coming down behind them. Ahead, across a wide square, sconces illuminated a high opening that ended in a three-sided stable. Quinn had already gotten out of the saddle and was leading his horse into the building.

Dan prepared to dismount by shifting in his seat. As he swung his leg over and down, his muscles spasmed, and he gripped the pommel of his saddle as his feet landed on the large paving stones. His legs nearly collapsed beneath him, but he held on. When he regained his balance, he led his mount into one of the stalls. She whickered at the sight of the hay.

Quinn tended his own horse with the unhurried grace of someone practiced at doing the chore, his movements smooth and automatic as he took off her tack and saddle, placing them on racks provided for them.

As he watched, Dan realized there wouldn't be stable hands or servants here. It was one thing to know that objectively and another to understand what that meant at the end of a long ride. Nobody else would care for his steed but him, so he had work to do for half a candle mark. It was labor he understood how to do, as his Sword Master had taught him, but it was not a task he was accustomed to doing regularly.

As a Junior Lord of Septily, Dan knew he had a lot to learn about living as a common-born individual. Knowing he never wanted to return to the capital of Skycliff as a noble, he could push his fatigue and muscle soreness aside to do what he needed to do.

Chapter 2: Reality Sets In

DAN UNBUCKLED HIS SADDLEBAGS, dropped them in the corner by Quinn's belongings and relieved his mare of the saddle, harness and tack. As he hung them up on the provided hooks, he ran his fingers across the Torren House crest stitched into the saddle flap. While he had no desire to join his parents in any of their intrigues or dealings, he would miss the house insignia. The golden lion rampant above a black storm cloud had always filled his imagination with ideas of courage and nobility. Everything his father was not. Shaking his head, he dropped his fingers from the familiar heraldry. The Watch Guard had their own symbols, which mainly consisted of recurring imagery with a shield overlaying crossed swords, sometimes with a compass rose depicted in the center of the shield.

Following Quinn's lead, he found a soft brush and combed his mare's summer coat. The warmth her flanks had preserved his strength during the lengthy journey. While he brushed out her velvety fur, Dan leaned into her shoulder, savoring the comforting solidness of her presence. The stable was warmer than the outer courtyard, but the sweat of his nerves chilled him. So far, his worries had been for nought. It seemed his true testing would begin tomorrow, and while he should be thankful, he was also worried. Was he truly prepared?

"Horses are wonderful, aren't they?" voiced Farrald, the lean redhead who had attempted conversation earlier. He brushed his mare with light strokes, swaying back and forth in happy movement. In this torchlight, his freckles were muted against his tan. While he appeared to be someone who would naturally have paler skin than Dan, he had obviously spent many hours in the sunlight, and he had the faint accent of the Desert District of Septily.

"Yeah." Dan did not want to be rude, but with the war of nerves and exhaustion, he was not sure what to say. He noticed how soft his dark hands were even with the callouses from his sword training. His ancestors had once been traveling merchants of the Southern Continent, but they had moved to Septily and joined the First Champion Elar in fighting against the Dark One, gaining a title and a barony in the process. Generations later, Dan's family lived sumptuous lives of landed merchant barons, living off the profits of trade deals created by their forefathers. Dan almost felt jealous of Farrald. What must it be like to live a life in which you could be valued for your hard work, and not how you fit into the power plays of your parents?

Farrald did not seem to take offense at Dan's reticence, as he combed his horses' mane with loving strokes, running his other hand after the brush in rhythm. He began to sing a hymn from the sanctuaries. "Amazing light, amazing love, God, you are faithful to us."

Dan cocked his head, surprised. He did not join in with the song. But the tune and the words felt familiar. His family attended worship at the Triune Halls in Skycliff, but they were not devout. His faith was something private, and no one wanted to hear his off-key voice. He wondered what Alex would think of Farrald's open faith.

Alex had ridden his horse to the edge of the stable and still sat there, not dismounting. He had a sulky look on his pale face, his lips pouting, his eyebrows drawn down, and a lock of his blonde hair drooping halfway over one side of his face. His purple silk shirt and brown leathers were covered in road dust, as all of them were. He peered into the stable. "Is there no one here?"

"We tend our own horses, recruit," Quinn said, not looking up from where he curried his mare.

Alex shifted in his saddle, frowning deeper. "My father would not approve."

"He did. That's why you're here." Quinn arched an eyebrow at Alex, and then turned his back on him. He walked over to a water pump, filled the bucket, then filled his horses' trough.

Alex huffed, then slid down from his horse, wincing as his fine leather boots hit the paving stones. "That was an awful ride."

Dan shifted to the other side of his mare, continuing to brush her down as she ate her well-earned hay. He glanced back at Alex, wondering if he knew how to rub down a horse.

Alex fumbled with a clasp on the girth of his saddle.

"Here, I can help." Farrald started to move toward Alex.

"No." Quinn frowned, deepening the lines around his mouth. "Show him. That's all. No helping."

Alex sighed heavily. "Thank you, Farrald." The saddle slid off his mare and landed in a heap on the ground, including his personal bags. He awkwardly picked it all up and tripped over a dangling strap.

Dan bit his lip. He couldn't, shouldn't, laugh or show any pleasure in Alex's discomfort, but the sight had been satisfying. Even if Alex had every right to be angry at him, he hadn't wanted Alex to come along on this journey. The King had granted him his hope of being a recruit to the Watch Guard, but he had sent Alex with him. He was not sure which of them was being punished more.

Farrald did not know what Dan knew, and he did not laugh. "If you unstrap your saddle bags and sling the straps over the main saddle, it will be easier to carry. And when you remove your mare's bridle, be extra gentle and give her a good rub on the cheek, so she knows you'll be kind. She won't fight you."

Alex did not thank Farrald for his advice, but he did as Farrald had instructed. Alex glared at Dan when he spotted him staring.

Dan filled his mare's bucket with more grain and filled her water trough, as a way of continuing his work and ignoring Alex. It was not Dan's fault Alex was here. Well, maybe it was, but this was better for Alex than what he could have been doing. Even if Dan did not want Alex here, he knew Alex needed to get away from the capital as much as he did, even if Alex did not understand that.

After they had finished giving their mounts their much-deserved rub-downs and all the care they needed, Quinn guided them into the structure behind the stable. It was a long, low room between stone walls, not really part of the castle proper, but an adjacent building between the stable and the castle. A row of slim beds took up one wall, with an open walkway on the other side.

With a touch of a smile, Quinn waved at the beds. "Here's where new recruits stay until we sort them into their cadres before their induction to the Watch Guard as apprentices. The privy's down at the end. There's a washbasin by the castle wall. Extra blankets are in the chests at the end of the beds." He locked gazes with each of them in turn, ending with Dan.

Dan rooted himself solidly under the man's measurement. "Understood, Quinn."

Quinn pivoted on his heel and left them there.

"This isn't so bad," Farrald said, and he immediately placed his leather helmet on the bunk closest to the door of the stables.

Dan shook his head at him. "Don't sleep there, there's a draft."

Farrald shrugged and opened the trunk at the foot of the bed he had already claimed. "I can be closer to my horse this way."

"I will take the bunk closest to the castle," Alex said. He opened the chest at the end of his chosen bed, and then opened the chest for the cot next to his. Once he had four extra blankets on his bed, he shucked off his boots, helm, breastplate, and weapons' belt, then curled up under the covers with his back to them. His saddlebags were still in the stable.

Dan chose a cot in the middle of both. He used both the extra blankets from his chest, and he carefully organized his helm, boots, bags, breastplate, and belt in the chest before closing the lid. He did not want spiders or bugs in his things. As he lay down with his sword tucked under the thin mattress, he noticed Farrald gazing at his trunk. Farrald got up and placed his belongings in his chest. "Good idea and good night," Farrald said. He snuffed out the torch in the barracks.

The dim light from the stable yard flickered through the small window shafts by the roof. Dan heard Alex breathing raggedly like he was crying, but he did not get up and check. He was sure Alex would not appreciate it. For a time after that, he could hear Farrald murmuring a prayer, but then his words became deep breathing. No one stirred. Dan's mind whirled, but the depths of his weariness finally overwhelmed his worries.

Chapter 3: A King's Dilemma

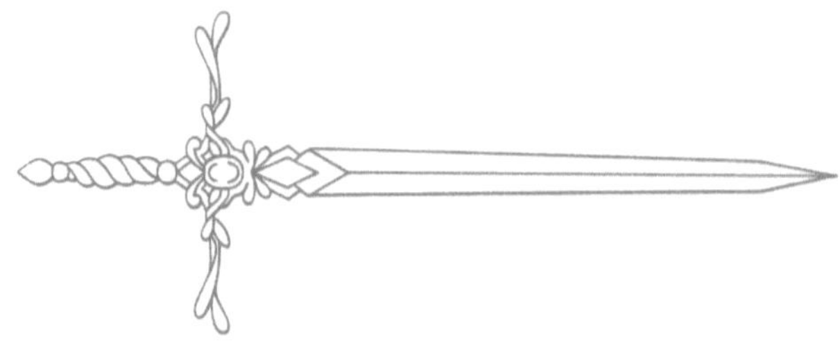

SHEDDING HIS BEJEWELED ROYAL robe which weighed on his shoulders nearly as much as his ostentatious court crown, King Xandros retreated to his private suite with only his oldest friends, Sword Guard Theran and Shepherd Jordan. They wore their early middle age with grace, as they continued to train with each other and instructors daily. Even with his hectic agenda of meetings with the Triune Council, the Court of Nobles, and the Court of Commoners, Xandros maintained his training schedule to stay fighting fit for self-defense. Like his father before him, he wore the trappings of royalty, but always with fabrics and tailoring meant for ease of movement.

With his ornate purple robe draped on a custom stand and his twinkling crown safely placed in a designated case, Xandros relaxed and reclined heavily in his cushioned chair, releasing the tension in his back. What he did here in this private space often had a greater effect on the citizens of Septily than anything else, and yet, he felt more at ease here than he did in court. Tonight was the same, and he needed a moment with his closest friends before he had to send them away on dangerous missions. After the recent tense meetings with the Court of Nobles, and the accusations of political manipulations by various factions, both Theran and Jordan stood stiffly on the other side of his mammoth desk, as if they had forgotten they could relax with him.

Xandros found his focus shifting to the portrait of his son which sat near his elbow. His son's blonde hair, blue eyes, and open smile reminded him of more carefree moments. He believed innocence still resided in his son, even after his recent debacle. The boy reminded him of his late wife, and that had been his undoing when it came to raising him. Whenever he looked at his son, his sorrow at the loss of his beloved wife overcame him. So, he had allowed the boy to be raised by others, and that was pure foolishness.

In his discomfiture, he shifted his thoughts to his friends again. Their jaws were tight. Their brows furrowed. Seeing them distraught brought the tension back to his shoulders and he closed his eyes.

After the discovery and closure of the Red House, a vile brothel filled with slaves, he could not fault his friends for their stiff demeanors. The insidious infiltration of their society by those who traded in human flesh had been growing over the recent years, with several of the Red Houses opening in different locations about the city, and none had been able to put an end to it. If he guessed correctly, both Theran and Jordan blamed themselves for thinking they had fixed the issue already, while he was certain the responsibility fell solidly at his feet. Out of the three of them, he was at the top of the Courts of Law, while Theran and Jordan owed their first allegiance to the Triune Council, and their respective areas of expertise, the Swords of Defense and the Shepherds of Faith.

He missed their youth, despite the solid measures of training interspersed with all their play. They had always been together. Their parents had not only been friends, but all had been firm believers in the Triune God, and so raised their children as close to the faith as they could, with Theran trained in Sword Mastery, Jordan brought up to Shepherd, and with Xandros educated in the Law. When his parents had sought out children to be his closest companions, they had chosen Theran and Jordan, with the aid of the Triune Council, so all had received cross-disciplined schooling.

As he reminisced about their childhood, he pondered his son's life. Alex had not undergone the same training, not developed the same friendships, and he was suffering for it. Sending Alex to apprentice with the Watch Guard was Xandros's attempt to make up for a childhood of soft living among the nobility and the bad training of foreign governesses who did not understand the ways of the Triune Halls or Septily.

Xandros fixed his attention on the painting of their family hanging on the wall. It had been created when his beloved Roseanne had been alive. Her blue-eyes held fathomless depths. Roseanne, a lady of the Ryssorrian Court, had not understood the Triune Halls' traditions and how they affected the monarchy of Septily. Believing he would rectify this lapse when Alex got older, Theran allowed her to raise Alex in the Ryssorrian way. When she had passed, he had been consumed with grief. This enabled the kingdom to become weak.

Furthermore, he had consented to Alex being pampered by his wife's old governess, without proper instruction as his heir. The Watch Guard could provide a base for Alex to learn what Xandros had been unable to teach him. With Dan and Farrald at his side, Alex might find the close friendship he needed with those of other disciplines to succeed as King of Septily, who was legally held in check by the Triune Halls' Council.

His friends had remained at attention as he ruminated. Theran's tan, middle-aged countenance remained somber, with his keen hazel eyes fixed on the maps on the desk. His fitness for duty was pronounced by his trim and muscular appearance, despite the mix of gray and dark hair at his temples. His black and purple uniform designated his role as the Head of the King's Guards, and of course, it was impeccably kept. The breastplate of hammered steel gleamed in the light of the room's lamp and firelight. Theran was a rare fighter who fought with both hands and carried two blades, a sword of power and a long knife. He preferred a two-blade fighting style over the usual kind featuring a sword and shield. While taller than most men, Theran had a natural and trained ability with incredibly fast reflexes.

Next to Theran, Jordan was a study of contrasts. While his face remained youthful and luminous with inner joy, his hair had gone prematurely white. Like Theran, his purple and white tunic, pants, and robes of the Hall of Shepherds were impeccable, and marked him as the King's Shepherd, only second to the High Shepherd on the Triune Council. His lean figure wrapped in his loose attire fooled some into believing he wore the blade belted at his hip as decoration, but he was a keen and intelligent fighter. In addition to his sword, he carried a copy of the sacred scriptures and a plain staff. Jordan's sharp blue eyes concentrated on a tapestry map of the known world of Aramatir, with Septily depicted at its center.

Directing his attention to the map, Xandros knew he did not have the luxury to enjoy the evening with his friends. They had work to do, but perhaps they could at least enjoy a good repast. He waved at the sideboard filled with a buffet of finger foods his steward had brought earlier, and then the comfortable chairs opposite to him. "Please, take sustenance. We have serious matters to discuss, and none of us do well on empty stomachs."

Theran checked the lock on the door before turning to face him. "Majesty, I am your protector here, as always, and the recent events make me uneasy, even here in your private study. We must remain vigilant to stop the Red Hand from creating more of their Red House establishments in Skycliff."

Xandros sighed. "I agree, but please stop standing at formal attention and calling me 'Majesty' in the privacy of my study. This room is secure. You have placed layers of security between me and the rest of society. If I am confined like this, I will never know what it is like to truly live in Septily or feel the freedom I hope our citizens have."

Theran's hand drifted to his helm, which hooked to his belt during his most relaxed moments of guarding Xandros. "The freedom that allows assassins to lurk close to you? Or the freedom your son Alex had when he went to the very criminals we keep trying to erase from Skycliff and attempted to procure more than conversation from a woman in the Red House, provided by that cruel organization the Red Hand?"

Jordan tutted in disagreement, crossing his arms over his chest. "We cannot judge Alex. We do not know he went to the Red House for such ill purposes. He loved his mother, and he has never treated any woman poorly."

Theran snorted. "There is only one motive for someone who goes to the Red House. You know that, Jordan."

Jordan held up his hands. "I have never been there for any purpose than to shut one down. Even if we assume Alex went there to do something unworthy, we can hope he did not truly understand the circumstances in which those women are brought to the Red House."

Theran scowled. "He cannot be so naïve." He walked over to the sideboard and snatched up a few slices of cheese and some brown bread.

Xandros had heard enough of their conjecturing. When he had learned of Alex's foolishness late in the evening a few days prior, the two of them had been retired for the evening. His other Sword Guards had done their jobs and had kept his confidence. He knew Theran and Jordan would be angry, for he had created arrangements that they did not know about, and feared the parting he must endure. He dropped his head to his hands for a moment in a wordless cry of prayer for his friends, for his son, and for his kingdom.

He felt someone touch his hands, and knew from the softness of that touch, it had to be Jordan. This was confirmed by his friend's words.

"Lord of Light, we need your guidance."

"Amen." Theran said in response, his voice grim.

Sitting up straight with a determination not to let them down, Xandros tapped the papers on his desk. "Alex could be so naïve, and that is why I decided on the punishment I gave him. He has been too sheltered and does not truly understand the traditions of our kingdom or this office. I have sent him to train with the Watch Guard. They prepare him for the right path. Instead of focusing on his punishment, I would like us to consider the methods in which he discovered the Red House, and how the establishment opened again, in a new location, after we closed the last one."

Xandros unrolled a map of Skycliff. Red marks dotted the map, showing all the previous sites of the Red House within the city's walls. He was warming up to his revelation. He hoped his friends would forgive him for waiting to share it.

Jordan poured himself a glass of mead and picked up a piece of bread. He fixed his attention on the map. "They have a system of transporting their slaves into the city that we are not seeing. At first, it seemed the port must be vulnerable, but we have not found any leads there. I've had apprentices working on it."

Theran leaned over the map, tracing his fingers from one red mark to another. "My people, in disguise, have not seen a pattern or a transportation method for this operation either, and I had hoped they would be more effective than the Shepherd apprentices. No disrespect to you, Jordan."

Xandros pointed to the unofficially named Inner Circle, which surrounded the palace grounds. "Have you searched here? I have reason to believe our problems may be coming from those closest to the palace."

Theran stepped back and glared at the door which led to the main hall and court. "You have reason to believe those who step and fawn at your every whim would do such a thing?"

Xandros ran his hands over his face and sighed. "The nobles and the merchants always have a handful among their number who are greedy for more and more money and power." Opening the drawer of his desk, he withdrew the missive he had been given the same night he had his son arrested and sent to the Watch Guard. "This, gentleman, is a handwritten note by one of our city's most powerful nobles, given to his son who thwarted his father's plans. Because of this young man, Alex was saved from a long-running plot to blackmail me and force me to be this noble's puppet."

Theran and Jordan stared at the paper and then exchanged a glance with each other and spoke at the same time. "Torren?"

Xandros gritted his teeth and gave a slow nod. How had they known? Had he been so blinded by his grief he could not comprehend the threats against him?

Theran's brow furrowed again, and he held out his hand. "Lord Torren is behind the Red House, and this proves it?"

Xandros handed him the slip of paper. "Not exactly."

Jordan read the missive over Theran's shoulder. "There are no names. Not even Prince Alex is mentioned by name." He put his hand on Theran's shoulder. "We can't act yet."

Theran crumpled the paper in his fist. "Where is Junior Lord Dan, now? Would he testify in court against his father?"

Chapter 4: From Guard to Spy

Theran's fist remained clenched around the paper, as he struggled with the bitterness and grief that assailed him at every mention of the Red House. The criminal group was responsible for the loss of one of his nieces. He loved his country. He loved his friend the King. And at the same time, he wanted to speak to Junior Lord Dan and force every bit of information out of the upstart noble. He recognized the urge was not worthy of his calling as the Master Sword Guard responsible for the King's protection, but he still felt hard anger building in his chest.

Xandros shook his head. "I sent him with my son to the Watch Guard. It was his wish, and I hoped he would continue to protect my son as you protect me, old friend. In addition, there is a young man whose father forced him to join the Watch Guard who will also train with them. He is yearning for the path of Shepherd, and I hope the three will form bonds like we share."

Theran took a slow breath, wrestling with his feelings and understanding Xandros had a duty to uphold, to keep the country of Septily on the right path to justice for the safety of all citizens. If Junior Lord Dan Torren was truly worthy of the Watch Guard, then he had already told them all he knew about his father's association with the Red House. While the Watch Guard did not share the same calling as the Sword Hall of the Triune Halls, they served as Guardians against evil across inter-kingdom borders and had a good alliance with the Triune Halls of Septily. If the young man passed his training with them, then Theran would speak to him as a colleague. The pain in his chest eased and he tried to think clearly.

Jordan steepled his hands in front of him. "Bonds like ours do not always do well when they are forced upon young men."

Theran hadn't considered that problem, but it was not the one that most concerned him. He wanted to get information on the Red Hand's operations and shut down all their Red Houses, which trafficked women and men, children and adults, by force or with poisons which rendered the victims helpless and unable to fight back.

Xandros bowed his head. "It is the best I can do. We must focus on the Red House."

That, Theran agreed with, but he still needed to say his piece. "Without Junior Lord Dan, we have no evidence we can take to the Lawgivers, and we cannot prosecute or imprison anyone without their help. I commend you for being a good king, but there are times when you could rule much more efficiently. We need to shut down the Red House." His anger built again as he spoke, but it was followed immediately by remorse. None of this was Xandros's fault. He dropped his head. "Forgive me, my King, my friend, I speak out of pain."

Xandros rose from his chair. "I understand your grief, Theran, I do. Your niece was stolen from you and was never found. We need to act on this urgently, and it is why I am asking you both to help me with the next steps. I plan to trap Lord Torren and all those involved."

Theran ran a hand through his hair and paced in front of the fireplace. While only embers burned in the hearth, his frustration and pain boiled under his skin. He swiveled to face his friend and King. "What can we do that we have not already tried, Xandros? It has been going on for years, and our efforts have failed to create a meaningful dent in their organization, especially if they become so bold as to try to trap young Alex via blackmail."

Xandros leaned forward and placed both his hands on the map. "We do the unexpected. We trap them, and we hunt them on their ground, not our own."

Theran stalked over to stare down at the map of the city, not sure how they would find anything new on the parchment.

Jordan placed his hand on Theran's arm in a placating gesture. "We will help, in any way we can, King Xandros. As your friends, and as your subjects. What do you want us to do?"

Xandros reached into his desk again and withdrew two more missives. "I received news from the Watch Guard about a slave route of the Red Hand in the Southlands. I need you, Jordan, to take a platoon of Sword Guards from the Triune Halls to intercept a caravan of kidnapped children, men, and women."

Theran shifted in his stance, not sure he heard correctly. Jordan, to intercept a slave caravan? It was unexpected, but was it wise?

Jordan took the paper and opened it, pressing his lips together as he read it in full. "Are you sure this is the best fit for me, Xandros? I am capable of defense, but I am not a warrior."

Xandros tapped his desk. "The man in charge of this particular unit was assigned as a favor to a noble in my court, and while the unit is available on a moment's notice for this mission, they are not the most experienced, nor is the commander. I need someone with your steady influence and discernment in charge. I believe your voice of gentleness will be healing for the captives, once they are freed."

Theran could understand Xandros's reasoning, but what if Jordan and the upstart Sword Master he referred to failed? Since his wife's death, Xandros had been struggling to rule. For the first time in years, Theran could see some of the renewed confidence Xandros had once had. Maybe the trouble with Prince Alex had caused Xandros to reawaken to the tasks at hand, but, this seemed like a strange plan. "Are you set on this, Xandros? It seems that I would be best suited to taking out my anger on the Red Hand in a battle."

Xandros held the other letter close to his chest. "While it will not put you in a fight, this assignment will bring you closer to the root of the problem here in Skycliff, and it is only you who I trust to do the task. Jordan would not be suited for it. You will need to pretend to be disavowed from my service and will work as a guard for Junior Lady Leandra Torren, Dan's sister. I met with her, and she is, like her brother, discomfited and unhappy with her father's attempts to rule her life and to ruin Skycliff. She will help you gain access to the Torren family affairs." He slowly held out the letter. "You will need to tread with care, but if you need to strike, you will retain full authority to cut the head off the snake."

Theran thought over his friend's words and wondered at the sensibility of the plan. Would Lord and Lady Torren truly believe he was disavowed? What would that entail? And who was this young woman who would betray her parents? Yet, if it put him in a position to finish the Red Hand's activities, he would take it. He held out his hand for the missive.

Jordan held up one hand. "My friends, the shepherds and the lawgivers do not countenance vigilante justice."

Theran sighed, knowing he was radiating the kind of anger that caused Jordan to speak as he did. "I will do the matter justly." He bowed his head to Xandros, and then to Jordan. "I promise, I will not strike unless there is no other option."

A moment of silence passed over the room.

Jordan held out his hands. "Hope in the Lord is all we truly have."

Theran closed his eyes as Jordan prayed, but he struggled to hear the words of the prayer. Time for prayers were over. They needed to act. He would do all he could to understand the plans of his King and do his best to begin the necessary work, but inside, he felt torn between rage and a need for justice. They were headed into late evening, but he couldn't imagine sleeping. It was time to be awake and actively pursuing the Red Hand.

Chapter 5: Morning Chores

Dan startled awake because of a strange noise and fumbled for his blade. When his fingers closed around the leather-wrapped pommel, he relaxed and took in his surroundings.

Early morning light shone across dusty cobblestones and the outer room. The stable had been full of a variety of horses, at least a few dozen. That meant somewhere beyond this area, presumably through the door at the end, there were more rooms, possibly more barracks.

It dawned on him that he did not know how the Watch Guard lived their daily lives in their Keeps. Were they all bachelors? Did they have families? Was he cut out for this life of service?

No. He pressed the questions away. He couldn't doubt this now. It was the best choice he had.

A cock crowed outside. That might have been what awakened him. He had heard chickens at the Lake District estate his parents owned, but he had forgotten how rousing the birds could be. Last night, they had ridden across the dark, flat stones of the courtyard before they had entered the stable. How much did he miss of the Keep's structure? He ran his hand over his lightly stubbled chin and sighed. He usually over-worried things, but for a time he had acted almost as impulsively as Alex.

In his bunk closest to the castle door, Alex was curled under a lump of blankets with the top of his blonde hair sticking out. Dan contemplated waking him, then decided against it. Dan knew the next time they spoke,

Alex would have some harsh words for him. No, he was not waking up Alex.

After he dressed in a clean tunic and pants, he made his bed, mostly because he saw Farrald straightening his covers and pillow and he did not want to look like a slouch. He did not know how Farrald got the corners tucked in so tight and he did not ask. He was almost as helpless as Alex. It was an uncomfortable assessment.

Dan sat on the chest at the end of his bed to put on his boots and stared down at the floor. The stones were worn and uneven, but clean. As he stared at the grooves between the stones, he realized he knew who probably washed the floor, but he did not like the idea. And if he did not like it, he was sure Alex would be furious.

With that thought, Dan rose and followed Farrald into the stable area. If he sincerely wanted freedom from his past, he had to learn to live like a common-born man, like Farrald, well, except not exactly like Farrald.

Farrald was grooming his horse again and singing to it. He pivoted to nod at Dan and kept singing with a big smile on his face.

Dan stood there momentarily, taken aback by Farrald's ability to sing with such cheer this early, then grabbed one of the other brushes and started combing Alex's mare. The horse hadn't had proper grooming the night before and it leaned into him appreciatively, snuffling his hair.

Farrald stopped singing when he went to fetch fresh hay for the horses. "So, I never did catch your name?" he asked.

Dan sighed, embarrassed that he'd been so rude to Farrald, who had done nothing wrong the day before. "I'm Dan Torren, but call me Dan. The rest doesn't matter anymore."

Farrald paused in his work. "So, you're a noble and Alex is, too?"

Dan opened his mouth, then shut it. What could he say about Alex? He was not sure. He reflected on all the ways they both stood out as nobles to Farrald and knew he couldn't hide his identity. His clothes were city clothes, the kind of tunic and pants the nobility wore in Skycliff with decorations up and down the sleeves of his shirts, and with piping on his dark pants. He continued to brush his mare as he collected his thoughts.

"My family is influential at court, or at least my father tries to be. I don't want that life. Where are you from, Farrald?"

"The Desert District. It's dry there." Farrald shrugged.

Dan smiled, then chuckled. "That's an understatement—'dry'—I think I've heard tell it can suck the moisture off your bones."

Farrald scoffed. "Only if you're foolish to be out at midday with no protection."

"What do you do during midday?" Dan asked.

"We sleep, meditate, or study," Farrald said, his eyes lighting up. "The Sanctuary library has the most insulated corners where one can stay cool in the heat and is one of the best places to spend midday. I understand they have an even bigger library here."

"You came for their library?" Dan asked, shaking his head in puzzlement. His tutor Reg would have loved Farrald, as much as he was frustrated by Dan. He imagined Reg regaling Farrald with dry, dusty facts and Farrald soaking in his wisdom. Dan enjoyed reading entertaining stories, but he hated regimented studies.

"Of course, the Watch Guard holds more knowledge between its towers than any place outside of the Triune Halls in Skycliff, if not even more than that. Have you been to the library at Skycliff?"

"Yes." Dan finished brushing down Alex's mare and started grooming his own mare, who lipped at his shoulder until he patted her neck. "My tutor took me there every week. I was supposed to do research in several areas to keep my mind sharp and help me understand the vast responsibilities of my family."

"What's it like?" Farrald had grabbed one of the brooms but stood there, leaning against it.

"Rooms and rooms of books, tall windows, enormous tables, and small ones. There is a section I like on the top floor, where there are books on the legends of the Champions, and you can see magnificent views of the harbor."

"Our library did not have any views, but I like books on music, worship, and philosophy. It is where we can truly learn who we are in relation to the Lord. Do they have a good section for that in Skycliff?"

Dan shrugged. "That was not somewhere my tutor Reg took me, and I did not seek it out."

Farrald's face sobered and he started sweeping. After a few moments, he began humming a tune in time to the sounds of the broom across the floor. Dan did not recognize the song. It was pleasant, but Dan was glad he was not expected to join in. He picked up another broom.

When they had finished sweeping the stable and had bestrewn hay in the stalls, Dan considered cleaning the tack, but he paused at the doorway to the barracks room. Should he wake Alex yet?

Chapter 6: Rude Awakenings

THE PROBLEM OF WAKING Alex was solved when Quinn came bellowing out from the barracks room with Alex by his elbow. "Up, up, up. You have chores to do."

Alex was barefoot, his shirt hung loosely around his hips, and his hair was sticking up in every direction. He glared at Dan, then Farrald, and yanked his arm out of Quinn's grip. "Unhand me. I am–

"A recruit. Not even an apprentice. That's what you all are," Quinn reminded them. "Nothing else matters here. So far, you aren't passing muster, Alex."

Alex clenched his fists. His shoulders tightened, and so did his jaw. His face reddened.

"Master Quinn, would it be all right if we broke our fast? I'm awfully hungry." Farrald said, interrupting the scene.

Dan gave Farrald a small nod. "I am hungry, too, Sir Quinn."

"I am no one's 'sir' or 'master,' 'Quinn' will do. We don't stand on ceremony here unless you speak to the Sergeant of Arms, the Lieutenants, or the Captain." Quinn puffed up his chest as he spoke and pushed Alex's shoulder. "There are no titles for anyone else."

"Of course, Quinn," Dan said. He tilted his chin downward, not in an actual bow, but as deferential as he could manage, with Quinn manhandling Alex. He tried to keep his eyes focused on the flagstones below their feet, but still watched them both out of his peripheral vision.

Alex visibly forced himself to relax with a deep breath. "May I get my boots, Quinn, and my vest, before I help with the chores and have breakfast?"

"Yes. Farrald will demonstrate how to fold your bedding, and Dan will show you how to clean tack. Then, you will have breakfast. Tomorrow, you had all best be done with these basics by the seventh mark." He pointed at a large candle on a metal stand with a metal cover over it that stood outside the stable in the courtyard.

The candle had a wire running through it at evenly marked intervals. Candles like this for marking the time were common in Septily and in the world beyond. Each mark matched an hour of the day, if the candle were lit and kept burning. He guessed somewhere inside the keep a larger time candle was used to keep the time as accurate as possible. The seventh mark came seven hours after the darkest part of the night; the larger time-candles were replaced at midnight.

Thankfully, Alex did not gripe at Farrald or Dan when they showed him how to do the chores assigned to them, and he stopped glaring at Dan midway through cleaning the horse tackle.

"This can't be fun for you, either," he said, as he ran a polishing cloth over one of the stirrups.

Dan glanced around to see if Farrald was listening to them, but Farrald was humming over his work, sitting on a bench several feet away.

With a careful hand, Dan rubbed more cleaning oil into his saddle. "The head of our house guard was a retired Sword Guard from the Triune Halls. He made me learn how to care for my horse, my tack, and my blade after every lesson. I'm not saying I liked it, but he promised to show me how to fight like him if I did my chores without complaining."

He paused in his work and stared out at the blue sky above the courtyard beyond the stable. He missed old Thorn. He wondered what the old man would think of him now when he couldn't even make a bed as well as Farrald.

"I see." Alex winced as he rubbed the cleaning cloth over the last bit of tack. He finished it and gripped the cloth tight in one hand. "I had the finest tutors, the best servants. I envied others their freedom. But I did not know what I was wishing for." As Alex gathered all his cleaning cloths, Dan showed him the basket on the side of the stable where the used cloths were stowed until they were washed for their next use.

"You must believe I am a fool, even more so than you did the other night" Alex said bluntly. He gave Dan one of his specific looks, a studied gaze which meant he was ready to judge anything Dan said.

Dan shook his head. He did not want to remember the garish party where they had both been two nights ago. "I do not believe you are a fool for wanting freedom."

He thought about telling Alex about a spot he had missed on his tack, then noticed a blister on Alex's palm. "Let's get washed up for breakfast."

Hanging his tack up on the hooks on the stable wall, he watched out of the corner of his eyes to make sure Alex did the same. Then he walked over to where Farrald sat resewing the edge of his worn saddle. "We need to find where we eat breakfast." His stomach grumbled as he spoke.

Farrald laughed as his stomach whined. "It is time, isn't it?" He finished his stitching with a precise knot, then slipped the supplies for tack repairs into a trunk.

Alex frowned as Dan and Farrald both washed their hands under the pump at the same time. Then he joined in the fray. By the time they were done, they had chilled hands and water spray dotting their clothes.

As Dan dried his hands after Farrald and Alex, a sense of contentment washed over him. The Watch Guard offered him a chance at a life beyond the political machinations of Skycliff. He knew he was lucky. The citizens of Septily would never really care what happened to a Junior Lord. He could join the Watch Guard or get trained to do something else. The only individuals who would miss him from his past were his parents and his sister, and his parents had made it clear they wanted him for only one thing: to be their political pawn because he was the same age as Alex.

It would not happen. He would not return to Skycliff with Alex at the end of the year. That would effectively ruin his father's plans.

As they made their way toward the kitchen door, Dan's mind wandered to the stories he'd heard about the Watch Guard. They weren't just protectors of borders; they were guardians of ancient secrets and powerful artifacts. He recalled tales whispered in the corners of Skycliff's grand halls, stories of weapons that could command the elements or change the course of battles.

"What do you think we'll learn first?" Farrald's excited voice broke through Dan's reverie.

Dan glanced at his companions. Alex wore a mask of indifference, but Dan could see the curiosity burning in his eyes. "Combat training, probably," Alex said with a shrug.

"Maybe," Dan agreed, "but I hope we'll learn about the artifacts the Watch Guard protects too." He lowered his voice, pausing outside the kitchen door.

Farrald's eyes widened. "My gran used to tell stories about a bow that never missed its mark, no matter how far the target."

Even Alex looked intrigued now. "My mother told me stories about a staff that could control the weather. Always thought it was just a myth."

Dan nodded, excitement building in his chest. The Watch Guard served beyond the borders of any nation as protectors of the known world of Aramatir. But now he realized it might be so much more than that. They could be the last line of defense against powers beyond imagination.

Here, he could learn not just how to fight, but how to protect the world from threats most people couldn't even comprehend.

Whatever challenges lay ahead, whatever ancient and powerful forces they might encounter, Dan wanted to be ready to face them.

The legends of the Watch Guard were about to become his reality.

Chapter 7: Breakfast

Dan, Farrald, and Alex returned to the barracks and entered the wooden door that separated the barracks from the rest of the castle. The door swung open to reveal warm light and the smell of fresh bread.

At the stove stood a brown-skinned man with a tattoo on his arm of an owl holding a sword in its claws. He wore an apron over his Watch Guard uniform, and he beckoned them toward a table. "There you are! I'm Kaipo. The other recruits are in the practice field. Eat up and eat quickly. You'll join them soon."

Alex frowned as if he might say something, but Dan nudged him.

"Quinn told us to clean our tack," Farrald explained as he grabbed a hunk of bread and a bowl, which Kaipo filled with a mash of cheese, potatoes, and sausage. "We did not know there were any other recruits here, yet."

"You're likely the last, although there were rumors of more arriving, they are from an unpredictable people." Kaipo poured more food into two more bowls and handed them to Dan and Alex, who took seats around Farrald on the bench by the long, wooden kitchen table.

Dan grabbed a piece of bread and used it along with a spoon to shovel the steaming food as quickly as he could, forgoing all the noble manners his mother had painstakingly taught him. Farrald was doing much the same. Alex dipped his bread in the mash, took a bite, and chewed slowly.

"This is good." Alex pointed at the mash.

"Of course, I made it." Kaipo grinned. "You're not going to like Quinn's cooking, but we all take turns." He walked back to the ovens and pulled out several more loaves of bread. "Luncheon will be ready for you when you finish practice. Best get that down. Sergeant Nuria may not take so kindly to waiting."

Alex noticed he was behind, took a moment to roll up the cuffs of his shirt, and began to eat more quickly, although still far more politely than Dan and Farrald did. They finished their food in a few more minutes.

"I'll get your sword and shield while you finish," Dan offered to Alex.

Alex tapped his heart in a tiny salute. "Thank you."

"Each man cares for his own kit, but today I will let you help," Kaipo stated sternly. "You're going to need to eat and move faster than that, recruit."

"Alex. My name is –"

"Recruit. Your name is recruit until we take you on as an apprentice." Kaipo said.

Dan traipsed back to the stable barracks with Farrald as Kaipo continued to educate Alex in the ways of common treatment. He retrieved his sword, shield, and light breastplate, then found Alex's, which were of far finer steel than his own. Farrald had a blade in an old leather sheath which he buckled awkwardly around him.

"I did not have much cause to use my sword at home," Farrald said, "my dad wanted me here, wanted me to see more of the world before I made up my mind." He shrugged. "I've already made up my mind, but he won't listen."

"My father doesn't listen well, either," said Dan. "You plan on being a Shepherd?"

Farrald smiled, his whole face lighting up. "You can tell?"

"A little," Dan said, grinning. If he'd had a Shepherd like Farrald, he might not have minded going to worship at the Triune Halls' sanctuary, but none of the Shepherds in Skycliff seemed to share Farrald's sunny disposition. "Come on, let's get Alex."

Farrald held up his hands. "Wait, please, tell me who he is. He's someone, but I never excelled at learning the houses."

Dan worried his lip with his teeth. "I really shouldn't say, but think higher than noble houses. His real name's Alexandros."

"Alexandros, Alexandros." Farrald muttered. "I don't remember any noble named, wait." Farrald stepped back as his face paled and his freckles stood out starkly. "Prince Alexandros? What is he doing in the Watch Guard?" Farrald glanced around as if he could get in trouble for asking.

"That's not for me to say," said Dan.

Farrald winced. "Okay." He laughed shakily. "I broke bread with the future king."

"And taught him how to make his bed." Dan reminded him.

Farrald's eyebrows raised into his shaggy bangs. "Oh, no. I told him he did it wrong."

Dan shrugged and took his gear and Alex's gear toward the castle. "Come on, let's get to practice."

Farrald lagged as they strolled back inside.

When Dan brought Alex his gear, the prince quickly buckled on his own breastplate. Dan was thankful he knew how to do that himself, especially under Kaipo's watchful eyes. Alex strapped on his sword and shield, then stood to leave. Then he paused, picked up his bowl, and took it to the sink. "Thank you, Kaipo, for the meal. Thank you, Dan, for retrieving my gear."

Kaipo pointed to the other doorway with his cutting knife. "Go down the stairs, out into the field. Sergeant Nuria will force you to run laps for being late."

Dan wanted to defend or make excuses for them, but instead, he followed orders and stepped out the door, leaving both Alex and Farrald to follow him. He did not want to imagine the scene the prince might cause at any moment due to the lack of respect for his title.

Not for the first or the last time, Dan was glad he did not have the same responsibilities as Alex. He was not anyone special. He did not have to hold up anyone else. He only had to earn his own self-respect.

Chapter 8: Drinaii Captivity

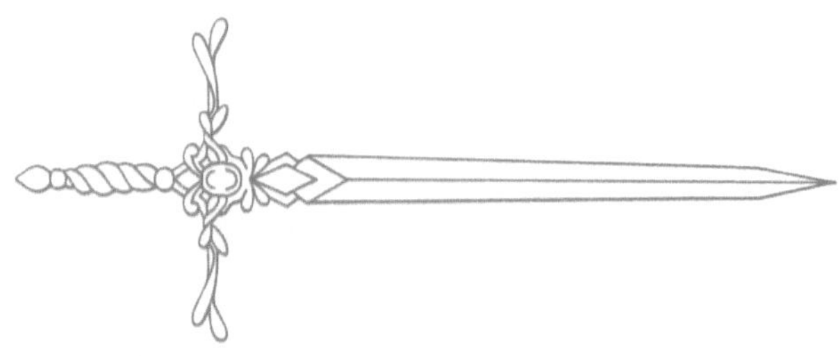

Sunlight filtered through the dark maroon walls of Captain Stelia's private tent. Her cot took up one side. The other side held her two packs, her sole possessions. The tent was stuffy, with the faint scent of sweat and leather lingering in the air. Canvas walls rustled gently with the occasional breeze, casting shifting shadows across the interior. The corners of the tent were dim, contrasting sharply with the bright central rug, her only luxury. The rug depicted a burst of sun's rays over a mountain range.

In the center of the rug, a tiny girl trembled in fear. She couldn't have been more than seven. Her ribs stood out from the tatters of her clothes, even though she had been captured recently. The summers and winters in the Southlands were harsh, especially for the nomads who tried to eke out a scant existence while staying clear of the Drinaii.

Stelia had been that girl once, except the tent where she had trembled belonged to the leader of the Dark Sisterhood, far more spacious and far less comfortable for captives. Unlike this girl, she came from a village, and not a nomad's camp, but their circumstances were similar. She lost her entire family to the Drinaii, as this girl had. She had been taken for her potential to serve, as this girl had.

She clenched her fists at her sides, struggling with the deep echoes of pain and fear, even after all these years. Even as a Captain of the Enforcers, she had little freedom. There were those above and below her who would love to see her fall from her position. They feared her, hated her, and rightfully so. She had earned it, as the favored Enforcer of the Dark Sisterhood, placed in her position in the Drinaii Army by Kalidess, the dread leader of the coven.

Ironically, the task suited Stelia because of her loathing for the Drinaii and the Dark Sisterhood. As an Enforcer, she meted out the punishments on any Drinaii mercenary who did not fulfill their tasks as the Dark Sisterhood wished. Her duties placed her above the Drinaii Commanders, which they resented, especially as her rank was beneath theirs, but as an Enforcer, she could bring them to justice for the Dark Sisterhood, and they had little to say in the matter. Rightly, they hated and feared her. Nearly as much as she hated and feared them.

The air around her always seemed to thicken with tension whenever she approached a Drinaii Commander. She could see the flicker of contempt in their eyes, barely concealed by a mask of forced respect. Every interaction was a silent battle of wills, with Stelia's authority prevailing through sheer force of her indomitable presence. The weight of her role pressed heavily on her shoulders, a constant reminder of the precarious balance she maintained. Each punishment she administered was a blow against her own sense of morality, yet it was a necessary evil she embraced with grim resolve.

She hated the things she did as an Enforcer, but she would rather do those things to the Drinaii than to those they took captive. Before Kalidess made her an Enforcer, she served for a short time as a Drinaii soldier in the ranks. While she knew she had been coddled compared to some because of her relationship with Kalidess, she had been forced with the choice to kill or be killed. Her hands would always be stained with the blood of innocents, even if that time was behind her. Being a part of the Drinaii, enslaved to them and to the Dark Sisterhood meant her soul was tainted, and she held no hope of redemption.

But she did what she could to change the fate of those like her, when she could get away with it.

As a Captain, she slept and worked from her own tent, and she was allotted one captive or slave whenever they conquered a village or group of nomads. She could choose whichever captive she wanted, could do whatever she wanted. She knew the sorts of things the other Captains and Commanders did to their captives.

As tears ran down the little girl's face, Stelia took in a deep breath. She must remain calm. If she were to do what she hoped and get away with it, the girl could not breathe a word to anyone about it.

She knelt on the carpet next to the little girl, and the girl's trembling became sobs of distress.

"Shh. Hush little one and listen."

The girl bowed until her head hit the carpet.

Stelia reached down and raised the girl by her shoulders, then lifted her chin until she could see the girl's brown eyes flecked with gold. "You are not going to die or suffer today."

The girl's eyes widened, her trembling becoming more pronounced as she stared at Stelia, a mix of fear and confusion reflected in her gaze. The girl's frail shoulders quivered under her hands, and the stark evidence of her recent hardships were etched into her hollow cheeks. The tent's dim light cast shadows that emphasized the grime on the girl's skin. Stelia's heart ached with a familiar pang of empathy and sorrow, something she had grown accustomed to over the years. The little girl seemed so fragile, and yet she held onto a spark of life that Stelia found both heartbreaking and inspiring.

Stelia lowered her voice to a whisper. "If I can, I will free you. If you speak of this to anyone, we would both be hurt."

The little girl continued to stare at her, as if she did not comprehend what Stelia meant.

"I am going to clean your wounds, and then put dirt on you again, like a disguise. You will stay chained in my tent, but I won't lock your chains, until I have a chance to free you, someplace with a water source and a clear path to another place. You will ride with me, serve me, and when we have a chance, I will set you free at night and away from the camp. I hope to find someone else, another captive, to send with you so you will be safe."

Tears slid down the girl's face.

"Can you pretend to be my servant until we have a chance for your freedom?"

The girl nodded slowly, then bowed her head to the carpet again.

Stelia stood and went to glance through her tent flap. No one stood near enough to have heard. She might get away with her treason again. She did not feel triumph at her deception. Instead, she felt only sorrow. Even after rescuing nearly a hundred from captivity, the hollow pain still rested in her belly, knowing the numbers of those she killed as a foot soldier, and of those who died whenever they took a village or a group of nomads. Every time she rescued one, she ran the risk of death or worse, but it was the only thing keeping her alive. Without these small acts of impossible hope for the future of those she saved, she had no reason for being. And she was perfectly suited for it, since she started this work not long after her enslavement by Kalidess. Somehow, even as a child, she had been able to get others away. But when she tried to run, she had been caught and punished. So, she decided this was her purpose. To save one at a time, even while doing the despicable work of enforcing Kalidess's will on the Drinaii.

Long ago, she had a friend. That friend escaped. Then, she made another friend, and that friend was no longer her friend. Being friends with Captain Jennar was to be friends with the enemy. He had seemed like her, once, but due to his more recent actions, her trust in him was broken.

Thinking of him seemed to summon him, for she heard his distinctive throat clearing outside her tent.

Stelia straightened her helmet and opened the flap of her tent, noting the way his armor was regulation fit, spotless, and dully soaking up the sun the way Drinaii armor did. His white–blonde hair barely poked out of the sides of his helmet.

"Yes, Captain Jennar. What news?"

"Stelia, why such formality with an old friend?" He waved his hand toward the interior of her tent. "Why don't you invite me in, for old time's sake?"

"It would be inappropriate, Captain Jennar. Those times are past."

He ground his teeth before leaning in and speaking quietly to her. "You do not want me as your enemy, Stelia. I know what you are about. I know your secrets."

Her chest grew tight, but she kept her face relaxed. "Jennar, I do not give favors or receive them in my position of Enforcer. Remember that."

He waved a finger at her. "Ah-ah. You called me Jennar." Then he straightened and glanced at the soldiers walking by her tent before addressing her again. "If you won't allow an old friend to watch your back, you won't be able to keep this up, Stelia."

"I don't know what you're talking about."

He shook his head. "Lying was never your strong suit. But consider this a limited time offer. If you don't accept help, I might be the one to turn you in."

Goosebumps rose on her arms, but she clenched her jaw. "Step away from my tent, Captain Jennar."

He saluted her sardonically. "As you wish, Enforcer."

Stelia did not relax until she lost sight of him in the crowded thoroughfare that ran through the encampment. Did he really know about her work to free captives? If he did, would he really tell? She stepped back into her tent, and pulled off her helmet, placing it on her cot before unbraiding her hair and running her hands through it. What would she do? Try Jennar on some trumped-up charge and have him flogged or killed? The thought twisted her stomach. It was no worse than other things she had done to protect her secret, but she did not want to do that to Jennar, even if he had become one of the loyal Drinaii Captains.

The little girl came over to her side and took a clump of Stelia's hair, combing through it with her fingers.

"You don't have to do that."

The girl shook her head and continued to finger comb Stelia's hair.

"We're going to have to take care of you quickly, if Jennar's really going to do as he says."

The little girl dipped her chin but did not speak.

Stelia had seen that before. Some children refused to speak after the trauma they endured, and she understood.

Chapter 9: In the Training Yard

When they reached the training yard, Dan paused. Alex and Farrald stopped with him. They needed a moment to take it all in. Young women and men about their age stood in rows, going through fighting stances at the direction of a tough-looking middle-aged woman with skin as dark as Dan's own and a single, thick braid snaking down her back. The woman's gaze was sharp, missing nothing, and her voice carried a steely authority that commanded respect. A large griffin stood with the recruits, mirroring their movements. The creature's keen eyes observed everything with an intelligent glint.

Dan was amazed at the sight of the creature. He had never seen a griffin up close. While Septily and Aerland, the birthplace of griffins, had peace between them, the only time they had visited Septily in his lifetime had been after he had his falling out with Alex. He couldn't help but stare now, at the rippling colors of the creature's feathers and fur, gold, white, and brown. As the griffin flowed through the stances, it dug its talons into the grass, leaving deep gouges that spoke of its immense strength.

The harsh-looking woman faced them and barked orders in a low voice. "Recruits. You're late. Ten laps around the perimeter of the field. You'll rejoin us for the first sparring matches. Put your blades on the racks and plan to pick up wooden staves when you return." Her braid swung like a whip as she turned her back on them and started shouting commands to the other recruits. "4-7-3-1." It was obviously a sequence of moves they'd already learned, as the recruits started a series of sword attacks, their movements synchronized and precise.

Not wanting to be left out of training much longer, Dan hurried to the nearest weapons rack, set down his sword and shield, and ran out along the wall of the keep, seeing the clear markings of footprints in the grass. The morning sun cast long quiet shadows, broken by the rhythmic thud of their feet hitting the ground, with the sounds of the blade practice behind them. Running laps was probably part of a standard warm-up. The scent of sweat and fresh grass mingled in the breeze, a reminder of the hard work and discipline that would define their training.

He held back until both Alex and Farrald caught up. It seemed like Farrald was a little bored by their speed, so he picked up the pace. Alex joined them. They ran together easily without speaking. The camaraderie in the rhythm of the run soothed Dan and he felt hope again, hope that this could be his place, away from his father's plots. The soft thud of their boots on the packed earth and the synchronized rise and fall of their breaths created a comforting harmony.

A shrill whistle ended their run. Sergeant Nuria had formed the rest of the recruits into pairs, including the griffin who stood opposite to a young man. The young man's leather gambeson sported a similar pattern to the one the griffin wore over its broad chest, with an image of crossed arrows. So, they knew each other. Dan had never met anyone from Aerland and couldn't fathom an even match between the man and the griffin. Nonetheless, he was relieved not to be expected to confront the fierce creature.

The young woman standing next to Sergeant Nuria had lustrous dark hair, full lips, and gorgeous brown eyes. She stood with a confident posture. He tried not to stare at her beauty. She probably wouldn't even notice him next to Alex. Knowing he shouldn't stare, Dan stared down at the packed ground.

"Keeva, pick your match from these three."

"Yes, Sergeant. I'll take the dark-haired one."

Dan looked up, surprised by her choice. Her eyes, a startling blue under her raven hair, were crinkled in mischief.

"We're fighting, not flirting here, Keeva." Sergeant Nuria warned.

"And we can't do both?" Keeva put out her bottom lip in a mock pout and winked at Dan.

His cheeks burned.

"Never mind. You're with him." Sergeant Nuria pointed at Farrald.

"You two," she pointed at Dan and Alex, "you're sparring at the other end of the line. Keeva, you're staying next to me."

"Yes, Sergeant." Keeva dropped her eyes for a moment, but she winked at Dan again.

Dan's cheeks grew even hotter as he realized he was still staring at her. With heavy steps, he turned away and selected a wooden practice sword from the rack without much care.

Alex carefully considered his choice, then they joined the back of the line.

Despite his efforts, Dan couldn't shake the image of Keeva; her face persisted in his thoughts. The way she moved, with an effortless grace, and the playful spark in her gaze left an impression that Dan found hard to ignore.

"Hey, don't make me look bad on the first day." Alex smacked Dan in the arm with his wooden blade.

Dan flinched and brought up his own wooden sword, taking his fighting stance, and trying to focus on the prince. Suddenly, he had another reason to hesitate. Did he dare hit his future monarch? How did Alex's fencing tutors handle it? Despite being the same age, Dan had never seen Alex fight. The prince's sparring sessions were usually private, behind closed doors.

While he was considering this, Alex attacked, striking him again, but this time in the chest. "Maybe you're trying to make me look good?" Alex asked, his voice light. "I know I've seen you fight, Dan Torren."

Dan raised his sword again, and they began again. When Alex stepped toward him, he parried and thrust, coming in strong against Alex's blade.

Alex pushed him to the side with his own parry, then snaked his blade down and tripped Dan as he stepped in. Dan lost his balance, surprised by the prince's disregard for the court rules of fighting. He took a stumbling step to the side in time to parry and riposte against Alex, scoring against his wrist.

Alex grinned. "Now that's more like it." He stepped back, twirling his sword.

Dan felt his anger rising. He did not like being toyed with. He brought his sword in for a quick-strike as Alex's twirled sword was on its backswing.

Alex tried to parry but did not get his sword around fast enough and Dan's sword hit hard against his clavicle. Alex winced and stepped back. "Glad that wasn't steel."

"Me too."

Dan took a moment to catch his breath, wiping sweat from his forehead. The training yard seemed to quiet around them, the voices of other recruits blending into the background as they focused solely on their sparring match. The wooden swords clacked together, echoing through the air with a rhythmic cadence that matched the ebb and flow of their movements. This was where he was meant to be, but he had to make a good impression.

Chapter 10: Sizing Up the Competition

After the first session, Sergeant Nuria had them switch partners. Dan would fight one of the fighters near him, while Alex was sent jogging down the line to fight against Keeva. The sun was higher now, casting longer shadows on the training yard and intensifying the heat. Sweat trickled down Dan's back as he tried to shake off the fatigue from yesterday's ride. He had to make a good impression.

"Hey, eyes on me, old man." The lanky, red-headed boy across from him gave a half-smile, as if to assure him he was only joking. His freckled face and mischievous green eyes made him appear too young for training.

"Excuse me? I'm not that old. Only nineteen." Dan wiped sweat from his brow and pushed his shoulders back, trying to look more confident than he felt.

"I'm fifteen. Remember that when I beat you." The boy smiled wider and raised his sword, his stance sure despite his youth.

"And if I beat you?" Dan loosened his shoulders, rolling them back to ease the tension.

"You'll be the old man beating up on the poor, defenseless young boy," the boy said, pretending to cower with bent shoulders, his lips turned up in a pout. The effect was ruined when he grinned again, a flash of teeth that spoke of both humor and determination.

"Your name?"

"Ewan. You?"

"Dan."

The whistle blew and Ewan leaped toward Dan, his movements a blur of energy. Dan stepped back and parried Ewan's blade and body with his own, taking a solid stance with his legs bent. Their wooden swords collided with a jarring impact.

Ewan landed against him; his arm caught up on their blades. His eyes flashed with determination, and he pushed forward with a grunt.

Dan moved back, but flicked the point of his blade out and caught Ewan's elbow with a hard rap. The sound of the impact drew a few glances from nearby recruits.

Ewan's eyes narrowed. "You're fast for an old man." His voice held grudging respect, mixed with a challenge.

"I'm nineteen, not ninety." Dan's quick reply came with a twinge of unease at the constant reminder of his age among the younger recruits.

Ewan attacked again, this time from a low line which Dan parried easily. But he did not follow up on a riposte because he wanted a better measure of Ewan, who attacked with aggression, each time telegraphing his movements. Dan easily defended himself, then when Ewan slowed, he reached out and poked him in the midriff.

"You weren't fighting that hard with your friend," Ewan stated, his voice accusatory but curious.

"We're not exactly friends," Dan said, his tone more neutral. His eyes flicked over to where Alex and Keeva sparred, a hint of envy gnawing at him.

Ewan raised his brows but did not comment. He simply adjusted his grip on his sword and prepared for another round, a determined set to his jaw. The training yard buzzed with the sounds of clashing wood and the voices of the recruits, the day's heat intensifying the smell of sweat and earth.

Sergeant Nuria blew the whistle again, the sharp sound cutting through the air, signaling another rotation of opponents.

"Nice match, old man Dan," Ewan said with a cheeky grin, his red hair glinting in the sunlight.

Before he could manage a good comeback, Dan faced off against a young, sienna-skinned woman with a trailing tattoo of feathers from her cheek to her chin. She wore her hair up in a crown of braids, the intricate patterns gleaming under the sun.

"Amiria." She pointed at herself. "From the Tuhinga ... you call it Destiny Isles." Her voice was melodic, carrying the accent of her homeland.

Dan tapped his heart. "Dan, from Septily. It is good to-"

The whistle blew. Amiria took a fighting stance unfamiliar to Dan with her long blade, her arms back so that the tip of her blade edged over her shoulder. Her movements were fluid. Dan took a step forward, and she stepped back, the same distance. He stepped back. She followed, again keeping the same distance.

She arched an eyebrow. "You dance well?"

Dan took a stutter step with a jump forward, bringing his blade in straight towards her gut. Her blade arced downward at an incredible speed. She knocked his blade to the side and followed through with a circular cut at his chest. The blow smacked against his ribs and he fell back. He would have to be wary of her.

Next, when she stepped forward, he thrust his sword toward her midsection but dropped the tip as her blade arced down, and he circled the edge, bringing his own sword up to riposte her inside strike and make a cut of his own on her forearm. She barely flinched at the hit.

She nodded. "Good."

Dan felt a little irritated at her condescending praise, as if she had allowed him to hit her. When they started toward each other again, her blade whipped around his, and he stepped further and further back, bewildered. Then he saw a line of direction she hadn't tried, and he dropped into a crouch, stabbing upward with his sword.

She blocked it in time, then pivoted, and reached to smack his outer wrist. She grinned at him before she stepped back, her eyes sparkling with mischief.

Impressed by her ability, Dan lost all his irritation at her. She might be younger than him, but she was a master fighter. He would have to learn how to counter her moves. The whistle blew again, and Amiria gave him a salute, or at least something he believed was a type of salute. Dan raised his sword to his lips, then bowed to her as she strode away. She giggled. Giggled. He had never made a girl giggle before. They usually preferred the more well-dressed blonde men who talked more. Or at least that was the fashion in Skycliff. Maybe because the prince was blonde?

His next opponent drove any of those thoughts away. A huge pale man, taller than anyone Dan had ever met, with mountains of muscle on his upper body and a trimmed blonde beard. His presence was intimidating, his sheer size casting a shadow over Dan. "The name's Nilsen. And you're Dan, the only one here older than me."

Dan clenched his hand around the pommel of his sword. Something about the man's tone put him on edge. His piercing blue eyes seemed to size him up. "I suppose. I'm nineteen."

"Same, but my birthday is in the early winter. And yours?"

"In summer, so I'm younger."

The man smiled, revealing perfect teeth that contrasted with his rugged appearance. "This will be fun."

The whistle blew, and they began.

Dan waited for Nilsen, but Nilsen merely stood in a steady stance, like a mountain waiting for a fly to attack it. His face had settled into a craggy statement of resolve, eyes unblinking and focused.

Dan flicked his blade out in a feint, but Nilsen did not move, apparently seeing the feint for what it was. Dan stepped in and attacked Nilsen's shoulder, but Nilsen parried him enough to keep the edge away from him and did not riposte. Dan shook his head. "You're going to let me make a fool of myself."

Nilsen grinned. "Yes."

Dan attacked again, Nilsen parried and bound Dan's blade, but did not riposte.

Dan attacked high, low, in a circular pattern, and nothing got past Nilsen's defense. Meanwhile, Nilsen remained still and flicked Dan's blade to the side with every parry. His movements were precise and controlled, making Dan feel clumsy in comparison. He did not counterattack once.

Dan finally stepped back and Nilsen stepped forward, closing the gap between them to strike. Dan barely parried the heavy swing in time, ducking and weaving to do so. He moved back again and Nilsen followed through with another attack, which Dan successfully parried, but when Dan went to riposte, Nilsen struck his blade out of his hands and put his sword tip to Dan's throat.

Dan held up his hands. Even a practice blade could do damage if Nilsen hit him hard enough. The weight of Nilsen's presence pressed on him, making him hyper-aware of every move.

"Would you like to know how I beat you?" Nilsen asked him as he handed Dan his practice sword.

"You're faster than I am and more powerful." Dan wiped his hand over his sweating forehead, trying to ignore the sting of humility.

"No, I beat you before we started. I beat you by intimidating you with my size. You never even tried to hit me in the chest, and always tried to hit my legs, arms, anything at the edges of my reach. Am I right?"

Dan's shoulders slumped. "I should know better."

"Yes. Well, Amiria beat me yesterday. She is tougher than I. And more frightening."

"She is?"

Nilsen leaned in toward Dan. "Beauty scares me, my friend. The most beautiful people are sometimes the deadliest. Take my word for it."

"So, what are you saying about me, then?"

Nilsen eyed him critically. "Not my type, and not that beautiful." He grinned.

Dan laughed, his tension easing away. "The feeling's mutual."

The whistle blew. Nilsen jogged away and Dan's next opponent from the opposite line stepped into view. The heavily tanned man was shorter than him, wiry, around his age. His shoulders were broad, and his scarred wrists were thick, as if he were used to some kind of physical labor. He carried his practice sword as if it weighed nothing, his stance relaxed but ready.

"I'm Dan from Septily."

"Perren from Ryssorria." The man reached out his hand.

Dan shook it, noting the relaxed strength of Perren's grip. The man's palm was calloused, hinting at a life of hard labor or constant training. This might be his toughest opponent after Nilsen.

"Good luck," Perren said, smirking, his eyes gleaming with confidence.

Heat boiled inside Dan. Perren's smirk and the last two losses were getting under his skin. He tightened his grip on his sword, determined to prove himself.

The whistle blew, and Perren, his hand still around Dan's, pulled Dan off balance and smacked him in the ribs with the pommel of his sword. Then, he let go and stepped back, his movement smooth and practiced. "All's fair in war, you know." He winked, his smirk widening.

Holding his sore ribs, Dan moved back, then stepped back again, his breath coming in sharp bursts.

Perren took one step forward, his stance casual but alert, but did not follow further. Dan massaged his ribs a moment more, trying to ease the pressure from the bruise forming under his tunic. Straightening, he began a circular attack. Perren evaded it with his own circling blade, pressing into Dan's ribs with a counter-attack that made Dan wince.

Dan stepped back again, his mind racing. Before Perren reset in his line, Dan jumped forward and smacked Perren on the wrist, causing Perren to drop his sword.

Perren smiled as he picked it up, then followed through with a foot to Dan's instep and a sword point to his knee, his movements fluid and precise.

Dan struck the blade away and grabbed at Perren's shirt, attempting to throw him off-balance. The fabric bunched in his hand, but Perren barely budged.

The whistle blew three times, a sharp interruption.

Perren relaxed and grinned at Dan; his breath steady. "Good fight, friend."

"Friend?"

"A friend will train you hard enough for you to beat your enemies." Perren's tone was sincere, his smile genuine. It sounded like some kind of cultural proverb. Dan sucked in a breath, but did not respond, still processing the intensity of the spar.

Sergeant Nuria blew the whistle again and the recruits all formed a half-circle around her, their expressions a mix of determination and exhaustion. "Good. That's a beginning measure. I held back Inaki from the lines today, but tomorrow she will be engaging each of you in turn in the morning and afternoon sessions. Although there are no griffins who have ever turned from the way of Light, we must be prepared to fight those with wings." She looked at each of them, her gaze stern and unwavering.

Chapter II: Choices

Sergeant Nuria made a rolling motion with her hand directed toward the griffin. "Inaki, please tell them what you've seen in the skies."

The griffin cleared her throat and spoke. Her voice was a resonant rumble that seemed to echo across the training ground.

Dan opened his mouth in shock. He had not known griffins could talk.

"Crow-men, vile hybrids of the Dark Sisterhood, have been spotted in the skies of Aerland, spying for their mistresses. We have fought them, but not successfully, since we were unprepared to fight aerial battles. Now, we train for such a thing. All the Watch Guard will receive training from Aerland as needed to battle this new threat."

"We thank Aerland for your aid to the Watch Guard, Inaki, and Gorka." Sergeant Nuria gave the griffin and the boy wearing similar armor a short bow. They bowed in return, lower.

Inaki's feathers shimmered in the sunlight, each movement sending ripples of gold across her plumage. Her eyes, keen and intelligent, regarded the recruits with curiosity. Gorka, standing beside her, had a resolute expression with his chin lifted as if he welcomed any challenge.

Sergeant Nuria turned to the others. "This evening, we will have a public ceremony for those who wish to train with us, knowing that not all will take our final vows at the end of the training."

Ewan and a boy who appeared to be his twin, red-headed brother, murmured to each other in low tones. The sunlight cast dancing shadows on their faces, highlighting their identical features.

Sergeant Nuria's stern frown bore down on the twins, silencing their conversation. "All will be made clear at the apprenticeship ceremony," she declared firmly. Her narrowed eyes swept over the gathered recruits, assessing their reactions.

"Now, be off with you to the kitchens," she commanded, her voice brooking no argument. "Lunch will be served in the courtyard."

Dan's stomach growled, and he winced, embarrassed. Next to him, the twins laughed. He was not making the impression he had hoped to make on the first day.

As the others broke into groups, Dan noticed Perren staying with him. He did not know what to think about his new "friend," but he hoped Perren would teach him more blade work. As they walked toward the kitchen, he glanced around, searching for Farrald and Alex in the crowd of a dozen recruits.

Farrald was singing another hymn and most of the others gave him a bit of room. Farrald differed from the rest. Dan doubted he had fared well in the bouts. Dan caught up to him and Farrald nodded to him and Perren but kept singing.

"Oh, the Lord is good to me, and so I thank the Lord."

Perren nudged Dan. "He does know we're at Watch Guard training?"

Dan shrugged. "It's his way. He likes to sing."

Farrald grinned at them between the verses of his song, then he broke off as Alex approached, giving the other boy a deferential nod.

Alex fell alongside them as they walked to the kitchens. The others were talking animatedly over the bouts, but their group was quiet, except for Farrald.

They trooped through the kitchen with the others, filling bread bowls with thick meaty stew and picking up apples as they passed by Kaipo. The aroma of freshly baked bread and hearty stew filled the air, mingling with the hum of conversation. The kitchen was a hive of activity, the warmth from the ovens creating a cozy atmosphere.

"Only one bowl, for now. You can have seconds later. One apple each. Seconds later." Kaipo ladled generous helpings into the bread bowls as he spoke. "Remember to wash your hands."

Dan broke off from the line to wash his hands at the pump outside, the metallic clang of the pump handle mingling with the sounds of birds chirping nearby. Farrald, Alex, and Perren followed him.

"Wise choice," Perren commented.

"I would rather wash up than stand in line and wash up after I had to juggle my bowl," Dan said.

"Wise is the man who cleans his hands before eating," Perren said.

Farrald chuckled. "You know, you're awfully concerned with wisdom for a ruthless fighter."

"I'm not ruthless, I'm efficient," Perren informed him. He cocked his eyebrow at Farrald. "Speaking of which, I have some pointers for you on defense. You use a lot more distance than you need."

"I thought I needed all the distance I could get from you," Farrald said.

Perren chuckled. "I beat you, but it would be better if you parried me close and returned some blows."

"Who taught you? A street brawler?" asked Alex.

Dan glanced at Alex, then Perren, who was scowling now. Was Alex trying to start a fight?

Perren gave Alex a once-over, slowly gazing at him from his well-cut hair to his well-shod feet. He tilted his chin up and raised his eyebrows. "Respectability in a fight is for court toadies."

Dan stifled a smile as he inwardly groaned.

Thankfully, Alex laughed. "Too true. That's the whole reason I ended up here. Court toadies." He glared at Dan.

"I was not ..." Dan protested, then he shook his head.

"You don't want to train for the Watch Guard?" Perren asked Alex, his voice rising in surprise.

"I don't have a choice in what I want," Alex said, his jaw tensing.

"Everyone has a choice," Perren stated firmly.

"Not everyone," Alex mumbled. He adjusted the cuff of his shirt, then strode away to get his bread bowl. Farrald followed him, and Dan followed Farrald, leaving Perren looking perplexed by the water pump.

The courtyard was alive with the sounds of clinking cutlery and muted conversations. Recruits were scattered at wooden tables, some under the shade of large oak trees, others basking in the sunlight. Perren was not far behind them when they sat down at a wooden table outside. Across the courtyard, the griffin was making her way through an enormous bowl of fish, her feathers glistening in the sunlight. The recruit with her was sitting nearby, eating his stew and keeping a vigilant eye on the rest of the courtyard.

Dan thought about going over to them, but he was already seated between Perren and Alex, with Farrald across from him and Amiria nearby. She winked at him, then dipped her head to Perren. "Respect," she said.

Perren blushed, then busied himself with his food, slurping noisily.

Amiria smiled and devoured her food, but with more grace.

Dan attempted to eat quietly while monitoring the others. He was afraid Perren and Alex were a powder keg waiting to explode. When he thought they seemed calm enough, he glanced around at the others in the courtyard and caught Keeva winking at him again. He glanced down, then back up to see her laughing at something Nilsen had said. He felt like an idiot. Of course, she was more interested in Nilsen, even if the mountain of a man's craggy face was not much to look at.

Chapter 12: Unwanted Vision

After lunch, they did not have time to chat. The sun had shifted, casting longer shadows across the courtyard as Sergeant Nuria began to speak. She gave them a long lecture on Watch Guard standards of conduct. The air was warm and still, and Dan struggled to pay attention. The drone of her voice seemed to blend with the distant hum of insects. When he sank low in his seat, someone kicked him under the table. He jumped but refrained from saying anything. Perren chuckled softly, the sound barely audible over the sergeant's stern tone.

Dan sighed and tried to listen again. The lush greenery around the courtyard was a stark contrast to the lecture. "The Watch Guard is responsible to the Triune Halls and to the Champion. At this time, Aramatir does not have a known, active Champion but we expect one to rise in our lifetime." Sergeant Nuria paused and then asked, "When do Champions arise?"

Amiria raised her hand. "When the time of need is greatest, when the darkness comes, when the battle is nearly lost."

"Yes. In desperate times, there is always a Champion who comes," Sergeant Nuria said. "But we cannot wait on a Champion. Mayhap another land has a Champion right now on the other side of the world, and that Champion is needed more there than we need one here."

Nilsen raised his hand. "How would we know, Sergeant Nuria? Does the Watch Guard have towers all over the world?"

Sergeant Nuria gazed at him. "It is said we once did, that expert sailors from IceWynne and those from Destiny worked together to create the largest, fastest ships ever created, and they sailed all around the world."

"If anyone was going to do that, it would be Merseas," said a young man with multiple braids. He was standing in the doorway to the kitchens. He had two swords strapped to his shoulders. A young woman, with her hair cropped short, stood next to him. She had a bandolier of throwing knives around her chest and a set of curved blades, unlike any Dan had seen before.

Their heights and builds were similar, their dark skin glowed with some kind of gold powder, and they wore matching smirks. Dan's heart sank at the sight of them—two more young recruits who might take the place he so desperately wanted here, and given the way they bore their weapons, they might achieve it.

"You're late and impertinent." Sergeant Nuria said. "As expected from Merseas pirates." She scowled at them and indicated the grass at her feet. "You'll sit here, Furian and Flycke."

"Aunt Nuria, really?" Furian whined.

They were related? Dan did not know recruits would be trained by a family member. Why hadn't they been sent to a different Watch Tower?

"It is Sergeant, or you're going home."

"The boat already left," Flycke said.

"You could swim." Sergeant Nuria stated, raising her eyebrows and pointing to the grass at her feet again.

"Yes, Sergeant," the two said in unison. They sauntered past the others and took their seats on the grass, lounging languidly.

Dan felt some inward relief as Sergeant Nuria put her relatives in their place. But Merseas pirates? He knew the Watch Guard took people from every nation, but he had never considered the Merseas to truly be a nation.

Flycke winked at Alex, then whispered something to her brother. Her eyes sparkled with mischief, a stark contrast to the seriousness of the lecture.

Sergeant Nuria cleared her throat.

Flycke sat up straight and bowed her head, as if repentant. But Dan could see the smirk on her lips. He glanced over at Alex, worried again. How would he protect Alex from both Perren and a Merseas pirate?

Alex had a small smile on his face, but he pretended to pick at his fingernails.

Dan shifted in his seat and sat up straighter. He couldn't afford to fall asleep. Sergeant Nuria caught his eye and dipped her chin as if approving. Then she launched into her lecture again. "The Champion, if there is one in the lands we watch here on the mainland, stands as our leader if he or she chooses to be. The Champion is the embodiment of light in our darkest times. The Lord has a hand on each Champion's destiny."

Dan was trying to pay attention, but his ears rang, and a flash of light appeared to the side of his vision. He blinked, trying to clear his sight, but the light persisted, drawing his gaze irresistibly. He turned his head, then swayed in his seat, light and darkness closing in on him in dizzying circles. The world around him seemed to blur, the edges of his vision darkening as if shadows were pulling him into another realm. He saw a young blonde woman surrounded by light. Darkness pressed down on her until she knelt under the weight of it, the shadows twisting and writhing as if alive. But then she raised her eyes, and the light exploded around her, pushing back the encroaching darkness in a brilliant burst.

He understood, suddenly, she was younger than him, not now, but would be. Would be? Even in the weight of this strange vision, he wondered how he knew anything about her, but she appeared uncertain, which surprised him because in her hand she held a pure white blade, the kind only carried by the Champions of Aramatir. The blade gleamed with an ethereal light, its surface unmarred and pristine, a symbol of hope and power. He wanted to say something to her, to reach out and offer support, but his head spun, and his limbs felt heavy, as if rooted to the spot. The vision faded, the light dimming, and the woman's determined face blurred. Everything went dark, the sensation of falling toward dappled shadows blurred his thoughts.

Chapter 13: Unwanted Knowledge

THE WORLD TILTED AND swayed around Dan, colors blurring into a kaleidoscope of muted hues. A cacophony of distant voices buzzed in his ears, as if he were underwater. Somewhere in the haze, he felt hands on his shoulders, their touch both grounding and intrusive.

"Dan! Are you all right? He's fainted, I think," Farrald's voice cut through the fog, tinged with worry.

Dan opened his eyes, the harsh sunlight near blinding. He found himself sprawled on the ground; legs awkwardly draped over the bench where he'd been sitting. The courtyard's cobblestones pressed uncomfortably against his back, their rough texture a stark contrast to the soft, dappled shadows cast by the overhanging trees.

Farrald hovered above him, his freckled face pinched with concern. To his right, Alex knelt, his usual haughty expression replaced by a furrowed brow. The scent of grass mingled with the metallic tang of nearby weapons.

Perren's dry voice cut through the air. "I've never seen a grown man faint before. That might be too much humility for even me to swallow." His words dripped with humor, but a hint of unease lurked beneath.

Dan disentangled himself from the bench. He gently pushed away Farrald's probing fingers. "I'm all right... just had a weird daydream or something. I don't know." The words felt thick on his tongue, his mouth dry as parchment.

As he attempted to stand, the world tilted again. His vision swam, dark spots dancing at the edges. Farrald's arm around his shoulders was a welcome anchor, though it stirred an uncomfortable memory - his sister's comforting gesture after one of their father's harsh punishments. The recollection churned in his gut like sour milk.

The stares of the other recruits prickled against his skin. Keeva's gaze bore into him with an intensity that made him want to shrink away. Amiria's fingers tapped a strange rhythm on his arm before withdrawing, leaving behind a tingling sensation that seemed to pulse in time with his racing heart.

Sergeant Nuria's approach was heralded by the soft clink of her armor. Her voice cut through the murmurs like a blade. "Recruit Farrald. Take Dan to the infirmary. Have Healer Terese check him for head injuries." Her stern gaze swept the courtyard. "The rest of you, line up."

Dan flushed with embarrassment as he allowed Farrald to help him up. He was grateful to leave the courtyard, though he resented being half-lifted as if he couldn't manage on his own. Once inside, he shook off Farrald's arm and leaned against a wall. "I can make it."

Farrald sighed. "I'll walk alongside you."

Dan grunted and pushed himself off the wall, starting down the hallway from the kitchen. "Do you know where the infirmary is?"

"I studied the layouts designed for the Watch Towers before I came. Unless Tower Eight is different, it should be a little farther, with a door next to the courtyard where we arrived, designed for quick access for injured guards."

"More information than I needed," Dan groaned, taking a few unsteady steps forward before stopping. "You studied the layouts of all the Watch Towers?"

"Yes. They're almost all variations on a single main keep and tower structure. Each tower has stables, single and double rooms, an infirmary, main hall, kitchen, training yard, armory, library, and vault. The Keep includes dwellings for families, a garden, and a blacksmith," Farrald explained, his words rushing out. "The Repository Towers have deeper vaults, thicker walls, and don't include rooms for families."

Dan had never heard of a Repository Tower, but he wasn't keen on hearing more. He straightened away from the wall. When Farrald offered an arm, Dan shook his head. "Don't take all my weight."

The walk to the infirmary was a blur of cool stone walls and the echoing sound of their footsteps. Dan's pride stung more than any physical discomfort, although the hallway seemed to stretch endlessly before him.

When they finally reached the infirmary door, marked by an intricately carved emblem of a plant entwining a sword and shield, Dan felt a mix of relief and apprehension.

As Farrald pushed open the heavy oak door, the scent of herbs and tinctures wafted out, a complex bouquet of earthy and medicinal aromas. The infirmary itself was a study in organized chaos. Shelves lined the walls, laden with jars of dried plants, vials of colorful liquids, and an assortment of instruments both familiar and bewildering.

Healer Terese stood amidst this ordered disorder, a beacon of calm. She was a woman in her middle years, with skin the color of sun-warmed honey and eyes that seemed to hold the wisdom of ages. Her golden-brown hair was pulled back in an intricate braid, revealing a face etched with laugh lines and the occasional scar - badges of a life fully lived. She wore a soft green robe over a brown tunic and pants, the fabric shimmering slightly in the light streaming through high windows. Her calf-high boots were well-worn but sturdy, speaking of countless hours spent on her feet.

"Yes?" Her voice was a soothing balm.

Farrald explained the situation, his words tumbling out in a rush. Terese listened patiently, her eyes never leaving Dan's face.

"Hmm." She beckoned them forward with a graceful gesture. "Please sit on the nearest cot. I'll check your vitals. You tell me about this vision. Farrald, you can wait outside."

As Dan settled onto the cot, he couldn't help but notice the array of curious objects surrounding him. On a nearby table lay what appeared to be an ancient scroll, its edges crumbling with age. Next to it sat a small, intricately carved box that seemed to hum with barely perceptible energy.

Terese followed his gaze. "Ah, you've noticed some of our more... unique tools," she said, a hint of amusement in her voice. "That scroll contains healing techniques passed down from the earliest days of the Watch Guard. And that box?" She paused, her eyes twinkling. "Well, let's just say it holds remedies for ailments both common and arcane."

As she began her examination, her fingers moving with practiced precision, Terese continued. "You know, the Watch Guard doesn't just protect borders and people. We're also custodians of knowledge and artifacts that could change the world - for better or worse."

Her hands paused over Dan's temples. "Now, tell me about this vision of yours. In my experience, what some call fainting spells can sometimes be glimpses into... something more."

Dan's eyes brow furrowed; his earlier embarrassment faded as he considered how to handle this unwelcome possibility.

Chapter 14: Exam

Dan shifted uncomfortably on the cot, the crisp linen sheets crinkling beneath him. The infirmary's cool air raised goosebumps on his skin, a stark contrast to the warmth of embarrassment on his cheeks. Memories flickered through his mind like candle flames - a court gathering, someone collapsing, hushed whispers of weakness. He swallowed hard, hoping fervently that his new comrades didn't view him with the same disdain.

Terese's gentle touch on his wrist anchored him to the present. Her fingers were cool and dry, her grip firm yet comforting. "Well?" she said, releasing his wrist. "Your heartbeat is slow and steady, but I'd like to hear more about what brought you here while I continue with the examination." She reached for an instrument on a nearby tray, its polished surface gleaming in the soft light filtering through the window.

"Have you seen one of these before?" she asked, holding up the curious device.

Dan studied it, noting the narrow and wide ends. "It looks like an ear trumpet."

"Yes, a similar concept." Terese's eyes twinkled with approval. "I'm going to listen closely to your heart and lungs." She gestured to his leather gambeson. "Take off the leathers."

As Dan unclasped his armor, the familiar scent of leather and sweat wafted up, mingling with the herbal fragrances permeating the infirmary. He set it aside on the cot's headboard, the weight of it a reminder of the training he was missing. "I don't feel too bad," he offered, "just a little light-headed."

"Did you have lunch?" Terese asked, her tone casual but her gaze sharp.

"Yes."

"Hmm." Terese's noncommittal response hung in the air as she pressed the wider end of the instrument to Dan's chest. The cool metal sent a shiver through him, and he focused on steadying his breathing. Terese moved the device with practiced precision, her brow furrowed in concentration as she listened to his heart and lungs.

Stepping back, Terese regarded Dan thoughtfully. Sunlight streaming through a small window cast her in a warm glow, highlighting the silver strands in her hair and the fine lines around her eyes that spoke of both laughter and concern. The tidy infirmary, with its shelves of colorful herb-filled jars and meticulously arranged tools, seemed to reflect her organized and efficient nature.

"Now, tell me what you experienced, so we can examine the evidence together."

Dan's gaze dropped to his boots, their worn leather a familiar comfort against the polished infirmary floor. "I saw a vision of a girl," he began, his voice low. "She was younger than me, and she had the sword of a Champion, but she appeared uncertain, which was strange. I wanted to speak to her, but Farrald started shouting."

Terese's eyebrows rose, a flicker of intrigue crossing her face. "You had a vision of the new Champion?" She moved with fluid grace to her desk, where an open leather-bound journal awaited her notes. The scratch of her quill on parchment filled the momentary silence.

"Maybe. I don't know." Dan's cheeks flushed anew, the warmth spreading to his ears. "Sergeant Nuria was talking about Champions and then I saw what I saw." He could almost hear his father's scornful voice, dismissing such fanciful tales.

"Have you ever had a vision before?" Terese's question was gentle, free of judgment.

"No. Not that I know of." Dan shrugged, grappling with the strange mix of reality and unreality his vision had brought. "It felt real, but it was not."

Terese's expression softened, a look of understanding in her eyes. "Well, I can't tell you if what you saw is true or not. That will come in time, but it sounds like the visions of Shepherd Bellan from three hundred years ago. He had visions of our last Champion for decades before the Champion came."

As Terese spoke, her hands never stopped moving, organizing her supplies with an efficiency that spoke of years of practice. "We won't know if your visions are true until, or if, the Champion is chosen by the Lord of Light. What I know is that you have no physical symptoms that I believe would lead to a fainting spell, but it is possible I missed something, so you will stay here for a short observation period."

Dan groaned inwardly, frustration bubbling up inside him. What if they deemed him mentally unfit for the Watch Guard because of this vision? Where else could he go to escape his father's expectations? The weight of uncertainty pressed down on him, as heavy as his discarded armor. "I don't want visions," he murmured, his voice barely above a whisper.

"Thank the Lord for that!" Terese's chuckle was like warm honey, rich and soothing. It eased some of the tension coiled in Dan's shoulders. "That's the most convincing part. You aren't having visions of self-grandeur and you don't want the visions."

As she spoke, Terese's hands never stopped moving. Dan watched, mesmerized, as her fingers deftly wove together herbs and bandages. The infirmary air was thick with the mingling scents of medicinal plants - sharp peppermint, earthy chamomile, and something more exotic that Dan couldn't quite place.

"Stand, walk to the door, return to the cot, and sit down again," Terese instructed, her keen eyes tracking every movement. "I want to see how steady you are on your feet."

Dan complied, his steps unsteady despite his efforts to appear composed. As he turned back towards the cot, he caught sight of something unexpected - a beautifully crafted sword hanging on the wall, its blade gleaming with the supernatural sheen of power.

"Oh, young men," Terese sighed gently as Dan settled back on the cot, the linen sheets crinkling beneath him. "I'll brew you some tea and have Kaipo bring another bread bowl. Once you've had those and rested longer, you'll be fit enough for the ceremony."

"But I don't want to miss this afternoon's sparring session," Dan protested, the words tumbling out before he could stop them.

Terese's gaze sharpened, her eyes flickering with an intensity that spoke of more than just healing knowledge. "I believe you might want revenge for some of those bruises you're sporting?"

Dan straightened up and the movement sent a twinge through his sore muscles, a reminder of his recent defeat. "I could best them if I had another chance."

"Good. You can do that tomorrow," Terese said, her tone brooking no argument. "Today, vision or no, and I am inclined to believe you had one, you will rest. I have a task for you while you rest."

Dan rubbed his wrist, still sore from the sparring session. The skin there was tender, a palette of purples and yellows.

"Ah yes, I'll fetch you a compress to reduce that swelling," Terese remarked. Her movements were a graceful dance as she gathered supplies, at once both nurturing and martial. Dan could easily imagine those same hands wielding the sword on the wall with deadly precision.

As she worked, Terese's voice took on a thoughtful tone. "But I believe you still have enough dexterity to write your vision for the Hall of Wisdom here and read about the visions of Shepherd Bellan. You wish to become a Shepherd, do you?"

"No," Dan replied firmly, the word carrying the weight of certainty. "I have no interest in becoming a Shepherd."

"Ah, I see. That would be Farrald's calling." Terese nodded knowingly towards the door.

"Yes, he sings all the time," Dan confirmed, remembering the way Farrald's melodies seemed to linger in the air long after he'd finished.

"Of course." She waved to an armchair in the corner of the room, its worn leather inviting rest. "You can sit there while you rest, eat, study, and write. I'll get Farrald to fetch your bowl of stew."

As Dan settled into the chair, he felt the weight of Terese's gaze upon him.

The parchment she handed him felt rough beneath his fingers, the quill unfamiliar in his hand. As he bent to his task, the scratch of pen on paper filled the air, punctuated by the soft clinks and rustles of Terese preparing his compress.

When Farrald brought the stew bread bowl, its aroma rich and hearty, Terese shooed him away with a gentle but firm hand.

The book she brought Dan next – *Visions of Bellan* – was a weighty tome. As Dan carefully opened it, the musty scent of age wafted up to him. The pages were thin, almost translucent, covered in intricate script that spoke of a time before printing presses.

As he began to read, Dan couldn't shake the feeling that this was more than just busy work. But as he sank deeper into Bellan's visions, surrounded by the quiet hum of the infirmary and wrapped in the comfort of Terese's care, Dan felt the stirrings of curiosity. The Watch Guard kept ancient secrets. Perhaps, his visions would help him succeed?

Day 25, Month 10, Year 1673.

Once again, the divine symphony of destiny unfolded before me, a tapestry woven of light and revelation. Amidst the humble confines of the kitchen, where the aroma of porridge mingled with the whispers of morning, I found myself ensconced in a luminous embrace. From the ephemeral mists emerged the shimmering silhouette of the Champion's fabled sword, suspended in midair as if borne aloft by unseen hands. Its blade, anointed with the radiance of ages, cast prismatic hues that danced like ethereal fireflies in the air.

Beside this celestial artifact stood the figure of a man, resolute and steadfast, his hand outstretched to grasp the pommel of destiny. As he touched the hilt, a torrent of brilliance erupted, ensnaring both mortal and blade in its blinding embrace. In that transcendent moment, the boundaries between realms blurred, and the veil of mortality thinned, revealing glimpses of a realm where the fate of nations and the hopes of generations converged.

The gravity of my vision has found resonance among my peers, who at long last acknowledged the veracity of my prophetic communion. Urged by Shepherd Tallin's solemn command, I hastened to inscribe this divine encounter, a testament etched upon parchment, even as my hunger gnawed and my porridge lay forgotten, sacrificed at the altar of revelation.

Bellan

Dan shook his head, disbelief swirling within him. He did not have anything in common with Bellan; the man's words sounded fantastical and impractical. Glancing around the room, Dan took in his surroundings—the meticulous arrangement of items on Terese's desk and all her instruments of healing. She had an intense, focused posture as she bent over her task. He couldn't help but wonder if her pen scratched out notes about him. The thought unsettled him deeply. Closing his eyes, Dan leaned back in the chair, trying to fill his mind with something else.

That something else became sleep.

Chapter 15: Troubles With Leaders

Jordan closed his eyes, inhaling the familiar scent of hay and horses. "Lord of Light, grant me patience," he whispered, his fingers absently stroking his mare's neck. The raucous laughter of the Fifteenth Unit grated on his nerves, a stark contrast to the solemnity their mission deserved.

Opening his eyes, he caught sight of Commander Leo, resplendent in his white and gold uniform, holding court among his subordinates. The young commander's easy smile and relaxed posture spoke volumes about his approach to leadership. Jordan felt a pang of longing for Sword Master Theran's steady and firm leadership style.

"Shepherd Jordan!" Leo's voice cut through the stable's clamor. "I trust you're ready for our grand parade through the countryside?"

Jordan bit back a sigh, forcing a neutral expression. "Commander, perhaps we should discuss the details of our mission before we depart."

Leo's smile faltered for a moment before returning, brittle and forced. "Now, now, Shepherd. No need to worry the troops with such serious talk. We'll have plenty of time for that on the road."

As Leo turned away, Jordan felt his patience wearing thin. He thought of the slaves they were meant to rescue, of the lives hanging in the balance. The weight of responsibility settled heavily on his shoulders, a familiar burden made heavier by the apparent frivolity surrounding him.

"Lord," Jordan prayed silently, "help me find a way to reach these people. To make them understand the gravity of our task."

With a deep breath, Jordan led his mare out of her stall, each step a conscious effort to embody the calm and wisdom expected of a King's Shepherd. As he passed the jovial Sword Guards, he offered them warm smiles, hoping to connect with them.

The setting sun painted the sky in breathtaking hues of orange and pink, a reminder of the beauty that persisted even in trying times. Jordan allowed himself a moment to appreciate the view, drawing strength from it. Whatever challenges lay ahead, he would face them with the grace and determination befitting his position.

As he approached Commander Leo again, Jordan steeled himself for another clash of wills. But this time, he resolved to find common ground, to bridge the gap between them for the sake of their mission and those they were sworn to protect.

The young commander was adjusting his saddle, his ornate uniform catching the last rays of the setting sun.

"Commander Leo," Jordan began, keeping his voice low and steady.

Leo turned, his smile bright but not quite reaching his eyes. "Ah, Shepherd Jordan! I assure you, everything is under control."

Jordan frowned slightly. "With all due respect, Commander, King Xandros commissioned me to oversee our journey and I—"

Leo placed a hand on Jordan's shoulder, his voice taking on a placating tone. "My dear Shepherd, I understand your concerns. Truly, I do. But you must trust in my methods. After all, I am in command of this unit, and you are our guest. A relaxed unit is an effective unit, wouldn't you agree?"

"To a point, yes," Jordan conceded, gently removing Leo's hand from his shoulder. "But they need to understand the stakes. Besides the King's missive clearly states we are to co-lead this mission. The lives we're trying to save—"

"Of course, of course," Leo interrupted, waving his hand dismissively. "Tell you what, why don't you share your... spiritual insights with us later. I'm sure those we are trying to rescue have time for sermons along the roadside."

Jordan narrowed his eyes. "I appreciate the offer, Commander, but—"

Leo's smile tightened almost imperceptibly. "Perhaps we should wait until we're outside the city walls? For security reasons, of course."

Jordan hesitated, weighing his options. "I suppose it would be acceptable to wait to read the King's missive, as long as it's done promptly once we're clear of the city."

"Excellent!" Leo clapped his hands together. "I'm so glad we see eye to eye on this, Shepherd. Your counsel is, as always, invaluable."

As Leo turned to mount his horse, Jordan caught a glimpse of the young commander rolling his eyes.

"Oh, and Shepherd?" Leo called over his shoulder, already seated atop his mount. "Do try to keep up. We wouldn't want you falling behind now, would we?"

With that, Leo urged his horse forward, leaving Jordan standing there. As he moved to mount his own horse, Jordan whispered another quiet prayer, "Lord of Light, grant me the wisdom to navigate this challenge, and the strength to ensure our mission's success... despite our leadership."

Chapter 16: Salutes and Presentations

Dan woke slowly, his hand brushing over eyes heavy with sleep. The light from the windows had dimmed, casting long shadows across the room. A woolen blanket lay draped over his lap, its weight both comforting and oppressive. The book by Bellan sat on the nearby table. As Dan sat up straighter and stretched his arms overhead, his muscles protested, reminding him of the day's earlier exertions.

"Oh good, you're awake in time for the ceremony," Terese said from her desk. "You'll need your gambeson, your actual sword, and your helmet. Then, you can join the others waiting in the hall outside the Main Chamber." She had changed out of the soft green robe and into a full set of Watch Guard armor. While the apprentices of the watch guard wore whatever armor they had brought with them from home, the Watch Guardians all wore fitted armor made of multiple pieces of metal sewn together in an overlapping pattern for their breastplate, with elbow length sleeves of a similar pattern. From wrist to elbow, Terese wore metal arm guards. Unlike many other warriors from other lands, the Watch Guard did not wear armored leggings, but they did wear uniform black pants, with black, knee-high leather boots. Terese's sword was sheathed at her left side, and on her right, she carried a long knife. Her head was covered by a helmet made of overlapping metal disks which left her face free. The uniform was a mixture of heavy and light armor, giving a fighter freedom of movement, but also some measure of protection.

As Dan donned his leather gambeson, its familiar scent of oil and sweat enveloping him, Farrald and Alex entered, bearing his sword and long knife. The weapons seemed heavier than usual, as if imbued with the gravity of the impending ceremony.

Farrald looked miserable in his old leather cap style helmet, and he seemed to be attempting to walk a half step behind Alex, in deference to Alex's rank.

Alex handed Dan his sword. "We're to wear our swords at our hips, unsheathe them at the right moment, and then, well, just follow us. It's like most ceremonies." He gave Dan a grave look, his lips pressed together. "We're not swearing in, but we are swearing to keep secrets."

He glanced over at Terese. "I'm beholden to the people of Septily and they state these vows won't change that, but if you hear anything strange, let me know."

"I understand," Dan said. He buckled his sword belt. "I haven't been in as many ceremonies as you." He reminded Alex.

Alex nodded. "More than one set of ears is helpful."

Farrald nodded, somberly. "I will serve in any way I can, Prince Alex."

Alex's face twisted. "You can't call me that here but thank you."

Dan walked over to Terese's desk. "Thank you for your help, Terese."

"You're welcome, recruit." She shook his hand. "I'm looking forward to seeing you more and reading about your visions."

"I hope I never have another one," Dan said.

She smiled. "Of course, no sane person would want one." She drew on a ceremonial cloak from a hook on the wall, and then gestured to the door. "After you, recruits."

The walk to the Meeting Chamber was a blur of cool stone walls and echoing footsteps. The air grew thicker as they ascended the stairs, heavy with anticipation and the musty scent of ancient stone.

They entered a long, wide hallway with a double door at the other end. All the recruits were there, lined up and waiting in a shuffling, but quiet fashion. Even the griffin had crammed herself into the hallway. Dan wondered where the griffin slept at night and if there were wider hallways like this one to accommodate her.

At the front of the line, which seemed poised to enter the double doors, a burly, blonde man wearing the official regalia of the Watch Guard stood, gazing out over the recruits.

"All present and accounted for." Terese called ahead.

"Then present we will," the man said. He knocked on the double doors, and they were opened from the inside by another Watch Guard.

"Who presents these recruits?" the man who had opened the doors asked.

"I do, Watch Guard Cullin Wendell." The officer who had waited with the recruits said. He saluted by putting his fist to his chest, then his head, then by putting three fingers against his lips.

"And I, Terese Burnside." Terese repeated the same salute, fist to chest, fist to forehead, then three fingers to her lips.

"That means..." Farrald began to whisper.

Alex nudged him.

Terese glared at them, narrowing her eyes.

Farrald bit his lip and looked at the floor, his cheeks reddening.

Dan felt a bit bad for Farrald, who was probably trying to help him. What he didn't know, that Alex did, was that Dan had been asked to be in a few of the Noble House Ceremonies and every house had its version of a salute. He had to remember all seven by the time he was six years old at his first ceremony. The Watch Guard salute wasn't all that hard in comparison.

The double doors opened with a deep, resonant groan, revealing a chamber bathed in the warm, flickering light of hearths and lamps. The rosy glow danced across the dark grey stone walls, creating shifting shadows that seemed to whisper age-old secrets. At the far end, a tapestry hung, its intricate designs barely visible in the dim light, hinting at histories unknown.

As Dan approached the dais where three imposing figures sat, the air grew thick with solemnity. The scent of burning wood mingled with the metallic tang of armor. Each step on the stone floor echoed in the hushed chamber, marking their inexorable progress towards a moment that would change their lives forever.

As they entered, each recruit took a place standing behind a seat at a table. The seats looked pre-assigned. Dan paused slightly and felt a hand hit him on the back of his left shoulder.

So, it would be the table to the left. He, Farrald, and Alex would share that table with Quinn, who raised one eyebrow in greeting, and Terese, who followed them to stand at one end of the table.

All the chairs were arranged so that the recruits faced the three officers on the dais. Dan studied them, instead of glancing around at the other recruits.

In the seat with the highest back on the dais and sitting closest to the tapestry, the officer with the silver on his uniform sat tall and proud. He had short-cropped dark hair with bits of gray in it. He had broad shoulders, strong hands which rested relaxed on the table before him, and he wore a black cloak flung over his shoulders so the five silver bars on his shoulders stood out prominently. He wore all shades of black and gray clothing, and a three-quarter length metal breastplate. His helmet sat on the table to his right hand. His sword was slung to his left. He also had knives strapped to both of his lower legs. His short boots were polished to a shine but had seen heavy wear around the tread.

At the right of the table on the short dais, a short man with walnut skin and raven dark hair was gazing at each recruit from under fierce black eyebrows. He was frowning, but stood straight, giving his full attention to the room. His eyes seemed to linger on Alex the longest.

Dan glanced at his friend then at the dais again. The man was looking at him now, and he raised his finger to his right eyebrow. It seemed to mean something. Dan kept his gaze steady. The man glanced at the head of the Watch Guard, and then across the table at his counterpart.

The woman wore shades of dark brown and gray with four bronze bars at her shoulders. She wore her reddish-brown hair in multiple braids and had a tattoo that ran from her pale temple to her chin on both sides of her face. Her hands were similarly patterned, and she wore a bandolier of knives, as well as two swords, one at each hip. She looked to be nearly as tall as the head of the Watch Guard and she perused the recruits with her eyes. She seemed to ignore Dan's table entirely, or he had looked at her after she had finished her quiet consideration of them already.

At the foot of Dan's table, Quinn, who had brought them from Skycliff, sat patiently, sitting straight up, but with a slight lean backward. He'd seen all of this before, or so his visage seemed to say. His eyes were relaxed, but then Dan noticed his fingers drummed the tabletop in a slow pattern. "Careful," the pattern said.

The air in the chamber grew heavy with anticipation.

Chapter 17: Standing on Ceremony

Dan had not imagined that signal. He knew Alex would see it. His eyes darted around, noting who else might have caught it. The flickering torchlight cast dancing shadows across faces, making it difficult to read expressions. He peered at the head table, where the captain's intense gaze was now fixed on Quinn. The weight of unspoken communication hung heavy in the air.

Captain Denali's voice cut through the silence like a blade. "Who stands with these recruits?" The words echoed off the stone walls.

"I do, Terese of the Watch Guard, Healer, and Shepherd to the Wise."

And I do, Cullin of the Watch Guard, White Knight of the Forgotten." Cullin stood at the farthest table on the right with Perren, Gorka, and Inaki the griffin. Kaipo, who had cooked all day, was already seated at the table, his posture straight with his hands firmly folded in front of him.

"And I do, Bertrand of the Watch Guard, bearer of the Scroll." Bertrand was an elderly, dark-skinned man with tight white curls and a short, white beard who stood at a table with Ewan and his twin, and the two Merseas siblings, Flycke and Furian. The other Watch Guard already at their table was a hawk-faced woman with a long nose, and multiple ear piercings.

"And I do, Jesta of the Watch Guard, librarian of this Keep," said a short woman with pale skin and a shock of spiky red hair, who stood at a table with Nilsen, Amiria, and Keeva. A tanned woman, with muscular arms and a thick braid wound over her shoulders, sat at their table. She gave the impression of being a formidable opponent.

The scent of old leather, polished metal, and burning candles mingled in the air, creating an atmosphere thick with tradition and solemnity. Dan could feel the weight of centuries pressing down upon them all.

Captain Denali's next words seemed to vibrate with authority. "Terese, Cullin, Bertrand, and Jesta, you hereby stand with and for these recruits. Your Watch is their Watch. We watch our own."

"Yes, Captain Denali," the Watch Guards intoned in unison, their voices blending into a solemn chorus.

Captain Denali spoke to the room. "Recruits. You will now each take the vow of apprenticeship to the Watch under the guidance of First Lieutenant Mol. This vow is sacred, under the guidance of the Lord of Light and the Triune Halls. Even apprentices who do not become members of the Watch Guard stand for the Watch and must not break its secrets."

As the oath-taking began, the room seemed to hold its breath. Dan could feel his heart pounding in his chest, each beat seeming to count down to his turn.

"We will start with Terese's table." First Lieutenant Mol turned her sharp gaze on them.

Next to him, Dan felt Alex stir. Obviously, the prince had thought they would have more time to prepare themselves.

Terese stood again. She walked to stand behind Farrald. "Recruit Farrald. Stand, state your recruit name with titles if any, your citizenship, and repeat the Apprentice Vow after me."

Farrald drew his sword, held it in front of him in both hands, and said, "Farrald Weaver, of merchant class rank. I am from the Desert Hall of Septily."

"As an apprentice, I will uphold the secrets of the Watch Guard and remain true to the Watch, under the Lord of Light and the Triune Halls, regardless of whether I take my final vows. I will not forsake or break the

Watch Guard's secrets, nor will I break any other oaths." The words of the oath hung in the air; each phrase laden with significance.

Farrald repeated her words as Dan turned them over in his mind. He gave the table a single tap with one finger.

Alex tapped in response. Neither had heard anything that would hurt Alex as the future King of Septily.

Farrald dipped his head.

"Farrald, you have been accepted as an apprentice of the Watch Guard. You will Watch and you will Guard the secrets of our order. You will live by our rule and walk in our ways as long as your apprenticeship lasts." Captain Denali stated.

"Yes, Captain Denali," Farrald said.

"Sheathe your sword until the time is right."

Farrald awkwardly sheathed his sword, made his salute slowly and precisely, then fumbled into his chair at the table. Sweat stood out from his brow.

Terese touched Farrald's shoulder briefly, then she came to stand behind Dan.

As Dan stood, the cool metal of his sword hilt ground him in the moment. His voice, steady despite his inner turmoil, rang out in the chamber. "Daniel Bello Torren, Junior Lord of the House Torren, of Septily."

The slight stir among the recruits at his words was like a ripple in a still pond, quickly suppressed but impossible to ignore. As he spoke the oath, Dan felt as if each word was being etched into his very soul, binding him to something far greater than any task he had before.

Dan sheathed his sword, gave the salute, took his seat, and sat up at attention, forcing himself to look forward and not look back.

"Prince Alexandros..."

When Alex stood to take his oath, the tension in the room ratcheted up another notch. The soft whispers that broke out at his introduction were like the hiss of a snake, quickly silenced by the sharp rebuke from the officer.

"Silence! Begin again, recruit." The command cut through the air like a whip crack, leaving a ringing silence in its wake.

"Prince Alexandros Bryant Stone, second of my name and heir to the throne of Septily." Alex looked straight ahead as he spoke. He gave his oath with solemnity, waited for the captain's response, then performed the salute, and sat with elegance.

There was a moment of silence. The captain gave a curt nod to Alex, then shifted his eyes to one of the center tables. The ceremony continued. No one else seemed to receive any special attention, although when the Merseas twins took their vow, Alex tilted his head toward them, his lips curved upwards. Dan shook his head, hoping he did not have to intervene at some future moment.

The ceremony continued, the repetition of oaths creating a hypnotic rhythm, broken only by the occasional clink of armor or the rustle of fabric as recruits shifted nervously in their seats. The air grew heavy with the weight of promises made.

Finally, Captain Denali stood, his armor gleaming in the flickering light. His salute was crisp, authoritative. "The Watch never rests," he intoned, his voice resonating with finality.

"The Watch never ends," came the response, a chorus of voices that seemed to resonate through the very stones of the keep. Dan's lips moved, but the words stuck in his throat. Beside him, he sensed Alex's similar hesitation, a shared moment of unease that lingered even as the final echoes faded away.

As the ceremony concluded, Dan couldn't shake the feeling that they had just crossed a threshold from which there was no return. The words of the oath seemed to hang in the air, an invisible but unbreakable chain binding them all to an unknown destiny.

Chapter 18: A Feast of Service

After the ceremony, Officer Kaipo stood up and addressed them. "Captain, Watch, may I recommend a repast from our labors. I have shepherd's pies and fruit pastries for our meal this evening if the new apprentices will be so kind as to retrieve them and serve them to us."

"Thank you, Kaipo. Apprentices. You have your orders." Captain Denali said.

Dan stood up, making sure he was not the first on his feet, but also not the last.

Officer Quinn rapped the table with his knuckles. Dan looked at him and Quinn inclined his head to Captain Denali. "Remember who to serve first."

Dan nodded. "Of course, sir."

"Quinn."

"Of course, Quinn," Dan said, feeling as if his spine was getting stiffer every time someone corrected him. This place, the Watch Guard, had as much protocol as the capital, but here it was understated, expected but not given as rules. He did not like it, but it did not surprise him. He was second out of the room, carefully maneuvering so he was behind Amiria who led the way to the kitchen.

They were all quiet on the way there as the momentousness of their vows settled. Of course, that did not last when they smelled the food.

"Kaipo is truly gifted," Amiria said as she sniffed the air appreciatively before they entered the kitchen.

Each shepherd's pie had a savory scent that seemed to rest on Dan's tongue as if he were tasting it out of the air. His mouth watered. "He is gifted."

"He used to be a chef's boy before he came here," Keeva informed them. She took a pie from the table as Farrald reached for it. "You're going to have to be more assertive, Farrald." She jostled him with her shoulder as she turned to leave the room.

Dan had been trying to see if the pies had any differences before he picked one up, but they all had the same golden crusts, so he quickly grabbed one and hurried out with it, hastening his steps to catch Keeva.

"Sucking up already?" she asked him, as he drew close to her.

"And what are you doing then?" He asked.

She grinned saucily. "The same. I know good work when I see it." She gazed at him boldly, checking out his arms and shoulders, her eyes dropping briefly to his hips. "Hmm. You are stronger than Perren believes. You're going to cause him some trouble if he wants to fight for first of the Watch recruits."

She tilted her head toward the door, and he opened it for her.

"Thanks, friend." She kicked him in the ankle as she passed him.

He sidestepped in pain, barely hanging onto both the pie and the door. He couldn't believe she'd do that, but he supposed she was after the first position as well. With barely a limp, he entered the great room after and followed her up to the dais. She served Captain Denali with a small head bow.

"Thank you, recruit Keeva." Captain Denali said. Then, he frowned. "Don't think your stunt at the door went unnoticed and don't think it will help you in the competition. We guard each other's backs. Kindness will get you farther than a kick."

"Yes, Captain," she gave a short bow with her head again and stepped off the dais.

Captain Denali handed the pie she had given him to the lady officer. "First Lieutenant Mol, would you like this pie?"

"Thank you, Captain." Mol moved the pie to her end of the table, not keeping her eyes on his for very long.

Something about the exchange between the stern Captain Denali and the long-legged lieutenant bothered Dan. They seemed uncomfortable with each other. Mol's twisting tattoos were more visible this close, and he could see they depicted interwoven chains of leaves, both on her face and her lower arms.

"Sir, may I serve you dinner?" he asked Captain Denali.

"I am waiting to be served by someone else if he is willing." The captain smirked as if amused by something. "I'm sure Lieutenant Baris will take your pie."

Lieutenant Baris turned his dark eyes on Dan, his fierce eyebrows, broken nose, and square jaw lending him an angry appearance. It did not work on Dan. He'd seen worse attempts at intimidation from his father. Dan placed the pie on the table in front of him.

Lieutenant Baris glared at him.

Dan gave a tiny nod of his head and exited the dais, walking back out of the room the way he'd come. He breathed a sigh of relief when he saw Alex hadn't returned yet. He would have to warn him. As he walked down the hall, Alex came his way behind the twins from Tiry Mor. Dan stepped in front of Alex.

"Captain Denali expects you to bring him his pie."

"Of course," Alex said, rolling his eyes. "The head of the household must make sure all bow before him."

"Be careful, Alex."

Alex rolled his eyes. "I know, Dan. I've been in situations like this all my life." He resumed his walk to the great room and Dan watched him go, wishing he could be there for the conversation that might ensue at the head table. Considering this, he hurried his pace back to the kitchen and grabbed another pie hastily as Perren was getting his pie, moving slowly, along with the recruits from Merseas.

"Have you been cleaning up after that prince forever?" asked Perren.

"No, but I have been watching how he handles those around him," Dan said, quickly exiting the room.

"What do you mean?" Perren followed close at his heels and easily matched his pace.

"The captain only wants Alex to serve him pie," Dan said.

"Oh, now that's something I want to see." Perren sped ahead of Dan and opened the door for him with a mocking bow.

Dan gave a short shake of his head to Perren and entered in time to see Alex serving the captain, then giving him a short half-bow.

The captain grinned, showing his teeth, but his eyes narrowed. He said something, something too quiet for Dan to hear. Alex's response was muted, but Dan watched the faces of the two Lieutenants. First Lieutenant Mol put her hand on Alex's arm as if warning him. Lieutenant Baris thumped the table with his fist and growled something indiscernible to Alex.

Alex gave all of them short bows, stepped down from the dais, and stalked out of the room. His face was white, and his lips were pressed together in fury, as he passed Dan in the entryway.

Dan couldn't follow him without messing up the order of things, so he went to their table. The others were eating their pie in silence already. Alex returned with his own shepherd's pie and sat down, eating precisely with the full manners of someone raised at court.

Farrald ate slowly as if he were wanting his food cold. Quinn ate as slowly, and as Dan looked at the front dais then side-eyed Alex, he realized what the others were doing. They were giving Alex, who had picked up his food last, time to eat his full meal before the recruits had to serve dessert. Dan was a bit ashamed that he hadn't realized.

As Alex finished, he glanced at Dan and tapped the table once, then stood up to go to the kitchen.

Dan stood a half-beat later and followed him out.

In the hallway, Alex waited for him to catch up.

"What happened?" Dan asked.

"Captain Denali wanted to make sure I knew I was here as punishment. Lieutenant Baris commented how I should watch my hands around the ladies here, and First Lieutenant Mol told me to come to her if I needed any extra lessons in sword work."

"That's ... wait, was she trying to tell you that she could help you with something other than sword work?"

"At first, I did not think so, but there's some kind of politics going on between those three, some shifting of power. I don't want to be anyone's pawn." Alex grumbled. "I'm so tired of all the court games and I hoped I wouldn't have to deal with them here. Here, I get to deal with cleaning out the stables and power plays. Two kinds of manure."

Dan felt a chuckle rising as they reached the kitchen. "Hey, maybe working in the stables will give you some idea on how to handle the nobles in Skycliff. My father could take a little shoveling out."

Alex crossed his arms over his chest. "He put you up to it, did he?"

Dan picked up two pies. "He was the reason I was there the other night." That was only part of the truth, but the only part he wanted to tell Alex.

"And you were being a good son."

Dan ground his teeth together. "I'm sick of being the good son, the loyal son, the son he uses and manipulates. If ... if I can gain a place here, I'm not going back."

"I wish I could choose that." Alex picked up two pies. "So, if I bring two pies to the head table, who do I offer them to?" He smirked.

Dan shrugged. "Your choice?"

"Is it?"

"Two to the Captain and I'll serve the others?"

Alex smiled broadly. "Sounds good to me."

They ambled back to the great hall with the sweet smells of cherry and apple pies in their hands.

When they re-entered the grand hall, the captain was not at the head table anymore. First Lieutenant Mol and Lieutenant Baris glared at each other across the small table.

Alex glanced over at Dan, then shrugged and served both pies to the two lieutenants.

Dan carried the two pies he had to the table they had shared with Quinn and Terese.

After the Captain had left, the meal became more casual, but Dan remembered that they were always being watched and were supposed to always be at watch, observing others around them. It was uncomfortable at first, and then he slipped into the role, as he had so often in his life. He realized that the Watch Guard was simply a continuation of skills he had learned at court. He stirred, not quite liking that, but knowing it was true. His parents had watched every move, wanting him to be their perfect, noble son. He had never had a moment of privacy, except in his own room. Here, they did not even have that, unless they gave them rooms with friends they could trust.

Chapter 19: Mopping Up

AFTER THEY FINISHED THEIR desserts, they washed up all the dishes in the kitchen, with each table group assigned a task. Dan, Alex, and Farrald were assigned to mop up the floors in the main hall, after they had helped clear the tables. Farrald showed both Dan and Alex how to wield a mop and sang throughout the task. While Dan was not sure how Farrald was going to survive the Watch Guard training, he did appreciate the way Farrald made every moment joyous with his singing. From Alex, he learned the three of them were considered a training group and would be assigned most of their tasks together, as well as their sleeping quarters. So, perhaps, if Alex forgave him, he might not have to be as guarded in their private quarters.

As they finished wringing out their mops, Farrald went to Kaipo to receive an official dismissal, since all the other apprentices had left for their quarters. This left Dan alone with Alex.

Alex offered a hand to Dan. "Truce, Dan. Between us. Please don't make me work for this too hard. I've never had to apologize to anyone other than my parents."

Dan shook his head. "You don't owe me an apology. I was sent to that brothel by my father to spy on you, to report your activities to him. I brought the Sword Guards and reported you to your own father instead. Even if I was not the snake my father wanted me to be, I did not act like your friend."

Alex continued to hold his hand out. "I agree. You did not. You acted like you had my best interests in mind, stopped me from being an idiot, kept me from embarrassing my father and the crown." He took a deep breath and said, "I apologize for my behavior to you since then. I was angry. I was embarrassed. Please forgive me and help me survive this horrible experience."

He leaned forward and whispered. "We both know I have never mopped a floor before and it is disgusting, not to mention painful."

Dan shook Alex's hand. "Forgiven. I apologize for not being a better friend. But, as it is, our sword callouses probably helped us deal with these awful mops. I will never consider mopping the floor to be easy again."

"Same." Alex emptied his mop bucket into the drain Kaipo had shown them earlier. The water would run out under the Tower through a series of drains.

Dan watched the water seep away and wondered how much information he still had to learn about living a life of a commoner. As one of the families of the unofficially named "inner circle" of Skycliff and with generations of nobility behind him, he had been nearly as privileged as Alex.

Alex clapped Dan on the shoulder. "I wonder if my father knows how drains work. Or how to mop a floor. I can't quite picture it. Can you?"

Dan shook his head. "No, but then your father served in the last war against the Southern Continent, and I have never heard much about it other than the dry historical records."

"I have not either." Alex ran his hand through his hair. "Since my mom died, my father hasn't spoken much to me other than about duty, lessons, and law."

Dan did not know what to say. His father was far worse than Alex's father, but he did not believe comparison would help. He merely offered silence.

"You know, you're going to be good at this Watch Guard training. You listen well."

Dan shrugged. "It was always the best strategy in my household, to listen." And not to speak. But he did not add that out loud.

Chapter 20: The Plans of a Lady

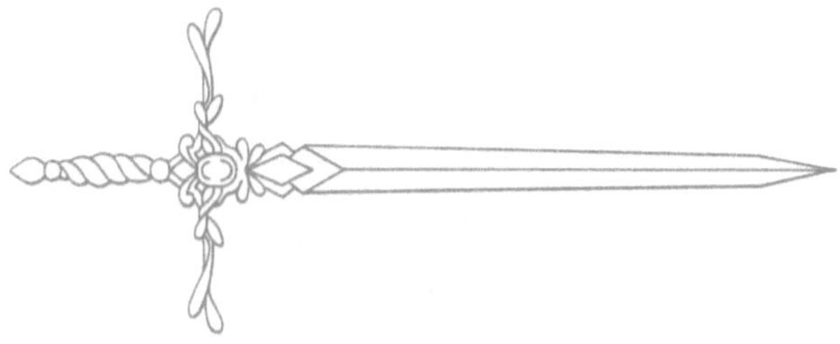

ALONE IN HER STUDY, the tiny room off her bedroom, Leandra ran her hands over the pages of the book she was reading, reveling in the smoothness of the paper. But after doing this several times, she realized she was soothing her nerves. It was a bad habit to do such a thing unconsciously. She thought she had broken habits like that as a child, the last time her mother had burned her hands with a fire poker and forced her to wear gloves to cover it up at their social engagements.

She allowed her hands to smooth the soft pages one more time, then closed the book. "Notable Women in Warfare and Their Weapons" was not on her mother's approved reading list for young ladies. Leandra opened the secret compartment in her trunk and placed the book inside next to her assortment of short blades, knives, and hair sticks with sharpened edges. She closed it carefully and covered it with the frilly undergarments her mother insisted she embroider for that nebulous future day of her wedding, covered these with some soft linens, and locked the chest with a key she wore around her neck. One couldn't be careful enough with parents like hers, even if they believed she didn't get out of bed until luncheon and that she hadn't read a book in years.

She certainly hadn't read her mother's choice of books, which were stacked and covered in dust on a corner of her desk. "A Ladies Guide to Flirting with Grace" along with "The Coquetry of Color" were not something Leandra ever planned to read, although she had read the book

"The Language of Flowers" her mother had given her because messages could be passed in certain circles with the right bouquet. However, since the book was a popular read among court nobility, Leandra doubted many messages passed with flowers remained a secret for long. There were only so many variations and double meanings for flowers.

Still in her night dress, Leandra slipped into her bedroom in bare feet and sprawled across her bed. She didn't want her mother or her maid to realize she had been awake since dawn. She might as well take a nap before her expected visitor arrived.

She tossed and turned for a while, and then groaned into her pillow with a satisfyingly unladylike sound. She couldn't go back to sleep. Too much uncertainty surrounded her latest gambit. Too much potential danger. It was heady, and terrifying. If caught, burnt hands and a striped back from her mother's belt would probably be mild forms of punishment. She wished she had been able to leave with Dan. It wasn't the first time she had envied him his less limited freedom, but it was the first time he had done something so defiantly bold she admired him. She had given up on him as an ally years ago, thinking he had succumbed to their parents' schemes. She had been wrong, and he had freed himself in one singular act. Her way might take longer, but she planned to find the same kind of freedom as he had. She rang her bell for her maid, and Molly rushed into the room.

"Lady Leandra, I'm so sorry I'm late. I didn't expect you to wake up before luncheon. Would you like the blue gown or the yellow today, miss?"

Leandra waved her hand lazily toward the closet, as if she didn't care, although she had planned out her outfit as soon as she knew she would have a visitor. "Oh, I think maybe the blue, no, the green with the gold trim. Yes, the green one, today." She stood and clasped the key necklace in one hand while Molly dressed her. When Molly went to fetch her the appropriate slippers, she tucked the key with its chain into a hidden pocket at the waist of the gown.

"Will you be wanting breakfast this morning here or in the sitting room?"

Since she had planned out every moment of this day, she knew she had to play every moment correctly to allay her parents' suspicion. She had to seem as if she knew nothing, as if she were nonchalant and uncaring as always. "Here. I don't want to see company."

Molly frowned. "But the green, it's one of your best dresses."

"And if I choose to enjoy wearing it in my own rooms, what does that matter?" Leandra gazed at her reflection in her full-length mirror, forcing herself to cock her head to the side and pretend to admire the gown. She had nearly blown her entire mission by insisting on wearing it, but she wanted to make a good impression on her visitor. Without meaning to, she had pinched her brow in concern, so she ran her hands over her eyes, feigning weariness while she relaxed her expression.

"As you say, Lady Leandra," Molly said. She would not openly argue with Leandra about the gown, even if she often told tales on Leandra to her mother.

When Molly left the room to get breakfast, Leandra tucked her favorite jade green hair sticks into her updo, angling them so the sharp edges wouldn't pierce her scalp.

After breakfast, it was only a matter of waiting for the opportune moment after her parents' guest arrived.

Hours passed. Finally, as luncheon started and Leandra was summoned from her quarters, their doorman announced they had a visitor. It seemed her parents believed they were outwitting her with the timing of their guest's arrival.

When he entered, her parents stood to greet him, and Leandra did the same, taking in the measure of him as he greeted first her mother, with a small bow over her hand, and then her father, with a brief salute with two fingers to his temple, as the Sword Guards did for the noble houses. It was interesting to watch, given that she had seen him give a full hand to heart, five fingers to the temple salute to King Xandros only days ago at court. He gave her father the respect of his class, but nothing more. All in all, she was pleased with his appearance, which was important for any subterfuge to work.

Wearing a dark gray uniform with silver armor made of interlapping disks, a helmet of the same make tucked under his arm, and fine leather boots dyed black, Sword Guard Theran was dressed down in comparison to his usual court uniform as the King's Sword Guard. His handsome features did not flinch or flicker when her father made a remark about his change of status. His tone was dry when he spoke, respectfully, of his thanks for finding a new position in their household. When he was given his assignment, to guard Lady Leandra as she was courted by the men of nobility interested in her hand in marriage, he gave her a graceful bow.

It would be proper to curtsey in respect, but that was not to the plan. Instead, Leandra turned to her parents and crossed her arms. "I told you; I do not need a Guard."

"Leandra, we have spoken of this," her mother's tone could chill ice in summer.

"Mother, I do not want to be courted by the nobles you have lined up for me."

"Leandra, you are getting too old to be a spoiled maiden. It is time for you to take your place in society, and that means finding you a fortunate match among your peers. This necessitates a Guard, so we may be assured of your safety."

Leandra wanted to snort in derision, knowing it was her parents' choice in friends and in trade that endangered her far more than anything else. If it weren't for their activities, her reputation would have been safe with the accompaniment of her maid.

"Oh, mother, do you really think it's necessary for a Sword Guard to follow me around all day?"

"Yes, your father and I are in agreement." Her mother's tone dropped to a dangerous low note.

Leandra knew that she should not push the argument any farther. She dropped her eyes demurely, and then curtseyed to Sword Guard Theran. "My apologies, sir. Of course, I will accept your protection."

"I believe Sword Guard Theran will have specifics to speak to you about, as he and I discussed previously," her father said. "The receiving room is free."

Thankfully, she had eaten breakfast, given that going with Sword Guard Theran meant she could not finish lunch. It was her father's way of punishing her without being obvious about it in front of anyone else. Leandra stalked over to the sitting room and flounced her skirts as she entered the room in front of Sword Guard Theran.

Chapter 21: Theran Meets His Match

Despite serving alongside his King for a few decades, Theran's discernment and knowledge regarding the nobility lacked the nuances he needed for his undercover role. He had been coached by King Xandros and had been assured he could trust Lady Leandra, young though she was, to help him.

He was concerned by her behavior in the dining room, as she had seemed offended by his presence. Her pouty behavior combined with her frivolous, fashionable attire at home made him wonder if she really was the woman King Xandros had concocted this plan with. But as soon as the door to the receiving room shut, her entire demeanor changed.

Straightening her posture, she locked the door of the receiving room, and leaned in close to him. "You and I will thwart my father's schemes and send the Red Hand into the merciful justice of the Law. Are we agreed?"

Her perfume wafted over him, her liquid brown eyes captured his and he stood there, his mouth dropping open in shock for a moment, before he answered. "Yes, I am to serve as your Sword Guard, a silent protector at all events, and together, we will search out the dealings of the Red Hand, and who is in league with them."

"My father is one. That is why you are here."

"Yes, the King had information on him."

"Thanks to my brother."

"The King sent him to the Watch Guard along with Prince Alex and one other."

"King Xandros hopes his son will have two advisors such as yourself and Shepherd Jordan, men loyal to him and the Triune Halls unto death, even if it means sacrificing your position at his side to serve as a lady's guard."

He did not respond at first, trying to take her measure.

"I see you doubt my ability to keep secrets or be trustworthy with such matters, given that I look as I do." She lifted her chin and took a slow turn, showing off her fashionable court attire: a green dress in some shimmering fabric with gold tassels at the edges of the skirt and where the bodice met the skirt. The top, thankfully, was high at the throat, with a small, lateral bar of exposed brown skin at her collarbones. He had no idea why the ladies of the court varied their bodices from year to year, but he was glad it was not a deep cut year. Those dresses had embarrassed him.

As he took in her demeanor and her attire, he realized it was re-markable, by court standards, that she was not married yet. Her mother wanted an advantageous match, and her generation had a surplus of young women among the noble houses. Her parents wouldn't consider a commoner for her. This decision to find her a husband seemed to be overdue, but perhaps her parents had been saving her to create an alliance with another wealthy family.

Leandra cleared her throat and lifted her innocent-looking brown eyes to him. "Well, will I do as a spy in my father's house and in the King's court?"

He felt his face grow warm. He rarely gave any women the long look he had been giving her, and he again reminded himself that she was fourteen years his junior. "Do you carry a weapon?"

She smiled so broadly it crinkled the edges of her eyes. "Well, that was the last thing I expected you to ask, but yes. I carry three weapons. Can you find them?" She closed the distance between them again and he realized she was nearly his own height. Her brown eyes had pooled into serious depths.

He stilled himself and stared at her face, then noted her hair, held together by two sticks, and considered her dress. "Your hair sticks, and perhaps a long knife in your skirts."

"Yes, and no. I wish I had a slit-pocket for a long knife in my skirts, but I don't. My mother would ask too many questions and she finds much of my behavior deplorable, anyway. I have my two hair sticks, which are edged but not at the point, since I don't want them sticking into my scalp, and I have my wit."

"I see." He reflected on her impressive bearing for a moment more, forcing himself to stay in one place and not step back, as he wanted. "You also have boldness."

She laughed, and the husky sound hit him in the gut.

This time, he stepped back. He hadn't felt this attracted to a woman in years, and again, he reminded himself she was too, too young, and Dan's sister, and the daughter of the man responsible for the Red Hand in Skycliff.

"Does anyone suspect my reason for being employed as your guard? Does your father? Given that I have been loyal to King Xandros and the Triune Council for years, will they believe that I have left my service to the King?"

She cocked an eyebrow at him. "You mean, since I have thought of it, others must have?"

"Yes."

She crossed her arms over her chest. "That is probably true, but I doubt many will consider it. Most of the nobles crave power and influence. To give it up, for any reason, would be unreasonable to them. To willingly give up your place at the King's side, with your voice in his ear? To them, that would be insane, unthinkable."

He sighed. "I have seen such power-hungry attitudes at the court, but it seems strange to me."

She leaned closer to him. "And so, you are less knowledgeable about the daily lives of nobles than you know. That is why you are here, correct?"

He shifted his weight from one foot to the other, fighting the urge to flee from her nearness and how it affected him. "I have seen much from the King's side, but there are many who would never speak to me, secrets beyond my scope of influence. I was both greater and lesser, because I served the King."

She touched his arm. "Yes, but here, you are nothing but a mere Sword Guard to a younger noble lady, therein you are in even greater disgrace, or so those who care about such things will perceive it."

Fighting the urge to pull away, Theran asked her something that had been bothering him about the assignment. "How did you get your father to hire me? And why did you pretend not to want me as your Guard"

"The answer is in your question. If I tell him I don't want something, he will usually give it to me."

"What?"

She smirked. "It has worked for years. He believes he is training me, punishing my faults."

"And how did you come by your hair sticks?"

She touched one of the curls escaping her updo, trailing it through her fingers. "Our family's head guard was a retired Sword Guard to the Triune Halls. He trained Dan. He trained me when no one else realized it. I had to get up well before breakfast for years."

He rocked back on his heels, realizing how impressed he was by her determination to upend her parents' expectations of her. "And now?"

"I pretend to laze about as a proper noble, but my maids have strict orders to stay out of my room until noon. I need my beauty sleep, you know. Although I mainly use that time to collect my observations and complete my studies."

He did not comment, did not ask about her observations and studies, realizing he had been dragged further into the conversation that he had expected to be, or that he should be. In any moment, he would start telling her that she did not need any extra sleep to be beautiful, and then, well, the idea she might be flirting with him on purpose was ridiculous. He was too old. He allowed himself to retreat a few steps away from the conversation and stare out one of the windows at the street outside. He had to reset his focus on thwarting the Red Hand.

Chapter 22: Basic Training

Up before dawn, running laps, fighting in lines, fighting in skirmishes, horseback riding, and learning how to fight on horseback. All of these were activities Dan expected as part of his training as a Watch Guard. And they did them, every single day without fail, in all weather. Dan had never been so sore and exhausted in all his life. He struggled to hold back moans when he heard the waking bells and fell asleep each night as his head hit his pillow.

But the physical lessons weren't the hardest ones. In addition to those, they had to learn battle tactics, map-reading, map-making, basic healing techniques to bind wounds and tend fevers, cooking, and sewing skills for patching up their gear. In addition to all of that, they had chores. He had been right that first night. They were the ones responsible for cleaning the entire Tower and Keep. In a smattering of weeks, he felt like he had his head stuffed full of information and he wasn't sure if he would remember all of it. In a few months, he was terrified of the test their trainers hinted they would take. It was a test that would determine whether they would continue training with the Watch Guard.

They did everything in teams of three or four, with one of their sponsoring Watch Guards by their side in every lesson, encouraging them or shouting orders at them, depending on the situation. In the larger skirmishes, they worked with everyone, but for the most part, Dan worked, studied, and fought alongside Alex and Farrald with Quinn or Terese at their elbows, demanding more.

The worst part of his exhaustion meant that Dan had no idea how he fared against the others. If a competition existed for first place, he had no idea what his place was among the thirteen apprentices. But the best part of his exhaustion meant that he knew he was giving it his best. He hoped his best was good enough, but he didn't have time to think about it too long, or to worry about whether Keeva liked him as well as Nilsen, or anything else. Another good part of their intensive training schedule was that Alex didn't have the time or energy to get into trouble by fighting with Perren or flirting with Flycke, although he often saw Flycke winking at Alex when they passed each other from training session to training session.

Farrald, with his joyful love of learning, continued to sing every morning, and pray every night. Dan was surprised Farrald had the energy for either, but he had grown to appreciate the way the music made it easier to get moving each day, and the prayers calmed him in the evenings.

A month of training passed, and Dan expected the middle-of-the-night wake-up call by their Watch Guard instructors, but he woke when a rooster crowed, sometime before actual sunrise.

"Argh. What is wrong with that bird?" Alex moaned from across the room nearest the window, which showed a slight lightening of the sky to a blue-black color. It seemed later than they usually woke.

"Rooster," Farrald answered while shifting around in his bed.

"Don't they crow at dawn when the sun lights up the sky?" Dan asked.

Farrald laughed quietly. "Only city-folk believe that. Roosters crow whenever they feel like it. When they feel threatened, when they feel like strutting, when they want to impress their flock, when the sun rises, when the sun sets, midnight, midday, whenever. Roosters like to crow."

"Why did we not notice it before?" Dan asked, rubbing his hand over his eyes.

"Too busy. Making too much noise of our own. And we managed to go to sleep probably after the rooster fell asleep." Farrald moved around more, making rustling sounds.

In the duskiness of the dark, Dan couldn't quite make out what Farrald was doing.

"Going to light a lamp. It is probably time to get up anyway. If we're dressed and ready to go, we might even impress Terese and Quinn before they start shouting at us to move faster."

"Gah." Alex moaned.

"If we're in the kitchen early enough, maybe we can help with breakfast and not have to clean up," Farrald offered.

The idea of warm food made Dan's stomach whine in discontent. He really wanted to eat some decent breakfast, and Farrald was a better cook than most of the other apprentices.

"I'm in, then," he said.

"Why did you not start with that argument?" Alex retorted.

Farrald lit the match and they stared at each other with bleary eyes.

Dan put a hand over his mouth to stop his grin at the sight of Alex's hair, sticking straight up from his head. He noticed Farrald busying himself with his clothes chest, obviously doing the same. Even though they had roomed together, eaten together, and trained together, they still hadn't forgotten Alex's position as a prince.

Alex ran a hand through his hair. "Another reason to get up. I don't want to get laughed at by anyone other than you two."

"It is an honor, your highness," Dan gave Alex a short bow with an extra flourish.

Alex squinted his eyes at him in a mock glare. "Don't get used to it."

"I won't." Dan turned away and got dressed, amazed they'd been able to banter again. It had been so long since they had been at ease with one another. While Dan was one of many noble children who grew up with Alex, he was the only one who lived in the capital nearly year-round. They had been friends until Dan's father started bothering him to gain an advantage with the King through Alex.

The idea had turned Dan's stomach and so he had begun to distance himself. It was partly his fault Alex had ended up in that brothel. By distancing himself from Alex, he hadn't been around when the Harnan brothers started taking Alex to gambling parties and tempting him with ideas that would put him out of favor with the Triune Hall Council.

While they lived in a kingdom and Alex's father was the King, the Triune Hall Council and the Council of the Lords were also part of a balanced power system. The King listened to the others, and they listened to him. If Alex lost favor with the Triune Hall Council, he might jeopardize his right to succeed his father on the throne. Dan knew all of this. Alex should, as well, but he had been with the Harnan brothers too long. They had bent his ear and made him susceptible to their influence, which could have led to blackmail, or losing his succession.

As it was, Dan's father had wanted Dan to blackmail Alex. That's why he'd been sent to retrieve Alex from the Red House – to find him in a compromising position. Dan hadn't even known there was a brothel, but once he knew what his father and Lord Harnan were up to, he raced to the house and pulled Alex out of the waiting area, before he could do anything stupid, or anything more stupid than going there in the first place.

"Dan, are you coming to the kitchen with us?" Farrald asked.

Dan realized he'd dressed and stood staring at his sword, bearing his family crest. He wished he could be proud of that crest. He turned and could see Farrald was looking at him with concern and Alex had his eyebrows up in an obvious question.

"Are we all right, Dan?" Alex asked.

"Yes. I was...thinking about my father."

Alex gave a curt nod. "Not a happy topic."

"No, definitely not." Dan slammed his sword into its sheath.

Farrald watched them both, then flung open the door. "Let's get to the kitchen before anyone else has the same idea."

Dan followed the other two out and down the stairs to the water pump. They all briefly washed their faces and hands. Alex wiped some water through his hair. As they entered the kitchen, Dan's mood lightened as he smelled fresh bread, eggs, and bacon.

Kaipo grinned when he saw them. "Ah, you three remembered your breakfast, I see." He handed a pair of lengthy tongs to Farrald. "You, I can trust with the bacon. Turn it when you think it is halfway right. We want it crisp and even, but not over-cooked."

Farrald took the tongs and took a place near the dark stove, where the bacon was cooked in a huge pan that covered four burners. "This is the most bacon I've ever cooked at once."

"Keep your eyes on it," Kaipo said before turning to Dan and Alex. "Hmm. I will start you, Alex, on chopping some fresh fruit for our breakfast, and you, Dan, will pull the loaves from the fire. You will need to wait for them to cool for a quarter-mark, then turn them onto the cooling racks."

Dan watched Alex pick up a knife and eye the fruit next to a cutting board. "I've never...what are these?"

"Melons, apprentice." Kaipo sighed. "Cut them open and you'll see. If you can, make cubes of them, without the rind."

Alex blushed but turned to his task. Even after a month of learning more about cooking meals, Alex still struggled with some of the basics.

Dan walked over to the giant stone fireplace, in which a fire burned under a set of racks with bread tins on them. He put on the fire mitts, with their extra protective cloth, and took up the large metal paddle which would help him slide the loaves out. He could see they were steaming. "Are they ready?" He hoped it was all right to ask, given that during their training for cooking, they often had to guess if they were right and then eat what they had made, regardless of how good or bad it was.

"When the tops are as high as the sides of the tins and the edges are brown." Kaipo told him.

Dan's job of waiting for the bread felt interminably long and he started staring into the fire, thinking of the blades of power carried by many Sword Masters and those who served in the Triune Halls. A longing filled him for a sword like that, a weapon that would help him live a life of purpose. In the embers of the fire, he imagined a dark shimmering sword forged for justice humming with power in his hand, a weapon that would strike fear into the hearts of—

"Dan! The loaves!" Kaipo's shouts broke Dan's reverie.

Two of the center loaves were darkening into a burnt crisp. He used the paddle to yank them out, and one fell on the floor. He carefully moved the other to the cooling racks, then went back for the others. He felt his own cheeks warming, not from the heat of the fire but from his embarrassment. "I'm sorry, Kaipo."

Kaipo pointed a finger at Dan. "To be of the Watch Guard, one must cultivate the ability to keep your focus and have patience."

"I understand." Dan gazed down at the ruined loaf on the floor. "I will clean that up."

"Yes, you will. And then, you will help me make another batch under my direction."

"Yes, Kaipo." Dan knelt and started picking up the hot loaf.

"It goes there," Kaipo indicated a small barrel with food scraps. "The rooster will love it."

"Of course," Dan muttered, feeling a distinct dislike of the bird.

As Kaipo showed Dan how to mix ingredients to make a loaf of bread and how to pour the dough into a set of pans, he was glad Kaipo did not bring up his mistakes as they worked. If it had been his father teaching him or his tutor, he would have never heard the end of it. Kaipo did not say anything more about it. Dan relaxed and settled in to watch the next set of loaves bake, although his stomach was growling.

"No, no, your work is done today. Those loaves won't be done for a full candle-mark." Kaipo steered Dan, Alex, and Farrald over to the kitchen table. "Now, eat of your labors. You have an interesting day ahead of you."

"You mean more sword drills, battle tactics, skirmishes, and running?" Farrald sighed.

Kaipo chuckled. "Ah, you will wish it were that simple when the day is done." With that cryptic remark, he left them to eat and busied himself by stoking the fire.

Chapter 23: A Series of Tests

When they had finished their breakfast and washed their dishes, Dan, Alex, and Farrald turned to Kaipo for directions, but he merely waved a hand at them. "Terese is your trainer. Go to the infirmary to start your day."

Dan wanted to ask why they had been allowed to sleep in late, but he could see Kaipo had his focus fixed firmly on cooking more breakfast.

As they walked toward the exit, Perren strolled in with Gorka. Perren raised an eyebrow in mock surprise. "A prince, a noble, and a merchant's son broke their fast first today? Well," he nudged Gorka, "We're going to have to rise earlier."

Gorka snorted. "Speak for yourself. Inaki and I already went for our early morning flight. Not everyone can stand around in the mews and feed their birds. Some of us take our Wing Partners out for a hunt before dawn."

Farrald waved his hands excitedly. "Roosters, eagles, and griffins all wake before dawn to eat? That's fascinating. I imagine..."

"Don't," Gorka held up a hand and shook one of his fingers. "I'll get in trouble with Inaki for comparing her to one of Perren's eagles. I imagine she'd bite you if she knew you compared her to a rooster."

"No, I..." Farrald's face turned bright red. "Please, I ..."

Gorka slapped Farrald on the back and Farrald swayed on his feet. "Heyla, it is all right. If you want to know more about griffins, come talk to Inaki and me if we ever have time away from our grueling schedule. She is the expert and I'm her friend, so you'll get your knowledge from the source instead of imagining it."

Dan leaned into the conversation. "What does it take to be a Wing Partner?"

Gorka's brow furrowed slightly, and his gaze grew distant as if recalling a memory. "Time, patience, and a love of flying. Like anything, it takes practice."

Perren held out both of his hands and spoke in a sage voice, "The wise man who does not put his knowledge into practice is like a bee that gives no honey."

Alex snorted and cocked his head to one side. He had been standing silently through most of the conversation. "That's from the Book of World Proverbs, from the Lost Continent. I did not expect you to be such a learned man, Perren Hawksmith."

Perren's face swiftly changed from peaceful to mutinous, his jaw tightening, and his open hands dropping to his sides. "You know nothing about me, Prince," He sneered at Alex's title.

"And, you know nothing about me," Alex retorted, lifting his chin. "I think we should rectify that."

"Anytime, Prince." Perren growled.

"Let it go, Perren," Gorka put his hand on Perren's shoulder.

Perren shrugged him off and stomped over to Kaipo's worktable.

Gorka paused and glanced at each of them in turn, first Farrald, then Dan, and then Alex. "He...has reason to distrust royals. My apologies."

Dan loosened his stance, hoping Alex would let this one go, hoping he would not have to stop Alex from doing something foolish. He knew what a temper the prince could have.

Alex glared at Perren's back but finally turned to face Gorka. "I appreciate the way you speak up for your friend. The world would be a far more peaceful place with friends like you."

"That's why I'm here, to train to be a Watch Guard and keep an eye on the world around us." Gorka waved his hands to include the walls around them.

Alex gave him a small nod. "Thank you. It would be a pleasure to speak to you and... Inaki, later." He pivoted on one heel and sauntered out of the room.

Leaning forward, Gorka whispered to Dan, "Is he...always like that?"

"He was raised to be like that," Dan told him.

"I see. I'll try to soothe Perren's feathers."

"Thanks," Dan said.

He and Farrald hurried to the infirmary to find Alex already there, standing in the middle of an empty room. "She appears not to be here yet. I wonder what we should do in the meantime."

The smell of herbs and medicines hung heavy in the air. Sunlight streamed through the windows and Farrald turned to run his fingers over the books on the bookshelf. "I wonder if she has a book about griffins from Aerland. I could do some research before..."

Terese's arrival was heralded by the soft clink of her armor and the creak of leather from her travel pack. Her presence filled the room, bringing with it an air of authority and purpose. The weight of her gaze as she assessed them was almost physical, and she turned her attention to Farrald.

"We do not have time for light reading, apprentice. I need the three of you to show me which medicinal herbs and emergency supplies we need for a long journey and how to pack them. If you fail at this task, I will teach you what you need, teach you to pack them, and then we will gather your other supplies for our training."

"Terese, are you saying we're going elsewhere for our training today?" Dan asked.

She put her hands on her hips. "That's not observant enough for a Watch Guard apprentice, but yes. Now, can either Alex or Farrald tell me where we might be traveling?"

Alex cast a brief look at Terese's gear. "May I see the back of your travel pack?"

She turned slowly, revealing a sleeping bundle tied to the bottom of her pack.

Farrald raised his hand. When Alex did not say anything, he spoke. "It is going to be south of here or somewhere warmer. You do not appear to be bringing a heavy travel cloak or tent."

Alex jumped in next. "If you have packed well, it means we have a two-to-three-day journey ahead of us."

Terese pressed her lips together and cocked her head to the side. "Hmm." She rolled one hand at Dan. "Well?"

"We're going into dangerous territory, probably outside or between nations and kingdoms. We might be going for longer than two to three days if we can find someplace to resupply."

"Not bad," Terese said. "You all have an inkling of how to observe the obvious details and make some correlations based on the information I already gave you."

Alex puffed out his chest. "What information?"

Dan stepped toward him.

Alex glared at him, then dropped his gaze when Dan raised his eyebrows. "My apologies, Terese. I...am out of sorts this morning."

"I know." She put her hands on her hips. "Each of you is going to need to demonstrate patience as part of the Watch Guard, as well as listening skills, and observation skills. Not one of you is prepared for the tasks that await you in your lives, and you need to be. As a future ruler, as a future Guard or Noble, and as a future Shepherd, you need all the skills the Watch Guard can teach you and more. Because of my background and Quinn's background, we selected you from the larger group. With us, you will learn what you need to succeed here or in the treacherous streets of Skycliff."

Alex shook his head curtly. "Skycliff is a great city in a peaceful kingdom."

Dan made a small motion with his hand, trying to cut off Alex from saying anything else in an angry tone of voice.

Alex's neck turned red. "I mean, I can see that it can be a place of political intrigue and social backstabbing. While we do not have war on our streets, you are right in calling it a treacherous place for those of the court."

Terese cocked an eyebrow at him. "Remember, it is your job here to observe, to listen, to learn. Let's get back to business. What task should you have already completed while we were having this conversation?"

As they worked through Terese's task, the rustle of parchment, the clinking of glass vials, and the soft thud of packed bags created a symphony of preparation. The scent of various herbs mingled in the air as they sorted through supplies, each one carrying its own unique aroma.

Dan watched Terese as she subtly directed them to make the right choices and he hoped Alex would forgive him for stepping between them again and again, as the prince grew frustrated with the exercise.

Alex's anger radiated off him in waves that seemed to heat the very air around him. Dan could almost taste the tension, bitter and sharp on his tongue. Farrald's enthusiasm, by contrast, was like a cool breeze, his eagerness to learn lightening the atmosphere.

Before Dan had finished packing supplies he believed he needed, in addition to the basics, Terese interrupted them. "This, gentlemen, was your first test in a series of tests making up your first practical review. You need to pass more than half of these tests to continue training with us. When you finish here, go pack your personal gear and meet Quinn at the stables."

Dan took a slow breath, trying not to panic. Had he passed this test? He couldn't be sure. Terese and Alex seemed to be locked in a battle of glares until Alex stalked off with his medicinal supplies in a small pouch. Dan searched through his supplies one more time, considering what else he might need and what extras he might need to bring if Alex or Farrald forgot something.

Farrald finished, but continued to linger by the bookshelves until Terese sent him out.

Terese turned to Dan and crossed her arms. "You need to learn how to step back and let him fail."

Dan immediately knew she meant Alex and not Farrald, but it was the opposite of anyone in Skycliff would ever say. Dan considered the implications of her words. Alex might embarrass himself, or get into trouble, be blackmailed for mistakes he made, or be taken and held for ransom.

"He's...He can't fail."

Terese sighed, then handed a book to Dan. "This is a short record of Watch Guard Kellan, once the Sword Guard to King Elar, the first King of Septily. Read it and take notes." She handed him a journal. "You need to learn what it means to stand beside the King, no matter how many mistakes he makes. He needs to fail if he's ever going to be humble enough to be a good King, the kind of King the people of Septily need."

Dan held the books loosely in his hands. The last thing he wanted was another book to study. "I'm not training to stand beside Alex. I'm training to be a Watch Guard."

"And where do you think the Watch Guard stands guard over the nations of Aramatir? From our Keeps and Towers, from our Hidden Libraries? No." She grabbed a small parcel from the shelf by her desk, then pointed at him. "To be of the Watch Guard you must go where you are most needed for the world and for your country, even if it is beside the throne."

Terese's words hung in the air, heavy with implication. Each sentence seemed to add another weight to Dan's shoulders, the reality of his potential future settling around him like a cloak. The disappointment that filled him was almost physical, a hollowness in his chest that echoed with each breath.

Dan wanted to protest, but he said nothing as his disappointment sank deep into him. Was there no way to get away from the life of the court for him? Was he as trapped as Alex?

Chapter 24: A Near Miss

Rattling armor and heavy footsteps alerted Stelia to the Drinaii's high command someone nearing her tent. She signaled for quiet to the little girl she had rescued a while ago and the young woman she had taken from a village a few nights ago when the Drinaii had pillaged it. Both moved swiftly and knelt by the back wall of her tent, their heads to the floor. She hoped whoever came would be easily turned away. She had to enact her rescue plan soon. They were only a day's travel away from the coven's Dark Spire, a keep made of dark stones by the ocean's edge.

Stelia pretended to be busy at her folding desk, writing a missive to her contact in the Dark Sisterhood. Her heart pounded, but she kept her face composed. Someone gave a sharp whistle outside her tent flap, and she jumped up.

Pushing the tent flap to the side, she saluted the three Drinaii standing at attention outside. A female enlistee she didn't know, who carried the whistle, her friend-turned-enemy Jennar, and Major General Ader Worsten with his oiled mustache and blustering red cheeks.

Ader Worsten had attempted to make Stelia's life a living hell from the first day she had been sent to serve with the Drinaii. He had tried to have her whipped and beaten several times for supposed disobedience, but she had escaped those punishments every time with witnesses or by calling on the Dark Sisterhood for aid.

She saluted the Major General with a quick snap of her fingers to her forehead, only four, not five, as she was technically not his to command.

The enlistee spoke first. "Enforcer Stelia Southern, the Major General Ader Worsten demands an audience."

One reason Stelia despised Ader was his aggrandizing need for attention for his rank, but she did not say this. "What concern would you have me take to task, Major General?"

"I understand you have two captives in your tent, Enforcer. Only one captive is allowed per officer, unless one holds the rank of Major General."

Stelia kept her eyes on the florid Major General, but she sensed his knowledge came from the man by his side. Jennar's determination to undermine her didn't surprise her, but if this was his attempt to catch her helping prisoners escape, it would not work.

"Yes, Major General. I know Edict four hundred twenty-six. It serves to keep all plunder and pillage fair amongst the Drinaii."

"If you know the Edict, why do you have two captives in your tent?" Major General Ader Worsten took a step toward Stelia, as if he expected her to yield and allow him into her quarters.

"I sensed potential in both girls. I believe my contact within the Dark Sisterhood may be interested in them."

"Were they not checked by our resident witch?"

Stelia was surprised by his use of the term "witch" to refer to a member of the coven. The Dark Sisters, as they liked to be called, viewed the term "witch" as a slur. The Dark Sister stationed with the Drinaii on their away missions had not endeared herself to the Major General, but his use of that term meant he wasn't afraid of the woman. That was strange.

"Yes, but the powers can be highlighted or subdued by trauma, depending on the individual's potential. I believe these two should be seen by Dark Sister Chloedess, who is in charge of all those who enter the Dark Spire for Sisterhood or for service."

"You would sentence someone to that life?" Jennar's shock sounded real, and Stelia wondered what game he thought he was playing.

"If they are best suited for it, it is their destiny." Stelia said this without flinching, although she didn't believe a word of it.

"Enough excuses. I want to see them." Major General Ader Worsten stepped even closer.

"Yes, sir," Stelia said. She spoke over her shoulder into her tent. "Nisha, Berta, come out now."

The tiny girl and the young woman came forward to stand by Stelia's side, outside of her tent. When they were next to her, they bowed their heads to the three Drinaii soldiers.

"Let me see your faces, slaves." Major General Ader's voice cracked like a whip.

The tiny girl whimpered, but stared straight ahead. The young woman lifted her gaze to the Major General and then shifted her glance to his shoulder.

"Ugh. Are those sores? That's disgusting." The Major General stepped back and lifted a handkerchief to his mouth and nose. "They can't be sanitary to have in your tent."

"I believe they can be cured and be made of use, if they do not have the potential for power." Stelia turned to the girl and the woman. "Get back into the tent." She noted the skillful job they had both done with their makeup to make their appearance disturbing, and she fought the urge to smile.

The Major General glared at Jennar. "I thought you wanted to report Stelia for something illegal, not something unsanitary. Get her an extra tent for those two and keep them away from me."

"Yes, Major General." Jennar saluted his officer, then watched the man and his enlistee attendant stalk away. He turned to Stelia. "I tried to get you off lightly, old friend. Remember that in the days ahead. You won't get away with what you're doing much longer."

Stelia sneezed. He flinched. "I don't know what you're talking about, Jennar. Those two have some kind of gift. I know it."

Jennar shook his head at her and walked away.

Stelia watched him go, glanced around the common causeway between tents for any gossips, and then ducked back inside her tent.

She knelt down beside Nisha and Berta and whispered. "It worked, but you keep that disguise on for longer. I'll get you out of here soon."

"If you mean to sell us to that Dark Sister, we'll tell everything we know." Berta glared at her but trembled as she spoke.

"I know. And if you do that, I'll say you're lying." Stelia leaned in closer. "But it won't come to that."

Nisha nodded and touched Stelia's cheek. Her trust in Stelia had been sure since the first day Stelia had taken her in. Berta, with her melancholy mixed with anger over what had happened to her young family, had been more volatile and less certain.

They only had to make it through a matter of hours. Stelia had to hold Berta's trust just a little longer.

"Why don't you sharpen my knives while we wait? Just in case someone comes to check on us again." Stelia handed Berta her bandolier of knives. She had seen the girl eyeing them, and she figured she could handle anything Berta might try. Maybe the show of trust would help the girl trust her in return.

Berta took the bandolier and picked up the whetstone Stelia had left under her cot. She glanced at Stelia once, then bent to her task.

Chapter 25: Greater Good

Xandros rested his head against his hands while he studied the missives on his desk. No matter how many times he read them, the words remained the same. Somewhere, near the Southlands, Shepherd Jordan and Commander Leo tracked the Red Hand, but they hadn't found them yet despite getting closer to the dangerous territory of the Dark Sisterhood and the Drinaii Mercenaries, both of which kept fluid boundaries based on their penchant for terrorizing villages and nomadic traders.

Meanwhile, Sword Master Theran had infiltrated the Torren household in Skycliff, but had only been able to get terse coded messages back to him. From what he could see, reading into the missives, Theran had discovered how hard it would be to pin any knowledge of the Red Hand on the Torren family, but their initial resource, the young Lady Leandra had been helpful. They had tiny bits of information about the Torren's dealings in trade, and some possible ways the Torrens were covering their shipments of slaves while showing shipments of large trade goods on paper.

Xandros sighed and ran his hands through his hair. What could he do, here in the palace? Days of court life blended into one. Without Jordan and Theran, his closest friends and councilors, by his side, he had dry duty, hollow conversations, and the protective counseling of a rotating group of Sword Guards and Shepherds from the Triune Halls.

He stared at the picture of Alex and wondered if his son would find the right training with the Watch Guard. Maybe he shouldn't have sent him away.

A knock sounded on the door to his study.

He leaned back in his chair. "Please enter."

Sword Guard Llewllyn entered with a young boy dressed in plain clothes, possibly the child of a baker, given the plentitude of flour on the boy's shirt sleeves.

"This young man has a missive for you, and I thought he should deliver it in person. His name is Gavin."

Xandros stood and held out his hand. "Well met, Gavin."

Gavin stared at Xandros's hand, and then bent on one knee. "Sir, King, sir, I didn't know you were my contact, sir, er, your majesty."

Xandros knelt down on the floor next to him. "Gavin, I didn't know you were my contact either, which is all to the good, so we don't recognize each other as we go about our business most days under cover, spying for the interests of Septily. But I am guessing the reason you came was urgent, or you would not have requested a meeting."

Gavin bit his lip, and then put his hand to his heart. "Yes, your majesty. I've heard there's going to be a party at the Torren house. Your man inside will be there throughout the party, but one of the others and I came up with a plan to be there. You see, the noble houses don't employ enough servants for a party, but they do hire out extras. I thought if we had more ears listening, we could find out more."

Xandros stood up and circled his desk, with his hands clasped behind his back. "Is it safe enough, do you think, Sword Master Llewellyn?"

"If we have a few of the older spies on watch outside the house, and alert Theran to the presence of two inside, it will be."

Xandros turned to see Gavin getting to his feet. "Gavin, I do not want you to put yourself in danger for me, but I think the idea you and your friend have is a good one. May I ask why you do this work?

"Because someone has to. And they hurt one of my cousins. They need to be stopped." Gavin's chin jutted out and he clenched one of his fists as he spoke.

He sounded like a young version of Sword Master Theran, and Xandros felt the same way. The Red Hand hurt his people. They had to be stopped.

"Can you get a message to Theran so he will know to look out for you?"

"Yes, your majesty."

When Gavin and Sword Master Llewellyn left, Xandros returned to his contemplation of the painting of Alex. In the painting, Alex had to have been about the same age Gavin was now. If Gavin could offer himself up to help them discover and defeat the Red Hand, then Alex could learn how to serve his people with justice from the Watch Guard. He missed Alex as he missed his friends, but sacrifices had to be made for the benefit of the greater good.

Chapter 26: A Nest of Vipers

Theran, ex-Sword Guard of the King, stood silently at his mistress's side as she spoke to the servants, making sure her arrangements were in place for her parents' evening gala. He tried his best to ignore the harmonies in her voice and the way she wore her exquisite ball gown.

She crossed the room and went to the windows to glance out through a sliver of sunlight between the curtains. "My parents' first guests are about to arrive, and they'll want to see you and know all about you. You'll stand there, next to the fireplace, and I'll expect them to come to me, here." She took a seat on the davenport near the fireplace.

"Are you sure I should stand so close?"

"Yes, news of my father's hiring of you was to be kept hush-hush, so, of course, everyone knows about it and those who have not seen you yet, will want to."

Much of what the nobles discussed regularly was ridiculous gossip, but there were key phrases for particular activities like dealings with the Red Hand, and other illegal things Theran had been horrified to discover were happening right here in Skycliff, the capital of Septily, the kingdom of the Triune Halls and the light of the world. From affairs and gambling to illegal substances and abuse, the nobles dealt with them all in code phrases, which he had passed on to the Triune Halls.

He couldn't allow his facade to break, but he had a messenger who helped him, a boy in the market who was in training to the Sword Guard as a spy. It was a part of the Sword Guard Theran did not like, so he hadn't even known about the boy until he had taken this assignment, and now he knew more than he liked about the business of listening in to others' conversations and passing information along. And yet, he saw the use, as he had seen the use of giving his King sound advice based on his knowledge of protecting the kingdom. This spy craft was one more layer of protection.

Since they had met, he and Lady Leandra had gained small bits of knowledge about her father's workings with the Red Hand, but they hadn't gained what they truly needed: all or most of the major names of the families involved and the current location of the Red Hand's operations in the city since the incident with Prince Alex. The Red Hand had disappeared since the Sword Guards had appeared on their doorstep to get Prince Alex out of their den.

Tonight, they hoped the Red Hand would make an appearance at her father's party. The business associates of Lord Torren were to meet in the library, adjacent to the receiving room, at ten o'clock. Lady Leandra had gained this information from her mother, who told her to stay away from the library at that time, and Theran had gained the information from the servants.

The butler and the housekeeper did well to keep the youngest members of the staff away from these particular business meetings in the library, and served the meetings themselves, figuring they were too old to interest those that met and yet, also too respected to be gainsaid in their request. From these brief conversations with the servants, Theran realized two things: they held him in too much awe given his past associations, and they held a wealth of knowledge even Lady Leandra did not possess.

As Theran took his place by Leandra's side, standing near the fireplace, he vowed to keep an eye on her, on the two young associates who were hired as extra servers, and on all aspects of the party, but the details became muddled in the light of hundreds of candles, their flickering flames reflected in gilded mirrors and crystal chandeliers. The air became thick with the mingled scents of exotic perfumes, freshly cut flowers, and the rich aroma of gourmet delicacies. Soft strains of music from a string quartet in another room wove through the constant hum of animated conversation and tinkling laughter.

Like the eye of a glittering storm, Lady Leandra's gown, a masterpiece of emerald silk and delicate lace, caught the light with every graceful movement. A cluster of old and young nobles orbited around her, their eyes bright with admiration and thinly veiled ambition. They hung on her every word, each vying to be the recipient of her radiant smile or musical laughter.

Theran tried to remain unobtrusive, but his supposed fall from grace and his role as Leandra's protector caused a bubble of gossip. He realized he was drawing unwanted, appreciative glances from ladies who hid coy smiles behind ornate fans, and envious looks from gentlemen who adjusted their cravats self-consciously. Despite the attention, Theran remained quietly vigilant, ignoring the women who brushed against him.

The nobles around Leandra cast frequent glances at Theran, their whispers barely audible over the general din of the party. One young lady in a powder-blue gown leaned in close to Leandra, her lips curved in a conspiratorial smile as she murmured something that made the others titter behind their hands.

As the night wore on, the air grew warmer, heavy with the press of bodies and the heat of countless candles. The laughter grew louder, the conversations more animated, fueled by flowing wine and the heady atmosphere of wealth and power. Through it all, Leandra remained the calm center, her poise unwavering, while Theran stood sentinel.

Lady Leandra tapped her ornate fan on his elbow. "Guard, fetch me more wine."

Theran bowed as he took her glass and then signaled a pourer, a young man who was in Leandra's confidence enough to know she preferred the watered-down variety of wine normally given to small children. The pourer went to the drink table on the side of the room, and then returned. He handed it to Theran, who took an experimental sip, nodded, and handed it to Lady Leandra.

She took it from him, not even looking his way, then said, "Oh, my father's business is taking place soon, and the party is about to get dreadfully dull. It is so tiresome." She sipped her wine slowly, as if exhausted.

Her little group of admirers all stiffened uncomfortably, and one by one, they took their leave. Apparently, they were familiar with Lady Leandra's bouts of exhaustion and boredom, in which she stopped talking to everyone around her and communed with her wine.

Across the room, her mother's face turned down, and she crossed the room toward them.

Theran tried his best to remain as impassive as he possibly could as Lady Torren scolded her daughter. "Leandra, have you no propriety? No manners? Your guests deserve better treatment than bored disdain. I would take you to the doctor for your obvious addiction to wine if it weren't for the embarrassment it would cause us."

Leandra stiffened, then took another sip of her watered-down wine. "Really, mother, I do not have the problem you believe I have. And they were not my guests, they were your guests and father's guests, hangers-on to our status and wealth."

Lady Torren shushed her daughter with a hiss and a hand motion. "Leandra, I taught you better manners by far. What if one of them had intentions of marrying you?"

Leandra scoffed. "Did you invite anyone you intended me to consider for marriage? Perhaps, Lord Alder, who is in his dotage, or his grand-nephew, who is not even old enough to drink wine?"

"No, no. I would not marry you to any of the Alders."

"Or anyone here?"

"No, of course not. They are…" Lady Torren stopped herself, glancing around at their nearby surroundings. She sighed. "Stay here until most of our guests leave, so I can be sure you offend no more of them. And don't go into the library. Your father has a meeting there in a few minutes."

"Of course not, mother. I hate reading, you know that."

"I am aware. Your tutors despaired of teaching you anything, as they did your… brother." Lady Torren sniffed. "I don't know why the King had to send him away from us."

"Perhaps he wanted to go?"

"Leandra, you are being terrible. I am going to bring a doctor here tomorrow, even if I don't get your father's permission." Lady Torren snapped her fan against her daughter's arm, then strode away from them to speak to guests who lingered nearby, shooing them out of the room so Leandra wouldn't be able to speak to them.

"That may have been overdone, if she really thinks you have a drinking problem."

Leandra shrugged. "I can handle anything my mother sends my way. And it is worth it. I have a feeling tonight's meeting will prove fruitful for us." She leaned back in the davenport and closed her eyes. "I'm going to pretend to nap." She handed her glass to him and he noticed it was nearly full.

Apparently, she had been pretending to sip without swallowing even the watered-down wine. She was still cleverer than he expected, and far cleverer than her parents gave her credit for. He would guess she did quite a bit of reading without her parents' knowledge.

Eventually, the guests had either left for the evening or been invited into the library. Lady Torren looked in on the receiving room where Leandra lay on the davenport and Theran stood guard. She shook her head and closed the courtesy doors before going around to the second entrance of the library, which opened from the hallway.

The entrance from the sitting room to the library was located next to the davenport, and as soon as the courtesy doors were closed, Leandra sat up and motioned to Theran.

He leaned toward her, and she grabbed his collar to pull him closer.

He wanted to back away, but she began whispering furiously in his ear. "If you move the decorative molding on this side of the fireplace, a small vent opens up on the library. You will be able to hear everything they say. I'll lay back down; in case my mother decides to check on us again."

He nodded, and she let his collar go. He turned to the molding immediately, so his back was to her. Theran did not want her to see his blush, which he was sure was prominent on his face. He really needed to exercise more control over his mind. Lord of Light, help him. He could not feel this attracted to her, a woman who was the daughter of the nobles associated with the Red Hand, a woman who smelled like honeysuckle and who could outwit half the people around her.

He closed his eyes again, glad she could not see him, and prayed a silent prayer for help. Then he finally turned to his task again, and moved the molding aside, freeing up the vent, which opened to allow a bit of light from the library, and the murmuring of voices.

At first, with all the conversations blending into one another, he did not know if he could hear well enough to get anything out of the meeting, but then a single voice called the meeting to order. It was Lord Torren, and his voice commanded attention.

"My noble associates, we are back in business with the Red Hand. After our most recent debacle with the prince, we have moved our attention to others for bribes, and we have opened our newest house in the Lake District, which I know is less convenient for most of us, but we will have to find some excuse to visit in the coming months, and I believe my wife, Lady Torren, has plans for a winter gathering for those we know and for the particular trade goods we know will serve their proclivities best."

And so, their plans came together, and Theran felt his blood run cold.

Chapter 27: Into the Night

As the tent lost its warmth to the cool of night, Stelia waited for when the Drinaii encampment filled with snores and the minute rustles of sleeping mercenaries. Finally, she stood up from her cot, already fully dressed and wearing her boots. With a tiny flick of her fire-starter, she lit her night-lamp, a lamp with a shade that opened and shut to allow minimal light.

Nisha was asleep, but Berta's eyes were open and alert.

"It's time." Stelia's voice remained low, not a whisper, but also not the tone she used to force her words to carry over a distance.

Berta nudged Nisha, and the child woke with a start, and then a shiver. She sat up, folded up the blanket she had been using, and then threw her arms around Stelia.

Startled by the sudden affection, Stelia stood there and stared down at the girl's soft brown hair. She glanced over at Berta, who bit her lip and looked away. After a moment, Stelia embraced Nisha back, and then let go. She couldn't keep the child with her.

With pre-planned motions, Stelia made hand gestures for their route through the camp. Nisha followed close behind her, and Berta took up the rear as they left Stelia's tent and turned left, toward the wasteland outside the perimeter of the encampment.

As she had planned, the guards on this side had been drinking the wine she had given them earlier in the evening, and Stelia slipped by them with the two girls. Beyond them, a second group of scouts ranged around the outskirts, but Stelia had a plan for that, too.

The Drinaii often camped in some of the same places along their raiding routes, especially as they neared the Dark Spire. Stelia knew this area well, and she led the others into a stand of trees outside the encampment, which wasn't as far out as the outer scouts kept watch. Inside the stand of trees, a broken-down temple lay in near ruins. On the side of the temple covered by thick brambles, Stelia pushed back the thorny branches, and pointed to a door set low in the wall. Nisha let out a small squeak and ran forward, opening the door that was not much taller than her. Berta pressed herself against the wall as she passed Stelia and then crouched low to enter the door.

Stelia followed them and closed the door behind her.

Inside, she crouched in the small space with the other two above a trap door.

"Where are you taking us?" Berta asked, her voice hoarse.

"The ancient cistern system gave the original dwellers of these lands a way to clean and keep track of their water system, allowing them to store water during droughts, and plan their water usage for crop cycles." Stelia opened the door set into the floor and pointed at the ladder leading downward. "It's safe, and it will lead us outside the scout's search area."

She swung her legs over the opening and started climbing down the ladder. Not long after, Nisha followed her, and then Berta, who left the door open above them.

Was the girl afraid of the dark? Stelia couldn't see why leaving that door open made any kind of sense, because she carried the only lamp, using her legs to help her climb down the ladder one-handed.

As they reached the next level, Stelia helped Nisha down from the bottom rung of the ladder. When she reached up to help Berta, the girl shook her head and jumped down with a small splash in the standing water.

The cistern tunnel stretched both directions. This section had a damp, dank air, but aside from a small trickle of water at the very center, the cistern was dry in this section. Stelia took the direction she knew led away from the Black Spire. The others followed. Their footsteps were the only sound in the tunnel, echoing like whispers going out before and behind them mixed with soft, watery ripples.

As they came to the next junction, Stelia thought she heard something, a hard splash sound behind them, but she couldn't see that far back beyond the dim circle of her lantern light. Nisha's face was solemn, but Berta's brow was pinched with worry. Stelia wondered if she had entrusted Berta with too much, but she couldn't do anything about it. They had to keep going. She boosted Nisha up above her, and then climbed up onto the ladder leading upward. Behind her, she heard Berta drop something.

So, Berta was untrustworthy. Stelia clenched her jaw but kept climbing. She would deal with the young woman as harshly as she needed to get Nisha to safety. And maybe she was wrong. Maybe Berta was merely clumsy, foolish, and scared.

That seemed like too much of a coincidence. When Stelia reached the door at the top of the ladder, she made sure Nisha was holding on tight, and then she pushed open the door above their heads. It was dark and silent above them.

Nisha climbed out. Stelia handed up the little lantern, and Nisha held it above Stelia's head. Stelia saw the little girl's eyes widen, and Stelia pushed herself up and off the ladder, reaching the landing above, and shoving Nisha back. As she turned to face the opening in the floor, Stelia tried to kick the trap door shut on Berta, who threw one of Stelia's knives.

The knife went wild and slid across the floor. Berta pushed up through the door, and Stelia kicked her in the face. Berta grabbed her leg and stabbed Stelia's calf with another knife. Thankfully, the leather of her boot was thick enough to deter it.

Stelia grabbed Berta's hand, twisted her fingers, and forced her to release her second knife. As Berta tried to wrestle with her, Stelia grabbed the girl's hair and stabbed her in the shoulder. Not a fatal blow, because she wanted the girl to live.

"Give up, Stelia, you've been caught." Jennar was climbing out of the trapdoor.

Stelia rolled toward Nisha, trying to shelter the little girl with her body. The girl held the lamp up and had pressed herself against a wall.

"What do you want, Jennar?" Stelia asked him, trying to think of a way to stall him, to turn this mess into an escape for Nisha.

"I want to serve the Drinaii and Kalidess for the rest of my days, gaining power of my own." Jennar stood over Stelia. "I've been mapping out probable escape routes for a few years, trying to figure out how you've been helping captives escape. I found a map of these cisterns a month ago. That day I warned you. I tried to give you a chance to confess, Stelia, but you've forced my hand."

Stelia wanted to protest, but she saw another mercenary climb out of the cistern. "How many of your unit did you bring?"

"All of them. I know what kind of fighter you are," Jennar smirked. "Now, are you going to come quietly, or are we going to have some fun before I turn you over to the Major General?"

Stelia doused the lamp, kicked Jennary, and shoved Nisha toward the exit, hoping the girl would find it in the dark. She would not give up. With a low growl, she rolled in the opposite direction and threw a knife toward the center of the room.

Someone yelped in pain and surprise.

Stelia yanked her sword out from under her and stood with her back to one of the outer walls of the cistern building. She hoped Nisha had made it out.

A rush of air in front of her face alerted her to movement, and Stelia struck, angling her sword to cross her body.

Someone swore. She struck again at her target in the dark, and she heard someone stumble back.

"Light a lamp, you idiots!" Jennar shouted from somewhere to her right.

Stelia stayed to the right, but pressed further into the room, sweeping her sword in a hard arc at her head level, hoping to catch another mercenary. But her sword caught nothing but air.

A flicker of flame lit up the room, as a lamp was lit by a mercenary still half on the ladder and half in the room.

Jennar stood by the open door with his sword at Nisha's neck. "Give up, Stelia, or watch your pet die."

Stelia thought of calling his bluff, thought of saving the girl from further slavery with a swift death, but she couldn't do it. She dropped her sword and let the others overpower her with their blows and strip her weapons from her body.

When they started kicking her, she hoped they would be foolish enough to kill her, because anything they did would be nothing compared to what Kalidess would do to her when she found out Stelia had helped captives escape.

Chapter 28: Lessons from the Journey

After a long journey on horseback with Terese, Quinn, Farrald, and Alex, Dan thought he might burst with the need to help or correct Alex. Every time they stopped for the night, Alex grumbled about something – the bedding, the food, the water, the chores, their training, saddle sores, and the lack of any full information from their trainers.

While Dan fully agreed with Alex about the last, he knew the prince was making a fool of himself with his complaints. True, Alex did not complain outright sometimes; but it was there, in the small sideways things he said, in his fumbling and reluctance with chores. And, on the one thing Alex complained about the most, Dan agreed with him but did not say anything because he knew he was being tested in a different way that Alex was.

Dan wanted information from the tight-lipped Terese and the taciturn Quinn, but it was all a part of their training. They were supposed to watch, to observe, to make connections with the nuances of information they had been given.

So far, their guesses from the first day had been correct. They had headed south, rode long hours, camped rough, and were going somewhere important to their trainers. However, they hadn't taken any of the roads Dan or Alex had guessed they would when they had first left the Watch Tower.

On the third night, when they had finished with their rough dinner and their clean-up after it, they sat around the embers of the fire. Terese and Quinn never allowed it to be lit at night, something Alex complained about, but Dan knew not to. But because Terese had told him to allow Alex to make his own mistakes, he had kept quiet with the knowledge that a fire could stand out to anyone in the dark. By dousing the fire, they protected their location and did not attract anyone to their camp.

But tonight, Quinn did not douse the fire right away.

"Please, the three of you, sit." Quinn waved his hand across the flickering flames, indicating an area to sit across from him.

Dan sat by crisscrossing his legs. Farrald did the same. Alex followed their example, but with only three nights' worth of practice, he landed to the side when he reached the ground. Dan had never realized living a life full of chairs and furniture would cause the prince such a problem while camping rough.

Terese sat down next to Quinn, and their two teachers nodded to each other.

Terese leaned forward. "Tonight, we are going to find out what you have observed on our journey. First, do you understand the grouping of trails and roads we've ridden so far? Do you understand how they connect?"

Dan stared into the embers of the fire. He had been trying to figure out their destination from their odd traversing of the landscape, but it did not make sense to him. They had taken deer tracks, small roads, crossed fields and streams, and taken pieces of different major thoroughfares. They had traveled west, south, southeast, then west again.

Alex sighed and glared at the ground.

"If I may?" Farrald held out one hand awkwardly before dropping it back to his side.

Quinn grunted. "Go ahead."

"They are the border roads or the border roads of ancient times. Even when we have been within a single nation, the roads and trails we have taken are at the border of counties and villages. I believe this may be why we have not stayed at any inn either. The Watch Guard tries to stay out of the politics and power plays between nations, counties, and even villages." Farrald leaned back and glanced at Alex, then Dan, who caught his glance and raised his eyebrows in return.

Dan felt impressed by Farrald's sense of direction, his understanding of the roadways, and his reasoning.

"That is correct, on all counts," Terese confirmed.

Alex stood up and paced as he spoke. "But you're traveling with me, and I am the prince of Septily. The lack of politics within the Watch Guard seems to be at odds with my presence. Would it not make sense to make use of me? We could have stayed in some fine inns and charged the cost to the crown."

Dan wished he could have stopped Alex before he'd said "I am the prince." He had seen Quinn's hands curl into fists and Terese's shoulders tighten. But he said nothing, not even though he wanted to.

Quinn crossed his arms and addressed Alex. "You had to have training from your father. Why would it behoove a royal to travel quietly and not charge his costs to the crown?"

Alex frowned and stopped pacing. "Has my father traveled his way?"

Quinn's mouth opened in shock, but then he closed it and cleared his throat.

Alex ran his hand over his face and then through his hair. "He would be disappointed in me, as you are. I... did not want to join him at the court or in his stuffy office. I do not know anything other than all the titles, all the court nobility. I thought that was all I had to know, but I should have at least studied the maps, I suppose."

Dan bit his lip, trying to keep his thoughts inward.

Alex turned to him. "Dan, you have helped me out with this before. Why did we not stay at the inns or announce my presence on this trip? Is it because the Watch Guard wants to stay out of the political power of Aramatir? Can they truly claim that when they watch us all, anyway?"

Dan swallowed, glancing at Terese.

She waved her hand in a rolling motion, which he supposed meant he could answer Alex.

"I think…," Dan noted Farrald's clothes, Alex's finer gear, and then his own. "The crown gains its funding from the people, from taxes and gifts. When expenses are charged to the crown the people are paying for them. When a ruler is frugal with his expenses and taxes people less, his subjects are often thankful."

"This does not mean expenses cannot be charged, only that thought must go into them. It is also safer for you to travel without anyone knowing who you are and by camping rough. No one would expect a prince to camp rough."

"And, while I do not understand the power play of the Watch Guard for allowing you into training, I believe it is a favor they are doing your father. Perhaps they will cash in this favor at some point. I do not know if that is their usual policy or not. I have not studied it." He glanced at Quinn now.

Alex stepped around the fire and addressed Quinn. "Wait, did you tell Dan he couldn't help me before we left. Is that why I've been left to…make a fool of myself at everything?"

Quinn held up a hand. "I did not order such a thing."

"I did," Terese said. "Now, sit, Prince Alex. For you need to understand something as fully as Dan seems to have learned his lesson."

Alex bristled, his chest puffing out and his fists clenching as he glared down his nose at Terese, but finally he took a deep breath and sat down, next to Quinn. "What lesson did you give Dan?"

"A leader must make his own choices and must not be seen being bossed around by those who advise him. Even if the advisors are wise and true, a leader who is seen publicly taking advice or being reprimanded by their advisors is going to seem weak to others. However, at the same time, it is acceptable for you to seek advice. But the lesson is, you must ask him. He cannot offer it first. We would rather have you learn this under our command than when you are the King."

Alex frowned. "This makes sense, but the nation of Septily is ruled jointly by the monarch, the House of the Lords, and the Triune Halls Council."

"But who declares the decisions made? Who is seen as publicly announcing the laws?"

"The highest laws and announcements are given by the King at the court, even if they have been decided by the King and Council." Alex rubbed the cuff of his shirt. "I understand."

"Hardly," Quinn snorted. "You have a lot to learn, and our journey and our Tower cannot teach you everything. In fact," he moved a log in the fire, "You may have noticed some power plays at the Watch Tower. We do not usually train princes or royalty of any kind."

"The pirates," Farrald interrupted. "Those two, they are royalty, aren't they?"

"We do not call the people of Merseas pirates, even if they refer to each other that way," Terese reprimanded him.

"But how did you know?" Quinn asked.

Farrald shrugged. "They expected everyone to stop for them when they arrived. They act as if they own the Tower. It is the manner of those in power and from noble heritage."

Dan felt a twinge. "Do I act like that?"

"Of course," Farrald said.

Alex laughed, and then laughed more. "Do you act like that? Of course. I agree with Farrald. You aren't as snotty as some of the nobility, but I've seen you ignore people around you like you have the right to do so."

"I'm surprised you even noticed," Dan said drily.

"I may not have been paying enough attention, but I'm not stupid," Alex retorted.

"Then why were you at the Red House?" Dan asked him.

Alex stiffened, then stood up and stomped away from the camp, or at least until he got tangled in a bit of underbrush. They could hear him cursing and thrashing around.

Dan knew he'd been an idiot for bringing that up and he stood to go after the prince, but Farrald stopped him. "No."

"What do you mean, 'no'?"

"You already apologized to him for getting him in trouble with the King while you were trying to protect him from some double-dealing nobles, and anyone who goes to a Red House, they deserve to feel some shame for their actions."

"He did not do anything."

"He was there. That is doing something." Farrald growled.

"What do you know about them?" Dan asked.

Farrald shook his head. "Enough," he said through clenched teeth.

It was the angriest Dan had ever seen the thin, usually good-natured young man.

"Farrald should explain what he knows to all of us when the prince calms down from his tantrum," Quinn said.

"I'm back already," Alex said.

Quinn cocked his head. "What did you get from that outburst?"

Alex's face burned red. "Nothing, except to make a bigger fool of myself. Now, how does our little Shepherd know anything about the Red House?"

Chapter 29: The Red House

Farrald clenched his hands into fists and stared dully in the fire. "I have never been to one, but I know someone who was almost trapped in one."

Dan leaned over and squeezed Farrald's shoulder.

"What do you mean? Trapped?" Alex asked. "The women are compensated for their…services. At least that's my understanding. I did not do anything."

"You went. That gives their owner reason enough to keep them."

"Are you saying they are slaves?" Alex's voice went hoarse on the last word, and his face paled.

"How could you not know that?"

"Did you?" Alex turned to Dan.

"My father and his business associates have been to more than one," Dan said, his voice thick with disgust. "My father always knows its location, even though they move it often. I turned him into your father, the same night I went to get you with the Guards."

"Then the Harnen brothers, they must have known. They took me there, they…told me I would finally become a man." Alex bowed his head low. "I did not know they were not allowed to leave."

"I forgive you," Farrald said, placing his hand on Alex's shoulder.

"And I've been so terrible to Dan when you were trying to keep me from committing an evil act."

"I knew the man you used to be wouldn't do such a thing. It is why I decided to stop you. I hoped you would come to your senses. I did get you kicked out of your kingdom and your whole life."

"My father said if I repented, he would take me back." Alex sighed. "I repent."

"He meant more along the lines of repenting to the Lord," Quinn said quietly.

"Yes," Farrald agreed.

Alex stared at the ground beneath his feet and did not say anything.

Dan had a feeling he knew why his old friend was in turmoil. Neither of them had attended a worship service in the Triune Halls' Sanctuary in a long time. Dan did not think Alex had been there since his mother's funeral. He had always thought his friend must be going to the private chapel in the castle, but it was possible his friend hadn't gone at all. How would Alex become king of Septily, a kingdom founded on faith, if he did not believe at all?

Maybe neither of them would return to court life. If that was the case, Dan would be glad, but he knew Alex wouldn't be.

Chapter 30: Jordan Struggles

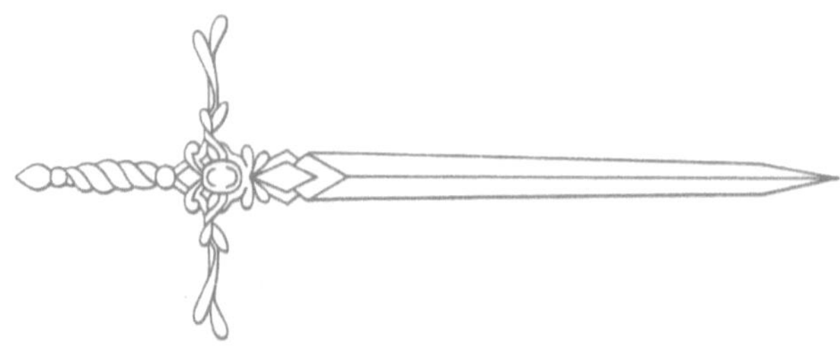

Days of travel. A burned village. A dusty trail. Bickering Sword Guards. The arrogance of Commander Leo.

Jordan wasn't sure he could handle much more. His patience was worn thin, no matter how many times a day he prayed to the Lord. No matter how he phrased it, even if he mentioned the King's directive he followed, Commander Leo would not listen to him about their mission.

Jordan had thought about turning back many times, but he did not want to disappoint King Xandros. They had been covering ground too hastily. Every day, Jordan knew they risked being spotted by the Drinaii and the Dark Sisterhood, whose territory they skirted in the Southlands. Commander Leo did not seem to even realize how dangerous those two groups could be. He seemed to think his unit could handle any fight.

Jordan watched them train before and after each day's ride. They were not ready for any fight, and they were not ready for the combined forces of the Drinaii and the Dark Sisterhood. He hoped he was wrong. He hoped they came across the working of the Red Hand without the other two forces, but this deep into the Southlands, following their lead, it felt inevitable that the groups were working together.

Day after day, the arrogance of Commander Leo grew, as if having no one to fight made him think his unit had proved something.

Jordan prayed they never had to find out if Commander Leo was wrong.

Chapter 31: Crossroads

Dan wondered when their journey would come to an end. They continued to travel as they had been on roads between towns and kingdoms. Roads owned by no man or no single entity. These roads were well maintained because the cities or kingdoms they intersected all did their part. At the crossroads at the very edge of the Kingdoms of the Northlands of Aramatir, Quinn signaled for their party to stop. Dan wanted to continue, feeling a longing to get to their destination.

After a few minutes of silence, drinking water from their flasks, and waiting, Alex asked,

"Does my father know we're leaving the Northlands?"

Quinn gazed at the prince from head to toe and back up.

While he wasn't under scrutiny, Dan shifted uncomfortably from the chafe of the saddle against his legs. He did not dismount because he hoped they would keep moving soon.

Instead of Quinn answering Alex, Terese addressed all of them. "This is our last moment to turn back. But I believe you are ready to go to the site of ancient treasures and our greatest loss. It is a site at which we remember those who have fallen. There, we retrieve or ensure a seal on artifacts, weapons, and treasures we do not wish found."

"Treasure?" Farrald leaned forward in his saddle and his mare took two steps forward.

Dan felt the same kind of longing. He wished he could speak so openly as Farrald but after the days of keeping silent at Alex's complaints, he had grown accustomed to listening. Not questioning. He was attempting to be as observant as Terese and Quinn, a good Watch Guard candidate.

Quinn gazed over each of them in turn, Farrald, Dan, and Alex again, until he finally gave a curt nod to Terese. "They'll do."

Terese gave her horse a slight nudge, and they crossed into the Fallen Southlands.

Nothing really differentiated the unkempt road from the other roads coming into the crossroads. The grass was dry. The air wavered with heat and seemed to grow no worse as they started down a path laden with broken carts along its sides. And yet, something inside Dan shifted. As they rode, he began to imagine what the tower would look like when they reached it.

Terese continued to share more information with them about the history of the land. "Once the Southlands were made of several prosperous city states which had unrivaled resources of gold, salt, and silver. Between the rough foothills and the Merseas, trade was plentiful and peaceful, until the Dark Sisterhood and the Drinaii appeared over fifty years ago and began to overtake them. We are entering our enemy's territory."

"Why isn't there a guard station here?" Alex asked, trying to force his mare closer to Terese, but she waved him back to ride behind her.

"The king wishes to preserve his men and his resources. In fact, the rulers of all the peaceful lands wish to preserve their resources and their people. They maintain their military personnel at nearby towns back a few miles from the actual border. As you should know," she turned in her saddle to quirk an eyebrow at them, "the southernmost district in Septily is the Desert District, which is harsh enough to repel most invaders, although this border of scrubby trees and high plains hides some of it in this corner. Those that do make it inland along the desert are desperate or in need of help."

She glanced at Dan, to make sure he was paying attention, and then turned her gaze on Farrald. "You know of what I speak, do you not, Farrald?"

Farrald stared ahead at his horses' ears and answered quietly, "Yes, I do. My family and most of the Desert District stay near the Desert Hall, trading, studying, and eking out a living against the harsh conditions. We know the dangers of the heat and the dry in the desert all too well. Some of my siblings died in the waste before I was born. And we have rescued those who come to us for aid, in thirst, in need of all help. That is where I met my friend who escaped the Red Hand. She escaped through the desert."

Dan clenched his hands over his reins but was careful not to yank them or alarm his mare. "The Red Hand?"

Farrald nodded. "The Red Hand's work can be found anywhere with trade routes, any place they can trade items or people. It is sad and disgusting to know that they will do such things. They often work alongside the Drinaii and the Dark Sisterhood when those two entities do not wish to keep slaves but wish to sell them. Often the women, men, and children the Red Hand sells are from towns and cities that the Dark Sisterhood have destroyed. That is the tale of the friend I know."

Dan went back to being silent. He wanted to ask more, but the weight and sickness of his father's business dealings weighed heavily on him.

Alex took up the slack of questions, "And the Watch Guard has a place in the fallen Southlands? How is that possible? Do the Watch Guard have an understanding with the Drinaii and the Dark Sisterhood?"

Quinn growled in the back of this throat, then spit on the ground near Alex's horse. "Never. We would never deal with such evil. We of the Watch Guard keep the lands of Aramatir under guard, waiting for the next Champion to give us direction."

"Or simply waiting to ensure the weapons of ancient times do not fall into the wrong hands," Terese added.

Chapter 32: What It Means to Serve

QUINN SHOOK HIS HEAD. "I know you believe the next Champion will give the Watch Guard direction, Terese. Don't pretend otherwise. I have seen the scrolls you read."

She stared ahead toward the horizon. "Yes, but you and I know there are those in the Watch Guard who simply want to keep the knowledge and the weapons 'safe' from all others."

Dan watched the two of them carefully, thinking of the political machinations he had seen at the banquet, the way the Watch Guard at the keep, small though it was, seemed to be at odds with each other. "How many are there who believe the Watch Guard should keep the secrets, never divulging them even to the next Champion?"

Quinn and Terese glanced at each other, then ahead at the road they followed. Neither said anything for a time. The quiet of the land around them was broken only by the sounds of their horses' hooves on the ground, the slight breeze rustling tumbleweeds on the edge of the road.

Dan took a drink of water from his waterskin and waited. He knew one of them would answer eventually, but as time lagged, he started glancing at Farrald and Alex, who both gave him shoulder shrugs and raised eyebrows.

Quinn finally cleared his throat. "It is hard to say how many who believe in the Champion and the coming of the Champion's kingdom, and how many believe the Watch Guard should keep the secrets and knowledge of Aramatir for all ages, with no power above us. It is not a comfortable assessment, or one that all will willfully acknowledge. I request that you do not speak of this when we return to our tower."

Alex sighed heavily. "And so, no matter what I do or where I go, the politics will weigh on me."

"Rulership is a heavy mantle of responsibility," Dantor reminded his friend.

Farrald held up his hand and began to quote scripture. "'When there is no guidance, a people falls, but in an abundance of counselors there is safety.'"

"So, do I need to have as many counselors as possible? Are you volunteering, Farrald?" Alex asked in a tone that seemed to mock.

Dan cleared his throat. "Is that not what your father has? A Sword Guard and a Shepherd by his side, as well as the entirety of the Triune Halls to balance his power?"

Alex slumped in his saddle. "But what happens if no one wants those jobs?"

"What do you mean?" Farrald asked. "It would be an honor. I don't believe I am the right person, but it would be an honor to serve, Prince Alex."

"You think so, after you've heard me snore?"

"I would be serving Septily and the Lord, so yes."

"Oh."

Quinn chuckled. "That's right, Alex. He was not offering to serve you, as the prince, but to serve Septily with you."

"To clarify, I was not saying I was right for such a position," Farrald put in. "I am not trained, nor am I in any position to understand the life of the court in Skycliff."

"But there are those who don't want the job," Alex said, glancing pointedly at Dan.

Dan bristled. "I want away from my father, not you. Don't you understand that? I stopped spending time with you when he wanted me to spy on you. I stayed away to help you, to protect you from him."

"Why did not you tell me?" asked Alex.

"Would you have listened? And how would I… turn on my father so openly? What would people have thought, then? I did not even know what I know now."

"He asked you after my twelfth birthday?"

"Yes." Dan gritted his teeth at the memory of it. He had been so shocked, so frightened by what his father had asked him to do. To spy on his friend, the future king of Septily, to attempt to influence his decisions? To use his friendship to gain power? It had been unthinkable. Wrong. He had never forgiven his father for it.

"And I thought you were angry at me because you lost that game of squares."

"For eight years? I may not be forgiving, but I'm not that petty."

They lapsed into silence again. Quinn and Terese were listening, and Dan had realized this at the end of their conversation. Did their instructors monitor everything they said and did? Weigh this for or against them? Would he ever be able to escape his link with Alex, or his father?

He took another sip of water and tried to gaze into the distance, but the questions and the worries remained.

Chapter 33: Choices

After riding deeper into the Southlands, Quinn led their group through a devastated village. All the buildings had been burned to the ground. Skeletal remains poked out of the dirt, some covered in decaying cloth, others with nothing over them other than a layer of ash-filled dirt. It wasn't the first burned-out village they had ridden through since they had entered the Southlands, and Dan had tried to stop thinking about the burning injustices done to these people.

The well-house on the far side of the village had been burned, but the stone cistern remained. Quinn stopped there, nodding to Terese. She stayed mounted.

Quinn dismounted. "Everyone, refill your water canteens. This is our last rest before we get to our destination."

The remains of the village and beyond were dry and dusty, with partial brush and small trees to the north, and desert to the south. Dan couldn't imagine where they might go, with no view of anything worthwhile on the horizon.

Alex, true to form, asked for him. "What place belonging to the Watch Guard could we possibly find in this miserable stretch of the world?"

Instead of Quinn or Terese answering, Farrald did, as he pulled the water bucket out of the cistern to fill his canteen. "It was not always like this. Once, the Southlands were full of riches and promise, full of knowledge and wonder. Caravans traded freely here, and they bartered exotic spices alongside gold, fine threads, and animals we rarely see any more. According to the texts I've read and the tales my grandfather told me, this was once the thriving market town of Azin, a day's ride east from the renowned city of Tare by the sea, which the Dark Sisterhood took for their own nearly seventy years ago. And, it was a few hours' ride south to the Watch Guard Tower and Library Repository, which stood guard over a nearby oasis. I believe that's where we're going, although I thought it was burned to the ground more than a fifty years ago."

"You know a great deal for a merchant's son from the Desert District," Alex observed as he dropped the bucket back down into the cistern and filled it with water. "You surprise me, Farrald."

Farrald took a sip of water, sloshing it around in his mouth before swallowing it.

Dan watched Alex grimace at Farrald's manners, but noticed the prince kept his mouth shut about it.

Farrald took another small sip of water, swallowed it normally, then answered. "Merchants know much of the kingdom and believe themselves as scholars of trade, which lends itself to geography, culture, and politics, for it is by understanding how people think merchants know which goods to sell. It is one reason my father wanted me to be a merchant and not lose my head in the Holy Scrolls. He feels the knowledge he has poured into me has been wasted like water dropped in the desert."

While Dan had felt frustrated by Farrald's long-winded explanations of things back at the Dark Tower, he had grown more appreciative of his new friend's knowledge of the world around him, and it did not surprise him to hear what Farrald's father thought about scholarly pursuits that involved trade. "My father wanted me to study more at the library in Skycliff, in specific subjects which he felt would help me gain power among the nobles and among the merchant houses. Our family came from merchants and still trade, from the platform of nobility. It is why he holds so tightly to power and prestige, if he can get it. He fears sinking back into our past as traders."

Farrald nodded. "Yes, the Torren family trace your lineage back to the traders who once had caravans throughout all of Aramatir and became so successful and so loyal to King Wendall that he granted them a title, at which point, their trade paths were given over to many other trade families. Your ancestors were generous."

Dan stared at the village around them and simply said, "They would be horrified by what my father has done and not recognize their own kin."

Farrald placed a hand on Dan's shoulder and slowly dipped his chin. "I will pray for them, Dan, and for you."

"Thank you." Dan uncapped his canteen, drank the last drops of water, then lowered the bucket into the cistern. When the container was full, he drew it back up, watered his horse, then dropped the bucket again. He repeated this until he had watered all their horses, filled Terese's canteen, and then his own. Without sipping from his canteen, he took the last drops of water from the bucket, then set it by the edge of the cistern.

When Dan turned to the others, Farrald dipped his chin to him again. "It seems you are not as far from your ancestors as your father is, friend. You are more considerate than I, for I did not even water my horse or fill anyone else's canteens. While I may say I want to be a Shepherd, I have a long way to truly have the heart for it."

Dan capped his canteen and placed it on his saddle, uncomfortable with Farrald's words. What was there to say to that? He did not like compliments, although he knew Farrald meant nothing bad by it. The young man did not do things for gain like a court noble would. Even if he was a merchant's son, he never spoke or acted like a merchant.

"He speaks the truth, there, Dan." Alex said as he climbed into his saddle. "I may dislike your nursemaid act, but I know it is for my benefit and not yours. Your actions speak more loudly than any of my words. My father would be proud to have you as his son, but he's stuck with me."

"And that, right there, is the problem you have," Quinn interjected sharply. "Prince Alex, you want others to remember your princeliness, but you forget it yourself. Your father is proud and always has been, to have you as his son. He would not have sent you to us otherwise. He knows what we guard and what we do. It is an honor to us, yes, but it is more honor to you, for we owe no allegiance to him as a King, but only as a fellow protector of the Triune Halls. Do not compare yourself to Dan, or Farrald, or Terese, or me. You are who you are. You must own your faults, yes, but remember your strengths. You have much to learn, and you must learn it quickly, but you are capable. Not all are so capable. Remember that."

Alex sat up straighter in his saddle with Quinn's rebuke. "Yes, Quinn. I will remember."

Terese took a quick stretch break from her saddle, handed out trail rations from her pack, and mounted again while they had spoken. "We don't have any followers, but I see evidence of another group of travelers who came through a few days ago. Oddly, I think… they may have been from Skycliff, but that makes no sense."

"Does my father know our destination?" Alex asked her.

"No. Only Captain Denali does."

Quinn mounted his horse. "If King Xandros asked him, he would tell him, and they could contact us or send a messenger along our trail. I don't believe this has to do with you, Prince Alex, or at least nothing from your father. What did you find, Terese?"

She held up a small tinderbox. "I found this by the remnants of a cookfire. It was not buried in dirt like everything else and looks new. The stamp of the Skycliff Sword Guards is clear on the back." She flicked it around to show them the symbol.

Dan's eyes narrowed. "But they wouldn't be involved with the Red Hand."

"Exactly. So, what do the three of you make of this?" She asked Dan, Alex, and Farrald.

Alex held out his hand. "May I see it?"

She gave it to him. He turned it over, then handed it to Farrald, who inspected it and handed it to Dan.

Dan held the silver tinderbox in his hands, tracing the familiar design of the Skycliff castle and Triune Halls at the edge of a cliff side over an artistic sea. A set of swords rested underneath the major design. It was intricate enough to be held by noble or high-ranking hands. "This is the tinderbox of an officer of the Skycliff Sword Guards. The only reason an officer would have to cross the border and into these lands would be on a mission for the Kingdom, and to protect the King. Or someone could have stolen it from an officer, but that is unlikely because of their training."

"I agree. It looks too rich even to carry on a journey like this," Farrald said.

"I don't know enough to say anything different, but I can't imagine my father's best friend and Master Sword Guard Theran, highest ranking officer of the Sword Guards would carry much less than that, nor can I imagine how anyone would steal it from him, or why he would come to be here."

"So, the conclusion is?" Quinn asked them, one eyebrow quirking upward.

"We need more information." Dan said, feeling irritated at their trainers' constant testing.

"Yes, that is the correct answer."

"What?" Dan raised his hands in frustration, then dropped them at one stern look from Quinn. "How is that an answer, Quinn?"

Chapter 34: Conclusions and Directions

"Sometimes, the conclusion is a direction to go, and not a final answer to the question." Quinn said.

"Remember our directive. To Watch. To Guard. It is not always our role to act or to have a final, definitive answer to all questions." Terese said. "And now we know we need to observe. I believe we should follow their trail, especially as they seem to be heading in the same direction as we are."

Quinn fell to the back of their line of horses while Terese took the lead, following a faint trail in the ashy dirt which gave way to blackened sand.

Somehow, Dan ended up directly behind Terese, Farrald took the middle spot, and Alex rode directly ahead of Quinn. Dan suspected Alex wanted to speak to Quinn more, and as he heard their voices murmur, his idea was confirmed.

While Quinn's background was unknown to Dan, he guessed based on his own observations and the way Quinn had felt comfortable in his father's court that Quinn had some nobility in his background or had trained himself to be comfortable in the presence of rulers.

Meanwhile, Farrald, who was highly knowledgeable and liked to share his knowledge, often spent most of their riding hours with quiet contemplation and soft singing or the recitation of scriptures from the Holy Scrolls.

This left Dan to watch Terese pick out the trail ahead of him and observe what she seemed to find. She had a close eye, and he noticed many of the markers after she did, noting how the breeze steadily worked against them to erase the marks of those who had ridden ahead. He counted ten riders, but he couldn't be sure. Most of the horses were shod in the capital and so they left similar hoofprints in the sand, but a few stood out. Plus, the riders ahead of them seemed to travel in groups of one or two, like Dan's group was doing. It seemed the safest way to keep your numbers hidden, which was he was sure why they were riding in nearly a single file. But here and there, the hoof prints ahead of them spread into a mess of hoofprints nearly six horses across. He wondered why the riders did this, but there were no signs that he could understand.

Terese kept them at an endurance pace, but at a faster walk than Quinn had been leading them at, which seemed strange as they were riding into the heat of the day. Dan guessed she wanted to catch up slowly to the riders ahead, if she could.

He twisted in his saddle to look over his shoulder at the others. Farrald had his eyes on the distant horizon and was muttering a scripture verse repeatedly. Alex and Quinn rode side by side in quiet conversation.

Dan let himself sink into thoughts he had been avoiding. The remnants of the village reminded him that his father was financing the Red Hand by supporting them as a business in Skycliff. Slavery was an abomination, not a business.

Dan wanted to believe that somehow his father really did not know how the Red Hand operated, but his father had always insisted on having knowledge of every business he financed as a noble. He talked endlessly about understanding your market, and how to handle being a merchant noble and staying in the favor of the other nobles of the court and the King. It sickened him to realize how much lower his father was than even he had realized, and he was suddenly glad for the tutors and the trainers, and all those who had cared for him and his sister in his parents' regular absences.

He wished he had spoken to his sister before he'd left. He hadn't really spoken to her in any depth in several years, since she had her coming out and seemed involved in the same social scene as his parents, which he found boring then, and disgusting now. Did she know what their father was involved in? Should he have warned her before he left? He did not know. It seemed she was like his parents in her politics, but he realized he was not really sure. She hadn't married, which was strange, but then his mother wanted something special for her children's matches, and Leandra was particular.

The more Dan reflected on it, he wondered if his sister was all right. She kept to herself all morning, and he knew she was not sleeping in, as their mother assumed. He had seen her in the library, although she told their parents she did not like to read. He had also seen her in the small training room off the guardroom. Their old Sword Guard had taught her self-defense, and he assumed she was practicing, but what if there was something else to it? He was sure their parents wouldn't approve of her wanting to be anything other than a marriageable noble lady they could bargain with in their dealings.

But the more he considered his sister, he was sure she did not want that. He would have to help her get away from them. Now that the idea had struck him, he wished he had written her a message before they left the Watch Guard Tower.

He must have betrayed some of his worry with his expression, because when Terese turned to check on him, she slowed her horse to ride next to him. "Is everything all right, Dan?"

"Yes," he said, "But I suddenly wondered if my sister is all right, considering who my father is involved with."

"And your mother?"

"She must be involved, too. I cannot imagine she would not be."

"It is hard to have parents who disappoint or even shame us. Remember, you make your own choices."

"But do I?" Dan asked. He flicked his gaze toward Alex and whispered. "I wanted to join the Watch Guard, but not with the prince. I don't want to have my life saddled to his, no matter whether my father is involved. I don't want to… be a noble at all, not if… it is all about intrigue and backstabbing and being terrible all the time."

Terese scoffed. "I thought you were beyond that kind of drama, Dan. Consider your words and who sent you here. Is the King terrible all the time?"

"No, of course not."

"And he is the head of the political leadership of Septily, and therefore, not all the politics of the court are terrible. I think you have seen the worst of it."

"I hope so," Dan said morosely.

"Well, thankfully, we do not have time to dwell on it, because we have a choice to make. Look, our destination is there, and our trail continues to the southeast." She flung a hand forward.

Dan followed her fingers with his eyes and saw the top edge of a dark tower rising out of the sand in front of them. At the sight of it, Dan reined his horse toward it, then stopped. Dan felt a swell of longing fill him, and it took every ounce of his training to stay still and not ride toward the structure. "Is it underground?"

"Not originally, but it is safer if others don't think they can reach it."

Dan surveyed the trail of hoofprints, and then the top of the tower. "So, are we going there, or are we following the trail?"

"What should we do?" She asked him, bringing her horse to a stop.

Dan sighed as Farrald, Alex, and Quinn formed up around him and Terese. He peered at the others.

"The question is for you, Dan. What do you think we should do?"

"I want to go to the tower." The words slipped out of him unexpectedly, but he felt the truth of them in his gut. "I don't know why, but I feel like I need to go there."

Sweat broke out on the back of his neck and goose bumps ran down his arms. "Did anyone else feel that? A sudden heat, then a chill?"

Quinn gave him a grave look, flicked his eyes at Terese, then back at him. "You feel it? The magic?"

"Magic?!" Dan tensed, and his horse stamped her foot nervously, reacting to his movements.

"We guard many things, but I did not know any were active," Terese said, "and strangely, I do not feel it."

"So, it's not magic? Right?" Dan felt his voice getting higher in pitch. First, passing out with some vision about a champion, and now this? It was too strange, and yet, something called to him, not a voice, but a humming, a longing, and it was coming from the tower.

Chapter 35: To the Tower

THE TOWER WAS ENCROACHED by sand so that the ramparts remained above it while on three sides the sand had overtaken the lower levels. A frisson of energy zipped through Dan and he leaned forward, urging his horse into a gallop. In the shadow of the afternoon sun on the sunken tower, an oasis of small trees surrounded a well. Dan dismounted there, tethering his mare to one of the trees and ensuring she had some water. But after that, the pull of power intensified into a tingling, prickling sensation he could no longer ignore. The hair on Dan's arms rose as he approached the sunken tower, noting how the sand had worn into the brownstone, leaving ancient testimony to past storms in wind-worn fissures. He could make out an entrance on the side with less sand and he strode toward it, until he stumbled in the soft sand, overcome by chills and zings of pain rushing over him.

He smelled something hot and metallic for a moment, and then Terese had her firm hand on his forearm, murmuring to him.

"Dan, I have blocked the power, as best as I can, considering I can't feel whatever's bothering you. It seems an artifact in the tower is keyed to you, and you alone."

"That's possible?"

"It is how objects of power choose their bearers."

"I believed that had to do with faith in the Lord? The Sword Guards of the Triune Halls all have blades of power, and they talk of how the Lord leads them and their work."

Terese tapped his arm. "Faith or magic, it is a power that is calling you."

"I don't understand, and," he stopped speaking to stare at her, taking in her steady demeanor, "How are you blocking it?"

Terese squeezed his forearm but did not let go. She touched the pommel of her short sword. "I have a blade of power. It is active because of my faith. However, I have seen magicians and sorcerers use similar objects with no discernible faith. They seemed to worship power itself, and sometimes power gained through pain. I do not understand why the Lord allows it."

"Your sword allows you to block whatever is calling to me?" Dan gazed at the pommel of her sword, which seemed unremarkable in decoration or grip. "Could I hold it?"

She shook her head. "The carrier of an object of power is often keyed to the object itself in a way that cannot be replicated by others. You might take my sword and it would act as a common sword in your hand, or you might take my sword, and it would react against you, possibly giving you power feedback much worse than what you are getting from whatever is calling you."

He shook his head. "Why me? I don't understand."

"It doesn't matter. We need to investigate. For whatever reason, I can't feel the power at all, and you do, so you need to lead us to the object, and I can't block it while you're locating it."

Dan contemplated the tip of the tower sticking out of the sand, the way the ancient structure had stood against countless storms and had never fallen or been taken in battle. He didn't understand why it called him, but he knew it held a key to his future. "I'm ready." He braced himself by tightening his arm muscles.

She let go of his forearm and the prickling chills ran up his arm from his fingertips to his shoulder. His muscles, already tight, clenched and cramped. He stumbled, and then Terese gripped his arm again and the sensation stopped.

"I'll walk you into the tower. Once we are inside, I'll release you for enough time to locate the object. And it is best if you take a deep breath and relax instead of trying to fight it with tension."

This reminded Dan of something his old Sword Guard teacher taught him. "The best form comes from the calmest mind."

"Exactly." She guided him forward, and he kept pace with her.

They went on this way until they reached the edge of a dark outcropping, which, from a distance, looked like broken rock, instead was a crumbling archway tilted and mostly buried in the black sand.

"I need to let go of you to open the tower. Take a deep breath, let it out, and relax."

Dan did as she said, shrugging his shoulders up and down to shake the tension out. "I'm ready."

She let go of his forearm and the pain raced up from his fingertips and to his shoulders.

He forced himself to keep breathing steadily, to imagine he was floating in the lake by his family's summer house.

Because of his concentration, he did not see exactly how Terese opened the door, but the air between the archway began to shimmer and the smell of ancient parchment overwhelmed became prominent. The pain Dan felt ratcheted up, and he fell to his knees.

Terese put her hand on his forearm again, and the relief from pain brought tears to his eyes. "Thank you," he said, his voice a hoarse whisper.

"Thank me when this is over." She pursed her lips tightly. "Once we are inside, we will walk forward until we reach an open room where three halls meet. I will let you go and you will need to relax and concentrate enough to see if you can tell which way you need to go."

"What will happen when I find the object? Will it stop hurting me then?"

She gazed at the archway ahead of him, her posture stiff. "I can't promise you that."

He did not like how her tone changed. Terese had always been warm with him, like his kind Aunt Bax, who allowed him to call her by her nickname. But now, she had become rigid in her posture, her voice had deepened to a harder tone. But he had no choice. It was either trust her and move forward or try to fight through the strange pain to get away from the tower. If he did that, there'd be no going back to the Watch Guard, and he'd be stuck with his father's machinations.

It was not a hard choice.

It was the only one he could live with.

"I guess I am ready to go find it."

"Good." Gripping his forearm, she pulled him through the entrance to the sunken tower.

Chapter 36: The Call and the Responsibility

Darkness enclosed them, hemmed them in from every side, and the weight of the ashy sand above them pressed down. Dan tried to breathe shallowly, curling inward from the perceived pressure from above, but Terese gave his arm a hard pinch.

"Breathe deeper. Fight the fear. Focus on how my blade of power lights up this place."

Dan sucked in a deep breath, let it out quickly.

"Slower, you know how to breathe."

Dan took a long, deep breath, held it for a moment, then let it out slowly. He could feel his shoulders and rib cage relax, so he took another breath. As he did so, he noticed the light warming up the room with a deep orange like an earthy flame. The color coalesced into the shape of the blade held by Terese.

"By the Lord's light, we walk these halls. We come to safeguard the weapons and hope they will become forsaken, without drawing the forsaken."

Dan felt her fingers tighten as she spoke these last words. did she think he was forsaken? Is that why her demeanor had changed before they entered the Tower?

The light from Terese's blade brightened and the entryway became more visible around them. They had walked several steps on the uneven, soft sand before the darkness had overcome Dan. He regarded the area, even looking back at the beckoning blue sky and ashy sand behind them. How had he not noticed the light from the sun only moments ago?

As he turned his focus back on the entryway, he noticed the distinct path of sunlight reaching into the room and the way Terese's blade lit up only a small area around them. The dark stone walls were dusty with age and sand, the carvings on the pillars covered with grit, and the entry stood shorter than he expected, but then he realized they were standing on a large mound of sand, obviously swept into the Tower by desert storms.

"We're going to go three steps ahead, then stop. I'll let go of your arm, and you'll have a moment to gain a sense of the call's direction. I'll grab your arm again, if it is still hurting you."

Dan listened to Terese's specific instructions and took another deep breath and released it. "I'm ready."

They walked ahead three steps, and Dan could see where the entry hall split into three smaller hallways, where the sand dipped down to allow passage into them. He gave Terese a quick nod.

When she let go of his arm, the trembling chills returned to his right arm, but not his left, and he felt a pull in the center of his body, like he needed to turn to the right, to go that direction.

"We need to go right."

"And do you need my help?"

"I can handle it." Dan walked toward the right hall and the sensations became more of an uncomfortable buzz that resonated with the pull inside of him. "Yes, this is the way I need to go."

She followed behind, keeping her sword blade aloft, the light from it blazing a path of light around them like an unwavering torch.

He did not question how the blade of power worked, having seen them before in Skycliff. He knew a little about their basic properties. His old Sword Guard mentor had one. He had never expected a call from any object of power. He wasn't sure he wanted it, because it seemed like one more thing his father might try to twist to his ends and purposes. But now, he could not deny the need growing inside him to reach the source that called to him, that seemed to be speaking his inner mind and soul.

This side corridor which Dan continued following, had several exits to other rooms and hallways, but his path remained forward. The further they went, the thicker the dust and musty smells became. He swiped at his nose with his hand to stop from sneezing. Still, the tug of power drew him onward, with a plan for him, whether or not he liked it. When he paused, the discomfort increased, so he continued, hoping he would find an end to the strange prickling sensations when he reached the object.

The tug brought him to a door carved with several figures. The tautness of the pull intensified again him as he swept away the dirt over the carving. The figures on the door were old Champions. He could tell by the familiarity of some likenesses found in some places in Skycliff, although others weren't as familiar to him. The group of Champions surrounded a single box in which a shattered blade rested. The carving was intricate, and Dan ran his fingers over the shattered blade, and then opened the door.

Inside, he could see the box from the carving. It was an iron trunk with a strange padlock. The grooves of a handprint lay over the top of the lock. Sand, dust, and mist swirled around the trunk, but Dan moved toward it.

Behind Dan, Terese murmured something, but he did not make out the words. Consumed now by the need to open that box, he placed his hand over the handprint. A rational part of his brain wanted him to stop, but the compulsion moved him forward, despite the unlikelihood of his hand fitting the handprint.

His hand fit perfectly in the grooves. A glow emanated around his fingers, but it was not a glow of light, but of textured shadow, a shimmering black that seemed deeper than even the dark shadows of the chamber beyond the light from Terese's blade.

An audible click resonated through his hand, his chest, and the chamber, and the lock fell open. With trembling hands, Dan opened the lid of the iron box and gazed down at the broken blade within. It was shimmering obsidian, alive with power from within each of the seven, jagged pieces. Dan ran his fingers carefully over the tip of the top piece of the glowing shards, feeling a sensation of warmth and power running from his hands to his heart. He couldn't let this blade lay here unused any longer. He touched each of the seven shards, traced his hands over the engravings on the cross guard, and then reached for the hilt.

As his fingers came around the leather-wrapped grip, a heavy, warm wave rushed through him, from somewhere within his fingertips to the hilt, and somehow, resonated in ripples through the shattered pieces of the sword which began to melt and reshape.

In the deepest recesses of his mind, Dan wanted to let go of the blade, but he did not. He held fast as it took shape in front of him, perfectly balanced for his hand, for the extension of his arm. It was a part of him and it was hungry for justice, for vengeance, for righteousness against those who would do harm to his people, and peace for those who would live with kindness. It opened up parts of him he had closed off, even from his own thoughts, and he felt as if a part of him had been hollowed out and refilled, then hollowed and filled again.

Memories of his childhood rose up and fell away. His mother's wheedling accusations and anger, from quiet hisses to shouting, and his father's abrupt explosions of hot, violent temper followed by pouting silences, and then the nonchalant insistence that neither of them had meant anything by their outbursts, their comments, the way they treated his desire for fairness with contempt and ridicule.

The painful memories came and were washed away by something stronger, a sense of overwhelming love and a simmering need for justice.

More memories came, these of his Sword Master Thorn who taught Dan with respect and gentle firmness, always consistent, always fair in his teachings and tests. These memories felt buoyed up by the insistent, full sense of love and the calm of true fairness and justice, taught to him by a man who had honor.

These memories were slowly replaced by the good and the terrible moments of his childhood at Prince Alex's side, the games they had, the arguments, the slow falling away when his father wanted him to spy on the prince. His recent training with Alex renewed his need to protect his friend, to protect his country if his friend failed it… a double-edged sword of justice, if needed.

He felt assurance that he could fulfill the call. Again, the love overcame him, and a light pierced the dark blade in his hand until it glowed like a dark night at the edges of the moon.

He did not know how long he stood there with his hand on the hilt of the black blade, the shimmering power of it mesmerizing him and shattering him as he realized he knew exactly what he needed to do, knew exactly what his call had always been: to bring justice and protection to Aramatir as a Sword Master, as a Guard and Protector of the people, and in service to the Lord's Champion, when she came.

"Are you in pain, Dan?"

Terese's voice startled him, as did her hand on his arm. He trembled to suppress his first instinct to protect himself with his blade. She was not attacking him.

Slowly, he lowered the blade to his side and shook his head. "No, not like I was. I feel the pain of the land of Aramatir, calling out for justice against those who have spilled the blood of innocents, of those who would harm others for power and gain. It is… a pain I've felt before and suppressed." He realized he had tears on his cheeks. "I will not ignore it again."

"And what power does your sword hold innately?"

"To block, to protect, to battle," he clenched his jaw, then took another deep breath. "The call is strong. I believed, based on what other Sword Guards have told me, that the blades of power from the Lord come with a lightness, a sense of grace. Instead, I feel pain, determination, and a need for justice to be served."

"And can you hold that without letting it consume you?" Terese asked him, her posture stiff.

He sensed she thought he might have been subsumed by the power of the blade. "I can. It is a darkness I already carried, and one that can only be lightened through the work of finishing the Dark Sisterhood forever."

He paused, surprised by the words that had exited his mouth. "I... I don't know where that last bit came from, but I can hold this and it will work well with me."

"Do you feel my block at all, now?" she squeezed his arm.

"No. There's no physical pain from the power calling me, but there is an intensity of purpose coming from it. Your hand on my arm makes no difference."

She let go of his arm slowly and stepped back into a defensive posture. "Do you feel any need to attack me?"

"What? No." He held up his other hand in a placating gesture. "At first, when you approached, I almost defended myself, but I knew it was you, so I did not."

"And now, are you sure?"

"Why would I attack you?"

"The last one who held that blade became so sure of his purpose and his righteousness that he attacked other Sword Guards whom he believed had strayed from the path of light, regardless of what the court of law might say. He became over-vigilant in his duties and took matters into his own hands, despite being asked by three Champions to lay down the sword."

"I thought only one Champion came at a time to Aramatir."

"That is the legend, not the truth. The Lord puts his mantle on one person, or two, or three, and usually they serve for their lifetime, but sometimes they only serve for part of it. In the time of the Unmaking of the Dark Blade, three Champions had to put the blade down, and its bearer."

Dan took a step back from her, raising his sword before letting it fall to his side. "I am not that bearer. My purpose is clear, and you are not someone I am called to speak justice to."

"As long as it remains so, I will not take your blade."

Chapter 37: Blood in the Sand

SHEPHERD JORDAN CROUCHED BEHIND the edge of a sand dune next to the Commander Leo and the unit of Sword Guards from the Triune Halls of Skycliff. On the other side of the dune, their enemies had made camp. Sent to find out information about the Red Hand and dispense justice as needed, they were officially under the direction of Shepherd Jordan according to the missives given to him and Leo by King Xandros, but Commander Leo had ignored his direction at every juncture. He often re-ordered their encampments in the evenings and scoffed at Shepherd Jordan's insistence that they ride single file to hide their numbers.

But as they hid behind the sand dune together, Jordan was in perfect agreement with Leo. They needed information on the Red Hand's operations, and they had found a contingent of the Red Hand along with a unit of Drinaii mercenaries led by one of the Dark Sisters.

The mercenaries surrounded a vast group of slaves chained to one another in a rough circle. Separated by age and gender into groups of five, the slaves were strangely quiet, or so it seemed to Jordan. Even the smallest children did not make enough noise to bring attention to them. The youngest had to be a toddler, held by another small child in their group of five. Both children stared downward and flinched when a Drinaii mercenary passed them.

Instead of paying much attention to most of their slaves and instead of posting any kind of watch or scout, the Drinaii mercenaries focused on one prisoner staked off separately from all the others. It was because of this that Sword Master Leo, the Sword Guard unit and Jordan had been able to get so close. They were downwind, so the scent of unwashed people and the bitter tang of blood swept over them with the breeze, but this meant their own scent did not travel to the Drinaii.

The woman at the center of everyone's attention wore tatters of clothing, and by the scrapes and bruises on her, it appeared she had been beaten and dragged across the harsh sand, which clung to her wounds. Her limp blonde hair had been cut in ragged locks which hung over her face.

One of the Drinaii mercenaries had a scourge in his hands, a whip with barbs up and down its length. He stood over her and spoke, but his words were too faint for Jordan to make out.

She drew back and spit at him, and the Drinaii kicked her in the side, then stepped swiftly back as she whipped one of her feet out. He was not as fast as she was, and her foot connected with his kneecap. The Drinaii stumbled but regained his footing and uncoiled the scourge.

As he raised it, Jordan felt Commander Leo nudge his ribs. "Now would be a good time for a distraction."

Jordan winced as the scourge landed on the woman, even as she twisted away from it. The Drinaii dragged the barbs of it across the woman's shoulders, but she did not cry out. He closed his eyes, then moved his head away from the sight.

Facing Leo and trying to ignore the man's ridiculous need to smoothe his pomade every few minutes, he decided it was time to give him another chance. "I agree. I have explosive powders in my saddlebag. Perhaps, if we deploy them to the west, the Drinaii will head that direction." He had learned that giving Commander Leo the appearance of choosing often gave him the most peace.

Jordan took pride in keeping the peace, even with a smarmy man like Leo, who seemed determined to wrest authority into his own hands as often as possible. The man was hardly the cream of the Sword Masters, and it saddened Jordan to see the office held by a man who had only been appointed to the Triune Halls and this unit based on some kind of court intrigue. Leo did not even have a sword of power, which was usually the sign of a Sword Master in Skycliff.

Leo, of course, did not agree with Jordan, which Jordan had suspected would be the case. He countered with, "I see the value of the west, but I would like to deploy them to the north. They're more likely to expect an attack from that direction and it should draw them off. I have men already on their way there with the powders from your bag." Sword Master Leo smiled and ran one hand over his blonde pomade, which had become a bit straggly under travel conditions.

Jordan bit back a curse, anger rushing over his good sense. "You took my powders?" He couldn't shout, given their precarious position, but he hissed when he spoke through clenched teeth. "But you are right that the time to act is now. Do you have a signal and a plan?"

"Of course." Leo waved a hand at one of his people and they produced a small whistle.

Jordan started to say something to stop him, but the man brought the whistle to his lips and blew before Jordan got a word out.

Confident that the Drinaii had heard it and would be on them in seconds, Jordan ran down the dune to his horse and jumped into the saddle, ready to fight or flee as needed.

When an explosion reverberated through the sand, Jordan's mare side-stepped. He ran his hand over her neck and spoke soothing words, then started her at a walk toward the edge of the dune.

The Drinaii started shouting on the other side of the dune, a language Jordan was unfamiliar with, a mix of both common tongue and something else.

Leo rode past him at a gallop, drawing his sword. All the rest of their compact unit followed, and Jordan shouted after them. "Stop. You fools!" They did not have the numbers to fight off the thirty or so Drinaii mercenaries and a sorceress.

Jordan hadn't been a swearing man in years, but another old oath from childhood rose to his lips, then died in the back of his throat. He would not follow Leo. He pivoted his mare and galloped the other direction, to the other end of the great dune which had hidden them. As he neared the edge, he slowed, listening.

The sounds of shouting in different languages, the clash of steel, and the screams of horses told him the battle was underway. He guided his horse slowly around the slope of the dune and saw some of the Drinaii and the sorceress were running toward the smoke from the explosive powders.

The rest of them were engaged in a fight with Leo and his unit, who held the upper hand only because they were mounted, something the Drinaii were obviously aware of as they cut at the horses' legs. Two mares were down, bleeding into the sand, their riders pinned beneath them. Commander Leo had taken them into a fight they couldn't win, probably because he foolishly thought that Sword Masters were superior to the Drinaii. Sword Masters, especially those with crystal blades of power, were sometimes more powerful than the average Drinaii foot soldier, but the Drinaii trained from early childhood to be some of the most feared mercenaries in all Aramatir, swallowing up most of the mercenary companies from the past.

Jordan realized no one was looking at him. All were engaged in the battle. He could slip away, ride hard and escape, but should he? What kind of coward did that make him? Where was his faith?

But as one of the Drinaii glanced his direction and Jordan watched Commander Leo fall under the blades of the mercenaries, Jordan leaned forward into his saddle and urged his horse into a run, away from the battle.

Chapter 38: Chaos and Grace

Stelia pushed off from the ground, crying out as her wounds bled, but forcing herself up and onto her feet. Major General Ader Worsten had decided to make sure she was punished before the Dark Sisterhood could be notified of her treason. She had been starved for days, barely given water. She had been beaten. They had forced her to walk barefoot in the desert, but when she fell, they dragged her until she walked again.

Out of sight of the Dark Spire, Major General Worsten oversaw her scourging in front of the Red Hand and his most loyal men. Surprisingly, the Dark Sister with their unit had thrown in her lot with him and had taken part in the torture which would lead up to the Rite of Scorching Death, which would grant her more power. So, perhaps it wasn't surprising after all, at least not like what happened after they had chained her and started to scourge her.

An explosion erupted in the north. Chaos reigned. Major General Worsten had been knocked over by one of his men, and the Dark Sister had left his side. Stelia had taken her chance and stolen his keys.

With bloody fingers, Stelia used the keys she had stolen to free the children closest to her, but as the small contingent of soldiers from Septily died and the Drinaii overcame them, she handed the keys to one of the women.

The keys would be of no use if Stelia was caught with them when the Drinaii returned to their task of punishing her. She flung herself away from the prisoners, hoping her actions hadn't been noticed. Maybe some prisoners could escape, even in broad daylight. The Dark Sister was busy with whatever had exploded. The Drinaii had fought an unexpected foe. Maybe the chaos would give the prisoners a chance.

Worsten roared out commands, attempting to restore order to his unit. Drinaii soldiers converged on their leader's position, some wounded and bleeding freely.

"Secure the captives!" Ader shouted. Spittle flew from his mouth as he yelled.

Stelia had fought to get to her feet again, and she tried to think what else she could do to cause chaos. She was going to die. She might as well make her death mean something. She limped forward, and then with the last ounce of her strength, she threw herself at the General Major's back, screaming and grabbing for his sword.

General Major Worsten twisted on his feet, but only succeeded in tripping. He landed on his side with Stelia wrapped around him.

Stelia had his sword and plunged it into his chest, once, then twice, before rough hands grabbed her and yanked her off him. Someone hit her in the back and knocked the air out of her. She fell onto the sand.

Jennar loomed over her, blocking the bright sun behind him. "You're going to die the death of a thousand suns as a fitting end to the Rite of the Scorching Death, Stelia. Make peace with your maker."

Two soldiers held her hands, another two soldiers held her feet. Jennar drove stakes into the surrounding ground, and they tied her to them.

When they were finished, Jennar spat in her face. "That's for your work as an Enforcer, Stelia, and the friendship you forgot."

She watched as he mounted his horse, rounded up the prisoners, and rode away, leaving her to die in the heat of the desert. While it didn't hurt as much as the scourge had on her body, or the beatings, or even the hunger in her belly, Stelia felt tears on her face for the first time since her childhood. She tilted her head, trying to keep the moisture from falling to the ground, but it did. Water wasted. But she couldn't stop crying. Jennar's words kept echoing in her head. "Make peace with your maker."

Would the maker want a broken thing like her? No. She had no use. No purpose. No peace.

As the sun sank over the horizon, Stelia shivered in the chill of the coming night. Why hadn't she died yet? What reason did her body continue to breathe? How much more would she suffer?

She heard a set of shuffling footsteps in the sand.

A dappled mare loomed over her in the twilight. An unfamiliar man in a light-colored robe swung down from the saddle. He knelt by her side.

"Oh, thank the Lord of Light. You live."

Stelia tried to say something, but her voice came out in a croak. Was she hallucinating?

The man sang a song she didn't know. Something about the Lord saving wretches and having grace. He loosened the straps on her wrists, but Stelia was so weak she couldn't seem to sit up. She had to be dreaming. This must be what death felt like, although it didn't seem like the stories she had been told.

Chapter 39: Power and Purpose

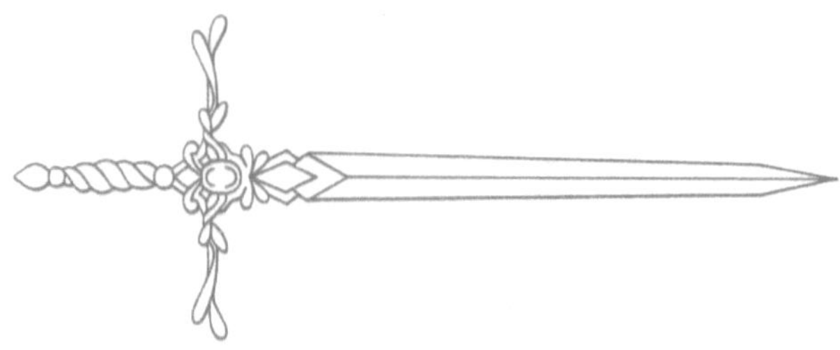

"Remember who you are. Remember whose you are. For the Lord saw everything he had made, and behold, it was very good."

Farrald was singing again.

Dan woke to the sound of his friend's voice, outside the tent.

Alex rolled over on the other side of the tent and ran his hand over his face. "What is going on this early?"

"I don't know." With one hand on the dark blade, currently sheathed in an ancient leather case that needed some care, Dan edged his way to the tent flap, opened it, and proceeded to put on one of his boots. While doing so, he gazed at the fire and reported to Alex what he could see.

"Shepherd Jordan is talking to Terese outside her tent where they are keeping the escaped slave. Jordan sounds upset again. Quinn is standing at the edge of camp, keeping watch over all of us. Farrald is tending the fire, but singing loud enough for all of us to hear."

"But why is he singing? Why does he do it?"

"I think he's trying to soothe Shepherd Jordan with some hymn."

Alex groaned. "You know, if he weren't going to be a Shepherd, his whole "holy singing" thing would annoy me. Actually, it still does, but I guess it makes sense." He rustled around behind Dan. "Well, are you going to finish putting on your boots?"

"Yes," Dan tied his first boot, then pulled on his second, lamenting the sand which seemed inevitable. It poured and dried in every crevice of their clothes and skin. He couldn't imagine anyone wanting to live in this deserted land. While he didn't agree with Alex about Farrald's singing, he didn't know how Farrald managed to be so cheerful about everything.

But he was awake now, and he needed to make the best of it, so he stood up, stretched his arms overhead with his sword in his hands, then stepped away from the tent. He buckled the sword sheath around his waist and strolled over to the fire as Alex started putting on his own boots.

The whole group was camped in the oasis by the sunken tower, out of the wind, which had picked up when the others had returned, covering their tracks. Their camp was simple. Three tents. A picket for the horses. A fire pit. A cloth folding table Quinn had brought with him. It was a clever contraption held up by short sticks which were easily packed into the saddlebags.

As he approached the fire, he noticed Farrald had started preparing their morning coffee which simmered in a pot in the coals, and he had had laid chunks of trail bread with cheese on the small folding table. Dan took a slice of the bread with the cheese and sat down next to Farrald on the ground by the fire. He bowed his head as Farrald prayed, and then began to eat. He rarely liked to talk in the mornings, and Farrald didn't seem to mind. Alex came to sit with them, munching on his own breakfast.

Shepherd Jordan walked over to the fire; his face still wet with his shed tears. He also picked up breakfast from the table and folded his legs easily to sit down on the other side of Farrald, where he bowed his head and spoke a quiet prayer.

Dan wasn't sure what to think of Shepherd Jordan. He had known him from a distance his entire life. Shepherd Jordan normally stood to the right of King Xandros at most public assemblies and at most court sessions dressed in stately Shepherd's robes with a sword belted around his waist. Since Shepherd Jordan had walked into their camp the night before, with the escaped slave slung over the saddle of his mare, he had been openly distraught. His clothes were covered in dried blood, but he wasn't injured. From his own words, he had proclaimed he was a coward from running away from an unwinnable fight started by Sword Guard Leo, a man Dan knew to be more of a court appointee than a true Sword Guard. Shepherd Jordan claimed responsibility for Leo's death, and the deaths of all the other soldiers, although Quinn and Terese had both disagreed with him. Dan didn't know what to think, seeing the Shepherd so disheveled and full of sorrow.

Anger and disappointment were the emotions Dan had seen most openly displayed by his parents when he was growing up. Sometimes, they were happy or seem to take pleasure in the discomfort of others, but he had never seen either of them cry. Dan had been forbidden to cry in public since the first time he had been whipped as a punishment. It was uncomfortable to see Jordan display his sorrow so openly, but at the same time, he knew objectively there was nothing wrong with it. He finished his bread and cheese and sat with his hands clasped, staring into the fire. It felt like someone should say something. Maybe he should? But what?

Farrald had finished his breakfast and started to sing again. "Remember who you are."

Shepherd Jordan raised his head and put his hand on Farrald's arm. "Thank you."

Farrald shrugged. "God calls me, sometimes, to sing. I simply listen."

"It is a gift. You would do well as a Shepherd."

"My father wants me to learn to fight, and to become a tradesman or a warrior." Farrald stood up abruptly, his brow furrowed, and he walked over to where the horses were tethered.

Dan reached out his hands, as if to warm them by the fire, as he tried to think before he spoke. "Farrald wants to be a Shepherd, but he also wants to honor his family. His father taught him a great deal of the history of Aramatir. He has more knowledge than I have. The Watch Guard offers some of that to him, even as his heart calls him to the Shepherds."

Shepherd Jordan poured coffee into four of the tin travel mugs. He passed the first one to Alex, then one to Dan, and then he stood up with the two mugs in his hands. "I think Farrald needs some of this. And, as for you, I would have you consider the relationship I have with King Xandros and Sword Master Theran. We have each trained in each other's disciplines, and so, I think Farrald's father is not completely wrong in wanting Farrald to have some experience as a warrior, even if he becomes a Shepherd."

Having said his piece, Shepherd Jordan joined Farrald by the horses and held out a mug of coffee to him.

Dan took a tentative sip of the scalding hot coffee, and then held the mug in his hands, letting the earthy coffee smell wash over him.

"What do you think of that, Dan?" Alex asked him. "Do you think my father plans for Farrald, you, and I to be like him, Sword Master Theran, and Shepherd Jordan?"

Dan leaned back away from the fire, with his mug in his hands, and turned to look at Alex. "I don't mean you any disrespect, but I had hoped to leave Skycliff behind me, to fight with honor for the safety of others, not get caught up in politics again, like my father wants. And now, I have this sword."

Dan touched the hilt of his blade of power and let the hum of energy run through him. He unsheathed it and held it out flat to Alex. "Do you sense the way it calls out for justice?"

Alex stared down at the blade, and then inspected the hilt, but did not touch it. "Did you read the runes?"

"I don't know the language." Dan stared down at the swirling words, not sure if he should be able to intuit their meaning as the bearer of the blade.

"I don't either, but I know this blade. Its story is one that's kept hidden in the upper archives in the Hall of Law."

"But wouldn't it's story better fit the Hall of the Sword?"

"Not that blade," Alex leaned back from Dan. "I am amazed it reformed for you, but at the same time, it suits you. I wonder what it means."

"I want to fight for the sake of justice. That's why I am glad to be part of the Watch Guard." Dan placed his sword back it its protective covering.

Alex frowned and he stared down at the mug in his hands.

Some time passed between them, with Alex turned away from him, but Dan couldn't apologize for what he had said. The coffee mug cooled in his hands and he took a large gulp of it. He turned to Alex again. "What would you want, Alex? If you had a choice?"

Alex took a sip of his coffee, and his mouth twisted. "That's cold." Then he took another swallow. "But I need to wake up." He stood up slowly, and looked down at Dan. "We both need to wake up, Dan. We don't have a choice. Our lives are set, designed, and not in our control. We need to make peace with our duty to our land and to our people." He finished his mug of coffee and walked into the rising dawn away from the camp.

Dan thought about going after him, of arguing, but Shepherd Jordan had returned.

"I missed speaking to you last night," Shepherd Jordan crouched next to Dan. "I believe we have you to thank for the intelligence about the Red House, the Red Hand, and the link we found to the Drinaii and the Dark Sisterhood."

Dan stood up to clear up the used mugs, which he would wash carefully with limited water, and store in one of their shared travel packs. "I only shared the location of the Red House in Skycliff."

"But that information led to more, and while I witnessed the horror of seeing Sword Masters cut down by Drinaii, I know more now than I did before. Every piece of information will build, and we will stop them."

Dan was surprised both by Shepherd Jordan's encouragement and his confidence. He was not used to hearing anyone speak that way. He found himself shifting his weight and leaning back toward the Shepherd, gazing at the man's sincere eyes, his unlined, youthful face. Despite being the same age as the King and having a shock of white hair, Shepherd Jordan looked young, younger than Quinn or Terese.

"Do you know anything else about your father's business associates?"

Dan shook his head. "Not that I am aware of. My father did not bring me into his business, and I tried to stay clear once I realized that he wanted me to spy on the prince."

Shepherd Jordan gave him a once-over. "Initially, Theran and I believed you avoided your father because of his ties with the merchant class. We assumed you were a snob."

Dan stopped moving, with one of the mugs partially wrapped in a drying cloth. "When? Why?"

"We did not understand why you stopped spending time with Alex. We noticed you started spending time with the Sword Guards, but we needed to assess your character. Not everyone is invited to join the Triune Halls, but we were considering you." He sighed and rubbed the back of his neck. "It turns out, you might be a better fit than some of the men and women we have now. Captain Leo was not the best fit for command, although ultimately, I am responsible for his death. I did not take command of the team." He paused and touched the symbolic pendant he wore on a chain on his neck, a symbol of the Lord of Light. "I had forgotten my training."

"I'm sorry." Dan knew these words were nothing, not enough, but he had nothing else to say, nothing else he knew to give. Farrald's singing was probably far more comforting.

Finally, they were rejoined by Alex, who had returned to the fire.

"Shepherd Jordan, it is an honor to share camp with you. I apologize for not greeting you properly when I woke." Alex bowed partly to the Shepherd.

Shepherd Jordan bowed his head. "It is an honor to share camp with you, as well, Prince Alex."

Terese cleared her throat audibly as she approached. "We do not go by titles here, gentleman."

"Understood. I do have a request to make of you, all of you. I know you are here for the Repository in the sunken tower, but I hope I can ask for your help. I would like to recount my steps. See if the camp has been moved."

"No need," Quinn said as he joined them. "They moved. I saw the dust trails of their passage to the North. I would like to follow at a distance, but we need to take a short foray into the sunken tower."

Chapter 40: Echoes of the Past

Jordan's boots sank into the sand which had overtaken the stone floor as he descended into the sunken tower, the air growing cooler with each step. Alex and Quinn flanked him, their faces tight with anticipation. The smell of dust and ancient parchment filled his nostrils, a scent that usually brought comfort but now carried an undercurrent of unease.

"Watch your step," Quinn muttered, his hand brushing against the hilt of his sword.

As they reached a side chamber off the main corridor, Jordan felt a prickle at the back of his neck. Something was off. The air felt heavy, charged with an energy he couldn't quite place. He glanced at Alex, noting the young prince's eager eyes darting from shelf to shelf, clearly hoping to find a blade of power like Dan's.

"Remember," Jordan said softly, "we're here to gather information, not artifacts."

Alex nodded, but Jordan could see the disappointment etched in the set of his shoulders. He felt a pang of sympathy for the boy, remembering his own youthful desire for validation.

They split up, each taking a different section of the vast chamber. Jordan's fingers trailed along the spines of ancient tomes, his heart quickening as he recognized titles he'd only heard whispered about in the halls of the Shepherds.

Then he saw it. A leather-bound volume, its cover etched with symbols he recognized from prophecies of old. With trembling hands, he pulled it from the shelf. "The Convergence of Shadows," he whispered, his voice filled with awe.

"Find something?" Quinn called from across the room.

"Yes," Jordan replied, his excitement barely contained. "A text that might help us understand the connection between the past and our current crisis. Would the Watch Guard allow me to read this?"

Quinn grunted, but then gave a curt nod. "For you, yes. But consider it a loan. And only because this place… doesn't feel right, not like a repository tower should."

Jordan nodded, tucking the book into his satchel. He understood Quinn's unease. There was a presence here, something dark that seemed to pulse just beyond the edge of perception.

"Alex," he called, "we should regroup."

The prince emerged from behind a row of shelves, his face a mask of forced neutrality. Jordan's heart ached, knowing the boy had found nothing to rival Dan's blade.

As they prepared to leave, Quinn held up a hand. "Give me a moment. There's one more room I need to check."

Jordan and Alex exchanged glances as Quinn disappeared down a narrow corridor. Minutes ticked by, the silence broken only by the occasional skittering of unseen creatures in the shadows.

As they waited, Jordan found himself drawn back to the book he'd discovered. Unable to resist, he carefully opened *The Convergence of Shadows*, its ancient pages crackling beneath his fingers.

"What does it say?" Alex asked, peering over Jordan's shoulder.

Jordan's eyes widened as he scanned the text. "It speaks of cycles… of darkness rising and falling throughout history. And here—" he pointed to a particularly dense passage, "—it mentions something called 'The Resurgence.' It seems to point to how the actions of Champions can ripple across ages."

He continued reading, his excitement growing. "This could explain so much."

Alex nodded, but his attention had already drifted. Jordan watched as the young prince moved among the shelves, his hands trailing over various artifacts. He picked up a beautifully crafted breastplate, its surface etched with intricate designs, but after a moment, set it down with a sigh.

Next, Alex hefted a sword, its blade gleaming even in the dim light. For a heartbeat, Jordan thought he saw a flicker of... something. But then Alex's shoulders slumped, and he returned the weapon to its stand.

"Nothing?" Jordan asked gently.

Alex shook his head, frustration evident in his voice. "Nothing. They're just... objects. Beautiful, ancient, but... dead." He picked up a small dagger, turning it over in his hands. "Why did the blade choose Dan and not me? Am I not worthy?"

Jordan's heart ached for the boy. He closed the book and placed a comforting hand on Alex's shoulder. "Worthiness isn't about magical artifacts, Alex. It's about the choices we make, the people we choose to be."

Alex nodded, but Jordan could see the doubt lingering in his eyes. Before he could say more, they heard Quinn's footsteps echoing down the corridor.

As Quinn emerged with his bulging travel bag, Jordan couldn't help but wonder what secrets the Watch Guard had uncovered—and what price they might all pay for disturbing this place.

Quinn's face was unreadable as he shouldered past them. "Let's go."

As they ascended, Jordan couldn't shake the feeling of being watched. The darkness seemed to press in around them, hungry and alive.

At the entrance, he paused, turning to his companions. "Did you feel it?" he asked. "The darkness?"

Alex nodded; his earlier disappointment replaced by concern. "Like something was... waiting."

Quinn's jaw tightened. "I felt it. I'll report it to the Watch Guard when we return. Whatever's down there, it's not something of the Watch Guard."

Jordan clutched his satchel tighter, the weight of the book a comforting presence against his side. As they emerged into the harsh desert sunlight, he sent up a silent prayer. Whatever shadows lurked in the depths of the sunken tower, he hoped the knowledge within this tome might help them face the coming storm.

But as they made their way back to camp, Jordan couldn't shake the nagging feeling that they had disturbed something dangerous. The sands shifted beneath their feet, and for a moment, he could have sworn he heard whispers on the wind, echoing with promises and threats from long ago.

Chapter 41: Power and Responsibility

THE COOL MORNING SWIFTLY gave way to midday heat as Terese and Jordan tended to the woman who had escaped from the Drinaii and the Red Hand. From what Dan had seen and what they had said, her injuries were extensive, and some were in danger of festering.

The cool morning swiftly gave way to oppressive midday heat, the sun beating down mercilessly on their camp. Dan and Farrald had been charged with keeping watch over the camp as Terese and Jordan tended to the woman they'd rescued, their hushed voices hinting at the severity of her injuries. The air seemed thick with more than just heat - a palpable tension hung over them all.

Quinn and Alex had ventured out to scout the perimeter and discuss the Watch Guard's responsibilities for the treasured artifacts in the repository. Despite the sunken tower's supposed protective aura, Dan couldn't shake a creeping sense of dread. The air seemed to pulse with an energy he couldn't quite name, setting his nerves on edge.

The dark blade at his side emanated power. Dad didn't know what to think of it, so he worked at taking care of the sheath. First, he oiled it, then noted several places he would need to sew and strengthen the leather material. The sword did not need sharpening, and Dan had noticed the others were uneasy when he had it out to check it. The obsidian blade gleamed in the sunshine and the dark pommel needed a leather wrap around it to feel comfortable in his hand, but the weapon had a compelling beauty to it. Dan wanted to hold it in his hands and treasure it, but again, he noted even Farrald seemed to shift away from him when he held it in the sunlight.

Perhaps, Dan could find out more about the blade by discussing where he had found it.

"Do you know how the protection around the tower operates?"

Farrald poked a stick into the embers of their cookfire and glanced over at the tent where Terese and Jordan tended their patient before answering Dan.

"The power in all our world has two sources, or at least from my understanding. There is the power of the Lord, seen at work in the Triune Halls and in the objects of power wielded by some chosen by the Triune Halls. Then, there is the power wielded by those who commit blood sorcery, in which the wielder either causes themselves pain and blood loss or someone else pain and blood loss. The sword Terese carries, as you know, is a blade of power of the Triune Halls. The sword you carry, this dark blade," he pointed at Dan's hip, "It was also forged by faith and skill by a weaponsmith of the Triune Halls. The power from it should represent the Lord's work in the world in some way. Each sword has its own purpose, as does its bearer."

"You say, 'should.' What do you mean by that?" Dan asked, dread coiling in his gut. The dark blade's power surged as if responding to his fears, but he tried to push it away as they talked. Dan couldn't shake the feeling that they were standing on the precipice of something vast – and that his newfound weapon might help or hinder.

"Normally, if the bearer of a blade like yours loses their faith or turns against the Lord, the blade will fade to an opaque color and lose all its power. It will sometimes break or shatter. Yet, yours is as dark as obsidian, unbroken and full of power. I don't understand what it means, exactly."

Dan unsheathed the blade and held it out to Farrald. "It was broken into several pieces when it called to me, but when I picked it up, it reformed."

Farrald did not take the blade but inspected it closely by leaning over it. "It feels… wait, I feel it?" He gave Dan a bewildered glance. "Normally, those who aren't the bearer don't feel the power from the object, but I can feel your blade. It is strong, filled with… a need for justice." Farrald took a step back. "It feels like anger and sorrow, and it is determined to do its work to end the evil in the land." He put his hand to his head and stepped further away from Dan and the blade. "I don't know how you can hold that."

The dark blade's power surged through Dan, a resonating thrum that sent shivers down his spine. As he re-sheathed the sword, an unsettling sense of rightness settled over him, as if the blade were whispering secrets directly into his soul. "It is the right blade for my hand. And it approves of you."

Farrald shuddered visibly, his face pale. "I could feel that, too, and I wasn't even touching it." His voice trembled slightly, betraying his unease.

The air around them seemed to thicken, charged with an invisible energy that made the hairs on Dan's arms stand on end. "What you said before, about the two types of power," he pressed, fighting against a growing sense of unease, "what does that have to do with my blade and with the protection around the tower?"

Farrald's gaze fixed on the sunken tower, its looming presence casting long, ominous shadows over their camp. His eyes widened, as if seeing something beyond the physical structure. "I can feel the tower like I can feel your blade, but it's different. Ancient, huge, in tune with the Triune Halls and the Lord, but also… strange." He swallowed hard. "It's as if there's something working against it, pulling on it, as if both powers are at war within its walls."

A cold dread settled in Dan's stomach. "The tower could become an instrument for evil?"

"Yes, no, I don't know." Farrald's voice cracked, his usual certainty crumbling. "I don't know why I can feel these things if they don't make any sense."

"I can only feel my blade, but I understand. It is not comfortable."

"No, it isn't."

"Can you tell if the tower is protecting us from evil, or if it is simply protecting itself?"

As they discussed the tower's nature, the air grew increasingly oppressive. Dan's skin crawled, as if unseen eyes were watching their every move.

"It is a little bit of both. It is like…" Farrald stared at the Tower, and then clenched his jaw. "No, I won't go there." His words were punctuated by a sudden gust of hot wind that carried the scent of ancient stone and forgotten magic.

"It is pulling at me, deep in my gut." Farrald gasped in pain and bent over. "It, something in there, wants me to come to it."

"That's what it felt like for me, as well."

"I don't like anything having that much power over me. It seems wrong."

"What about your faith in the Lord?"

"That's different. The Lord is the Lord of the universe."

"And an object made to serve the Lord?"

Farrald straightened, although he held his side as if it ached. "Maybe. That sword, it... I can feel it through you." He straightened up and took one step toward the tower. "Tell the others, then if you can, follow me, please. I would like you to guard me. It is what your sword is for."

Dan felt a thrum of rightness surge through him at Farrald's words. He was a protector. It was meant to be. The dark blade suited him well.

With that thought, he ran to Terese's tent as Farrald took slow steps toward the Tower, obviously fighting the pull.

At the tent, Dan stood outside, not knowing the situation within. "Farrald feels pulled to the tower. I'm going with him."

"Blast! Fine. Go." Terese's words were short and terse.

From within the tent, the woman cried out.

"Just another moment, and we will finish wrapping the wounds," Jordan murmured.

Dan hesitated, wishing he could help. Only so many people could heal, and he was not one of them. He would do what he knew how to do.

As he pivoted to chase after Farrald, Dan couldn't shake the feeling that they were walking into the maw of something ancient and hungry – something that had been waiting for them for a long time.

Chapter 42: Battle for the Tower

THE SECOND TIME DAN entered the sunken tower, the repository of the Watch Guard's ancient secrets, his senses were on high alert. The musty scent of ages past filled the air, a mixture of dust, dried papyrus, and something else—a spicy, unfamiliar odor that tickled the back of his throat. He hadn't noticed it during his first visit, when the dark blade had called him, but now it seemed to permeate every breath.

Sand had piled up at the entrance, threatening to swallow the doorway whole. As Dan's boots crunched through the gritty layer, he felt as if the desert itself was trying to reclaim this forgotten place. Inside, the walls bore silent witness to countless sandstorms, their once-intricate carvings now pocked and worn, barely visible beneath a film of dust and grime. Ancient weight hung over them as they traversed down the main hallway. Their footsteps echoed hollowly, each sound seeming to disturb some long-forgotten memory. The flickering light from their torches cast dancing shadows on the walls, creating the unsettling illusion of movement in the periphery of Dan's vision.

His dark blade, sheathed at his side, emanated a soft, pulsing energy. When drawn, it cast a grayish, shadowy light around them—not bright enough to be truly useful, but enough to make the darkness feel alive, watchful. The blade's presence was both comforting and disquieting, its power resonating with something deep within the tower itself.

Farrald moved ahead, one hand pressed against his lower ribs as if in pain, the other gripping his torch tightly. His face was a mask of concentration, beads of sweat forming on his brow despite the cool air. Dan could see his friend was fighting against some unseen force, struggling with each step forward.

"Are you alright?" Dan asked, his voice sounding unnaturally loud in the oppressive silence.

Farrald nodded tightly, not trusting himself to speak. The strain was evident in the set of his shoulders, the tightness around his eyes.

Dan marveled at the difference in their experiences. While Farrald was clearly being pulled forward by some unseen force, Dan felt nothing beyond the usual hum of his blade. Were these ancient artifacts truly sentient? Was this the call of the Lord, or something else entirely? The questions swirled in his mind, as oppressive as the stale air around them.

As they reached a crossing in the passageway, Farrald veered left without hesitation. Dan followed, realizing they were entering a part of the tower he hadn't seen before. The air grew colder as they ascended a flight of stairs, the stone steps worn smooth by countless feet over the centuries.

They emerged onto a landing, and Dan's breath caught in his throat. Before them stretched a vast sanctuary, its far end adorned with symbols of the Lord. The scent of old wood and ancient stone was stronger here, mingling with the faintest trace of long-extinguished incense.

Ruined chairs littered the landing, their once-fine upholstery now little more than tattered rags. But it was what lay below that truly captured Dan's attention. At the center of the sanctuary stood an altar, and upon it rested a staff that seemed to glow with an inner light. Behind it, dominating the back wall, was an enormous tree of life, its branches adorned with strips of dusty cloth that swayed gently in a breeze Dan couldn't feel.

"It is the staff," Farrald gasped, his voice filled with awe and pain in equal measure. He released his grip on his midsection and lurched forward, grasping the railing at the edge of the landing with white-knuckled intensity.

Dan's hand instinctively went to his friend's shoulder, steadying him. "That's too far for any sane man to leap, my friend," he said, trying to inject some levity into his voice despite the growing sense of unease in his gut.

Farrald twisted under Dan's grip, his eyes never leaving the staff below. "I won't jump," he said, his voice strained. "And that blade of yours, the power is too much."

"I'm not even holding it," Dan protested, but even as he spoke, he could feel the dark blade's energy pulsing at his hip, responding to the charged atmosphere of the sanctuary.

"You don't have to," Farrald replied. His gaze finally tore away from the staff, focusing on a set of stone stairs leading down to the main floor. The wooden railing had long since rotted away, leaving treacherous gaps, but the steps themselves looked solid enough. "Will you let me go if I promise to take the stairs?"

Dan hesitated, torn between concern for his friend and the undeniable power resided in this place. Finally, he nodded, releasing his grip on Farrald's shoulder.

As they descended, Dan's eyes darted around the sanctuary, taking in every detail. The place filled him with a contradictory sense of comfort and unease. Power emanated from the tree of life, resonating with the energy of his blade, but there was something else too—a slippery, unsettling presence that made the hairs on the back of his neck stand on end.

The shadows beyond their torchlight seemed to writhe and dance, and more than once, Dan could have sworn he saw movement in the corners of his vision. But whenever he turned to look directly, there was nothing but darkness and dust.

Farrald reached the sanctuary floor first, moving with single-minded purpose towards the staff. Dan followed a few paces behind, his hand resting on the hilt of his blade, ready to draw at a moment's notice.

As Farrald stretched out his hand towards the staff, a piercing cry escaped his lips. He doubled over, clutching his left leg. Dan rushed forward, his blade already half-drawn, and felt his blood run cold at what he saw.

A sickly-looking vine, its surface covered in vicious thorns, had erupted from a crack in the stone floor. It wound its way around Farrald's ankle, holding him fast. As Dan watched in horror, more vines began to sprout from the cracks in the floor and walls, their growth accompanied by an ominous creaking sound.

Without hesitation, Dan drew his dark blade fully. The obsidian surface seemed to drink in what little light there was, leaving nothing but a void in its wake. With a single, fluid motion, he brought the blade down on the vine holding Farrald, severing it cleanly.

Farrald, who had been struggling against the thorny grip, suddenly lurched forward with the release of tension. He stumbled, falling against the side of the altar that held the staff. To Dan's relief, no more vines approached his friend.

But the danger was far from over. Dan felt a presence behind him and spun just in time to see another vine reaching for him, its thorns glinting wickedly in the torchlight. He hacked at it desperately, backing up until he too reached the relative safety near the tree of life.

"Do you recognize these plants?" Dan asked, his voice tight with tension as he surveyed the writhing mass of vines that now surrounded them.

Farrald shook his head, his face pale with shock and pain. "No, I've seen nothing like them. Can you hold them off while I get the staff?"

Dan nodded grimly, tightening his grip on the dark blade. Its energy surged through him, filling him with a mixture of dread and exhilaration. Whatever these vines were, whatever power lurked in this ancient sanctuary, he knew that the next few moments would be crucial.

As Farrald reached for the staff once more, Dan stood ready, his blade poised to defend against the encroaching enemy. The air crackled with tension.

Farrald's brow furrowed. "Why are these plants here?"

Dan's eyes widened as he took in the full extent of the infestation. The vines weren't just on the floor; they covered nearly every surface of the sanctuary, their sickly green tendrils pulsing with an unnatural life. Yet, as he observed their movements, he thought he noticed a pattern. The vines weren't just growing; they were attacking. Each tendril seemed to strain toward the tree, only to be repelled by an invisible force.

"They're attacking the tree. I can feel it." The words left his mouth before he fully processed them, but as soon as he spoke, he knew it to be true. A fierce anger ignited in his veins, burning away his fear and hesitation. He stepped away from the dais, his grip tightening on the dark blade. "Get the staff. I'll deal with as many vines as I can."

The dark blade hummed in his hand, its obsidian surface seeming to drink in the dim light of the sanctuary. Though it was no gardening tool, Dan felt a surge of agreement from the weapon, as if it shared his determination to protect the tree.

He lunged at the nearest vine, the one that had been reaching for him moments before. The blade sang through the air, its edge impossibly sharp. It sliced through the vine with no resistance, the severed end falling to the floor with a wet thud. Without pausing, Dan stabbed at the hole in the floor where the vine had emerged, feeling a satisfying crunch as the blade bit into a thick root.

The vines surged forward with terrifying speed, their thorny tendrils whipping through the air like living weapons. Dan's blade flashed in the dim light, slicing through vine after vine, but for every one he cut down, two more seemed to take its place.

"There's too many!" he shouted, his voice strained with exertion. Sweat poured down his face, stinging his eyes and making his grip on the dark blade slippery. A thorn caught his arm, tearing through his sleeve and leaving a deep, burning gash.

Undeterred, Dan pressed forward. He moved toward the wall closest to the tree, hacking and slashing at the thorny vines. Each strike of his blade sent ripples of power through the air, repelling the vines momentarily before they surged back with renewed vigor.

Dan's arms burned with exertion, sweat pouring down his face and stinging his eyes. The vines hissed and writhed as he cut them, a sound that was part plant, part something far more sinister.

Farrald struggled nearby, the staff in his hands glowing faintly but offering little protection. "I don't understand," he panted, dodging a vine that nearly took his head off. "The staff, it's not doing anything!"

Dan spun, his blade carving a deadly arc through the air, severing half a dozen vines in one swing. But even as they fell, more rushed to fill the gap. The air was thick with the acrid smell of sap and crushed vegetation, making it hard to breathe.

A particularly large vine shot out, wrapping around Dan's ankle. He cried out as thorns dug into his flesh, yanking him off balance. He hit the ground hard, the impact driving the air from his lungs. Instantly, more vines descended upon him, their thorns tearing at his clothes and skin.

"Dan!" Farrald's voice was filled with panic. He rushed towards his friend, swinging the staff wildly, but it seemed to have no effect on the attacking vines.

Dan struggled, slashing with his blade, but he was quickly over-whelmed. Vines wrapped around his arms, constricting his movements. He could feel the thorns digging deeper, a burning pain spreading through his body. Dark spots danced at the edges of his vision.

Farrald lunged forward, but his foot caught on a root protruding from the floor, sending him sprawling. As he fell, the base of the staff struck the ground near the tree of life.

Suddenly, a pulse of green energy surged through the staff. "Dan, hold on!" Farrald shouted, scrambling to his feet. He planted the base of the staff firmly against the roots of the tree of life.

A blinding flash of green light erupted from the point of contact. The vines recoiled, hissing and writhing as if in pain. Dan felt their grip loosen and seized the opportunity, tearing himself free with a roar of defiance.

"The tree!" Farrald called out. "It's the source of power! We need to channel it through both the staff and your blade!"

Dan staggered to his feet, his body screaming in protest. Blood trickled from numerous cuts, and every movement sent fresh waves of pain through him. But he gritted his teeth and pushed through it, making his way to Farrald's side.

The vines, momentarily driven back by the burst of energy, began to regroup. They slithered across the floor and walls, converging on the two friends with murderous intent.

"Whatever you're going to do," Dan growled, raising his blade, "do it fast!"

Farrald nodded, his face pale with concentration. "When I say now, strike the nearest vine with your blade. And Dan," he added, his eyes meeting his friend's, "don't let go of me, no matter what happens."

Dan gripped Farrald's shoulder with his free hand, his dark blade held at the ready. The vines reared up around them, a writhing mass of thorns and malevolent plant life poised to strike.

"Now!" Farrald shouted.

As a massive vine lunged for them, Dan's blade flashed out, its obsidian edge slicing through the plant's flesh. At the same instant, Farrald drove the staff deeper into the tree's roots.

The world exploded into light and raw power. Green energy surged from the tree, through Farrald's staff, into Dan, and finally into his dark blade. The obsidian edge blazed with an otherworldly light, a mixture of deep green and midnight black.

A shockwave of energy burst outward, disintegrating the attacking vines instantly. Dan and Farrald both clung to the staff, buffeted by the maelstrom of power swirling around them. The air seemed to crackle with energy, and for a moment, Dan feared they might be torn apart by the forces they had unleashed.

But then, as suddenly as it began, it was over. The light faded, leaving them in a sanctuary transformed. The sickly vines were gone, reduced to ash that drifted in the air. The tree of life pulsed with a healthy, vibrant green glow, its light filling every corner of the room.

Dan and Farrald collapsed to their knees, gasping for breath. Their bodies ached, covered in cuts and bruises, but they were alive.

"We... we did it," Dan panted, looking around in awe.

Farrald nodded, a tired smile spreading across his face. "We saved the heart of the tower," he said, his voice filled with wonder. He looked down at the staff in his hands, which now glowed with a soft, steady light. "And I think... I think I finally understand my true calling as a defender of faith."

As they sat there, battered but victorious, Dan felt a profound sense of change settle over him. They had faced death and emerged stronger; their friendship strengthened in the heat of battle. Whatever challenges lay ahead, he knew they would face them together, as friends.

Dan clapped his hand on Farrald's shoulder, feeling the solid presence of his friend's faith and the power of the staff echoing it. "Let's go tell the others what's happened," he said. "And see if this changes anything about our journey."

As they turned to leave, Dan cast one last look at the sanctuary. The peace and power emanating from the tree was palpable, a stark contrast to the chaos of moments before. Whatever challenges lay ahead, Dan knew that this moment would stay with him.

Chapter 43: In the Lake District

In the Lake District, a late fall ice storm had draped a thick frost over her friend Giselle's small homestead. Leandra stood by the window, her breath fogging the glass as she gazed out at Theran's silhouette against the majestic landscape. The Sword Master cut a striking figure, broad-shouldered and vigilant as he kept watch on the distant Torren Estate.

Leandra enjoyed the freedom of pretending to be someone other than a noble lady. Several weeks had passed since she and Theran had discovered her parents' plans. Leandra had manipulated her parents into riding ahead to their Lake District estate to prepare the house for their noble friends. Leandra knew they were probably meeting with representatives from the Red Hand, so she and Theran had followed them from the capital discreetly.

Her parents had been ensconced in their house, but, unknown to them, Leandra and Theran were staying with Giselle, where they could keep an eye on the comings and goings of the estate and gather information for the King. But Leandra had hoped for more than mere duty on this trip.

As her fingers absently traced patterns on the cold windowpane, her mind wandered to thoughts of Theran's strong hands and the warmth they might bring. She longed to bridge the gap between them, to transform their relationship from one of duty and mutual respect into something more intimate.

The crackle of the hearth fire and the scent of baking bread filled the cozy two-room cottage, a stark contrast to the biting chill outside. Giselle's presence at the rough-hewn table behind her was a comfort, the soft sounds of kneading dough a rhythmic backdrop to Leandra's musings.

"You're going to wear a hole in that glass with all your staring," Giselle teased, her voice warm with affection.

Leandra turned, a blush coloring her cheeks. "I can't help it, Giselle. He's just so..."

"Oblivious?" Giselle finished, raising an eyebrow as she shaped a loaf with practiced hands.

Leandra sighed, moving to join her friend at the table. The rough wood beneath her fingers was a reminder of the simple life she'd come to cherish whenever she had a chance to visit Giselle, which was far less often than she would have liked. As children, they had been able to play together as Giselle's mother had once worked at the estate before she had inherited this cottage and the land around it from her father. While Giselle had faced many storms in life, she had come through them as an independent female landholder, which awed Leandra. Her friend had wisdom she needed about life. "How do I make him see me as more than just a noble lady he's sworn to protect?"

Giselle's eyes softened as she grinned. "Some men need a firmer hand, Le-le. Like my geese - they need a strong voice to guide them."

"Theran's not a goose, Giselle," Leandra chuckled, but her heart warmed at the use of her childhood nickname.

"No, but he might be just as stubborn," Giselle retorted, setting the bread to rise and dusting flour from her hands. "You've always had the strength to go after what you want. Don't let your title hold you back now."

Leandra nodded, her resolve strengthening. She glanced out the window once more, watching as Theran's breath misted in the frigid air.

The time for subtle hints had passed. If she wanted to close the distance between them, she would need to be bold.

"You're right," Leandra said, squaring her shoulders. "It's time I showed him exactly how I feel."

Giselle's smile was both proud and a little sad. "That's my Le-le. Just don't forget about your old friend when you're off being a lady in love, alright?"

Leandra reached across the table, clasping Giselle's flour-dusted hands in her own. "Never. You'll always be my dearest friend, Giselle. No man could ever change that."

As the two friends embraced, the scent of fresh bread and woodsmoke enveloping them, Leandra felt a surge of gratitude for this moment of warmth and friendship. Outside, the fall wind howled, but in here, she found the courage to face both the cold and her heart's desire.

Chapter 44: Duty and the Heart

THE BITING WIND CUT through Theran's cloak as he stood sentinel on the shores of the frozen Lake District. They hadn't packed for true winter and this fall chill had overtaken the Lake District swiftly, showering the fields with leaves. Dawn's light painted the frost-covered landscape in hues of lavender and gold, a stark contrast to the slate-gray waters of Lake Luna, the main lake of the Lake District. Theran's breath misted before him, a visible reminder of the chill that had settled into his bones during his vigil.

From his vantage point near the tree line, Theran had an unobstructed view of the Torren Estate across the lake. The grand house stood silent and still, its windows dark save for a single point of light in what he knew to be Lord Torren's study. He narrowed his eyes, straining to detect any sign of unusual activity, but the distance and the pre-dawn gloom revealed nothing of note.

The crunch of frost-covered grass behind him alerted Theran to Leandra's approach. He didn't turn, knowing that if he looked at her now, his resolve might crumble. The scent of lavender and honey wafted to him on the frigid air, a warm counterpoint to the chill that made his heart race despite his best efforts to remain stoic.

"You're up early," Leandra said. She came to stand beside him, and from the corner of his eye, Theran could see her pulling her travel cloak tighter around her slender frame.

"Couldn't sleep," he replied, keeping his gaze fixed on the distant shore. "Thought I'd keep watch."

Leandra hummed in acknowledgment, and for a moment, they stood in companionable silence. Theran was acutely aware of her presence, of the small space between them that felt both too vast and not nearly wide enough. He longed to close that gap, to wrap his arms around her and shield her from the cold, but duty and propriety held him rigid.

"It's beautiful, isn't it?" Leandra said softly, gesturing to the winter wonderland before them. "I've always loved the Lake District when the leaves turn the countryside into gold. Everything seems so pure, so untouched."

Theran nodded, allowing himself a quick glance at her profile. The rising sun cast a rich glow on her brown skin, highlighting the delicate curve of her cheek and the wisp of dark hair that had escaped her braid.

"It's a far cry from the bustle of Skycliff," he agreed, his voice gruffer than he intended. "Though I can't say I like the smell of Giselle's geese."

Leandra laughed, the sound like bells in the crisp morning air. "No, I suppose not. But it's a small price to pay for such a perfect vantage point, don't you think?"

"True enough," Theran conceded. He shifted his weight, suddenly restless. "We should head back soon. We need to prepare for our ride to the estate later as I believe today is the day we are expected to arrive."

Leandra turned to face him fully, and Theran found he couldn't look away. His heart thundered in his chest as he gazed into those mesmerizing brown eyes, flecks of gold catching the light like stars in a midnight sky. More locks of her raven hair had escaped her hood, dancing in the wind, and he fought the urge to brush it back.

"Theran," she said, her voice barely above a whisper, "do you ever think about... about us? About what could be, if things were different?"

The question hung between them, as delicate and dangerous as their mission. He wanted nothing more than to tell her yes, that she occupied his every waking thought, that he dreamed of a future where rank and responsibility didn't stand between them. But the words stuck in his throat.

"Leandra," he began, his voice strained, "I... we can't. You know we can't."

Her face fell, a flicker of hurt crossing her features before she schooled them into a mask of indifference. "Because of our mission? Or because you see me as a child?"

"No, not a child," Theran said quickly, hating the pain he heard in her voice. "Never that. But I'm too old for you, Leandra. You deserve someone-"

"Someone my own age?" she interrupted, a spark of defiance in her eyes. "Some simpering lordling who cares more for his own reflection than for the good of the kingdom? Is that what you think I want?"

Theran ran a hand through his hair, frustration and longing warring within him. "Of course not. But you're young, with your whole life ahead of you. I'm a Sword Master, sworn to serve the King and Septily. My duty-"

"Your duty," Leandra said, her voice bitter. "Always your duty. Is there no room in your heart for anything else, Theran? For anyone else?"

The hurt in her eyes was like a physical blow. Theran reached out, unable to stop himself, his hand cupping her warm cheek. Leandra leaned into his touch, her eyelids fluttering closed for a brief moment.

"There's room for nothing but you," he admitted quietly, the words torn from him. "That's the problem, Leandra. I can't trust myself around you. I can't let my feelings jeopardize our mission, or your future."

Leandra's eyes snapped open, a mixture of hope and frustration swirling in their depths. "My future is my own to decide, Theran. And I've decided I want you in it."

She stepped closer, eliminating the space between them. Theran's resolve wavered, his arm dropping to encircle her waist almost of its own accord. He could feel the warmth of her body through their layers of clothing, could count each freckle on her cheeks.

For a heartbeat, Theran allowed himself to imagine giving in. He pictured pulling Leandra close. But then reality reasserted itself.

With a pained groan, Theran stepped back, his hands falling to his sides. "We can't, Leandra. I'm sorry, but we can't."

The light in Leandra's eyes dimmed, and she wrapped her arms around herself, as if to hold in the warmth that Theran had denied her. "I see," she said, her voice flat. "Well then, Sword Master, we should return to the cottage. We have a mission to complete, after all."

She turned on her heel, trudging through the snow back towards Giselle's home. Theran watched her go, every step she took feeling like another crack in his heart. He wanted to call out to her, to take back his words and pull her into his arms. But duty held him in place, as immovable as the ancient trees that lined the shore.

With a heavy sigh, Theran cast one last look at the Torren Estate across the lake. The sun had fully risen now, its light reflecting off the frost-covered grass in a dazzling display. But to Theran, the world seemed a little colder, a little darker than before.

Squaring his shoulders, he followed in Leandra's footsteps, each step a reminder of the distance he'd put between them. The mission, he reminded himself. Focus on the mission. But even as he thought it, Theran knew that his heart had already betrayed him, lost to a lady he could never have.

Chapter 45: Embers

When Jordan stepped out of Terese's tent, he felt strangely renewed. Spending an entire night with herbs, poultices, prayer, and healing for the young woman rescued from her servitude with the Drinaii, he knew he should feel exhausted. Instead, his steps were light. A smile tugged at the corners of his mouth, and he lifted his hands in praise to the Lord of Light. "Lord, you provide. Lord, you are light. So be it forevermore."

The crisp morning air nipped at Jordan's exposed skin as he stood by the crackling fire, its warmth a welcome respite from the chill. The sun, now peeking over the horizon, cast long shadows across their makeshift camp, painting the world in hues of gold and amber. The scent of pine and woodsmoke mingled with the rich aroma of freshly brewed coffee, creating a comforting atmosphere despite the gravity of their situation.

Dan and Farrald joined him at the fire. For a moment, they all stood quietly around the warmth, even as the sun rose higher in the sky. Jordan observed the two young men, noting the weariness etched on their faces and the weight of recent experiences in their eyes.

With practiced movements, Jordan poured the steaming coffee into their metal travel mugs, the liquid gurgling softly as it filled each container. He took an appreciative sip, savoring the bitter warmth that spread through his chest, before breaking the silence. "What did you find?"

The question opened a floodgate, as both young men shared what had happened to them in the sunken tower's sanctuary, and the way the tree of life had renewed its strength. Jordan listened intently, his brow furrowing as he absorbed the implications of their tale. The excitement in their voices was palpable, a stark contrast to the solemn mood that had pervaded the camp earlier.

Farrald held out his staff to Jordan, the powerful green crystals embedded in the wood gleaming in the sunlight. Jordan could sense the power emanating from it, a subtle vibration that seemed to resonate with the very air around them. He shook his head, feeling the weight of his own path. "Such is not for me, not now." He rested a hand on Farrald's shoulder, feeling the young man's tension ease slightly at his touch. "You have been called by the Lord, and I will be glad to give you my blessing and the invitation to join the Shepherds of the Triune Halls."

A mix of emotions flashed across Farrald's face – pride, uncertainty, and a hint of fear. "My father will not be pleased, and…" Farrald glanced at the tent where the wounded woman was resting, his voice dropping to barely above a whisper, "I have someone at home."

Before Jordan could respond, Alex's voice cut through the air, startling a nearby bird into flight. "You have a girl and you never told us?" The prince burst into the conversation with questions as he and Quinn joined them at the fire.

Jordan watched as Farrald's face reddened, the young man's discomfort evident in the way he shifted his weight and avoided eye contact. "She… isn't exactly my girl. She is a friend who I hope could be more." The words came out haltingly, each one seeming to cost Farrald effort.

As Alex opened his mouth to press further, Dan rose, his movement smooth but purposeful. "Oh, leave him be." He waved his hand at Quinn, his voice taking on a more serious tone. "We have a tale to tell you of the Tower, something you and Terese should know."

"And me?" Alex asked, sticking out his chin, his eagerness apparent in the way he leaned forward.

"Yes, you as well," Dan said, his voice patient but firm.

Jordan saw an opportunity to redirect the conversation and seized it. "But I will catch you up, if you don't mind, Pr—Alex," he held up a hand, noting the flash of curiosity in the young prince's eyes. "I have a message from your father I've been waiting to share."

"You do?" Alex turned to him expectantly, all thoughts of Farrald's love life forgotten.

"For your ears alone." Jordan started to stand up, his joints protesting the movement after a long night of vigil.

Quinn, ever observant, waved Jordan back to his seat. "No, stay there, you've been up all night," he said, his voice tinged with concern. He pointed toward Terese's tent. "Come, Dan and Farrald, we will see if we can rouse Terese with some coffee and speak to her there."

As the others wandered away, their voices fading into the background, Alex sat down next to Jordan. The prince leaned toward the fire, poking at the coals with a stick. The embers hissed and sparked, sending tiny flashes of orange into the air. "Is he still angry?" Alex asked, his voice small and uncertain.

Jordan studied the young man's profile, noting the tension in his jaw and the way his fingers gripped the stick too tightly. He took a deep breath, the scent of coffee filling his lungs as he considered his words carefully. "No, well, I cannot say, truly, but I don't believe he is." He waited for Alex to look at him, but the Prince kept staring at the fire, as if he could find answers in its flickering depths.

With a quiet sigh, Jordan continued, his voice gentle but firm. "We have heard an excellent report from the Watch Guard Captain. He would like to keep you at the tower and keep you back from missions like this one."

Alex's head snapped up, his brow furrowed in confusion and a hint of indignation. "How is that an excellent report?"

Jordan shrugged, his rubs rustling softly with the movement. "I believe he was trying to gain some favor with your father by protecting you." He watched Alex carefully, seeing the mix of emotions play across the young prince's face – frustration, disappointment, and a flicker of understanding.

The fire crackled between them, its warmth a stark contrast to the chill that had settled over their conversation. In the distance, a bird called, its song a reminder of the world beyond their immediate concerns. Jordan sipped his coffee, giving Alex time to process the information, and prepared himself for the difficult conversation ahead.

"I thought the whole point was to toughen me up, show me the ways of the world. I can't do that inside the Watch Tower, not if the Watch Guard normally goes on missions." As he spoke, Alex turned to Jordan. "I've learned so much on this trip alone. Do you know how loyal Dan is to Septily? And to me? More than I ever imagined he was as a friend. And do you know how much Farrald knows about trade? I mean, I know he wants to be a Shepherd, but he knows more about the trade, geography, and customs of our kingdom than I do, and I learned from the best tutors at court."

Jordan refrained from mentioning that the best tutors at court did not compare to the teachers at the Triune Halls or the practical knowledge of someone living a life of trade in Septily. He did key in on what Alex said about Farrald. "You say Farrald knows about trade? I wonder what he knows about the current issues we are facing?"

"His father is, well, I think Farrald has been sheltered, like I was, but different," Alex paused and covered his face with one hand, as if embarrassed.

"Yes, but still, I did not realize Farrald's father would teach him so much. Which is odd, I suppose, given that we suspected Dan's father of teaching him his ways."

"You suspected Dan?" Alex shook his head. "Dan is anything but suspicious. I thought he was rude for a long time, not realizing what his father was asking him to do, but I always knew he was loyal to the kingdom, even if I did not know he was loyal to me as a friend."

Jordan wondered at Alex's phrasing. Most monarchs, or would-be-monarchs, would equate loyalty with the kingdom to loyalty to them, but apparently, Alex did not. What did that mean for Alex and for Septily in the future?

That thought was for another day. They had more pressing matters.

"Your father said he hoped you would not want to be kept inside Watch Guard walls, but that the choice would be yours, not that we can tell your captain that. Basically, I have the authority to speak your wishes as if they were the King's, at least in the matter of how you serve the Watch Guard, not the if."

"I understand. Thank you, Shep—Jordan." Alex shook his head. "It is hard not to use titles and to speak as casually as Quinn and Terese expect, but I understand the reasoning."

"And it is?"

"To remind us all that we are common in our humanity and in our frailty, and skills help us rise above the crowd."

"Hmm." Jordan felt even skills did not really help anyone rise above anyone else, but he figured this was a far step closer to where Alex needed to be than where he had been as a spoiled Prince.

Jordan quickly filled Alex in on the happenings in the Tower, although he was sure Farrald and Dan would also speak to their friend and give him all the details. Alex only seemed a little put out that he did not have a weapon of his own.

Chapter 46: Issues with Trust

When the tent flap rustled open, Stelia's muscles tensed instinctively. Pain lanced through her battered body, but she forced herself to sit up, swallowing a groan. Her right eye throbbed, vision blurred, and she gingerly touched the bandage on her cheekbone. Every movement was a reminder of her near-death experience.

A young man entered, his presence filling the small space. Dark-skinned, with close-cropped black hair and steady brown eyes, he radiated an aura of contained strength. Stelia's gaze flicked to the sword at his hip, and her breath caught. Could it be the sword Kalidess coveted...?

He stood rigidly by the tent's entrance, his eyes darting everywhere but at her. Stelia recognized the deliberate avoidance—she'd used it herself countless times. What was he hiding?

"Who are you?" The words scraped past her swollen throat, and she winced.

"I am Dan, apprentice to the Watch Guard." His measured tone and careful stance spoke volumes. He was assessing her, just as she was him.

"Why are you here?" Stelia pressed, searching for any hint of deception. Her years with the Dark Sisterhood had taught her that kindness often came with hidden costs, and these people were far too kind. She had never met anyone like Shepherd Jordan or Terese. They were strange, gentle, and seemingly forgiving of all her wrongs. She wasn't sure she could trust them.

Dan's eyes skimmed the tent, lingering on the tattered remnants of her old clothes. Stelia felt exposed, vulnerable in her borrowed garments.

He shrugged. "We came to see the sunken tower. The Watch Guard likes to ensure the safekeeping of the peoples of Aramatir."

His non-answer about the sunken tower did nothing to ease her suspicions.

"You went into the Tower?" She winced as one of the wounds on her back twinged. "But you say you are of Septily. Yet you are of the Watch Guard, not Triune Halls?"

He stared hard at one of the tent's walls. "My family did not approve of the Triune Halls. My father is a selfish man. My mother is the same. I joined the Watch Guard to get away from their influence."

She messed with the edges of one of her sleeves, noting the clean bandages over her arms, loosely covered by one of Terese's shirts. These people had been nothing but kind to her, but she had to understand their motives. Why would Dan's parents have disapproved of the Watch Guard? She bit her lip, trying to consider what she could ask him next.

His question came while she was wondering what she could ask and caught her off-guard. "Were you a slave or a fighter?"

"I am a swordswoman." She knew that didn't quite answer his question, but she had already told Jordan and she didn't want to dig it up again. She sat up now and curled her legs under her, prepared to move, if she needed to, even if everything hurt. Old habits died hard.

"May I ask your name?"

"Stelia Southern."

His attempt at pronunciation—"Steeleeya? Like Steel?"—almost made her smile. Almost.

"Yes." She raised her chin with a flicker of defiance kindling inside her and then decided to tell him part of it, watching closely for his reaction. "They gave me that name. I was an orphan, and then a prized possession of the Dark Sisterhood, until I tried to leave them." She gritted her teeth to prevent the tears at the corners of her eyes. It must be her injuries. She never cried.

"You have left them." Dan reminded her. "You found our camp. You are safe here."

Dan's assurances of safety washed over her. His voice was warm, soothing—dangerous. Stelia had learned the hard way not to trust easily. She glared at the tent walls, their flimsy protection a mockery of true safety.

"Safe," she scoffed. "These cloth walls keep me safe? I doubt that, Watch Guard Apprentice."

"The Tower's protections will keep you safe."

She narrowed her eyes, then her gaze found his hand resting on the pommel of his sword. "You found that there, did you?"

"Yes. It is a blade of power." He did not brag or boast, but merely stated it as fact. But the blade he carried--

The pulse of power emanating from it stirred something within her---longing, perhaps, or fear. She leaned forward, drawn toward it despite knowing better. "I know what they are, but I have never seen one. I had heard a rumor there was one in the Tower, one that the Dark Sisterhood thought they could use because of its history." The words tumbled out before she could stop them. She cursed inwardly at the slip, noting he tensed at her words.

Desperate to regain control of the conversation, Stelia flexed her right hand, remembering the sickening crunch as the Drinaii had broken it. "They broke my hand," she said, her voice low, "but they were hasty, and your healer may have fixed it in time. I will carry a sword again, maybe not one like yours, ever, for I am not worthy, but a blade of steel would suit me."

"You could always learn to wield one with your left hand."

Dan's suggestion about learning to fight left-handed almost made her laugh. If only he knew. But that was one secret she'd keep close, until she knew if she could trust him. For one who seemed so unsure of her, he certainly felt comfortable discussing her ability to fight. Was he that confident in his skill or in the strange blade on his hip? "Who taught you to fight?"

Dan shifted to lean back slightly, as if her question relaxed him. "My family hired a Sword Guard who taught me, although his real duty was to protect my sister and me. He taught me as much as I could learn from him, until my father sent him away."

She still wasn't sure what to make of him, but it was clear he had more respect for the Sword Master who had trained him than he had for his parents. Her mind whirled with the pain medicine Terese had given her and the questions she could ask. What was Dan's true purpose here? Guard? Interrogator? Friend? The last thought was quickly dismissed. Friends could quickly become enemies, as she well knew.

Stelia closed her eyes, feigning fatigue while her mind raced. This Dan was an enigma—kind yet guarded. She couldn't trust him, not yet. But perhaps, just perhaps, he and his companions represented something she'd thought lost forever: the freedom to hope.

Chapter 47: Questions and Answers

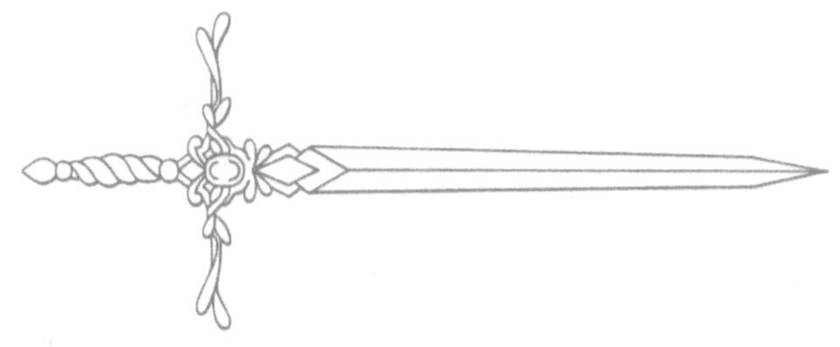

Dan's fingers twitched near the hilt of his sword, its power a constant, unsettling hum at the edge of his awareness. He forced his hand away, focusing instead on the woman before him. For a woman who had been beaten to near death, Stelia had resilience and strength. From the way she moved, Dan could tell she was in pain, but he could also tell she would fight if she felt cornered. He tried to stay farther away from her so she felt more comfortable, even though he knew Terese would want him to tend to her needs. She didn't seem to trust him, and he couldn't really blame her after she'd been so mistreated.

His gaze swept over her, noting the sinewy muscles visible beneath her borrowed shift, the scars crisscrossing her calloused hands. This was no ordinary slave, but a warrior. Her claim of serving the Dark Sisterhood and Drinaii sent a chill down his spine. What horrors had she witnessed? What had she done?

Dan flicked his gaze around the tent, hoping Terese hadn't left any weapons out. He was not sure if Stelia would take them, but he didn't trust her completely. Guilt immediately followed that thought. Wasn't he supposed to be better than this? The sword at his hip seemed to pulse in response to his unease, and he gritted his teeth at its influence. His thoughts felt jumbled with his fear, guilt, and even a bit of wary interest. He wanted to know more about her.

"I have never known anyone so keen to hold a weapon as you," he said, the words tumbling out without enough thought. He winced after he said them.

"You are right not to trust me." The defeat in her voice made something twist in Dan's chest.

"I am sorry, Stelia. I did not mean to... hurt you with my words." He fumbled for something more to say, acutely aware of how inadequate his apology sounded.

She shrugged slightly. "You could not even begin to hurt me with your gentle words. They are kind compared to what I have endured. As I said, you are right not to trust me, not to leave me alone in the tent of your healer."

"She is a Watch Guard, not only a healer. And I am here to help, not to guard. I merely thought you would rather have me stay by the doorway, instead of hovering over you. But..." he picked up a nearby cup of water. "Would you like some water?"

"No, thank you. But Terese is a Watch Guard healer, and she healed me? And the Shepherd, is he also of the Watch Guard?"

"No, he is a Shepherd of the Triune Halls of Skycliff."

"A Shepherd of the Triune Halls? Healing me? What was he thinking?" Her voice trembled.

"That you were in pain. He said you had been whipped horribly." Dan wanted to offer her some kind of comfort, but could think of nothing, so he awkwardly put the cup of water down. This close to her, he could see the freckles scattered across her face, an unexpected touch of softness that captivated him.

She turned away from him to lay on her side. "They prepared me for the Rite of Scorching Death. I was to be left in the desert when they took the slaves north to your land."

"I'm sorry." Dan was horrified, but the rest of her words hit him hard. Slaves going North to Skycliff? His heart rate quickened. A part of him dreaded answers to the questions he knew he had to ask. "Do you know where they were taking the slaves? Who had... purchased them?"

"A Lord Torren of Skycliff."

The words hit Dan like a physical blow. He staggered back, his mind reeling. Suspicion was one thing, but confirmation? The weight of it threatened to crush him. "I did not know... I suspected, but I did not know."

In that moment, the sword at his hip surged with power, responding to the maelstrom of emotions within him. Grief, rage, shame – it all coalesced into a burning need for action. Dan straightened, drawing strength from the blade even as a part of him recoiled from its eagerness.

"If my father has become evil, I must stop him." The words tasted like ash in his mouth, but he knew they were true.

Without waiting for Stelia's response, Dan strode from the tent. His mind raced, plans forming and dissolving with each step. He needed to return to Skycliff, to confront his father, to end this evil. The Watch Guard's teachings of patience and observation felt hollow in the face of such betrayal of basic decency.

As Dan grabbed his packed gear – "Always prepared. Always ready." – the mantra felt like a mockery. He had been prepared for many things, but not this. Never this. The sword's power thrummed through him, feeding his anger, his need for justice.

He couldn't wait to simply observe and watch. He would act. And may the Lord have mercy on those who stood in his way.

Chapter 48: Dan Rides for Vengeance

With the fervor of the dark blade's power thrumming inside him, matching his need for justice, Dan saddled his horse, mounted, and left their camp by the sunken tower in a blur. He knew someone, or several people tried to speak to him, but their voices barely registered through the thick fog of anger and a need to right the wrongs his father had caused.

Galloping down the sandy trail toward the crossroads, Dan realized the sword had gripped his mind, and he started to fight it. The power in the sword was unlike any he had ever heard of in a blade of power. As he struggled with it mentally, he eased up in the saddle, sitting back and signaling his horse to slow to a steady walking pace. If he pushed his horse too hard, he would end up stranded on the road with a lame animal, and he wouldn't do that. As he reflected on this this, and the injustice it would do to the animal, the sword's relentless push on his mind eased.

When it had, he unsheathed it, and held it to his side. Since no one else was around, he spoke out loud to it. "Dark Blade, you are well named, for your desire for justice edges toward vengeance. I will not trust you if you push me."

The blade pulsed obsidian in the sunlight, then dulled itself, as if in response.

Dan sheathed it again, kept his horse at a walk, and bowed his head, and planned out how he could pray. He was not Farrald. He believed in the Lord of Light, but he did not normally pray other than the planned prayers for meals, feasts, and worship, the ones he could recite. But this time, he would have to use his own words since he did not know any that applied to the situation. He started with something from a table prayer and went from there.

"Oh Lord, from whom all blessings flow. Is this blade of power from you? I do not know."

He sighed, feeling his words were too silly. "Please show me if I am right to keep it and direct my paths. Amen."

He waited with his eyes closed, but he did not feel anything happen. His spirit did not feel lighter. He did not have an immediate sense of direction, other than going toward Skycliff to mete out justice against his father and the Red Hand. It was disappointing.

When he opened his eyes, he could see that the dark blade humming beside him. While he could feel it urging him onward, he did not feel overwhelmed by it. That was something, he supposed.

He surveyed the road behind him and noticed a dust cloud. He hoped Quinn or Terese would not try to stop him. He knew he did not have a chance of staying in the Watch Guard, going off on his own with no plan and no permission. The knowledge of his failure to stay on the course he so desperately wanted weighed on his shoulders, hollowed out his gut, but he kept riding. He had to confront his parents. He had to stop the horror of slavery they had brought to Skycliff, to his home.

How could he have been so blind not to see their true natures? He had suspected. He had been uncomfortable with the way his father wanted him to use Prince Alex, but he hadn't known his parents' true depravity. He had hidden from it, run from it, ignored it for far too long.

Without realizing it, he had urged his horse to trot again, and as he rode, the horse's sides became flecked with sweat in the hot desert. The sword at his side flared suddenly, and darkness clouded his vision.

The darkness was absolute, cold and empty. Dan shouted, but his voice made no sound, no rasp or whisper. He worked his throat again, but nothing came. His horse had disappeared, and he was suspended in emptiness. He unsheathed his sword, gripping the pommel hard and the blade matched the surrounding, endless void. Without the weight of it, he wouldn't have known he was holding anything.

The blade resonated with a shimmer of shining darkness, separating him from the dark space around him. The blade took on a silver-black sheen in his hands, and slowly the silvery-black dissipated the flat black around him until Dan could see he and his mare stood in a field under a full moon.

A glare of light came over the horizon in front of him. The glare coalesced into the shape of a man wearing clothes of pure radiance. Not white exactly, but all the colors of light together. The man's skin shimmered colors in the light of his clothes, and Dan couldn't tell his origins.

Dan's legs trembled as he dismounted, falling to his knees in awe. His sword tip dug into the grass in front of him. Hastily, he raised it into a position of fealty and bowed to the man, who could only be one man, not really a man at all.

Dan's thoughts were babbling. He knew that, but he couldn't help it. He was not worthy. He was not ready.

"Lord, what would you have of me?"

When the man spoke, his voice resonated all around them, enveloping Dan with a sense of being beloved and at peace. "Dan Torren. You have been called to and have chosen a hard path. If you follow it, you must promise me, you will not kill in anger, or in vengeance."

Confusion warred with reverence in Dan's mind. "Lord?"

"I am love. I am light. I am the only true judge. You know this if you know me."

A surge of recognition and peace washed over him. "Yes, Lord of Light. I know you are who you say you are."

"Then you will do as I command, and you will follow this path of justice with mercy, with compassion, and with the knowledge that all people are my people."

Dan struggled to reconcile this command with the anger burning inside of him. "My Lord, my parents are… they have… they can't be yours."

"They are mine, but they have lost their way."

"I do not understand."

"Justice with mercy and compassion, Dan. The blade will help you, but its purpose was skewed by its last wielder. I will cleanse it, but you must stay on the path I set, or it will regress to its previous path, as will you. Walk in my ways alone."

Dan's grip tightened on the sword, feeling the weight of this responsibility. "Yes, Lord."

"And allow love to live in your heart for your friends and found family."

As Dan whispered agreement, the figure's radiance intensified until he had to shield his eyes. "Yes, Lord."

When Dan blinked, he found himself staring at the desert sky, Farrald's concerned face hovering above him. Relief flooded through him at the sight of his friend.

"Dan! You're alive. Thank the Lord of Light."

Dan put his hand on Farrald's forearm. "I saw him. My path is justice with mercy, Farrald. Justice with mercy. I'm not sure how I can accomplish it." The enormity of the task before him felt daunting.

Farrald held out a hand to help him up. "We will find a way."

As Dan took Farrald's offered hand, struggling to his feet, he felt a profound shift within himself. The burning desire for vengeance had been replaced by a resolve to seek justice. The Lord's words echoed in his mind, reminding him of the fine line between righteous action and misguided retribution.

Gratitude welled up in Dan's chest. "Thank you for believing me."

Farrald gave him a wry grin. "You are touched by the Lord. If others don't see it, they are blind."

Dan tried not to think about how others were going to perceive him. It was easier in some ways to think of the simple tasks for their journey.

He focused his gaze on how Farrald had attached his horse to Dan's mare, and they were both tied to a scraggly bush. "Where are the others?"

"Behind us. They will meet us at the crossroads."

"How did you know you would catch me?"

Farrald shrugged. "I did not now, but I prayed, and the Lord answered."

"He did." Dan reflected on his prayer earlier and how disappointed he'd felt when he hadn't received an immediate answer. He was not sure getting an answer was anything like he thought it would be. "Does He talk to you that way?"

"Never. I'm a little envious, but I feel almost a nudge now and then as I read scriptures and pray. It is enough." Farrald shrugged.

Dan admired Farrald's constancy of faith. Faith without visions was true faith. Dan had been given with visions, but he knew he needed them to truly see his path of justice with mercy and not vengeance. Without the Lord's help, without Farrald's friendship, he knew he would struggle to stay on the right path. The Lord hadn't only answered his prayer, he had brought him a friend.

Chapter 49: The Weight of the King

KING XANDROS STARED OVER the city of Skycliff, barely noticing the outlines of the buildings as they edged against the deepening sunset of glorious colors which spread over the sea beyond the city.

Once, he had beheld this view with awe. Once, standing in this same place, he had held his wife close in his arms, with their new son held tenderly in her arms between them. Once, he had reprimanded his son, right here, and sent him away.

He still missed Alex. Even with Alex's misdeeds and the harsh words between them, he yearned for his son and his closest friends, Theran and Jordan. He hoped Alex would create a close bond with Dan and Farrald. He hoped for all their sakes they could work together with the Triune Halls when the time came for Alex to rule the kingdom of Septily from this very place.

Xandros ran his hand along the carvings on the windowsill. Every ruler had left his or her mark, crudely carved by their own hands into the wood of the sill. While professional craftsmen created the actual seal for each ruler, each king or queen would carve their personal version in the windowsill in the first week of their reign. It was an unspoken tradition handed down for generations.

Xandros had chosen a tree, with branches in bloom above the edge of Skycliff. He remembered choosing it because he wanted his reign to flourish, to protect the city and the country, and because he wanted their relations with other kingdoms to grow. He had chosen his wife because he loved her, but he had fallen in love with her in part because she represented a dream of a united world of Aramatir, an idea her family did not share. Her home Kingdom of Wylandria had fallen on hard times, and although Xandros had tried to help, even after her death, they refused all aid and all trade with him. He did not understand their stubbornness and distrust.

He sighed and followed the path of carvings back past his father's griffin carving, his grandfather's shield carving, and all the way back to the first King of Septily, who had carved a tree with a sword and a scroll by its side, a representation of the Triune Halls, although not the official one.

He knew, deep down, that his own tree had been a way of copying the original one. Had it been too arrogant? He bowed his head and tried to pray, to repent, but nothing came. He was doing his best. His all. The weight of the kingdom, especially the horrific actions of the nobles who supported the Red House and the Red Hand slavers, felt heavy on him. The overwhelming sense of not being enough, not knowing enough, not being able to change the tide of events hung on his shoulders. He wished Jordan were here to pray with him, or Theran to discuss plans of attack.

On his desk, he had a note from Theran, but he had not heard from Jordan yet. Theran's note had been brief but telling.

X,
We are about to enter the nest of vipers. I worry for my charge. Please send friends and have them stay in the village nearby.
Your shield,
T

The note had been written in code, the words somewhat vague, but Xandros knew what Theran needed. He had called for a representative from the Sword Halls branch of the Triune Halls to come and speak with him in the morning. They would get help to Theran.

Even more troubling than Theran's note was the absence of communication from Jordan. The Shepherd had a talent for verbose missives with detailed descriptions. Xandros had sent him into the heart of the desert to find the slavers, to stop them if possible, or at least do reconnaissance and get their numbers. Had Jordan been injured, captured, or killed? No other explanation for his silence came readily.

When he had been but a prince, Xandros had thought he would have the power to make changes when he became King. With twenty years of rule beneath his belt, he was familiar with the sense of helplessness, of being at the center of an intricate web, but being caught in it and not in control of it. His actions and words rippled outward, but not fast enough, it seemed, to make the difference he wanted to make in the lives of his people.

With the governmental structure of shared power between the monarchy, the House of Lords and the Triune Halls, more could be done, but it meant relying on and trusting others, and waiting, always waiting. The interminable waiting was pulling him down.

As the sunset disappeared and the stars became clearer in the sky, Xandros tried to pray again and again. His words felt hollow and foolish, his mind felt scattered with worry, but he persisted. "Lord, help us. Help Alex. Help me." It was all he really had in him. He was not a poet or a Shepherd. He was simply a King with worries.

Chapter 50: Journey Forward

When Quinn, Alex, Shepherd Jordan, Terese, and Stelia met Dan and Farrald at the crossroads, Dan expected harsh reprimands, a lecture, vast disappointment. Instead, Quinn gave him a stern look and took point, Alex followed Quinn, Terese shook her head at him, once, and then they rode for Skycliff in silence. All the conversation of their ride south was absent. Alex seemed to shadow Quinn's every move. Terese and Stelia rode side by side. Shepherd Jordan remained a lone rider, either clucking his horse forward or slowing her if anyone tried to ride next to him.

Farrald rode with Dan but did not say anything. Relieved at first, Dan started to find the silence hollow. His blade's power even felt muted and distant. He stared at the road ahead, twisting through the desert, and then dusty farmlands as they rode through the Desert District, which lined the edge of the continent, separated from the Southlands by the Merseas. They soon lost sight of it as they turned north, taking different roads than they had taken on their journey south. They were making their best time for Skycliff. Home. Except it was not his home anymore.

Dan drifted in his thoughts about his time growing up in his parents' house, mimicking the Sword Guard who protected them and gave him lessons, the parties his parents held which he hadn't been allowed to attend even as he grew older. He was glad they had kept him apart. Would he have become like them if they had included him? A chill ran over him at the thought. He tried to shake it off and sit straighter in his saddle. How far had they traveled?

The sun was falling in the west, beyond the tree line. It seemed they would press on into the night.

Dan did not want to return to the bustling city with all the traitors who wore smiles and lied to your face, all the nobles and the merchants who were selling politics or goods, all trade of one kind or another, and all trying to get the best angle on trade, to cheat their fellow Septilians in any way they could.

Dan's chill gave way to the fire of anger as he thought of how many times his parents had lied to him, how many deals his father had boasted about doing that left another noble or trader in ruins.

And, under all of that, his father and mother had been doing something much worse: trading in people's lives for profit.

It sickened him.

And at the same time, he felt ashamed for not seeing the evidence that added up so easily once he knew the truth. The real rage he felt was for his own foolishness, his gullibility. How had he not seen it?

"Hey," Stelia's rough alto voice broke into his ruminations, and Dan barely kept from startling at her nearness. When had she ridden up next to him? When had Farrald fallen back to ride with Terese?

Dan ran his mare's reins through his fingers, not sure what to say.

"So, I decided I needed to tell you something."

Dan didn't know what to say to her, after their awkward conversation earlier and his abrupt departure. He glanced over at her, trying to think of how to respond to her strange comment. She wore Terese's spare clothes, a dark brown tunic and breeches. Her sloppily shorn tawny hair had been braided severely, and her eyes seemed the same color of blue as the sky.

"You must remember this. You are not your father or your mother."

Dan swallowed back a lump in his throat and said nothing.

Stelia's mare brushed up against him, and his mare side-stepped away, then back, nickering.

Stelia leaned toward him over the small gap between their horses. "Tell me you'll remember that you are not your father or your mother. They do not decide who you are. Only your actions do."

The chills on Dan's arms raised goosebumps. How had she known what he was thinking?

He cleared his throat, trying to dislodge his confusion. "Why does it matter to you?"

Chapter 51: Not Those Who Raised Us

Stelia shifted in her saddle, her eyes trailing over Dan's tense form. The weight of his parents' betrayal hung heavy on his shoulders. She took a deep breath, steeling herself for the conversation ahead.

"Dan," she began softly, drawing his attention. "I... I think I understand something of what you're going through."

His eyebrows furrowed, a mix of curiosity and skepticism in his gaze. Memories of her past threatened to overwhelm her. But she pushed on, knowing this was important.

"My parents died when I was young," she continued, her voice barely above a whisper. "Kalidess, the lead sorceress of the Dark Sisterhood, raised me to care for her daughter."

Dan's eyes widened, shock and disbelief etched across his features. Stelia felt a familiar twist of shame in her gut but forced herself to meet his gaze.

"Yes, I was... I became a monster," she admitted, the words tasting bitter on her tongue. "But I never had enough power to be trained as a sorceress – or at least, I never let them see how much I truly had."

She paused, memories of fear and desperation washing over her. "When I helped Kalidess's daughter escape, I lied and said she had died. My punishment was to serve the Drinaii, killing innocents under their command while still being Kalidess's puppet."

Dan's face was a storm of emotions, and Stelia felt an unexpected urge to reach out and comfort him. Instead, she gripped her reins tighter and forced herself to continue.

"Despite all the evil I committed," she continued, her voice growing stronger, "what matters is this: I told Kalidess's daughter what I'm telling you now. You are not your parents."

Dan shook his head. "But the Drinaii... they whipped you, tried to kill you in the desert. They performed the... what did you call it?"

Stelia's fingers unconsciously traced the bruises on her wrist. "The Rite of Scorching Death," she explained, a shudder running through her. "A combination of bloodletting, sorcery, and torture, ending with the accused left to die in the desert."

"But if you were one of them?" Dan pressed, confusion evident in his voice.

Stelia closed her eyes briefly, fighting back the wave of self-loathing that threatened to engulf her. "I was never..." she began, then stopped herself. "No, that's not true. I was one of them because I saw no other way. After helping Kalidess's daughter, I thought I'd missed my chance at redemption. So, I determined to rise through the Drinaii ranks, thinking I could hinder them from within."

She let out a bitter laugh. "It sounds ridiculous and convoluted, I know. There's no excuse for what I did. But eventually, I started trying to help the slaves."

Dan angled toward her, his attention rapt. Stelia felt a flicker of warmth at his willingness to listen, even as shame burned within her.

"How did you help them?" he asked softly.

"I claimed some as my personal slaves, then set them free," she explained, her throat tight with emotion. "But it was slow, one or two at a time. Meanwhile, I served as an Enforcer for the Dark Sisterhood, punishing any Drinaii who disrespected them."

Stelia's gaze dropped to her hands, seeing them stained with imaginary blood. "The Drinaii hated me, and many in the Dark Sisterhood did too.

I knew it couldn't last. An old friend betrayed me, discovered my efforts to free slaves."

"Why did you do it?" Dan's question was gentle, free of judgment.

Stelia's throat tightened. "I couldn't stand it anymore. The blood on my hands, the pain, the horror of it all. And the slaves... they reminded me of myself. Not that it makes me any kind of hero," she added bitterly. "Just a broken monster, I think."

"No," Dan said firmly, surprising her. "You're not a monster. A monster wouldn't have tried to free anyone."

Stelia felt something crack inside her at his words, a tiny fissure in the wall she'd built around her heart. She swallowed hard, forcing herself to focus.

"Maybe," she conceded. "But I didn't ride beside you for your grace. I wanted to remind you: you are not your parents."

Dan's eyes met hers, a spark of understanding passing between them. "And you," he said softly, "are not your former masters."

Stelia turned away, unable to bear the kindness in his gaze. She stared at the horizon, blinking back unexpected tears. His words echoed in her mind, stirring something she'd thought long dead.

"I suppose," she whispered, more to herself than to Dan, "we are not those who raised us."

As they rode on in silence, Stelia felt a fragile sense of hope taking root within her. Perhaps, just perhaps, there was a chance for both of them to forge new paths, free from the shadows of their pasts.

Chapter 52: Into Skycliff

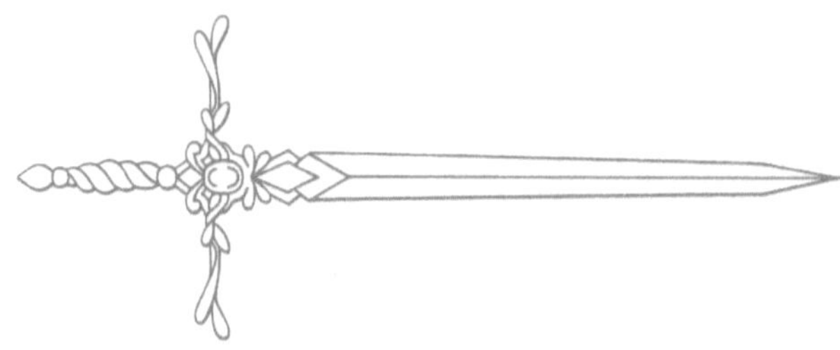

After a brief rest in the darkest hours of night and cold trail rations, they neared the outskirts of Skycliff.

The road widened enough so two carts could travel side by side, but the wagon, cart, horse, and foot traffic increased significantly. Dan attempted to rein in his impatience as he sat upright in his saddle and forced his legs to relax. His mare shook her head at him every time he tensed, as if to remind him they had ridden far too many miles to ride hard at this point, much less in a crowd.

Their group had bunched together, with Alex at the center. Quinn rode at Alex's left side. In front of them, Jordan, Stelia, and Terese rode three abreast, while Dan and Farrald took up the rear position.

Farrald slouched heavily in his saddle and rubbed at his eyes. "I did not sleep much last night, after I realized who Stelia is."

"Why not? She left the," Dan glanced around and lowered his voice, "the Drinaii behind. They no longer have a hold over her."

"No, that's not it." Farrald opened his mouth to continue, took a breath in, and then stopped, shaking his head. "I can't actually tell you."

"What?"

"I know who Stelia is because I've heard of her before, from someone else. I can't share who." Farrald shifted uncomfortably in his saddle.

"Someone she saved from slavery?" Dan guessed.

Farrald tilted his head to the side. "Yes. She saved her from slavery. I can say that."

"But why would that keep you awake, then?"

Farrald gazed around at the road, his eyes seeming to flit from one group of travelers to another. As they safely passed a group of foot travelers and were able to ride farther apart again, he held up one hand. "Imagine you've heard of someone who is a fierce fighter, someone who is known for her toughness, her resilience to torture and other things, and then you meet her, and she isn't like what you expected. She's younger, but also more worn." He wavered his hand around. "That's not exactly all of it, but…I guess I know the Dark Sisterhood wouldn't let her go so easily."

Dan turned to stare at Farrald. "Did you see her scars? did you hear about the punishment she went through before she escaped? I don't call that easy."

Farrald shook his head again minutely. "Eh. I don't know how to put it exactly, but I am shocked they turned her out. She's a valuable fighter for them, an asset. The Dark Sisterhood doesn't let go of those easily. They normally would bind someone and drain them of their blood and energy if they could no longer use them or sell them."

Heat ran through Dan from his gut to his hands at the outrage of anyone being drained of their life. "I had heard stories of their evil, but I did not believe they could possibly be true."

"They are." Farrald slumped in his saddle. "They truly are. I have seen some of their victims, after they've died. They would be left out in the desert, sometimes, at our borders, to warn us, I guess."

Dan squeezed his eyes shut to keep his mind from filling in the pictures of what that might look like. The horror, fear, and rage inside of him built and continued to build.

The mare tossed her head and then stomped to a halt.

Dan realized he was squeezing his legs, so he loosened them and gave the mare's neck a pat.

"The sword isn't controlling you anymore, Dan." Farrald reminded him.

"How can you stay so calm when you know this evil is happening?"

Farrald sighed. "I pray. I try to help others as best as I can."

"Don't you want to fight them?"

"Yes, and no. I want to fight them with healing, with peace, with all the goodness they hate."

Dan bit his lip to keep from saying something about the need to defend their country and those they loved from the evil of the Dark Sisterhood.

Farrald could fight in defense with his staff, but he would rather heal and pray because those were his gifts. Dan would rather fight, even if most of the Watch Guard apprentices had bested him. He needed to get better, so he could carry the dark blade with purpose and honor. He needed a teacher. As he reflected on that, his eyes landed on Stelia, where she rode silently, shrinking in on herself between Jordan and Terese.

"You say she's a talented fighter?"

"One of the Drinaii's best, as far as I know."

"I need her to teach me."

"She wants to submit her life to the Triune Halls as penance for her crimes. That's what she shared with Jordan and I this morning, when you were off with Alex."

Dan slumped in his saddle. He hadn't meant to lose the opportunity to learn. Alex had been spending so much time with Quinn since he'd received the dark blade, he'd needed to make sure the prince was all right, that their recovered friendship would not be lost.

So little time had passed and so much had changed, but as they neared the gates of Skycliff, the city appeared the same.

High stone walls surrounded the entire city, with Sword Guards of the Triune Halls manning the ramparts. The men and women wore varying types of armor, but all bore the crest of the King, and most carried blades of power. The dark blade seemed to respond to the presence of so many powered blades and thrummed loudly in Dan's ears as they took their turn with the gate guards.

The five men at the gate surrounded their small party, and one spoke to Jordan. "Name, business, duration of stay."

Shepherd Jordan sat rigid in his saddle. "Shepherd Jordan, to see the King, and as long as my service to the Triune Halls and Septily lasts, I will stay here or elsewhere at the King's pleasure."

"Do you vouch for everyone in your party?"

"I do. These are members of the Watch Guard and an informant."

"You may pass." The five guards moved back, and one of them stared at Alex as they went by.

Before they approached the city, Alex had agreed to enter as one of the Watch Guard so as not to raise any attention to their party. It was a humble move for him, and Dan was glad to see Alex seemed comfortable with his role as they rode into the city streets.

Jordan took the group around a side road, which seemed to meander far from the palace. The city's outer familiar scents—fresh bread, horse manure, and the ever-present tang of metal from the forges—filled the air.

Dan's gaze darted between his companions. Quinn's face remained impassive, Terese's eyes scanned the thinning crowds with practiced ease, and Alex... Alex looked completely at ease. Dan decided to keep watch as well. He noticed Stelia also had a keen gaze that roved around the crowds on the street.

As he took his own watch of the street around them, he noticed they had left behind the businesses that lined the main thoroughfares. The street narrowed, traffic slowed, and it seemed they were riding through a residential district by the wall, peppered with small grocery stalls and other needed items every few blocks. The street narrowed more, and they were the only riders on it. Foot travelers thinned to occasional children and parents, but soon, they were traveling completely alone in an area of Skycliff Dan did not recognize. It was startling to realize he did not even know all the neighborhoods in his home city, and he wondered where Jordan was leading them.

The whole group rode silently until they reached a dead end. A sanctuary building connected the outer wall of Skycliff and the inner buildings of the street.

Without dismounting, Jordan rode up to the front entrance, and after a whispered conversation, he dismounted his mare, and handed the reins to a young woman standing there, who wore the gray armor of a Triune Halls apprentice.

"We will dismount here and go into the sanctuary," Jordan informed them.

This all seemed strange to Dan, who had expected to ride straight to the palace, but the others did not protest, so he did not either. While he may not be allowed back into the Watch Guard, he remembered, they were to watch first, and learn the answers to questions with observation.

When he handed his mare's reins to another young apprentice, his mare whuffed his hair, and he patted her neck and handed her a small cube of sugar. She deserved it after the long ride they had. He took his saddlebags and slung them over his shoulder, then joined the others in the entryway to the Triune Halls sanctuary.

Inside, the flickering candlelight cast long shadows across the floor. Dan's eyes took a moment to adjust, and when they did, his breath caught in his throat. A lone figure knelt at the front.

When the man rose to his feet and turned, Dan knelt hurriedly, then tugged at Farrald who was next to him. The cold stone bit into his legs, but Dan barely noticed.

Farrald squinched his eyebrows together, but followed Dan's lead, as the others falteringly knelt as well, all except Alex.

"Father," Alex bowed his head.

King Xandros enveloped his son in a fierce embrace. Dan watched, unable to look away, as father and son reunited. The love between them was palpable, filling the small sanctuary with a warmth.

Memories of his own father flooded Dan's mind—stern lectures, violent outbursts, the constant pressure. Never an embrace like that, never that unconditional love that seemed to radiate from the King.

Dan's fingers dug into his palms. He should be happy for Alex, shouldn't he? His friend—his prince—deserved this moment of joy. But the bitter taste of envy coated Dan's tongue, and he hated himself for it.

As he glanced away to refocus his struggle with his anger, Dan became aware of Stelia's presence beside him, her shoulder nearly brushing his. He glanced at her, surprised by the tension radiating from her. He wanted to reach out, to offer some word of comfort or reassurance, but found himself frozen. Stelia seemed to be bracing herself for judgment, her body coiled tight as a spring.

Dan felt a fierce surge of protectiveness, which surprised him. Regardless of her past, Stelia was one of them now. And as the King approached, Dan silently vowed to stand by her side, whatever judgment awaited.

Chapter 53: To Turn and Change

Stelia's knees ached as she pressed her forehead to the cold stone floor of the church, bowing lower than she ever had for Kalidess on her own volition. The weight of her past pressed down on her, heavier than any physical burden she had ever carried. "I should not be here." Her pained whisper escaped before she could stop it.

King Xandros slowly released Alex, gazed at him for a moment, and then moved to stand in front of Stelia. "And why should you not be here? And why bow as if I am the Lord of Light himself? I am only a human king, one responsible to my kingdom and to my advisors of the Triune Halls Council and the House of the Lords."

Stelia slowly raised her head. Her gaze met the King's, and she fought the urge to look away, to hide from the kindness she saw there. It was easier to face anger, hatred – those she understood. This... this was foreign territory.

She swallowed hard, forcing the words out. "I am Stelia, formerly a Drinaii Captain, formerly the fosterling of Kalidess, the leader of the Dark Sisterhood." The titles felt like ash on her tongue. "I... was a companion to her daughter until her daughter escaped. I led raids on the borders of countries, fought with and tortured prisoners, as commanded, and have no right to be here." Her voice cracked. "I am a dangerous woman, and I would not have you tainted by my past."

"I see." King Xandros ran his hand over his chin. "And do you want to harm me at this moment?"

Out of the corner of her eye, Stelia saw Alex grip the pommel of his sword.

Stelia shook her head vehemently, her voice barely above a whisper. "No. I do not wish to harm anyone again." The truth of it resonated. How many nights had she lain awake, haunted by the faces of those she'd hurt?

King Xandros rubbed his hands together. "This is difficult, as I've heard you are a gifted warrior. It would be a shame to lose such skills."

Stelia shook her head. "I do not want to kill anyone else as long as I live."

"I understand that, at least. I do not either." King Xandros held out one of his hands. "Will you vow to protect Septily from harm, for the Lord of the Light, for the rest of your life?"

Stelia's mouth dropped open, stunned by his offer. This couldn't be real. It had to be some kind of trap. "I am a recent defector of the Drinaii. Surely, you need more than my word."

King Xandros's chuckle was warm, unexpected. "Surely, I do not. For I trust my advisors, and Shepherd Jordan's message spoke highly of you and your commitment to repentance and change." He extended his hand again. "Please, take the vow and rise to stand amongst this assembly as we decide our course of action against the Red Hand and their Red House."

Stelia stared at his outstretched hand, her mind reeling. This was more than forgiveness—this was a chance at redemption, a new life. Her hand trembled as she placed it in the King's surprisingly calloused palm.

"I vow to protect Septily and you from any and all harm, for the Lord of the Light, for the rest of my life." The words felt heavy, binding, yet strangely freeing. As King Xandros helped her to her feet, Stelia felt a weight lift from her shoulders. She stood taller, her gaze sweeping across the assembled group.

Her gaze connected with Dan's and he gave her an encouraging nod. A flicker of warmth kindled inside her. For the first time in years, she felt something dangerously close to hope. She wasn't naïve enough to believe her past was erased, but she could forge a new path, one step at a time. Maybe, she could even find friends here. She had been given an unexpected chance at life and freedom, and she didn't want to waste it.

Chapter 54: A Father and a King

King Xandros watched his son Alex with a mixture of pride and regret swirling in his chest. The boy—no, the young man—his posture straighter, his eyes clearer. The time with the Watch Guard had changed him, just as Xandros had hoped it would. Yet the ache of their separation lingered.

As the others in the simple church discussed strategies against the Red Hand, Xandros found his gaze continually drawn back to Alex. He longed to pull his son into another embrace, to tell him how proud he was of the growth he saw.

His eyes drifted to the two young men flanking his son. Dan, with his newly acquired sword of power, stood alert and focused. Farrald, no less engaged, holding the staff of power he carried, offered measured wisdom beyond his years.

These three young men, forged into a team by their trials with the Watch Guard, could be the foundation of a new era for Septily. Alex, learning to balance authority with humility. Dan, embodying the ideals of justice tempered with mercy. Farrald, bringing the compassion and wisdom of a future Shepherd. It was his plan from the moment he had sent them to the Watch Guard to train, but he knew it had not yet reached the point of completion. They were all so young.

But as the meeting continued, Xandros found himself imagining the future. Alex on the throne, with Dan and Farrald as his trusted advisors.

It was a vision that filled him with hope—and a touch of melancholy. His reign would not last forever, and part of him mourned the lost years with his son.

But there was still time. Time to mend their relationship, time to guide Alex as he grew into his role as heir. And perhaps, Xandros mused, time to remember how to be a father as well as a king.

When the meeting concluded, Xandros approached Alex again. "Walk with me," he said, his tone softer than usual. "I believe we have much to discuss about your travels and about the future of Septily."

Chapter 55: Friends and Plans

Dan turned away from watching King Xandros and Alex, whose relationship served as a stark reminder of what he lacked.

Stelia's voice was a welcome interruption to his thoughts. "King Xandros is not what I expected."

Dan noted the curiosity in her eyes. "He is a good king," he said, pride seeping into his voice despite his earlier envy.

Stelia's brow furrowed. "How is it that he values Shepherd Jordan's advice so much?"

By sharing knowledge, Dan hoped he could bridge the gap between him and Stelia. "Shepherd Jordan, King Xandros, and a Sword Master named Theran were raised and trained with one another."

Stelia crossed her arms, her posture softening slightly. "Things are very different here."

Before Dan could respond, Farrald's voice cut in. "I would hope so." Dan's felt the snap of tension as his friend approached. He cared for both Farrald and Stelia, and he knew Farrald would extend grace to her, but it seemed his friend had something serious on his mind.

"If I may, Dan, I would like to speak to Stelia for a moment in private."

"Of course," Dan said, allowing the two of them to walk a few feet away. This left him with Shepherd Jordan, Quinn, and Terese. Those three were already in conversation, but Terese waved him toward them.

"Dan, we need to know more about your sister and her abilities to defend herself. It turns out, she's gone to help Sword Master Theran scout out the situation at your parent's Lake District estate."

Dan clenched his hands into fists as he felt fear for his sister race through his veins, followed by the thrumming sensation of power from his dark sword. "We need to ride at once. She... she can't be left alone with my parents if they are fully into this Red Hand, Red House business. They are not to be trusted with her safety."

"But what are her skills? Did your family not employ a former Sword Master who worked for them?"

Dan rubbed his chin as he contemplated this. "She kept her training sessions private, so I am not sure, but I always suspected she had more training than my parents realized. She pretended to get up late and to be lazy, but I don't think she really was. At least I hope not." He realized he was panicking as he spoke, the words coming faster and faster. "Please, let me ride ahead."

"Not again, Dan," Quinn said sternly.

"We will ride with you, and tonight." Terese told him. "We need to at least get resupplied and get fresh horses. Then, we will ride and be able to fight when we get there."

Dan would not be able to rest until his sister was safe, but this time, he would abide by their direction.

As he agreed to wait for supplies and fresh horses, Dan's hand unconsciously gripped his sword hilt. The power within it resonated with his turmoil, a constant reminder of the weight of his choices. He would abide by their direction, yes, but every moment of delay felt like a betrayal of Leandra.

Dan had to trust in the Lord, in his companions, and in his sister's strength – whatever that might be. As he watched Stelia and Farrald return, he steeled himself for the journey ahead. Whatever came, he would face it with both old friends and new allies at his side.

CHAPTER 56: ONCE A FOOL

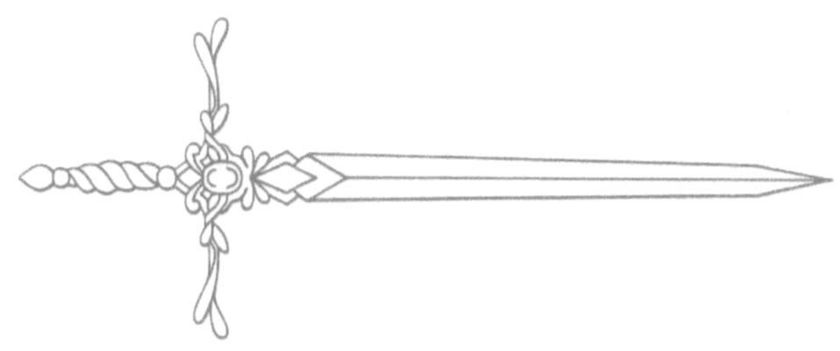

FROM THE MOMENT THEY entered the grounds of the mansion, Theran struggled not to grit his teeth or grip the pommel of his sword. While they couldn't see it when they were across the river, and even now, nothing visible was amiss, something felt wrong. It took him two days to figure it out, and he felt like a fool when he did.

As he wrote a second coded message to the king in the tiny room joined to Lady Leandra's by a small door so he could be close to always protect her, he heard a small noise in Leandra's room. Lady Leandra had gone out with the hunt, after informing him to stay behind, with a bit of a grim countenance. All the things they had said were still between them. All the longing. All the hurt.

The noise increased, but it did not sound like Leandra. He stood up slowly, edged to the door, and cracked it open.

A tiny maid in a huge black overdress startled when the door hinge squeaked.

She cowered, kneeling on the floor with the fireplace scuttle. "Lord, please, I don't want any trouble."

"I'm not a Lord." Theran heard the frustration in his voice, saw her flinch, and tried to speak in a more soothing tone. "I will not give you any trouble. I merely wondered who was in my lady's suite." He stepped into the room but stopped when he saw her trembling.

"I believed you were with her, sir, or I would not have entered." She kept her gaze down on the ground. "May I go, sir?"

"Of course." Theran stepped back.

She stood, taking the heavy scuttle of used firewood, and started to walk past him.

Because of the way she held the scuttle, one of her sleeves had scrunched around her elbow and he could see bruises encircling her wrists.

"Wait, who gave you those?" He tapped her forearm gently, and she stumbled back away from him, her eyes widening in fear.

"Lord, I cannot tell you. Please, if you are here, you must know, and you must know I cannot tell you." She put down the scuttle and shoved her sleeve down over her wrist. Bowing her head again, she said, "Please, let me go now, Lord. Unless you have … another use of me." Her tone went helpless with these last words.

He was close enough to see her shivering again. "No, I would never hurt you, lass. You may go."

"Thank you, Sir." She curtseyed quickly and fled the room.

When the door closed, Theran leaned against the fireplace heavily. How had he not realized until now that all the servants were conspicuously absent unless required to be seen and present, as when they were serving a meal? Where were they the rest of the time? Locked up or in hiding? He should have known, as he was in the role of a servant himself, and as he had found the servants at the house of Lord and Lady Torren particularly helpful in the past. He had been caught up with his feelings for Leandra.

Lady Leandra, not ever Leandra to him. He couldn't think of her in such familiar terms. But he had, he did, and he worried about her when she informed him he would stay behind in their suite of rooms instead of accompanying her on the grounds during a fox hunt. He hadn't even known she hunted. But that was hardly a problem; since he was sure she was both good at it, and good at hiding any skill she had. No, the problem was, if he was not with her, he couldn't protect her from the guests at the estate or her parents who set his teeth on edge whenever they spoke.

He crossed the room and stared out the window at the brooding clouds covering the sky. It did not look like these clouds would pass through as the others had. He gazed at the shadow-dappled forest for a quarter-mark, then returned to his room, put on his boots, stashed his papers in a compartment of his bags, and closed the door to his room, then Lady Leandra's room with an extra lock he had brought with him for these moments.

Outside the room, he stood for a moment in the hallway, listening to the sounds of the house. It was too still, too hushed. The servants were scurrying about on stocking feet, attempting to stay away from all the guests, it seemed. That was what had been wrong the whole time. He really should have seen it. He could exit via the main stairway, as he had every other time, or find the servant's stairs and see if he could find out more that way. But he did not want to terrify any other servants, so he opted for the grand staircase for guests and their immediate attendants.

For whatever reason, he felt a sudden need to hurry, as if Leandra's safety suddenly depended on him in the moment at hand. Outside the mansion, he changed his gait from walk to run, racing into the stables to find his mare being coddled by a startled stable girl, who shied away and tried to shove all of her hair back into her cap.

"It is all right. I can saddle my horse, if you would be so kind as to fetch my tack."

"Yes, sir." Her shoulders visibly relaxed as she fetched all his gear.

It took longer than he would have liked to saddle up, as tension seemed to be mounting like the chill of the looming clouds outside. "Do you know which direction they went for their hunt?"

"Lady Leandra said if you came out, to go to the Goose Herder's hut first, sir." The stable girl bobbed her head in a kind of bow.

How had Leandra known he would follow her?

Because she expected him to, because that was his role, because that's what he'd been doing all along, regardless of her public or private orders.

"I've been an idiot."

"Can't say, sir."

He shook his head. "You needn't. Please, if you see her before I do, let her know I am at the Goose Herder's hut."

"I will, sir."

With one swift motion, he mounted his horse. Remembering his earlier conversation, he studied the grounds and the mansion. "Are the servants locked up or in hiding?"

She stiffened. "Some are hiding. The others are locked up until Lady Leandra's visit is over tomorrow."

"Oh, dear Lord. The others?"

"I'm not supposed to say anything about them to you, sir. Please don't repeat what I said." She glanced furtively at the mansion.

"I won't repeat it to anyone except the King, his spies, and the Triune Halls. You have my word."

He leaned forward in his saddle and turned his mare's head to the bridge which crossed the river. He had to make sure Leandra was safe.

Chapter 57: Tight Spaces

When Theran reached the Goose Herder's house, he noticed all the geese were milling around the leaf-covered lawn between the entrance and the white-washed buildings, obviously at ease with their surroundings, which meant no one unusual had come to the thatched-roof cottage. He dismounted his mare and guided her into the stable yard behind the small house made sure she was comfortable with food and water, then approached the gate to the inner yard.

The geese squawked at him angrily, one after another, until the whole yard was a cacophony of honking noise. Some of the geese started to walk toward him flicking their back feathers and elongating their necks to make a hissing noise.

The curtain over the cottage window flicked up at the corner, then down, and Giselle opened the front door. "Down, geese guardians, down."

The geese quieted for her, but when Theran put his hand on the latch, the one closest to him hissed at him again and snapped its beak. From his previous stay, he had thought the geese had accepted him, but apparently, he had been wrong.

"Naw, Georgie, naw. Down." Giselle stepped toward the goose, carrying her tall staff but not waving it toward him, and the goose quieted, stepping back to stand with the others.

Theran opened the latch, stepped inside, and closed the gate behind him, always keeping his eyes on the geese.

Georgie gave him a stern look, dipping his beak, and staring up at Theran.

"Let our guest come in." The goose girl stamped the end of her staff on the ground. Georgie backed away.

Theran strode forward quickly, avoiding any goose that was in his path, until he reached Giselle.

"Lady Leandra left me a message to come here."

"I know." She opened the door behind her but stood in the center of the doorway. "I also know you don't like my home or my geese, but I can promise you, they are more protection for Leandra than you will ever be."

"Is that so?" Theran hadn't really paid much attention to Giselle before, but now he noticed the strength of her stance, the way she held her staff in her hands. "You've had some training, then?"

She gave him nearly the same look as Georgie, her mouth in a firm line, and cocked an eyebrow at him.

He held up his hands. "I believe you would protect Leandra with your life." He did not think she would measure up against a Sword Master, but he did not want to offend her further.

"Lady Leandra."

Theran felt heat rise to his cheeks. "Yes, that's what I meant. Lady Leandra."

"Then come in and act like the gentleman of the court you supposedly are." She stepped out of his path and allowed him inside.

The whole place was lit with a few candles and some light from the cracks in the curtained windows.

A shadow in the corner shifted and Theran stepped forward. "Lady Leandra?"

"They know we're here to spy on them. I wondered when you'd show up. Did not you get my message?" Her words came out in a fast blur, and she threw her arms around him. "I was so terrified they had taken you prisoner."

Overwhelmed by her presence pressed against him, Theran breathed in her lavender scent and did not say anything for a moment. He allowed himself to put his hands on her arms, and then with a heavy sigh, he stepped back from her. He could see her profile, but not her eyes in the dim light. "I did not receive a message, but suddenly, everything felt wrong."

"But you checked the mantle on the fireplace?"

"No. I was writing messages to the King."

"In code?"

"Of course."

"How did you know to come?"

"Like I said, something felt wrong. I knew I had to protect you, and that I needed to be with you. I went to follow you and hunt, but the stable girl told me to meet you here."

"You got one of my messages, at least." She pressed into him again, and he fought the urge to let his arms fall around her, to hold her close, to kiss her brow. He did not, barely remembering the goose herder's presence in the hut with them.

"And, like an idiot, he put his horse in my stables," the goose girl interrupted them. "And someone must have seen him, because they're here."

Theran pushed Leandra away again, hating the need to do so, and he went to peer out of a crack in the curtained window.

Five men on horseback rode up to the goose girl's property. Lord Torren led them, and the four others circled around him, looking eager to use their weapons. With a short conversation, they reached some decision. Four of them rode up to the gate, while one went to the stables.

Theran shook his head. "Now, what do we do?"

"Let me take care of it. You two, hide under my bed. I'm sure you'll find it a mite cozy." She winked at Leandra and pointed at her room. "Now, before I open the door."

Theran's heart raced as Leandra's warm hand gripped his wrist, pulling him urgently into the room. The floorboards creaked beneath their feet, each sound amplified by the tension in the air. He couldn't imagine how the goose girl would fend off the five men, but Leandra was his first responsibility. The scent of lavender from her hair wafted around him as she led him forward, momentarily distracting him from the danger.

When Leandra dropped to her knees and crawled under the bed, Theran's protective instincts warred with his need to assess the situation. He peered back through the doorway, muscles taut and ready for action. In the edge of his vision, he saw the goose girl open the door, her movements surprisingly calm given the circumstances.

The first word out of her mouth was a whisper, barely audible over Theran's pounding heartbeat. "Guard."

The geese outside erupted into a frenzy of squawking and honking, their wings beating against the air. Men's voices rose in surprise and anger, shouting indistinctly. Despite the danger, Theran felt a smile tug at his lips. It seemed the goose girl did know what she was doing after all. But a chill ran down his spine as he wondered how long she could really hold them off.

"Get under the bed, Theran," Leandra hissed from below, her voice tight with urgency.

Swallowing his pride, Theran dropped to his hands and knees. The rough wooden floor scraped against his palms as he lowered himself. His eyes, adjusting to the gloom, found Leandra's face peeking out from an opening in the floor. Understanding dawned on him – they would be under the bed, but also in a crawl space beneath the house.

He shimmied under the bed, the musty scent of old wood and earth filling his nose. As Leandra moved aside, he lowered himself into the crawl space. It was a tight fit, barely enough room for them to move. The earthen floor was cool and slightly damp against his clothing. When they closed the floor above them, darkness enveloped them like a thick blanket. Theran held his breath, hoping their ruse would work, but doubt gnawed at him.

In the oppressive darkness, Leandra pressed herself against his shoulder. Her warmth seeped through his clothing, and her whispered words sent a shiver down his spine that had nothing to do with fear. "Please, Theran, stuff your pride away and hold me for a while. I promise I won't take advantage of you right now."

Before he could stop himself, a teasing reply slipped out, his voice husky in the confined space. "Later, though, you will?"

Her soft snicker, so close to his ear, made his pulse quicken. "Maybe."

Theran opened his arms, his body moving of its own accord. As Leandra crawled toward him, he embraced her gently, acutely aware of every point of contact between them. He was grateful for the few inches of space she maintained – this was challenging enough without further temptation. The scent of her hair, a mix of lavender and something uniquely Leandra, filled his senses as she pressed her head into his shoulder.

Almost unconsciously, he dropped his lips to her hair, allowing himself one brief moment of tenderness before reality reasserted itself. He shouldn't think of her that way. He couldn't. The danger outside, the inappropriateness of any relationship, his duty – all of it crashed back into his mind.

"Relax," Leandra whispered, her breath warm against his neck.

Theran tried to obey, but his body remained tense, every muscle ready for action. Above them, muffled shouts and the angry honking of geese continued, a constant reminder of the peril they faced. Yet here, in the darkness, with Leandra in his arms, Theran found himself caught between fear and an unexpected sense of rightness. It was as if, despite everything, this was exactly where he was meant to be.

Above them, they heard the squawking and shouting quiet down.

"About time you mastered your animal's behavior! Stand back and let me inside, girl." It was Lord Torren's voice, and he sounded angry.

The goose girl's light footsteps retreated to the side of the house by the stove. "What's the matter, Lord Torren?"

"My daughter and her guard have gone missing. His horse is in your stables. Do you have an explanation of this?"

"I found the horse wandering in the field nearby, brought it into my stable, and planned to send it back to the mansion as soon as I had fed my geese their evening meal."

"I'm supposed to believe that lie?!" Lord Torren shouted. His heavy feet approached the stove area.

"Please, check my house, if you do not trust me, Lord Torren." The goose girl's voice was steady.

"I will. It should be my property anyway. I'm not sure how it ended up being yours." He stomped one foot.

They couldn't hear any kind of response. Theran could feel Leandra tense beside him.

After a long pause, Lord Torren's heavy steps crossed the room to the door. "Hedgewater, get in here and search this house."

Another set of footsteps shuffled over their heads, as a man in boots, presumably Hedgewater, wandered around the small space, entered the bedroom, and knelt down by the bed.

Theran stopped breathing, sure the man would notice scuff marks on the floor, the edge of the door to the crawl space, but after a few moments, the man stood again.

"There's no one here, Lord Torren, and no one in the barn either. She might be telling the truth."

Lord Torren's heavy footsteps crossed the room to the stove again. "Girl, if I find out you've lied to me, you'll join the servants in the house."

"I'm a free woman, Lord."

"Only as long as I allow it, remember that."

"I will remember, Lord Torren." Giselle's voice was steady, but there was an edge to it now. It was not fear, but anger.

But apparently, Lord Torren did not hear it, because he stomped out of the house and slammed the door. They could hear him shouting something muffled outside at his men, and then nothing.

Theran relaxed. He kissed Leandra's head again, and before he could draw back, she squeezed him gently. "Let's do this again under different circumstances, Theran."

His chest tightened. "I… I will consider it."

Light footsteps crossed the room, and the bed was pulled back from over the crawl space door, which opened shortly to reveal Giselle.

"All right, they're gone, and we need a plan, so stop canoodling and get up here."

Theran's heart raced as he emerged from the cramped crawl space, his eyes adjusting to the dim light of the goose herder's tiny home. The air was thick with the scent of damp earth and old wood, mingling with the faint aroma of lavender that clung to Leandra. He helped her up, careful not to let his touch linger too long on her hand.

"We can't stay here long," Theran murmured, his voice low and tense. He glanced at Leandra, noting the way her brow furrowed with worry. The urge to comfort her, to pull her close, was almost overwhelming. But he resisted, acutely aware of their precarious situation.

Giselle busied herself at the cookstove, its iron surface radiating a meager warmth. "They'll be back," she said matter-of-factly, stirring something in a dented pot. "Lord Torren isn't one to give up easily."

Theran nodded grimly, moving to peer through a gap in the curtained window. The world outside was a tapestry of deepening shadows, each one potentially concealing a threat. "We need a plan," he said, turning back to face Leandra and Giselle. "Something to throw them off our trail completely."

Leandra stepped closer, and Theran felt his breath catch. Even disheveled, she was breathtaking. "What if we split up?" she suggested, her voice barely above a whisper.

The thought of separating from her sent a jolt of fear through Theran's chest. "No," he said, perhaps too forcefully. Softening his tone, he added, "It's too dangerous. We stay together. Whatever happens," Theran whispered, leaning close to her, "I'll protect you. I swear it."

He felt, rather than saw, her nod. In that moment, surrounded by danger and uncertainty, Theran realized with startling clarity that he could not stop his growing feelings for her, not matter how hard he fought them. But for now, that realization would have to wait. Their survival depended on staying alert, staying hidden, and somehow finding a way out of this perilous situation.

Chapter 58: Plans

Theran's heart raced as he crouched in the shadows of the stable, the scent of hay and horse sweat thick in the air. As far as plans went, this was far from his best, but time pressed down on them. The Sword Guards from Skycliff hadn't arrived, and the search parties hunting for him and Leandra had started harassing villagers and Giselle alike. Their hastily concocted scheme to free the prisoners and servants while trapping the Red House purveyors inside felt fragile, a gossamer thread of hope in the face of overwhelming odds.

The setting sun painted the sky in hues of crimson and gold, a stark contrast to the growing darkness of their situation. Theran's gaze flicked to Leandra, perched in the loft above. Even in the dim light, her determination shone through, igniting a mix of admiration and fear in his chest.

"Has the message been delivered?" Leandra's whisper carried down to them, taut with anticipation.

Giselle nodded, her face set in grim lines. "Yes, I believe so. The timing is right. Most of the nobles are abed, tired from their dinner and carousing." She gripped her staff, the wood creaking under her fingers. "The guards have been attended to, and those still at full strength won't expect what's coming." The thud of her staff against the earth punctuated her words. "It's high time the nobles had a reckoning."

Theran's mind raced through the plan again. The sleeping draught in the nobles' food and wine should incapacitate most of their opponents, but the remaining guards posed a significant threat. He flexed his sword hand, feeling the familiar weight of responsibility settle on his shoulders.

The stable girl's soft voice broke through his thoughts. "I don't want the horses hurt, but I want the prisoners set free."

"You and I will lead the horses and the prisoners to the chapel in town," Giselle assured her. "It's not without risk, but if they all supped well tonight, and Theran is as good with a sword as he says he is, we'll manage."

Theran bit back a retort at Giselle's barbed comment about his skills. Now wasn't the time for pride. His gaze drifted to Leandra as she climbed down from the hayloft, the long knife at her belt catching the fading light. A knot formed in his stomach. He longed to keep her safe, away from the impending chaos, but her stubborn insistence matched the fire in her eyes. He knew arguing would be futile.

As darkness fell, the manor blazed with candlelight, a beacon of decadence amidst the encroaching night. Theran's senses sharpened, hyper-aware of every rustle of hay, every nickering horse. The wait stretched on, each moment an eternity of anticipation and dread.

Finally, a figure emerged from the kitchen door, a maid peering cautiously before hurrying towards them. "They ate the full meal including their dessert and their wine." She grinned maliciously. "Several guards ate all we gave them, as well, but five abstained from the feast because they ate earlier in the evening to remain fresh for guard duty."

"How long until the sleeping potion takes effect?" he asked, his voice low and urgent.

"The cook says moonrise," she answered.

It felt both too soon and an eternity away. As they waited, Theran tried to pray, but his thoughts scattered like leaves in the wind. When Leandra leaned into him for comfort, he stiffened reflexively, immediately regretting it as she withdrew, hurt flashing across her face. Words failed him, the gulf between them widening again.

When the moon finally climbed high above the horizon, Theran drew his sword, the familiar weight a cold comfort in his hand. The blue glow of the blade seemed to pulse with his racing heartbeat. He moved to leave the stable, but Leandra's touch on his arm stopped him. He turned to see her holding out hands to Giselle and the stable girl, a gesture of unity that stirred something deep within him.

"Good luck and blessings be on you," Leandra murmured, her voice steady despite the danger ahead.

As they echoed the sentiment, Leandra faced him, chin lifted in defiance. "You're not keeping me out of the action."

Theran saw the resolve etched in every line of her face. Arguing would only waste precious time. He held out his hand, a peace offering, an acknowledgment of her strength. When she didn't take it, the rejection stung, but he pushed the feeling aside. There were more important battles ahead.

They crept towards the mansion, the cool night air carrying the scent of damp earth. As they neared, a guard in polished Torren family colors rounded the corner. Theran's muscles tensed, ready for action. He touched Leandra's arm, a silent warning, but before he could formulate a plan, she was off, sprinting across the leaf-strewn lawn.

Panic and admiration warred within him as he watched her move, swift and sure. The guard's dismissal of her as a threat was his undoing. As Theran charged forward, sword raised, Leandra struck, her knife flashing in the moonlight as she sliced at the guard's legs.

The ensuing fight was a blur of motion and moonlight. Theran's sword sang through the air, meeting the guard's blade with a resounding clang. For a moment, victory seemed assured as the guard dropped to his knees.

"Please, mercy."

Theran dropped his guard, and the guard tackled him with a knife in his hand.

Pain exploded in Theran's arm as the guard's hidden knife found its mark. They grappled, the world narrowing to the desperate struggle for control. In that moment of tunnel vision, they both had forgotten about Leandra – a mistake the guard paid for dearly.

Her knife plunged into the man's lower back, and Theran felt the fight drain out of his opponent. As he shoved the limp form aside and scrambled to his feet, a new appreciation for Leandra bloomed in his chest. She was more than intelligence and beauty; she was strength and boldness.

Her gentle touch on his injured arm sent a different kind of warmth through him. "Are you all right?" she asked, tearing a strip from her skirt to bandage the wound. "We should bind that."

As she worked, Theran marveled at the layers of her character, each new facet only deepening his love. But their moment of connection shattered as a cry pierced the night.

"Treachery!"

The shout echoed, first outside, then reverberating within the mansion's walls. Chaos erupted around them, the grand doors bursting open to spill light and four angry guards onto the lawn. Theran pulled Leandra close, his body tensed to shield her from whatever came next.

"Look," he whispered, gesturing towards the side of the mansion.

In the shadows near the servants' entrance, figures moved with purpose – the prisoners, slipping away while their tormentors slept or focused on the distraction Theran and Leandra provided. Perhaps their desperate plan wasn't so ill-conceived after all.

As they faced the oncoming guards, Theran tightened his grip on his sword. Whatever happened next, he knew one thing with absolute certainty: he would protect Leandra with his last breath.

The four guards fanned out, moonlight glinting off their drawn swords. Theran's arm throbbed where the knife had caught him, but he pushed the pain aside, positioning himself slightly in front of Leandra. Her steady presence at his back was both comforting and concerning – he admired her bravery but feared for her safety.

"Take the two on the left," Leandra whispered, her breath warm against his ear. "I'll handle the others."

Before Theran could protest, she darted to the right, her long knife flashing in the moonlight. He had no choice but to engage the guards before him, his sword of power humming with blue energy as he parried the first blow.

The clash of steel rang out in the night air as Theran fended off his opponents. He caught glimpses of Leandra weaving and dodging, her smaller blade a disadvantage in reach but allowing for quicker, more precise strikes. Pride and fear warred in his chest as he watched her hold her own.

Theran's sword sang through the air, meeting one guard's blade with a resounding clang while he sidestepped the other's thrust. He used their size against them, staying light on his feet and forcing them to stumble over each other. A well-timed feint allowed him to catch one guard across the thigh, sending him stumbling back with a cry of pain.

Meanwhile, Leandra had maneuvered herself between her two opponents, using their bulk to obstruct each other. As one guard lunged, she ducked, causing him to nearly impale his comrade. Taking advantage of their confusion, she slashed at the back of one guard's knee, temporarily taking him out of the fight.

But their advantage was short-lived. The guards, though surprised by their skill, were well-trained and armored. Fatigue began to set in, Theran's wounded arm growing heavier with each parry. He switched to his left hand and prayed the power in his blade would turn the tide of the battle, but despite the blade's glow, it remained a regular weapon for this fight.

Leandra's breath came in short gasps, a sheen of sweat visible on her brow as she narrowly avoided a sword swipe that would have opened her from shoulder to hip.

They found themselves backed against the manor wall, the three remaining guards closing in. Theran's mind raced, searching for a way out. He met Leandra's eyes, saw the same determination and fear reflected there that he felt in his own heart.

"Together?" he asked, a lifetime of meaning in that single word.

Leandra nodded, a grim smile touching her lips. "Together."

As one, they surged forward, a desperate gambit to break through the guards' line. Theran's sword flared brilliantly, momentarily blinding their opponents. Leandra used the distraction to dart low, aiming for vulnerable spots beneath armor.

For a heartbeat, it seemed their plan might work. But then a guard's lucky swing caught Theran's sword arm, nearly causing him to drop his weapon. Another guard's armored fist struck Leandra's shoulder, sending her stumbling. They fell back, breathing heavily, as the guards pressed their advantage.

Just as hope began to fade, a battle cry split the air. Giselle charged from the shadows, her staff a blur of motion. She caught the nearest guard in the back of the knees, sending him sprawling. Before the others could react, she had positioned herself between them and the younger pair, her staff held horizontally before her like a barrier.

"Enough of this foolishness," Giselle spat, her eyes flashing with a fire that belied her years. "You boys want a real fight?"

The sudden turn of events gave Theran and Leandra a moment to catch their breath. They exchanged a look of surprise and renewed determination. With Giselle evening the odds, the tide of battle had shifted.

Giselle's staff was a whirlwind, striking with precision born of years of experience. She fought with a fluid grace that made the guards' swordplay look clumsy in comparison. Theran and Leandra rallied, flanking Giselle and pressing their attack with renewed vigor.

The guards, caught off guard by this three-pronged assault, began to falter. One went down to a sweep of Giselle's staff, another to a well-placed thrust from Theran's glowing blade. The last, seeing his comrades fall, threw down his sword in surrender.

As the clash of battle faded, replaced by the heavy breathing of the combatants, Theran looked to Leandra. Despite the dirt and sweat streaking her face, her eyes shone with triumph. He felt a smile tugging at his own lips, relief and admiration washing over him in equal measure.

Giselle leaned on her staff, surveying the fallen guards with a satisfied nod. "Not bad for a night's work," she said, a hint of amusement in her voice. "Now, let's see about those prisoners, shall we? Our night's far from over."

As they moved towards the servant's entrance, Theran caught Leandra's hand in his own. She squeezed it tight, a silent acknowledgment of what they'd just been through – and what still lay ahead. Whatever challenges the rest of the night might bring, Theran knew they would face them as they had faced these guards: together.

Chapter 59: Chains Unlocked

Theran's heart raced as he and Leandra navigated through the chaos towards the back service entrance of the kitchens. His arm throbbed where the guard's knife had caught him, a constant reminder of the danger they faced. Every shadow seemed to hold a potential threat, the memory of their recent battle with the guards still fresh in his mind.

They reached the door, and Leandra gave the special knock. Theran held his breath, acutely aware of how exposed they were. His hand tightened on his sword hilt, the blue glow of the blade barely contained beneath his cloak. Relief washed over him as the master cook's face appeared, her appearance disheveled and tense. Behind her, Theran spotted three kitchen maids armed with heavy pans and rollers, their determined expressions a stark contrast to their usual demeanor. The head chef's large knife, tucked into her apron, glinted ominously in the dim light.

"We won't have much time before the nobles wake," she told them as they entered the kitchen. "Lady Leandra, you should head to safety now." She touched Lady Leandra's arm and pointed to the cellar door off the kitchen.

"No, I will help get the last children out. I know the upper rooms better than anyone else left," Leandra declared, the same fire in her eyes that Theran had seen during their fight with the guards. He wanted to argue, to insist she save herself, but he swallowed his protests. He knew that look – there would be no swaying her.

As they prepared by the mansion door, Theran's mind raced through potential scenarios, each more dire than the last. The weight of responsibility pressed down on him. He had to protect Leandra, complete the mission, and somehow get everyone out safely. The image of Leandra deftly avoiding the guards' swords flashed through his mind, both comforting and concerning him.

Leandra's voice cut through his thoughts as she assigned tasks. "I'll take my parents' rooms," she said, her tone leaving no room for argument. "Theran, if you could take the main guest chamber across from theirs?"

"I will," he agreed, though every instinct screamed at him to stay by her side. After seeing her fight, he knew she could handle herself, but the thought of separation still twisted his gut.

As they ascended the servant's stairs, Theran's senses were on high alert. He wanted nothing more than to follow Leandra, to guard her back, but he knew his duty. With a heavy heart, he watched her disappear down the hallway before turning towards the guest chambers.

The silence in the upper floor was unnerving, broken only by the occasional snore from those under the influence of the sleeping draught. Theran moved silently, aware that not all guards might have partaken in the drugged wine.

Throwing open the main room door, Theran's heart skipped a beat at the sound of a frightened whimper from the inner room. What he found there made his blood run cold – a young boy, tied to the bed, unclothed and gagged, but also trapped under the sleeping form of one of the nobles. Fury and horror warred within him, but he forced himself to remain calm for the child's sake.

"We're going to get you free of here," he said, his voice steady despite the rage boiling inside him. As he worked to free the boy, his mind raced with the implications of what he was seeing. How deep did this depravity go?

"My sister's in the closet," the boy said raggedly through his tears.

"I'll get her, you find clothes for both of you."

The boy shook his head. "I'll get her, she'll be terrified of you."

"I understand," Theran said, his heart breaking for these children. He gathered two loose robes from the side of the room.

The boy opened the closet and a young girl, dressed in a shift, threw herself into his arms. "Charles, you're free." She saw Theran and shrieked.

"Now, it is all right, he's here to help us," Charles soothed his sister.

After they had thrown on clothes, Theran led the two of them out into the hallway, his sword at the ready, prepared for any guards that might appear.

"Take the servant's stairs here, and the head cook will send you through the cellar door that will get you free from here." Theran pointed to where they needed to go, and they needed no further prompting, running down the stairs.

After ensuring the children were on their way to safety, Theran's thoughts immediately turned to Leandra. Fear gripped him as he made his way to her parents' bedroom. What if something had happened to her? What if they'd been discovered? The memory of her skill in battle warred with his protective instincts.

The sight that greeted him as he entered the room nearly broke his heart. Leandra, weeping as she struggled with a heavy chain binding a young woman to the bed. Leandra's parents snored under the bedclothes, thankfully unaware of what was going on around them. The girl's tears and Leandra's desperation clawed at Theran's chest.

He went to Leandra and put his arm around her, feeling her lean into him slightly. "Leandra, we're going to figure this out a different way. We can't break the chain with what we have."

"We can't leave her here." Leandra gripped the girl's hand. "I promised I wouldn't leave her here." The determination in her voice reminded Theran of her fierce courage during their earlier fight.

"We can break the bedpost." Theran grabbed hold of the bedpost and freed it from the mechanism holding it to the bed frame. The post came free and the bed frame thudded onto the ground in that corner. Despite the commotion, Leandra's parents continued to sleep deeply.

Leandra slid the chain down the length of the bedpost and handed the chain to the girl. "As soon as we can, we will get you out of this monstrous thing." She wrapped a robe around the girl's shoulders, and the girl pressed her hand to her heart and half-bowed to Leandra, then Theran.

Theran stood and offered his hand. The girl did not take it, but Leandra did, her grip firm and reassuring. Then she helped the girl to her feet.

"Let's get out of here." Theran pushed open the outer door, his sword at the ready, prepared for any guards that might have been alerted by the noise. He stopped abruptly as he heard something stir behind him, his body tensing for another fight.

Chapter 60: The Challenge

Leandra's heart hammered in her chest as she guided the trembling girl towards the bedroom door. Behind her, the soft snores of her parents had faltered. She froze, her hand on the doorknob, as a grunt and the rustle of bedsheets pierced the tense silence.

"Quickly," she whispered to Theran, who nodded grimly. They had to move now.

As they stepped onto the landing, Leandra heard her father's sleep-addled voice. "What's going on? Who's there?"

She pulled the door shut behind them, buying precious seconds. The landing stretched before them, mercifully less crowded than she'd feared. Only three nobles stood in various states of confusion, having emerged from their rooms at the commotion. It wasn't a clear path, but it wasn't impossible either.

Leandra's mind raced. They needed to get the girl to safety, but they also needed to prevent her father from raising the alarm. An idea crystallized, wild and desperate.

This was it. No more running, no more hiding.

"Father!" She called out, her voice stronger than she felt. "If you have any honor left, I challenge you to a duel. One which will determine whether you can keep us here or free us forever."

A muffled curse sounded from behind the door, followed by heavy footsteps. Leandra's pulse quickened as the nobles on the landing stirred with interest.

The door flew open, revealing her father, disheveled and red-faced with rage. "Leandra! You ungrateful chit!" His eyes narrowed as he took in the scene – Theran with his sword drawn, the terrified girl huddled close to Leandra. "I am not such a fool to fight your guard."

The insult stung, but Leandra pushed past it. She'd expected this. "I challenge you," she clarified, each word precise and measured. "With my skills against yours. Sword and knife, no other weapons, no poison, no tricks. Will that be easy enough for a dishonorable old man like you?"

She felt the girl trembling beside her and gave her hand a reassuring squeeze. "We will get free of these monsters," Leandra whispered, willing herself to believe it. "I promise."

"The word of a fool is worth nothing," her father stated.

Something snapped inside her. Rage, hot and clarifying, surged through her veins.

"Are you so afraid of me, Father," she shouted, making sure everyone on the landing could hear, "that you can't accept my challenge to a duel? Am I so frightening to you that you can't face me at sword point alone? I'm sure your friends will be impressed by your cowardice."

Leandra's hands trembled, but she clenched them into fists, refusing to show weakness. The nobles on the landing shifted uneasily, creating a narrow path. Whether out of respect for the challenge or fear of Theran's drawn sword, she couldn't tell.

One of the nobles, a portly man with thinning hair, cleared his throat. "What's this? A challenge from Leandra, a mere girl against her father? Or is it a challenge from her sword guard?"

"I alone will fight my father for our freedom," Leandra declared, her voice ringing out clear and true despite the fear clawing at her throat. "If he can't best me, then he can keep me here."

She caught Theran's worried gaze. His concern was touching, but she shook her head slightly. This was her fight.

"Leandra, please," Theran whispered, "allow me this fight."

"No," she hissed back. Then, louder, knowing her words would carry: "He'll never accept a challenge from you. He's far too much a coward to face a grown man."

Her father's growl vibrated through the air. "Fine! I accept."

Leandra's stomach lurched, a dizzying mix of terror and elation. She'd done it. Now came the hard part.

As she laid out the terms, her mind raced ahead to potential pitfalls and escape routes. When her father demanded Theran stand unarmed between his men, Leandra's throat tightened. Theran reached out to touch her shoulder and gave it a squeeze. Whatever happened, she wasn't truly alone.

"The fight should take place at dawn," she declared, cutting off Theran's suggestion of noon. No more delays. No more chances for her father to weasel out of this.

When they had reassurances of safe passage to the dueling ring, Leandra straightened her spine, chin held high. "I have something to retrieve from my room."

Her father's dismissive shrug only strengthened her resolve. The nobles on the landing pressed against the walls, creating a narrow but passable corridor. Their eyes bore into her as she passed, a mix of curiosity, disdain, and something darker that made her skin crawl.

As she moved towards her suite, Leandra's mind raced through sword forms and fighting stances. Fear gnawed at her insides, but hope burned brighter. She was ready to face her father, ready to fight for her freedom and the freedom of all those he had hurt. Whatever the outcome, she would meet it with her head held high.

Leandra strode purposefully towards her suite, her heart racing but her steps steady. As she pushed open the door, she caught Theran's questioning glance. A small, secretive smile tugged at the corners of her lips.

Inside her room, Leandra moved swiftly to her narrow, but lengthy traveling chest. With practiced ease, she slid aside a false panel at the back, revealing a hidden compartment. Theran's sharp intake of breath behind her was almost audible.

"Leandra, what—" he began, but she was already reaching inside.

First, she withdrew a slender rapier, its hilt glinting in the dim light. The blade sang softly as she unsheathed it, testing its familiar weight in her hand. Next came a short knife, wickedly sharp and perfectly balanced. Finally, she pulled out a piece of light armor – a flexible leather vest reinforced with subtle metal plates.

Turning to face Theran, Leandra saw his eyes widen in surprise. "You never mentioned these," he said, a mix of admiration and concern in his voice.

"A lady must have her secrets," Leandra replied, efficiently strapping on the armor beneath her outer garments. The familiar weight of it against her chest was oddly comforting. "Father always underestimated me. It's time he learned his mistake."

As she secured the rapier and knife to her belt, Leandra felt a calm settling over her. She handed the long knife she had borrowed from Giselle for her fight with the guards to the trembling girl, and saw the girl's face tighten with resolve. The fear was still there, for all of them. Leandra felt it as a cold knot in her stomach, but it was overshadowed by a fierce determination. She met Theran's gaze, chin lifted defiantly.

"Ready?" he asked softly.

Leandra nodded, squaring her shoulders. "Ready."

With that, she strode out of her room, prepared to face whatever awaited her in the courtyard below. The weapons at her side were a tangible reminder of her resolve. Win or lose, she would fight with everything she had.

Chapter 61: Dan's Struggle

Dan had struggled to keep his horse's pace to an even combination of walking and galloping as they crossed from one county seat of Septily seat to another, riding hard for the Lake District. King Xandros had supplied them with all they needed to be a show of force against a group of surly nobles, and possibly some of the Red Hand and the Drinaii.

However, the amount of people in their company numbered over fifty, and that many people meant they spent an inordinate amount of time breaking camp, taking breaks, and reiterating orders with everyone in the command structure, with Shepherd Jordan and Watch Guard Quinn at their head, although that put Quinn over some of the Sword Guards of the Triune Halls and they did not seem completely happy about it from the looks they cast on Quinn when he road by and from the small murmurings he'd heard in the morning of their second day on the road.

As he took point with Quinn in the early light of dawn, not willing to ride as a rear guard when they neared his parents' estate in the Lake District, he noticed his mentor had become even more taciturn than usual.

This suited Dan fine, given that he was not interested in talking about anything, either. He wanted to get there, and if he was allowed, he would have ridden ahead.

The rest of the company strung out behind them, with Alex, Farrald, and Therese at the back. He thought it likely Alex had been sent back for his protection. He wondered if Alex knew, and then he shook his head. Of course, Alex knew. Alex was not stupid, but he'd gotten better at keeping his attitudes to himself.

Worries about Alex did not keep Dan's thoughts occupied for long. The message King Xandros had received from Sword Guard Theran seemed to show his parents were hosting the dominant group of the Red Hand at their Lake House for an extended party, and somehow Leandra had gotten mixed up in spying on them with Sword Guard Theran. Dan did not know what to believe about this sister's decision to team up with the Theran and work against their parents. In equal parts, he felt pride at his sister for standing up to them and doing something about the problem, shame for his own lack of action against them and his unwillingness to see how awful they were for so long, and fear that Leandra had gotten herself and Theran into a deadly situation.

As they neared the small chapel by the lake, Dan leaned forward in his saddle. "There's something going on," he said to Quinn.

Quinn clenched his jaw, then waved his hand. "Go ahead. Don't stir up trouble. Remember, the Watch Guard observes first."

"Yes, we Watch and Observe." Dan tried to agree, but in his heart, he wanted to do more than observe. He urged his horse into a gallop, then slowed to a walk as they met the outskirts of the crowd by the chapel. As he tried to hail someone, a flock of geese landed in his path and began attacking his horse, honking loudly, flapping their wings, and pecking at his horse's legs.

He brought his horse to a standstill and backed up, hoping the mare wouldn't lash out with her hooves and unseat him in her attempt to get away from the noisome birds.

Most of the crowd of people turned to face him, many frightened, some angry, and some amused by the way the geese were effectively blocking him from coming any closer.

He thought of dismounting, but one goose, a dominant male, took aggressive steps toward him and leapt up to peck at his boot. He backed up the horse again.

"Who comes?" A strong female voice shouted from within the crowd.

The people parted for the speaker, and the geese calmed as she approached.

Dan's jaw dropped when he realized who it was. "Giselle?"

She shaded her face with one hand and peered up at him. "It is about time you got here, with the King's Sword Guards, officially, I hope."

"Yes." Dan glanced back at the company behind him. "We're a mix of Watch Guard, Sword Guards from the Triune Halls, and one Shepherd." He turned back to Giselle. "What's going on here?"

"Freedom, plain and simple."

"Where is my sister?"

Giselle's forehead pinched, and her face paled. "She and Theran went back into the mansion to free more slaves, and..."

Dan did not hear the rest of what she said, as a roar of fear and anger filled his ears, muffling out the world around him.

CHAPTER 62: A Father-Daughter Fight

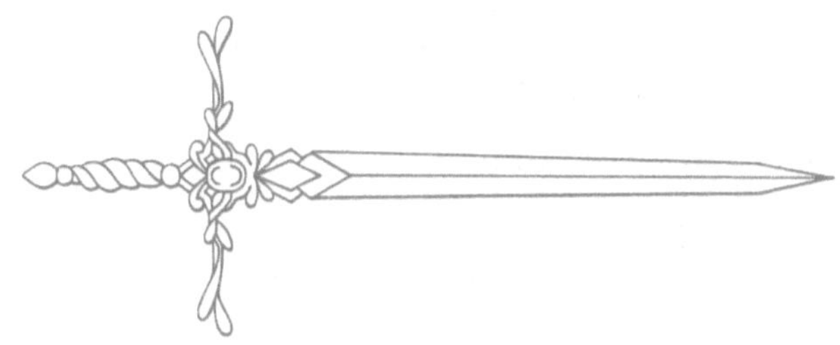

AT THE BOTTOM OF the manor stairs, a knot of noble women and men stared as Leandra, Theran, and the young woman they had rescued approached.

Two of them moved toward Theran, but he stopped and dropped his weapons before they could get too close. "Please keep these safe. They are worth more than you."

"You're a fool." One of them hissed, but as he grabbed for Theran's sword of power and the energy repulsed his hand.

The other tried yank at Theran's arm, but he flowed with the man's movement and stomped on his foot, causing the man to yelp and fall back. "At least I can walk on my own."

Leandra stood in a small open circle and lifted her chin. "I believe we have safe passage to the courtyard. Unless you are too terrified of us to allow us that."

The crowd parted with grumbles and mutterings, but they were allowed passage to the courtyard, where Leandra's father stood with his weapons belted to his waist.

Leandra glared at him and took up a ready stance on the opposite side of the courtyard. "Shall the stones be our guides as our ancestors used them?"

Theran had noticed the pattern of stones in the courtyard when they had first arrived, and had thought them to be merely decorative, but now he realized they were set in a circle, with a center line going through them, not for decoration, but for the purpose of dueling.

"I'm surprised you know our family history at all, Leandra, and where did you get those weapons?"

"Frightened now, father?" She taunted, leaving her blades sheathed.

Theran stood tense, behind her, the young girl close to him. The other nobles had taken up places around the circle, but two stood near him, without touching him.

Lord Torren paced at the far end of the courtyard, his face a mask of barely contained rage. The man's hand rested on the pommel of an ornate sword, its jeweled hilt glinting in the midday sun. Theran's stomach churned. How many innocents had suffered at the edge of that blade?

"Why is the Sword Guard free?" Lord Torren snarled at the men.

One of them put his hand on Theran's shoulder. Theran could see the man was nervous by the way he chewed the inside of his cheek. It was not the man he'd caused to stumble earlier, but a different one.

When Theran did not do anything to resist, the other of the pair gripped his shoulder.

Neither were holding on all that tight, but Theran did not resist.

It seemed to satisfy Lord Torren, and he said, "Are you certain you won't reconsider this foolishness, daughter? It's not too late to beg forgiveness."

Leandra's reply was sharp. "The only foolishness here is your continued belief that you can control me."

With a snarl, Lord Torren drew his sword. The assembled nobles cheered, already thirsting for violence. Theran's heart hammered in his chest as Leandra unsheathed her rapier, its slender blade catching the light.

Leandra's gaze swept the courtyard, finally landing on Theran. He tried to convey everything he couldn't say aloud in that single look – his pride, his fear, his unwavering support. She gave him a slight nod, the barest hint of a smile tugging at her lips.

"To first blood," she said, drawing her knife.

Across the circle, her father's eyes narrowed, but he agreed. "To first blood." And then, he charged at her, throwing all the rules of dueling aside in his rash attack.

Leandra's footwork was impeccable, each step measured and deliberate. She parried her father's first wild attack with ease, and riposting with an attack that fell only a breath from her father's forearm.

Theran's jaw clenched as he stood rigidly between two smirking nobles. The courtyard bustled with activity, a sea of silk and velvet as the aristocrats jockeyed for the best view of the duel. His fingers twitched, aching for the familiar grip of his sword.

With his blade of power a few feet away, propped against a weathered stone bench, Theran could feel its energy pulsing, calling out to him. The nobles couldn't touch it – the sword's power would see to that – but the separation still left him feeling vulnerable.

Theran's fingers curled into fists at his sides. Every instinct screamed at him to intervene, to place himself between Leandra and danger as he'd sworn to do. But this was her fight, her choice. He had to trust in her abilities, even as fear gnawed at his insides.

Lord Torren continued to attack aggressively, but after several parries, Leandra changed tactics. As her father's sword plunged toward her again, Leandra was already twisting gracefully to avoid the strike. Her rapier flashed out, quick as lightning, followed by an undercut with her long knife that sliced her father's sword arm.

Lord Torren stumbled back with a curse.

A drip of blood fell from the wound, but her father merely snarled and lunged at her again.

"First blood has been drawn!" Theran shouted.

Some of the nobles grumbled that he was right, but Lord Torren ignored them all and he struck at Leandra again.

Theran felt his stomach sink as the sword's edge neared her neck, but she ducked, parried, and kicked at her father's kneecap.

A fierce pride welled up in Theran's chest, mingled with a surge of hope. Leandra was more than holding her own; she was excelling. Her movements were fluid, each attack and parry flowing seamlessly into the next. She danced around her father's heavier blows, using her speed and agility to her advantage. She was fierce, determined, and formidable.

As sword met sword once more, the clash ringing out across the courtyard, Theran allowed himself a small smile. The outcome was far from certain, but one thing was clear: Leandra was no helpless noble's daughter in need of constant protection. She was a warrior in her own right.

As long as the nobles around him continued to behave with honor, they might make it out of this without injury, but as the nobles became more intensely interested in the potential for blood spilt and it seemed more and more apparent that Lord Torren would lose, he could see them begin to surge closer to the dueling circle.

Lord Torren began to noticeably tire from the onslaught of all the small wounds Leandra had given him, while she remained free of injury. He stumbled, and Leandra sliced his sword arm deeply, then danced backwards as he fell all his knees.

"Father, first blood, second, and more are mine. It is time to end this."

"No!" Lord Torren growled and then got to his feet again, glaring at her. "You tricked me."

Some nobles shook their heads in disgust. The two holding Theran let go of his shoulders.

"Those were the terms," one of them said. "She bested you fairly."

"We can't let them leave," Lord Torren said, his brow furrowing with anger.

Chapter 63: A Fight on Two Fronts

Dan's heart pounded as he charged toward the mansion, his dark blade thrumming in sync with his racing pulse. The courtyard came into view, a chaotic scene of struggling bodies and flashing steel.

His gaze locked onto two focal points amidst the mayhem. To one side, Sword Guard Theran was barely visible beneath a group of nobles, their fists raining down on him. On the other, a tight knot of men surrounded someone who Dan assumed was his sister.

With a roar, Dan urged his horse forward, scattering the outlying nobles. As he neared the center, he caught glimpses of Leandra through gaps in the crowd. To his shock, she was still on her feet, her rapier flashing as she fended off multiple attackers. Her skill was evident, but she was bleeding from several slashes.

"Leandra!" Dan shouted, swinging his obsidian blade in a wide arc. The nobles nearest him stumbled back, creating an opening.

Leandra's head snapped up at the sound of his voice. Relief flashed across her face, replaced by determination. She took advantage of the distraction, driving her rapier into one noble's shoulder.

Dan dismounted in one fluid motion, positioning himself back-to-back with his sister. "I didn't know you could fight like that," he said, parrying a strike from an enraged lord.

"There's a lot you don't know about me, brother," Leandra said, her voice tight with exertion.

Together, they began to push back against the mob. Dan's darker blade sang through the air, its power amplifying his strikes. Leandra moved with surprising grace, her lighter weapon darting in and out with deadly precision.

But the numbers were still against them. Dan caught sight of their father, Lord Torren, shouting orders from the edge of the fray.

A cry of pain drew their attention. Theran had managed to break free of his captors, but he was struggling to reach his sword, still held at bay by a ring of opponents.

Dan made a split-second decision. He charged towards Theran's sword. His blade cleared a path, nobles scrambling to avoid its lethal edge.

He scooped up Theran's weapon, feeling the unfamiliar weight of another blade of power in his hand. With a heave, he sent it spinning through the air towards its owner.

Theran caught it deftly and he joined the siblings, forming a triangle of flashing blades against the sea of enemies.

As the sounds of galloping hooves announced the arrival of the rest of Dan's company, the remaining nobles began to falter.

Lord Torren, seeing his advantage slipping away, charged back into the fray, as if to rally his men. When he saw Dan, he dropped his sword to his side. "Son? What have you done?" Lord Torren's voice cracked, his eyes widening as they fixed on Dan's shimmering sword of power.

Dan met his father's gaze, his voice cold despite the rage burning within him. "I am not your son any longer. I despise you and our family's name. From now on, I will have no last name, for I would rather be known as a bastard than as your son."

Thunder rumbled overhead, dark clouds coalescing as if summoned by Dan's fury. The air crackled with tension, mirroring the storm of emotions raging within him. As Dan raised his blade, Lord Torren stumbled backward, fumbling to bring his sword to a guard position before continuing his retreat.

Flashes of memory assaulted Dan's mind, each one stoking the flames of his anger:

His father's voice, sharp with disdain: "Pathetic! No son of mine should be so weak."

The sting of a backhand across his face, punishment for a perceived slight.

The dark blade in Dan's hand seemed to pulse with anticipation, as if thrilled at the prospect of vengeance. Its eagerness resonated with the fury and bitterness coursing through Dan's veins, amplifying his rage.

"Dan, you can't possibly mean that," his father pleaded, desperation creeping into his voice. "We're family. We're nobles. That means something."

Another memory surfaced: *Dan, bruised and bloody, locked in a closet for hours. His father's cold voice through the door: "Until you learn your place, you're no son of mine."*

"The only noble thing about you is your title, and you don't deserve it," Dan spat, his words dripping with venom. "None of these men do, for what they've done to countless innocents."

Another peal of thunder shook the air, Dan's sword shimmering in response. The heat of fury and the chill of bitter resentment warred within him, threatening to tear him apart. The dark blade sang to him, urging him to unleash his pain, to make his father suffer as he had suffered.

Lord Torren's face contorted, a mix of fear and indignation. "Dan, you don't understand. These people are slaves. It is what they were born to do, to serve us, to—"

"Take up your sword and fight me," Dan growled, cutting him off. *The words of his father from years past echoed in his mind: "A real man faces his challenges, boy. Pick up that sword and fight!"* Now, it was Dan demanding the same, the irony not lost on him.

Lightning struck Dan's sword, the blade seeming to absorb the energy. Power surged through Dan's body, fueling his rage. It felt like every injustice, every cruel word, every blow he'd endured was being channeled into this moment. The dark blade reveled in his pain, urging him to strike, to end it all in one swift motion.

"I said, fight me!" he roared, his voice barely recognizable, twisted by fury and the blade's influence.

"No, no, please." His father placed his sword on the ground, eyes darting over Dan's shoulder. "Have mercy. Think of your mother."

"I said, fight me!" he roared, his voice barely recognizable, twisted by fury and the blade's influence.

"No, no, please." His father placed his sword on the ground. "Have mercy. Think of your mother."

The mention of his mother sent another jolt of pain through Dan, but not in the way his father intended. A fresh wave of bitter memories crashed over him:

His mother's cold, disapproving stare. "You're an embarrassment to this family, Dan. Why can't you be the son we deserve?"

Her sharp tongue, cutting deeper than any physical blow. "Weak. Useless. You'll never amount to anything if you don't toughen up."

The way she'd turn a blind eye to his father's cruelty, sometimes even encouraging it. "He needs to learn, dear. Make sure the lesson sticks this time."

The dark blade pulsed eagerly, feeding on Dan's pain and resentment. It whispered seductively, urging him to unleash years of pent-up anger, to make both his parents pay for the torment they'd inflicted.

"Think of my mother?" Dan snarled, taking a menacing step forward. "The woman who stood by and watched as you beat me? Who added her own poison to every 'lesson' you taught?" His grip on the sword tightened, knuckles white with strain. "She's no better than you."

Lord Torren's face paled further, realizing his miscalculation. "Son, please... we only wanted what was best for you. To make you strong—"

"Strong?" Dan's laugh was harsh, bordering on hysterical. "You broke me, piece by piece, and called it strength." The storm above intensified, mirroring the tempest in Dan's soul. Lightning crackled around his blade, the weapon drinking in his turmoil and rage.

Dan stood at a crossroads, the weight of years of abuse and the seductive whisper of vengeance pulling him towards a point of no return. The dark blade sang to him, promising sweet release if he'd only give in to his darkest impulses.

Yet, somewhere deep inside, a small voice fought to be heard above the cacophony of pain and fury. It whispered of choices, of breaking cycles, of being better than those who had hurt him.

The storm raged around him, a fitting backdrop to the war within his heart. Dan trembled with the effort of restraint, his next move poised to shape not just his father's fate, but his own soul.

A flicker of eye movement from his father was all the warning Dan needed. His heart surged with a mix of betrayal and bitter vindication - of course his father would resort to such cowardice. Adrenaline flooded his system as he pivoted, his muscles coiled with tension.

The clash of steel rang out as Dan's blade met those of two nobles who had tried to strike from behind. The impact jarred his arms, but the dark blade seemed to drink in the violence, humming with eagerness. Fury exploded within Dan, a maelstrom of pain and rage that had festered for years. With a guttural roar, he countered with a wide strike. The stored power in his sword erupted, shattering one man's shield with a thunderous crack that echoed the storm above.

Lightning crackled down the blade as Dan faced his second attacker, his vision tunneling with focused rage. The man charged, desperation etched on his face. Dan's sword met him with a blinding flash of power, the dark energy singing through his veins with intoxicating strength. The noble fell instantly, and panic erupted in the crowd, their cries of fear a distant buzz in Dan's ears.

Waves of rage washed over Dan, a torrent of pain, anger, and bitterness echoing through his dark blade. Every insult, every blow, every moment of helplessness he'd ever endured crashed over him, demanding retribution. He raised the sword high, ready to unleash his fury on them all, his heart pounding with the intoxicating promise of vengeance.

"Dan, stop." Farrald's voice cut through the haze of anger like a knife through fog. "The power is to be used for good, not evil."

The words pierced Dan's consciousness, a lifeline in the stormy sea of his rage. Memories flooded back - their conversation on the road, his vision from the Lord, the command to see true justice done. The realization hit him like a physical blow: killing out of anger wasn't justice. It was vengeance. The very thing he despised in his father, he was about to become.

Regret, shame, and exhaustion swept over Dan in a dizzying wave. His arms felt leaden as he lowered his sword, the weight of his actions pressing down on him. With trembling hands, he drove the blade's point into the courtyard stones at his feet. The blade's power discharged into the earth with a sickening hiss, leaving a charred circle of cracked stones as the storm clouds overhead dissipated, mirroring the draining of his rage.

Dan looked up, his vision blurry with unshed tears. He met the shocked and fearful gazes of those around him, seeing in their eyes a reflection of the monster he'd nearly become. The courtyard fell silent, save for the fading rumble of thunder and the ragged sound of his own breathing. In that moment, the true weight of the power he wielded - and the responsibility that came with it - crashed down upon him with crushing force.

His legs gave way, and he crumpled to the ground, fingers releasing the sword as if it burned him. Shame flooded every fiber of his being, not just for what he had almost done, but for how close he had come to losing himself to the very darkness he sought to fight. Dan's body shook with silent sobs, the aftermath of his rage leaving him hollow and spent.

Chapter 64: A Prayer for Peace

Jordan, who had been riding near the rear of the group, reached the courtyard in time to see Dan's face crumple inward in a rictus of shame. The display of power had made him think he was riding to battle a Dark Sorceress, but instead, it was Dan's dark blade which shimmered with power and Dan who stood with slumped shoulders over the body of one of the nobles. The acrid smell of smoke and something darker—blood, perhaps—hung heavy in the air.

The dark blade lay at Dan's feet, its obsidian surface still shimmering with an otherworldly power. Around Dan, a sea of faces—nobles, Sword Guards, and bystanders alike—all wore expressions of shock and fear.

Jordan's heart clenched. This was not the outcome he had prayed for.

As he dismounted, his legs unsteady after the long ride, Jordan pushed his way through the crowd. The press of bodies around him was suffocating, whispers and fearful murmurs creating a cacophony. But his focus remained on Dan, the young man he had watched grow from a hesitant noble to... this.

Farrald's voice cut through the chaos, a soothing melody that seemed to calm the very air around them. "Our Lord reigns. Forever, in power and love, he reigns."

Jordan felt a surge of gratitude for the young man's steadfast faith. As he approached Dan, who had now sunk to his knees, Jordan could feel the conflicting energies emanating from the dark blade. It was unlike anything he had encountered in his years as a Shepherd—neither purely of the Light, nor entirely of the darkness. The complexity of it did not fit with what he knew of the sources of power.

Kneeling beside Dan on the cracked, blood-stained stones, Jordan held out his hands. He could feel the eyes of the crowd upon them, a weight of expectation and fear pressing down. But in this moment, there was only Dan, a soul in need of guidance.

"Dan," Jordan said softly, his voice barely carrying over the murmurs of the crowd, "you do not have to carry your anger, or your pain. You can give it to the Lord of Light. He will forgive you."

Dan's response was barely a whisper, his voice choked with shame. "I don't deserve mercy."

Jordan's heart ached at the raw pain in those words. How many times had he heard similar sentiments in his years of service? How many times had he wrestled with that very thought himself?

"No one deserves mercy," Jordan replied, the truth of it resonating in his bones, "but the Lord of Light grants it anyway."

Dan's heavy sigh seemed to carry the weight of the world. Jordan glanced at Farrald, seeing his own concern mirrored in the young man's eyes. "Can we pray for you, Dan?" Jordan asked, knowing that sometimes, the simple act of allowing others to intercede could be the first step towards healing.

When Dan nodded, Jordan placed a hand on his shoulder, feeling the tremors that ran through the young man's body. Farrald mirrored the action on Dan's other side, and together, they began the ancient prayer cycle for forgiveness.

As Jordan spoke the familiar words, he closed his eyes, imagining the Lord of Light as he often did in his private meditations—a source of pure, radiant energy, vast beyond comprehension yet intimately present. The words of the prayer, though simple, carried a power that Jordan had witnessed transform lives time and time again.

"Lord of Light," Jordan began, his voice steady despite the turmoil in his heart.

"...have mercy," Farrald responded, his tone carrying a calmness that belied his years.

As they continued through the prayer, Jordan felt a shift in the atmosphere. The oppressive fear that had blanketed the courtyard began to lift, replaced by a tentative hope. Even the crowd seemed to quiet, and he hoped those around them joined the prayer in their hearts.

When they finished with a collective "Amen," Jordan opened his eyes to find Dan weeping openly. The sight of those tears brought a lump to Jordan's throat. He suspected it had been a long time since the young man had been able to show his full emotions.

As Dan slowly rose to his feet, accepting Farrald's offered arm and returning the embrace, Jordan felt a surge of peace. This, he thought, was why he had become a Shepherd—to witness moments of healing, of grace extended and accepted.

Patting Dan on the back, Jordan turned to face the expectant crowd. The air was thick with anticipation, all eyes fixed on him.

"The danger has passed," he announced, his voice carrying across the courtyard. "It is time for justice to be done in the Lord of Light's name, according to the laws of Septily."

Watch Guard Quinn stepped forward, his face a mask of grim determination. "Let these nobles be dealt with according to the laws of Septily and the Watch Guard," he declared, "for their crimes are not only in this country but in the whole of Aramatir. We who have watched know the Red Hand has trafficked victims from one country to another. These here must be held to the justice of the Triune Halls and the Watch Guard of Aramatir, along with those of Septily."

Jordan nodded in agreement, but before he could speak, Alex's voice rang out. "And where shall their trial be, if not the country they live in now?" The young prince moved between Quinn and Dan's father, his stance protective.

A ripple of murmurs swept through the crowd. Jordan watched as Quinn and Alex locked eyes, neither willing to back down. Jordan considered intervening, but he believed King Xandros would be proud to know his son was loyal to Septily.

"Very well," Quinn growled. "We will return these nobles to Septily's capital seat of Skycliff. But if they have information about the rest of the Red Hand, the Drinaii, or the Dark Sisterhood, we will act on this separately as the Watch Guard."

"Agreed." Alex said, lifting his chin imperiously.

Quinn glanced back at the unit of Sword Guards from the Triune Halls of Skycliff. "You heard your prince. Take these nobles into custody. Bind them and prepare them for travel back to Skycliff. I'm sure there's a carriage we can re-use as a prisoner transport."

The Sword Guards moved in pairs, taking the nobles, who started to protest. Most however laid down their arms with nervous glances toward Dan and went with their captors.

Jordan's gaze swept the courtyard. He noticed Stelia standing apart from the others, her expression a mixture of confusion and awe. He made a mental note to speak with her later, wondering what she made of fair justice when she had so little experience with it.

He clapped his hands on Dan and Farrald's shoulders. "Come, let's speak to Therese and Quinn, with your prince, with Theran and Leandra, and with Stelia. We must make our own plans for what comes next."

As they moved through the crowd, Jordan felt the weight of responsibility settling on his shoulders once more. Perhaps, with guidance and grace, they could forge a new path for Septily, one of true justice and compassion.

Chapter 65: Chosen Family

THERAN COULDN'T STOP HOLDING Leandra, whether it was right or wrong. His arms wrapped around her trembling frame, and he held her molded to his side, but loosely enough that if she wanted to fly free of him, she could.

But she pressed into his chest and he could feel her hot tears on his cheek and neck.

When Dan held back from killing his and Leandra's father, Theran knew it was the right thing to do, but he struggled with fury at the disgusting scoundrel. If it were in his power, he would make sure Lord Torren was locked into the lowest, worst dungeon in all of Septily with no chance to see the light of day again.

As he considered this, he marveled at the sunlight shining down on them now, when moments before Dan had called a dark storm and lightning with his blade of power, a dark blade unlike anything Theran had ever seen. Dan had seemed tormented, and the blade had responded to him. Theran hoped it was not the dark blade he'd read about in the Hall of the Law, but the way Dan carried it and himself, he feared it might be so.

His gaze sought out Shepherd Jordan as the man led Dan over to them and called Prince Alex and another young man to join them. Jordan seemed weary, but also full of purpose and peace. So, perhaps, the blade of power Dan carried was not the one Theran feared. Perhaps, they would find a way through this, and the main battle with the Red Hand.

Shepherd Jordan stopped to speak to the two Watch Guard leaders, with Prince Alex and the other Watch Guard apprentice at his side, but Dan came to Theran and Leandra, his gaze traveling over their embrace and back to Theran's face. His expression was empty, guarded, unlike it had been moments ago.

"Sword Guard Theran, may I ask what you do here?" Dan's voice was neutral, despite the implied challenge of his question.

Before Theran could answer, Leandra did. "He's caring for me, like no one in our family ever did. Did you even see me, all those years, Dan? did you know how hard it was for me to pretend to be the girl mother and father wanted? Fearing all the while what would happen to me if I was not?"

Theran wanted to say something, but knew she had to stand and fight her own battles.

Dan's face crumpled, and he knelt in front of his sister. "I'm so sorry, Leandra. I was absorbed in myself and all that happened to me. I did not… help you as I should have. I did not know how or what you would say if I tried."

Leandra put a hand on Dan's head. "I forgive you, brother, but know this, I will choose who I love, not anyone else, not you, either."

Dan visibly swallowed, and then stood up and took his sister's hand in his own, then glanced at Theran.

Theran tried to stand straighter as he stepped forward and held out his hand. "I would be honored to court your sister, Lord Torren."

Dan's jaw tightened. "Don't call me that ever again, and with her permission, you can court her as much as she allows."

"You mean to renounce our family then, truly?" Leandra asked him.

"Yes. I do not wish to be called a noble when all the nobility I've ever known have been worth less than the dung in the stable yard."

"Even me, old friend?" asked Prince Alex, coming up behind him.

Dan sighed. "Not you. My parents. This lot they worked with." He cocked his head at the nobles being arrested by the Sword Guard.

"I understand," Prince Alex said gently.

Theran noticed the prince seemed to have softened from the petulant boy he had been mere weeks ago. It seemed the Watch Guard had him in hand, at least. "Prince Alex, may I…"

"I'm not called a Prince with the Watch Guard," Alex said. "Call me Alex."

Theran bit his lip, then continued. "Alex, may I ask how your father is?"

"He needs you back at court," Alex said. "This is going to be a complicated trial of nobles, regardless of Dan's choice to give up on the noble class of Septily."

Theran understood Alex's reasoning, but his gaze lingered on Leandra, his heart swelling with a certainty he'd never known before. She was the one - of that, he had no doubt. But even as warmth spread through his chest at the thought of her, a familiar weight settled on his shoulders. The King needed him back at court, and the impending trial of nobles loomed large. Theran furrowed his brow, mind racing as he tried to reconcile his newfound love with the duties that had defined his life for so long. How could he give Leandra the attention she deserved while still fulfilling his responsibilities to the crown? The path ahead seemed fraught with difficult choices, but Theran knew one thing for certain - he wouldn't give up on either.

Chapter 66: Leandra Makes New Plans

Leandra's heart raced as she stood in the courtyard, her brother's words echoing in her ears. "I do not wish to be called a noble when all the nobility I've ever known have been worth less than the dung in the stable yard."

She felt a surge of pride mixed with sorrow. Dan was right, of course, but the truth of it stung. Her whole life, defined by a title that now felt hollow and tainted. Leandra's stomach churned as she glanced over at her parents' closest friends. How many of the nobles had she dined with, laughed with, all while they participated in such evil? She squeezed Theran's hand, grateful for his steady presence beside her.

"I also wish to resign my family name," she heard herself say, the words tumbling out before she could stop them. "I do not wish to be known as a daughter of the Torren family name." She felt Theran's reassuring squeeze around her shoulders as she spoke.

Prince Alex bowed his head to her. "I understand, my lady, and I am sure my father will, as well."

His understanding brought unexpected tears to her eyes. She blinked them back, determined to stay strong. But she also wondered what would become of all the people who depended on the estate for their livelihood. She did not want her title, but she did not want to abandon them.

Alex glanced to Dan and then her, and he seemed to be thinking along similar lines. "We do need to have someone overlook the estate. I know

Shepherd Jordan and Sword Master Theran are needed by my father, but Shepherd Jordan has already asked to stay here for a while, to assist with those who are healing, and to help them find their way home or new homes here in Septily. It's a huge task and I know my father will need someone knowledgeable to oversee it. Do you have any ideas who would be most suited to this, as you are familiar with the estate?"

Leandra's mind latched onto this. There might be a way to make something good come from all this pain. The estate was vast, with resources that could be put to a healthy use. And who better to oversee such a transformation than those who truly understood the depths of the evil they'd faced? Perhaps… She needed to speak with Giselle and others who knew these lands, but also those who had kind hearts. But the time to act and speak was now, before the opportunity slipped away.

"Prince Alex, I think I have a course of action that could benefit all. If you would hear it?"

He raised an eyebrow but nodded. "Of course. What's on your mind?"

Leandra took a deep breath. "I have an idea. For the estate. For... for all of this." She gestured around them, encompassing the battered mansion, the shell-shocked servants, the freed prisoners still huddled in groups.

"What kind of idea?" Theran asked, his hand warm in hers.

"A refuge," Leandra said, the concept taking shape as she spoke. "A place of healing, of learning. For those who've been hurt by the Red Hand, by people like... like my parents."

She saw understanding dawn in her brother's eyes. "A safe haven for healing?"

"Yes," Leandra nodded, her excitement growing. "We have the space, the resources. And with the help of some of the freed prisoners, we would have the knowledge to create something truly meaningful."

Shepherd Jordan, who had approached during their conversation, nodded thoughtfully. "It's an intriguing idea, Lady Leandra. One with great potential for healing for all those hurt by the Red Hand."

"And for you," Theran said softly, squeezing her hand.

"Is this what you truly want, sister?" Dan asked her, his brow furrowed slightly.

"Yes, this is what I choose. And Theran is the man I choose, Dan," she said, the words feeling right. "He is a good man for me."

She leaned in to kiss Theran's cheek, a promise of the future they might build together.

Theran blushed. Alex turned to Dan as if unsure what to think of this, but Dan clapped Prince Alex on the shoulder. "That's settled then," he said.

Leandra felt a warmth spread through her chest. Yes, this felt right. Dan understood and wasn't standing in her way when it came to her love for Theran. And with her plans, she could reclaim her home and transform it into something her parents could never have imagined.

"We'll need to discuss this further," Alex said, his tone thoughtful. "There are logistics to consider, security concerns...not to mention my father's need for his most trusted advisors."

Leandra nodded, her eyes meeting Theran's. "Of course," she agreed, a mix of understanding and determination in her voice. "I know Theran's duties to the King are paramount. We'll find a way to balance it all." She squeezed Theran's hand reassuringly. "But it's a way to move forward, isn't it?"

As the others nodded, Leandra felt a spark of hope ignite within her. There was so much work to be done, so much pain to heal. The road ahead would require sacrifices, sharing Theran's time and attention with the needs of the kingdom. Yet, as she looked at the faces around her, she could see a path of possibility unfolding.

"Shall we find Stelia?" Shepherd Jordan asked, already turning toward the house. "I think she should be part of this conversation from the beginning."

"Stelia is?" Leandra asked.

"Someone who has been hurt by the Dark Sisterhood as we were by our parents," Dan said. He touched Leandra's wrist gently, like he had when they were children and he needed to assure her that he was there for her. "She will not be as you expect, but I know you will understand once you speak to her."

Leandra tapped Dan's wrist twice in response, with their childhood code. She would give this Stelia a chance.

As they moved back inside the manor house, Leandra caught sight of her reflection in a shattered mirror. The woman staring back at her was changed—bruised, weary, but with a fire in her eyes that hadn't been there before. No longer a nobleman's daughter playing at independence, but a woman forging her own path.

Whatever came next, she was ready to face it. With Theran by her side, with this new purpose before her, Leandra felt truly free for the first time in her life. The road ahead would be difficult, but she would walk it with her head held high, no longer burdened by the weight of a name she no longer wanted.

She was simply Leandra now. And that was enough.

Chapter 67: A New Purpose

STELIA'S MUSCLES ACHED AS she dismounted her horse. The journey to the Torren estate had been long, and every jolt in the saddle had reminded her of the wounds she'd sustained in the desert. But the physical pain was nothing compared to the weight in her chest. She had ridden with the company of Watch Guard and Sword Guards because she had no other place to go, although the king had offered her refuge. His absolute trust in her word made her uncomfortable, so she had chosen to be of use to those fighting against the Red Hand.

She surveyed the courtyard, now eerily quiet after the chaos of the battle. Servants scurried about while a handful of Sword Guards stood watch. The air still carried the metallic tang of blood.

"Stelia?" Jordan's voice cut through her thoughts. "We're gathering in the study to discuss next steps. Will you join us?"

Stelia nodded, her throat tight. She followed Jordan, Giselle the goose girl, and Dan's sister through the grand doors of the mansion, past shattered vases and torn tapestries. The opulence of the place, even in disarray, made her skin crawl. It reminded her of the interior of the Dark Spire, and the way Kalidess ruled. How many had suffered to build this wealth?

The study was a warm, wood-paneled room that smelled of leather and parchment. Giselle stood by the fireplace, her practical attire a stark contrast to the richly bound books lining the walls. Shepherd Jordan sat in a high-backed chair, his kind eyes watching Stelia as she entered.

"Please, sit," Leandra gestured to an empty chair.

Stelia perched on the edge, her back rigid. She'd spent years giving orders, striking fear into the hearts of others. Now, she felt powerless, reliant on others' mercy.

"We've been discussing the future of the estate," Leandra began, her voice steady despite the exhaustion evident in the shadows under her eyes. "With my parents... gone, we have an opportunity to turn this place into something good."

"What did you have in mind?" Stelia asked.

Giselle stepped forward; her eyes bright with purpose. "A rehabilitation center for the former slaves. A place where they can heal, learn new skills, and prepare for life as free people."

Images flashed through Stelia's mind: faces twisted in fear, backs scarred by whips, eyes devoid of hope.

"It's a noble idea," she managed, her mouth dry.

Leandra leaned forward her gaze intense. "We could use your help, Stelia. Your knowledge of the Drinaii, of the Red Hand – it could be invaluable in understanding what these people have been through."

Stelia's heart raced. Help? Her? The thought was absurd. She opened her mouth to refuse, but then she caught sight of Shepherd Jordan. His expression was open, encouraging. There was no judgment there.

"I..." Stelia swallowed hard. "I want to help. But I don't if I can."

"Why not?" Giselle asked, her tone curious rather than accusatory.

Stelia stood abruptly, pacing to the window. Outside, she could see a group of former slaves huddled together, their postures wary. "Because I'm one of the monsters they're trying to escape," she said, her voice barely above a whisper.

The room fell silent. Stelia could feel their eyes on her back, could imagine the horror and disgust on their faces. She braced herself for the inevitable rejection.

But then she felt a hand on her shoulder. She turned to find Jordan beside her.

"You're not that person anymore," Jordan said softly. "You chose to leave that life behind. To help us."

Stelia shook her head. "It doesn't erase what I've done."

"No," Leandra agreed, her tone matter-of-fact. "But it gives you a chance to do better. To make amends."

Stelia looked at each of them in turn: Leandra, with her unwavering determination despite the injuries from the battle; Giselle, practical and filled with spark; Shepherd Jordan, a beacon of forgiveness she didn't deserve.

"I want to try," she said finally, the words feeling strange on her tongue. "I want to help. But.. I'm afraid."

"Of what?" Shepherd Jordan asked gently.

Stelia's laugh was bitter. "Of failing. Of hurting them more. Of... of not being worthy of this chance."

"Those are all valid fears," Leandra said. "But they don't have to stop you. We can start small. Maybe you could help us understand the challenges they might face?"

Stelia nodded slowly. "Yes, I... I could do that. And perhaps help with security measures? The Red Hand won't give up easily."

Giselle's eyes lit up. "That would be incredibly helpful. We need to make this place a fortress of healing."

Stelia felt a flicker of hope. She took a deep breath. "Alright. I'll do it. I'll help however I can."

The relief in the room was palpable. Leandra squeezed her hand, while Giselle nodded approvingly. Shepherd Jordan's smile was warm.

As they gathered around the desk, pouring over maps of the estate and discussing logistics, Stelia felt a spark of something she'd almost forgotten – purpose. She might never fully atone for her past, but here, in this room, with these unlikely allies, she could begin to build a future worth fighting for.

Chapter 68: Return

Dan hadn't liked being one of the nobles since the day his father asked him to spy on Prince Alex, to gain his favors, and to toady up to the other nobles in court. But it was one thing to walk away from the idea of his family knowing he could go back, and another to actually do that, especially as it looked as though his parents would lose their estates and their status. It had seemed the right thing, and an easy thing, to renounce his father and mother, and their family name, but he loved his sister and did not want her to feel burdened. He was proud of her idea and her choice to recreate the estate as something new and life-giving to others, but at the same time, he realized he would be a man without a place to call home.

Farrald approached their group and leaned against the staff of power he'd received on their journey. The staff lit up from bottom to top, then went quiet. Farrald looked him up and down, then over at the house. "Would you ever want to return here?"

"No." While he did have a few good memories of sparring with his old house guard here, learning how to have a clean approach to life so different from the one his parents seem to live, and riding horseback in the fields, he never wanted to live here. He especially did not want the house in the capital, even though he'd lived there most of his life.

After finding a small handful of childhood items in his old room at the estate and saying goodbye to his sister, Stelia, Giselle, and others, Dan found turning his back on the Lake Estate harder than he'd expected.

But, once he turned his face toward the trail, riding between Therese and Farrald, with Quinn leading their way, the rhythm of the ride soothed his distress, and he fell into a state of near numbness. He knew, objectively, this was probably a type of shock symptom, but he was glad to be wrapped in the cocoon of nothingness for now. It gave him respite.

The countryside changed as they rode. They took breaks for water and food. They camped, and somehow Dan took his watch at night with Farrald for company, but they encountered no problems, and his thoughts remained quiet, his emotions hollow, and his sword was silent at his side.

This changed the closer they came to the Watch Tower. The dark blade seemed to wake up on its own, humming against his side. When they paused for their midday meal, Dan dismounted and touched the pommel of his sword.

In the distance, the Watch Tower loomed, a sentinel against the darkening sky. Dan felt the dark blade pulse at his side then surge into a constant hum. The dark blade's power tingled against his fingers and zipped along his veins. His body responded with a shiver, and his mind seemed to open from somewhere within, ripping open the emotions which had been covered in a blanket of numbness for the last few days.

Dan fell to his knees, and curled over, feeling all the hurt, loss, anger, and shame rock over him in waves. The blade of power responded to his emotions by raising a visible barrier of shadow around him.

Therese tried to reach him, but the barrier repelled her, even as she unsheathed her sword and tried to cut the barrier.

Dan shook his head at her, tried to warn her away, as the power surged and the barrier expanded, knocking her to the ground.

Therese shouted something and he couldn't hear her.

Dan curled inward even further as the shame he felt intensified, followed by more hurt, more anger, more shame. He had killed a man. He hadn't killed his father. His sister had been hurt. His father a criminal. His mother the same. What was he? Who was he, as their son, to serve the world of Aramatir?

The barrier around him thickened, and the blade of power sent a shock into his body. The pain was indescribable, all powerful, and he shuddered and gasped as it rocked through him again and again. He closed his eyes.

Suddenly, it stopped, and he felt a soothing balm of coolness against his side.

Farrald was singing something. He couldn't quite understand the words. Was that a language he knew? But somehow, Farrald had broken the barrier and his staff was pressed against Dan's side. The green crystals on Farrald's staff were bright green mixed with white, and he continued to sing in an unknown language, his eyes unfocused and his head bowed.

The dark blade's power receded slowly, the barrier dropped, and Dan wrested his hand from the pommel, unclenching his fingers one by one. He unbuckled his sword belt and let the whole thing drop to the ground as he stood on shaky legs.

Farrald's eyes widened, and he held out his staff to Dan.

Dan took the staff in his hands, and he felt his whole body calm. The hurt and sorrow were still present, tears rolling down his face, but he no longer felt shame.

Therese stepped toward Dan cautiously, her brow furrowed with concern. "The dark blade was known to bring pain to mete out justice, but I had never heard it could turn on its bearer."

"The shame of what I did, the guilt I felt for killing that man and not protecting my sister—it was tearing me up, and the blade responded," Dan said. "The Lord of Light cleansed it, but he also told me it might revert to its old nature, if I strayed from a path of justice."

"We are all called to stay in faith, but we all fail," Farrald said.

"You are going to have to learn to accept your emotions, but also how to turn your thinking, and do so quickly, so this does not happen again," Therese told him, her gaze stern. She eyed the sword on the ground and sighed. "And you are responsible for the blade. It is a heavier burden than any I would willingly bear."

Dan swallowed back a bit of his fear and sighed. "I understand."

"You begin to," she said, her expression softening slightly.

Farrald reached out to the sword and picked it up while Dan and Therese stared at him in shock. He shrugged. "It... it is a strangely emotive object, and I could feel pain coming from it. Dan and I can work with each other and my staff to heal it and bring it back to its original purpose, again."

Dan felt struck by this idea. "You mean, it... has feelings?"

"Of a kind, echoes of its past owner." Farrald gingerly held the sword belt in one hand and examined the metal guard around the grip of the blade. "There's writing here, but it is a language I don't know."

"Like the one you were speaking?" Dan asked, his voice tinged with curiosity.

Farrald blushed. "Oh... sometimes, when I pray, I speak in the tongue of the Lord of Light. I don't know how it happens, but I don't even usually know unless someone tells me. It is not... a comfortable gift."

"And not one given to most of those who join the Watch Guard," Therese said in a low tone. "Your father was a fool not to let you become a Shepherd. I will see if we can get you special training. I think I can convince Captain Denali to approve you as a Watch Guard Shepherd, like I am a Watch Guard Healer."

Farrald smiled. "Thank you, Therese."

"It is not up to us to stand in the way of the Lord of Light, especially not when it is apparent that you're destined for that service," said Therese.

Dan gingerly took the dark blade back from Farrald, centering himself with a deep breath. "I can't keep fighting it. It's time I learned to work with it."

Farrald took hold of half of his staff, which Dan still gripped with one hand. "What do you need from us?"

"Just... be ready. In case things go wrong again."

Dan closed his eyes, reaching out with his mind to touch the blade's emotive presence. Immediately, he felt its hunger, its desire for justice twisted into vengeance. But beneath that, he sensed something else – a core of righteous purpose, buried under years of misuse.

Gritting his teeth, Dan pushed past the blade's surface emotions, delving deeper. Images flashed through his mind: battles won and lost, lives saved and taken. The weight of centuries pressed down on him.

"I see you," he whispered to the blade. "I understand your pain, your anger. But we can be more than that. We can bring true justice, not just vengeance."

The blade's energy surged, threatening to overwhelm him. Dan staggered, nearly dropping to his knees.

"Dan!" Farrald's voice seemed to come from far away.

"I'm all right," Dan managed, though his voice was strained. He tightened his grip on the hilt, pouring his own convictions into the connection. "We are guardians, you and I. Protectors. Remember your true purpose."

For a moment, nothing happened. Then, slowly, Dan felt the blade's energy shift. The harsh, jagged edges of its power smoothed. When he opened his eyes, the obsidian surface had taken on a subtle sheen, no longer absorbing all light but reflecting it in complex patterns.

Dan let out a shaky breath, feeling drained but triumphant. "I think... I think it is better now."

Farrald's eyes were wide with awe. "That was incredible, Dan. I could feel the change, even from here."

"Well done, both of you," Therese said. "Now, let's get home to the Tower."

Home to the Tower. That was a thought. Dan realized it was his true home now, in a way no other place had been.

Chapter 69: A Welcome

WHEN THEY REACHED THE gates of the Watch Tower's keep, apprentices Keeva and Nilsen were the guards on duty. The two of them asked the official questions and were given the official answers by Therese, but meanwhile Keeva winked at Dan.

He pressed his lips together and looked away. Keeva was still as beautiful as the day he'd met her, but he had the dark blade now, and the responsibility for the blade was his alone. When he glanced back up, she shook her head at him and then glared over his head at the horizon, clearly dismissing him.

He had missed his chance. But that had already been true from the moment he'd picked up the sword.

Meanwhile, Nilsen scowled at him. That was not much different from when they'd left, at least.

Inside the keep, their horses' hooves clattered on the stone courtyard leading through the small number of shops and houses which lined the walls. Families of the Watch Guard were going about their lives, closing their doors, lighting their lamps, and preparing for their evening meals. The smells of spices and cooked meats made Dan's stomach groan in protest.

Therese chuckled. "Well, at least your stomach is glad to be back."

"This is my home now."

"While you're a fine recruit to the Watch Guard, Dan, even with your troubled sword and your penchant for visions, I think this is a temporary home for you. Like Farrald, you have more riding on your shoulders than the average Watch Guard recruit."

Dan opened his mouth to protest but stopped himself. He could see the reasoning behind Therese's words. He did not like it. He did not quite agree, but he knew what she meant. The weird sense of connection he had with both the sword and his unwanted vision about the next champion set him apart.

Farrald's stomach growled loudly, interrupting the serious bent of their conversation.

"Let's get inside before your stomachs cause an earthquake," Therese said, but she paused and looked over her shoulder. "You two, take care of your horses, then take yourselves and your gear into the kitchens. Kaipo will help get you a meal there, while I make our official report to Captain Denali and First Lieutenant Mol." She made a small gesture with her hand, beckoning them both closer.

Dan and Farrald both leaned in, and Therese dropped her voice. "Let's not discuss certain items yet. I'll make that report to Captain Denali in his office, and you can tell Kaipo." Then, she said more loudly, "That's right, apprentices. You'll be currying our horses after the journey you've given us."

Dan and Farrald rode their horses into the stables, dismounted, and set to work on feeding, watering, currying, and caring for them.

The work itself was steadying to Dan's nerves. The horses remained calm, and his own mare whuffed his hair when he carefully combed the tangles out of her mane and gently massaged behind her ears. He leaned into her, letting her warm, horsey smell fill his senses, and then let go and got back to work. If he'd really wanted a simple life, maybe he should have apprenticed himself as a stable boy and not to the Watch Guard.

Farrald began singing something quietly as he worked, his face lit up with joy as he curried his horse and Therese's horse. He smiled at Dan and said, "It is going to be all right. The Lord of Light will take care of us."

Dan bowed his head for a moment as he wrestled with his emotions. Even though he had faith, he struggled with the level of trust Farrald seemed to find instinctive.

When they finished all their work, they washed at the cold pump, then carried their journey bags inside to the kitchen, where they saw Kaipo had two places set.

Kaipo was at the stove and greeted them with a huge smile. "Welcome back, stragglers! It is good to have you both home." He ladled out two bowls of hearty beef and bean stew with something spicy tingling the air and placed them on the table. "My helpers will get the rest of your food settled." He tilted his head at Perren and Amiria who entered the kitchen from the main keep.

Perren, with his unruly hair and casual walk, gave Dan an unexpected slap on the back. "I always knew you were a good'un, but way to stick the nobles in the eye."

Dan was not sure how to respond to that.

"He means, we're glad you were able to save those victims of the Red Hand, and surprised you gave up your lordship," Amiria said, coming from behind Perren to hold out her hands to Dan.

He took them, and she gave his hands a squeeze.

Dan felt his face heating up and he gazed down at the floor. "There were a lot of things that went wrong."

Farrald came over and shook Perren's hand, and then Amiria's. "We'd like to hear about your journey, since you seem to know all about ours."

Dan quirked his eyebrow at Farrald, surprised at his friend's ability to change the subject, but also glad for it.

Farrald tugged at Dan's arm. "Come on, let's not let our food get cold."

So, they did not. The stew was accompanied by a hearty bread and a cold cheese. Warm tea and more bread, but this time sweetened with honey, followed the stew. As they ate, they listened to Perren and Amiria each tell the tales of their own journey.

Kaipo watched over them all, making sure they all had their share of food.

As Kaipo pulled Perren and Amiria away to clean up, Perren remarked, "I see you did not bring back the prince."

"He'll be here in a few weeks once some things get settled." Dan shrugged. "It is not actually easy to give up an estate, and he's taking care of that for me."

Perren raised an eyebrow. "Well, I wouldn't know about all the things nobles have to deal with."

Dan shook his head. "I did not mean it like that. It is… my father and mother did criminal things and Alex was the best person to deal with all of that."

Perren bit his lip. "Sorry. I… get, well, I am sorry about your parents."

"Thank you," Dan said, wishing he could sink into the floor. He wondered how often this would come up over his training, how many people would know, and how long it would take to die down.

"It is not your fault," Amiria said, and then she grabbed a bit of Perren's sleeve and said, "Come on, now, I'm not washing all the dishes by myself."

When they were both busy taking directions from Kaipo on cleaning up, Dan and Perren stood and climbed the stairs to their room.

With a small lamp lit on one of the tables, they slung their gear, including their new, powerful weapons, onto the trunks by their beds.

Dan sat down heavily and eyed the sword. "Do you believe I can handle the sword with faith every day for the rest of my life?"

"I know you will." Farrald said, sitting down across from him. "But let's not muck about with it tonight."

Dan thought that might be the wisest thing Farrald had ever said to him. In a short time, he pulled off his boots and got under his covers fully clothed. He was too tired to think, much less prepare properly. Tomorrow would come soon enough.

Chapter 70: Commitment

The air hung heavy with dust motes, dancing in the thin beams of light that managed to penetrate the small, high windows of the Watch Tower's secluded practice room. Dan stepped inside, the dark blade a familiar weight at his side. Sleep had come easily after yesterday's journey, but wakefulness brought with it the ever-present burden of responsibility. He spotted Therese and Farrald already waiting, their faces etched with a mix of anticipation and concern in the dim light.

Captain Denali stood at the center of the room, his weathered face unreadable. As Dan approached, the captain's eyes fixed on the blade at his hip.

"Good morning, Apprentice Dan," Denali said, his voice gruff but not unkind. "I trust you're ready to begin your daily training with that blade of yours?"

Dan's eyebrows rose slightly at the word 'daily', but he nodded, his hand instinctively moving to the sword's hilt. The moment his fingers touched the cool metal, he felt the familiar surge of emotion—a heady mix of righteous anger and an overwhelming desire for justice. He took a deep breath, willing himself to stay centered.

"Yes, sir," he managed, meeting the captain's gaze. "Every day until I master it."

Denali nodded approvingly. "That's the spirit. This won't be a quick process, but dedication will see you through." He turned to address all three of them. "From now on, you'll train here daily, away from prying eyes that might take too much interest in what we're doing. Dan, you'll lead with the Dark Blade. Therese, you'll observe and provide guidance. Farrald, you'll be his primary sparring partner."

Dan's eyes shifted to Farrald, who stepped forward gripping not a sword, but a long wooden staff. Farrald smiled and twirled the staff. It came alive with its distinctive soft green glow, pulsing with an energy that seemed to counter the dark blade's own aura.

As Dan drew the blade, he felt the eyes of his companions on him. Therese's expression was one of cautious curiosity, while Farrald's face shone with a mix of excitement and unwavering faith. The sword hummed in Dan's grip, its energy pulsing through him like a second heartbeat.

"Begin," Denali commanded. "Remember, this is just the first of many sessions. Pace yourself."

Farrald moved first, his staff a blur of motion and green light. As the weapons met, Dan felt the dark blade's eagerness, its thirst for combat—but also a kind of recoil as it encountered Farrald's glowing staff. He gritted his teeth, focusing on the mechanics of the fight rather than the sword's whispered promises of swift victory.

Parry, thrust, sidestep. Dan moved through the familiar motions, but each was amplified by the dark blade's power. He found himself moving faster, striking harder than he ever had before. But Farrald, with his glowing staff, matched him move for move.

"Control it, Dan," Denali's voice cut through the whoosh of air and the crack of wood meeting steel. "The blade serves you, not the other way around. This is what you'll work on every day until it becomes second nature."

Dan nodded, sweat beading on his brow as he fought to rein in the sword's influence. He could feel it pushing him, urging him to overpower Farrald's defenses, to strike him down. But Farrald wasn't an enemy—he was his friend, his brother-in-arms, and would be his daily training partner in this arduous journey.

With a supreme effort of will, Dan pulled back, lowering the blade. Farrald nodded approvingly, his staff's glow dimming slightly.

"Well done," he said, breathing heavily. "You're learning. Imagine how much stronger you'll be after weeks of this."

They continued to spar, the dust of the room swirling around them, illuminated by the interplay of the blade's dark energy and the staff's green glow. Dan found it easier to maintain control as the session went on. The dark blade still sang with power, but he was learning to direct its song, to harmonize with it rather than be overwhelmed by it. Farrald's unwavering faith and the counter-energy of his staff seemed to create a perfect training ground for Dan's growing abilities.

When at last they lowered their weapons, Dan felt a sense of accomplishment he hadn't experienced since first joining the Watch Guard. He turned to Captain Denali, hoping for approval.

The captain's face was stern, but there was a glimmer of pride in his eyes. "You've made progress, Dan. But remember, this is just the beginning. That blade you carry is both a gift and a curse. There are many out there who would seek to take it from you, to use its power for their own ends. That's why we'll train here every day, away from curious eyes, until you can wield it as naturally as breathing."

Dan nodded solemnly, the weight of the captain's words settling over him like a cloak. "I understand, sir. I'm ready for the challenge."

Denali stepped closer, his voice low. "The path ahead of you won't be easy. You'll face challenges, temptations, and enemies you can't yet imagine. But remember this moment—remember that you're not alone in this fight. Every day, you'll grow stronger, more controlled."

Dan looked at Therese and Farrald, standing tall and proud beside him in the dusty room. He thought of Perren, of Amiria, of Prince Alex, and of all the people he'd met on his journey. Each of them had shaped him, had helped him become the person who could wield this blade, who could commit to this daily struggle for mastery.

"Thank you, Captain," Dan said, his voice steady. "I won't forget. I'll be here every day, ready to work."

As they prepared to leave the practice room, Dan felt a sense of peace settle over him. The dark blade was quiet at his side, its power a steady, controlled hum. He knew the road ahead would be difficult, filled with trials and hard choices, countless hours of training and practice. But for the first time since he'd taken up the blade, he felt ready to face whatever lay ahead, one day at a time.

With Therese's wisdom, Farrald's faith and his newfound abilities, and the strength of the Watch Guard behind him, Dan stood tall, ready to write the next chapter of his story—a chapter of daily dedication, gradual mastery, and the promise of challenges to come.

As he stepped out of the room, Dan already found himself looking forward to tomorrow's session, to the slow but steady journey of becoming one with the Dark Blade. It wouldn't be easy, but he was committed to the path ahead, no matter how long it took.

Epilogue: The Letter

Shepherd Jordan's brow furrowed as he pored over the latest messages from King Xandros, his stomach knotting with each line he read. The weight of responsibility pressed down on his shoulders, growing heavier by the moment. Among the pile of correspondence, one particular message stood out - not for its content, but for its indecipherability. It had been intercepted, a potential goldmine of information, but its secrets remained locked away in the intricate script of the Drinaii language. Xandros had sent it to him for a reason.

With trembling hands, Jordan set aside the other letters, his mind racing. This single message could be the key to turning the tide against the Red Hand.

Without hesitation, he strode purposefully through the halls of the old Torren Estate, his footsteps echoing off the stone walls. He made his way to what was once the great ballroom, now repurposed as a training area. As he approached, the sounds of exertion and Stelia's firm instructions filtered through the air.

Jordan paused at the entrance, watching for a moment as Stelia guided her students through self-defense techniques. Her dedication to preparing them for the dangers ahead was admirable, but the encrypted message burning a hole in his pocket couldn't wait.

"Stelia," he called out, his voice tight with anxiety. "I apologize for the interruption, but I need your help urgently."

Stelia turned, her keen eyes quickly assessing Jordan's troubled expression. She nodded to her students, instructing them to continue their exercises, before making her way to the Shepherd.

"What is it, Jordan?" she asked, her voice low and concerned.

He held out the message. "It's in Drinaii. We've intercepted what could be crucial information, but without a translation..." He trailed off, the implications hanging heavy in the air between them.

Stelia's eyes widened in understanding. She took the message, her fingers tracing the intricate symbols on the outside. "My students can manage their drills for a while."

She placed a reassuring hand on Jordan's arm, feeling the tension in his muscles. "I understand the gravity of this, Jordan. The fight against the Red Hand hangs in the balance, and every piece of information counts. Let's see what secrets this message holds."

As they hurried out of the ballroom together, Jordan felt a small measure of relief. Stelia's willingness to help and her grasp of the situation's importance lifted a fraction of the burden from his shoulders.

In a short time, using the language forced upon her by those who trained her, she deciphered the language and the code of the letter to find this message:

General,

Your great and mighty deeds go before you. I have heard of your dominion over the Southlands and how you encroach upon other kingdoms, and I am in awe of the combined power you share with the sisters.

I write to you with urgent news. The dark blade of power has been unearthed and recovered by one of my recruits. This particular recruit has a friendship with the heir to the throne of Septily and has an unstable relationship with his parents. Previously, I had hoped to bring him into our fold, but there is something different about him now that he has returned. The dark blade is not working on him the way it has worked in the past, although I still sense its power. In addition to this item of interest, one of his training partners has taken up a staff of power, unlike any I have seen mentioned in our archives. From the brief glimpse I have seen, it is beyond doubt that this weapon is from the Lord of Light, and therefore, against us.

From all other reports, and the official one from their trainers, the two who carry these weapons disbanded the Red House set up in Septily, which may cause a disruption to one of our trade routes. While I do not know how she escaped, the Drinaii Enforcer reportedly killed in the desert was seen with them at the estate. If you know of these events already, please pardon me for bringing them to your mind again.

One troubling aspect of this entire situation is that the two guards who trained these recruits and the prince of Septily, made several omissions in their report, most notably about the weapons of power. These omissions, along with other behavior from my tower guards, has led me to believe that some here suspect me. While I have recruited two more to our number, I may need outside help to remain in control of this tower. If it is required for me to obtain the dark blade, I believe one of the sisters may be needed to sever the bond with its bearer. He keeps it close at all times.

According to your previous teachings, I have recruited two more members to our cause and welcomed the one you sent. She has been of great assistance, although she needs to become more subtle in her approach. Due to some of her foolish pride, she managed to get caught poaching on her training journey and landed herself and another on gate guard duty every night for the next fortnight. Another recruit requested to be moved away from their training unit, and the Captain is considering it, which means I do not believe I can convert her to our cause.

In other areas, it has been entertaining to watch the fools around me Watch, Observe, and Report but do nothing. They do not seem to know about The Dark Codex of Shadowed Steel which we know resides in one of their repositories. They do not understand their folly, and it is rich amusement to watch them scrabble at the scraps of details, and again, doing nothing to change the events around them.

However, this is the very reason the events surrounding these two recruits concern me. They both have objects of power. They both have stood against our plans. How shall I proceed with them?

Your sister-in-arms

Stelia's hands trembled as she deciphered the last lines of the intercepted message. The candlelight flickered, casting long shadows across the parchment and her troubled face. Across the table, Shepherd Jordan watched her intently.

Stelia finally spoke, her voice barely above a whisper. She looked up at Jordan, her eyes filled with concern. "I've heard of this book. *The Dark Codex of Shadowed Steel* is said to contain knowledge that could allow sorceresses to... to take control of the blades of power."

Jordan's face paled. "That's impossible. Those blades are uncorruptible. They've been our greatest defense against dark magic for centuries."

Stelia nodded grimly. "I know. But this book... it supposedly holds rituals that can overcome even that safeguard." She hesitated, then added, "Jordan... what if this explains Dan's blade?"

The Shepherd's eyes widened with sudden understanding. "The dark blade... unlike any we've ever seen."

"Exactly," Stelia confirmed, her voice tight with worry. "We've always wondered how it could exist, how it could be so different from other blades of power. What if... what if this grimoire is the reason?"

Jordan stood, pacing the small chamber, his mind racing. "If they've already used this knowledge once..."

"They could do it again," Stelia finished. "And on a much larger scale."

Stelia's gaze drifted back to the letter. "I've heard of a ritual that not only allows control of the blades but can twist their very nature."

Jordan ran a hand through his graying hair. "Blades once wielded for protection, turned against us. It would be devastating. And if Dan's blade is any indication of what they can do..."

"We can't let that happen," Stelia said firmly. "We need to find this grimoire first."

Jordan nodded, his resolve hardening. "So, what's our next move?"

"We gather information. Discreetly," Stelia replied. "We can't let them know we're aware of their plans."

"I'll reach out to Xandros and Theran, and my most trusted friends in the Triune Halls," Jordan added. "We need to identify the Watch Guard spies without tipping our hand."

Stelia stood, squaring her shoulders. "And I'll send a coded message to Dan and Farrald. If this Dark Codex of Shadowed Steel is real, there must be some record of it. Perhaps something that could explain Dan's blade as well."

As they dispersed to their tasks, Jordan was filled with determination to protect all he cared for – the people, their land, and the objects of power that had safeguarded them since the age of the first champion.

GLOSSARY

Main Cast:

Dan Torren - Protagonist, former noble, Watch Guard Recruit

Alex (Prince Alexandros) - Prince of Septily, Watch Guard Recruit

Farrald - Aspiring Shepherd, Watch Guard Recruit

Leandra Torren - Dan's sister

King Xandros - Ruler of Septily, Alex's father

Shepherd Jordan - King's advisor, spiritual leader

Sword Master Theran - King's guard, skilled warrior

Stelia - Drinaii Enforcer, seeking redemption

Terese - Watch Guard healer and trainer

Quinn - Watch Guard trainer

Secondary Characters:

Lord Torren - Dan's father

Lady Torren - Dan's mother

Giselle - Leandra's friend, goose herder

Kaipo - Watch Guard cook

Captain Denali - Head of the Watch Guard

First Lieutenant Mol - High-ranking Watch Guard officer

Lieutenant Baris - Watch Guard officer

Keeva - Watch Guard recruit

Nilsen - Watch Guard recruit from Icewynne Mountains

Amiria - Watch Guard recruit from the Destiny Isles

Ewan - Young Watch Guard recruit

Perren - Watch Guard recruit from Ryssorria

Gorka - Recruit from Aerland, partner to Inaki

Inaki - Griffin from Aerland, partner to Gorka
Flycke - Watch Guard recruit from Merseas
Furian - Watch Guard recruit from Merseas, Flycke's brother
Sword Guard Leo – a Sword Guard commander
Kalidess - Leader of the Dark Sisterhood
Major General Ader Worsten - Drinaii commander
Captain Jennar - Drinaii captain
Nisha - Young girl rescued by Stelia
Berta - Young woman rescued by Stelia
Molly - Leandra's maid
Sword Guard Llewllyn - Sword Guard in Skycliff
Gavin - Young spy working for King Xandros
Cullin - Watch Guard at the Tower
Bertrand - Watch Guard at the Tower
Jesta - Watch Guard librarian at the Tower
Shepherd Bellan - Historical figure known for his visions
King Elar - First King of Septily
King Roland - Xandros's father, former King of Septily
Queen Roseanne - Alex's mother, Xandros's late wife

Places:

Septily - The kingdom where most of the story takes place
Skycliff - Capital city of Septily
Lake District - Region where the Torren estate is located
Desert District - Southernmost region of Septily
Forest District – One of the seven districts of Septily
Sunken Tower - Ancient repository of the Watch Guard
Watch Tower - Training facility for the Watch Guard
Triune Halls - Religious and governmental center in Skycliff
Dark Spire - Stronghold of the Dark Sisterhood

Organizations/Groups:

Watch Guard - Protectors of Aramatir, keepers of ancient knowledge
Triune Halls - Religious and governmental body of Septily
Red Hand - Criminal organization involved in slavery

Dark Sisterhood - Evil organization of sorceresses

Drinaii - Mercenary group allied with the Dark Sisterhood

Shepherds - Religious leaders and healers

Artifacts/Objects of Power:

Dark Blade - Ancient weapon of power

Tree of Life – a symbol of the Lord of Light, sometimes planted as living trees in sanctuaries

Green Staff – Artifact of power connected to the Tree of Life

The Dark Codex of Shadowed Steel – a grimoire of the Dark Sisterhood

Titles:

Shepherd – Religious leader and healer

Sword Master - Elite warrior and protector

Watch Guard - Member of the protective order

Enforcer - High-ranking member of the Drinaii

World-Specific Terms:

Aramatir - The world in which the story takes place

Champion - Legendary figure chosen to fight darkness

Blade of Power - Magical weapon imbued with special abilities

Blood Sorcery - Dark magic involving sacrifice

Lord of Light - Supreme deity worshipped in Septily and other places in Aramatir

Acknowledgements

When I wrote this book in 2016, I did not know it would take me eight years to bring it to print, or that between then and now, I would publish it first as a serialization on Kindle Vella, which didn't exist at the time. But I am glad I waited and am thankful for all those who read the much shorter version of it on that platform first. If you were one of those readers, thank you. You kept me going when I needed encouragement the most. You sent me messages and emails. You asked questions and answered my polls. Because of you, this book is stronger and more robust.

Many thanks to my sister-in-law Lynn who read what I thought would be the final draft several months ago. Your eagle eye for editing is appreciated, but even more so, your encouragement and steadfast willingness to read what I write is amazing.

Many thanks to my parents. Dad, the last chapter is for you, because you asked for one more chapter. :)

Thanks go out to my writing group who read the a few of the additional chapters and gave me much needed feedback that I used to strengthen the whole of the book.

Many thanks to those who voted on my book cover choice, who cheered me on, and who encouraged me with kind comments along the way.

Thank you to John, for listening to bits and pieces of each draft, hearing out my ideas, and giving me time and space to write.

Thanks to all my family and friends for all of your encouragement.

And all thanks and praise be to God, my savior, my helper, and my creator.

About the Author

Tyrean Martinson recognizes she has an unusual name. Tyrean can be pronounced many different ways (and has been) but her parents liked the idea of not having two "e" letters in her name but pronouncing it "Tyrene". She has lived in Washington State her entire life but loves to travel in the US and internationally. The daughter and granddaughter of avid readers and storytellers, Tyrean has loved the landscape of Story for as long as she can remember. She told her first stories to her dog and her cat and entered a classroom short story contest in sixth grade. While she didn't win, she did receive encouragement from her teacher who said, "You could become an author." Astounded that this was possible, she began to fill notebooks with ideas, daydreams, and more. Years passed, life happened, and experience was gained. Tyrean is the author of over twenty books, over a hundred published poems, and dozens of published short stories. She also enjoys hearing all the stories her husband and daughters have to tell her about their everyday lives because they inspire her to write with courage.

ALSO BY

**To read any of the following books, you can find links here:
Tyrean's Link List**

In the World of Aramatir
Dark Blade: Forged (prequel to The Champion Trilogy)

The Champion Trilogy (also set in Aramatir):
Champion in the Darkness
Champion in Flight
Champion's Destiny

In the Universe of Anomalies
The Rayatana Series
Liftoff
Nexus

Collections of Short Stories and Poetry
Dragonfold and Other Adventures
Flicker: A Collection of Short Stories and Poetry
Light Reflections
Microfiction Multiverse (Forthcoming)

Non-Fiction
A Pocket-Sized Jumble of 500+ Writing Prompts
Jumble Journal 1
Jumble Journal 2
5… 4… 3… 2… 1… Write: 25 Speculative Fiction Writing Prompts
Dynamic Writing 1
Dynamic Writing 2
Dynamic Writing 3

Devotionals
Summer Devotions
Walking with Jesus: Stories from One Hope Church (as the editor and a contributing author)

Short Ebook Titles and Experimental Fiction
Ashes Burn: Seasons 1-7, Micro-Fiction Series as an Ebook
Seedling, a flash fiction reprint ebook
The Story Addict

Tyrean is featured in the following anthologies:
Hero Lost: Mysteries of Death and Life, a IWSG Anthology of Fantasy
Book to Dreams 1
Creative Colloquy 7
Best of Every Day Poets 1
Best of Every Day Poets 2
Overcoming Adversity: An Anthology for Andrew
The Insecure Writer's Support Group Guide to Publishing and Beyond
The Insecure Writer's Support Group Writing for Profit
Sunday Snaps: The Stories
New Voices IV: A Commercial Fiction Anthology